ANTHEM

TIM BINDING

ANTHEM

PICADOR

First published 2003 by Picador
an imprint of Pan Macmillan Ltd
Pan Macmillan, 20 New Wharf Road, London N1 9RR
Basingstoke and Oxford
Associated companies throughout the world
www.panmacmillan.com

ISBN 0 330 48745 0 (HC)
ISBN 0 330 42758 X (TPB)

1 3 5 7 9 8 6 4 2

A CIP catalogue record for this book is available from
the British Library.

Typeset by Intype London Ltd
Printed and bound in Great Britain by
Mackays of Chatham plc, Chatham, Kent

FOR CELIA

ONE

When he saw Roach walking towards him, neck stiff, head straight, eyes hidden by the incongruity of the dark oval glasses, feet ploughing through the wind-strewn rubbish, Henry's first inclination was to run up and knock him over, saying remember me now? but then his eye travelled down from the man's slightly soiled cashmere coat, to the gripped fist in the gloved hand and the steering handle attached to the black Labrador and he realized that his head was held in that immovable manner not because he was proud as it had seemed at first, as it had always seemed, proud beyond his calling, but because he could not see; for that is how blind men walk, uncomfortably erect, their head stuck on the untrustworthy vehicle of a body which might lead them they know not where. Richard Roach blind now. What a burden that must be. Still there was the urge to push him over, savour the look of worried incomprehension as he tried to grapple with the unknown, not realizing it was history grabbing at his lapels, knocking the wind out of his complacency.

But he did nothing, not because of the state of his old adversary, but for the dog and her patient stoicism. It would not be fair to treat such a creature like that. Once, on leave, he'd driven a girl he'd fancied out to a pub in Kent, his dog grey-faced, sitting in the back seat like an awkward aunt. Jealous of the attention he was paying the young woman, the animal had gone for a blind man's dog the moment they had walked into the public bar, snapping at his legs and hindquarters, while the Alsatian sat calm, regarding her with immovable contempt. 'Some creatures just shouldn't be allowed out in public,' the landlord had said, looking at them as if they had attacked the man themselves, and shamefaced they'd carried their drinks to the wintry table outside. The girl's name? He had no memory of it. He could hear her laughter, though, the light sound of it, like frozen crystal; follow his own accompaniment too.

A coin flickered down.

'Money for nothing?' a vanishing voice muttered. One of his regulars.

Roach drew closer. Blind! Was it possible? Five years since he had last seen him. Had his sight been failing then? Was that the reason for his dismissal? It didn't seem so at the time. 'I'm sorry, I don't remember you at all,' that's what he'd said. Well, he'd remember him now all right, if he gave him a healthy shove.

He picked up his violin, and as Roach passed him started to play one of the old songs, one of the ones that Joe had taught him, slow rollicking songs of the sea, one of the ones he knew Richard would recognize, and with those first opening bars, it was as if a wave had leaped ahead of itself, washing over the shoes of an unsuspecting beachcomber. The blind man's feet veered sharply to the side. He stopped, tilted his head, sniffing a whiff of the past, uncertain as to its provenance, his hand tightening, pulling the guide handle up abruptly. There was but a short distance between them now, but they stood with a line drawn between them, as if, yes, as if they were divided. Ah, he had him now.

Henry lifted his bow clear of the strings and drew the back of his hand over his broken lip. Only one whole face between the two of them, Richard with his eyes kaput and him with his seared skin and his bottom teeth scattered halfway across the world. The dog stood unmoved, taking no notice of him, or rather, no inquisitive notice. He was an object to be avoided, just as Henry had once been to her master. If only he'd had a dog then. If only he'd been blind!

He ran through a couple more bars, the mournful echo bouncing off the tiled walls. The man jerked his head, one way, then another, as if trying to catch the notes in his mouth.

'Soapsuds?' he called. 'Is that you?'

Henry sank back. Yes, that was him. A busker, not down, not out, simply getting by. You could work it like that if you wanted to, but only if there was nothing else; didn't smoke, didn't drink, no pals, no excess baggage, just observation and opportunity and self-imposed ostracism. Money fell into his case more often than one supposed, other things left there too, British Rail sandwiches, canned drinks, bars of chocolate. One night he'd had a fifty-pound note chucked in; a week later three men had stood in a semicircle and sprayed their evening's drinking over the day's takings. He'd picked the money out, gone down to the washroom, run the cash and the case under the tap, and treated himself to a cheap curry, one of those cut-price, two-dish-only places; no knives, no forks, just a white plate and a paper napkin for his fingers. They knew him there, knew him for his nods and smiles, and fastidious ways. Not much more. There was not much more to know. He moved in and out of the city like a wreath of smoke, keeping himself to himself, like Joe used to do, leaving nothing but a lingering presence, a darkening, a flare of vanished heat. The bottom-rung hotels, doss houses, park benches, that's where he stayed. When he was particularly flush he would walk down to Victoria bus station and catch a night coach up north, sit staring at the darkened country and lonely motorway lights, spend a day or two playing unfamiliar streets, tramping the roads, at night staying out in the open whatever the weather, sheltering under a dripping stone wall, stretched out on some rough patch of field, marvelling at the hidden world of stealth and movement, before coming back to London, mostly skint.

The man hadn't moved. Could he sense Henry looking at him? The rush hour passed between them, shoals of restless fish, bunching in and out in hurried flurries. Then, speaking softly to his dog, Roach turned and walked out towards the tunnel's exit. There was a tap on Henry's shoulder. Alf stood behind him, his cap tipped on the back of his head, exasperated hands on hip.

'Come on. You know better than to hang around on Kaiser Bill's shift. Now if it were this time tomorrow . . .'

He gave him a wink. Henry felt obliged to smile. They all knew of him, the booking clerks, the railmen, the station managers, knew his dark suit and his white neckerchief, knew the distance he commanded, as if what they saw, though recognizable as itself, was not quite of theirs, as if he emerged into their world without history or parentage, from a fog, unforgiving and unknowing. And it was true, there was an unsettling movement about him, hard, impenetrable like a shark's, understanding that it was only motion that kept him alive, and that even while he slept he moved, swimming against the current of his dreams. So they would take hold of his elbow, place a hand in the small of his back and escort him out of the station, the younger ones more insistent than their elders, as if his fall was too visible a presage to their uncertain future. 'You coming quietly?' they would ask, feeding on the bones of their own meagre joke, knowing that in all the years he had stood implacable against the commuter tide he had never spoken one word. It wasn't that he lacked the facility, though some seeing the flame imprinted upon his puckered skin had come to that conclusion; he was simply keeping the promise he made, never to utter again the sounds that marked him as human, and he had stuck to his pledge without much difficulty these five years. Not once had he tried, not in anger, not in drink, not even when alone in front of his mirror in one of his stark overnight rooms or taking his weekly soak in the public baths behind Oxford Circus. Other sounds he made, grunts, exclamations, sighs of satisfaction, but speech? Nothing could coax it from him. Why, he had even been picked up in that pub in Soho on the strength of his singularity (she had seen it as some sort of challenge to prise a word or two out of him and who was he to deny her competitive spirit?), laid out upon her athletic bed and never spoken a word, not even when she brought him finally to orgasm, not a drop.

Alf began to steer him away. For the first time in their long association Henry lifted up his arm, if not in anger, then through impatience, brushing the man aside as he gathered up his case and followed Roach up the Khyber Pass and out into the road, up towards Euston station. It was a terminal he rarely visited, and once within its domain felt the old slow swirl of undisturbed memory churning at his feet. He watched as man and dog crossed the concourse, saw the evening paper and the bar of chocolate stuffed into the cashmere coat, stood on the brim of the platform entrance, following Roach's careful but well-practised descent. Well, no change there, then. Perhaps he lived in the same town as before. Nothing remarkable about that. But blind! And buying a newspaper? Temptation was holding out a ripe fruit in her hand, but he was no longer seduced by the prospect of such succulence. Let him go.

Down on the platform, Roach disappeared inside the carriage. Henry turned and made for the glass doors, a couple of station personnel following him at a deliberately indiscreet distance. Outside the night was wet and dirty, the wind chill at his collar, the damp cold as it seized the fingers of his clenched hand. Better out than in, though. He'd didn't care for Euston, never played there; new foundations covering old ground and the bodies buried underneath. It hadn't been much better the first time around, that old great arch looming up out the gloom like a war memorial standing over its forgotten dead. He had passed through that arch into another world. Then the arch had been destroyed and with it the possibility of returning to the country that had lain behind it. There'd been no going back.

He jumped on a bus, which dawdled and traffic-jammed its way down to Oxford Circus. The lights had already gone up in Regent Street, measly stringy things, hardly worth the bother, the Christmas crowds already taking hold around Liberty's and further down, around the windows of the children's Mecca. He wondered if the train set was there still, the one that ran around the first floor, and then realized that in all those years of knowing of it, he had never seen it.

*

They had gone up to London to see the Christmas lights and the window displays and to visit Hamleys. The biggest toy shop in the world, in the biggest city in the world, that's what Mum had said, the biggest city in the world. How big is the biggest? he asked and Mum said, Well, if you tried to walk round it, it would take a million trillion steps, and he knew then that it must be very big for he had counted the number of steps from the top of the road to their house and that was a hundred and ten. Sitting in the carriage going up to London, he was looking out the window, looking at the Ovaltine girl, standing in the field with her cut-out arms carrying sheaves of wheat and a basket of brown eggs, her hair whipped to the train's passing, her smile following him as they hurtled past, when Mum leant across and told him that if by any chance they should get separated, and such things could happen in the big city, he must stay put. He must not try to find her but must stay where he was and if possible ask a policeman or a kind-looking woman to stand with him. Do you promise? she said, holding his head and looking at him straight, and he held up his fingers like Grey Wolf had told him to and promised. And then she took his reading book from him and said, And if you need to tell anyone where you live, you can take out your book and show them, and she began to write his name and address on the inside in thick black pencil. *This book belongs to Henry Armstrong and I live in Anglefield Road.* And as she was writing the door was pulled open and the guard stood there asking to look at their tickets, and Mum had handed the book back to him while she dug them out of her purse, and he took his mackintosh down from the string luggage rack and stuffed the book safe into his pocket.

When they got out they walked through a huge hall where there were models of trains in glass cases, like at the Science Museum. It sounded like a museum too, the hollow echo of their footsteps, the great empty spaces, Mum speaking to him in a whisper. He wanted to look at the models but Mum coaxed him away by telling him that at the toy shop they had a model railway which ran around the whole of the first floor. When they stepped outside it was like London was floating on a thick cloud, dark and murky, and he started to cry because he'd been told that they going to see the sights and watch the Christmas decorations light up, and he could see nothing. They had to ask their way four times to the bus stop and when they got there they waited and waited, it seemed for ever, and when the bus finally came it wasn't the right one, so they had to wait some more, until it came finally, rumbling, slow and carrying a funny glow all about it, like it had a coal fire inside. She had promised him that they would climb the stairs and sit up top, right at the front, over the driver, but when it came there was standing room only, so they had to shuffle in downstairs, Mum holding on to the railing above and he on to the nearby seat, not that there was much danger of them losing their balance, they were moving so slowly. We could walk it faster than this, Mum complained to the conductor as he rolled out their tickets. The conductor shook his head. Beggin' your pardon, lady, but you'd be lost in five minutes. We've missed three turnings this morning already and that's from someone who's been driving this route a six-year. Mum bent down and peered out the window. That won't help you none, neither. There's naught there to see. I'll tell you when.

When they heard him shout 'Piccadilly Circus' and squeezed their way to the platform ready to jump down, the conductor bounded down the stairs, his money satchel jangling. He ruffled Henry's hair and said, Better wrap his tubes up, love. Need a gas mask for that filth, and Mum had taken out this handkerchief from her handbag, big and white it was, and folded it into a triangle, and wrapped it over his mouth and nose and tied it with a knot around the back, like he was a outlaw in the Wild West, ready to hold up the stagecoach. They stood on the pavement, hearing the bus slowly fade away. It was like seeing a great ship slip away from the mist-wrapped quayside, watching the warmth and safely vanish into the gloom, leaving them marooned on an unknown island, with nothing but shapeless sounds and swirls and speechless shadows floating past. The air smelt damp and rotten. Mum stood there, not quite knowing which direction in which to set out. This is no good, she said, and took him into this tea shop they were standing outside, to ask the way. We might as well have a cup of tea and a sticky bun, while we're here, what do you say, Henry? and though he wanted to get to the biggest toy shop in the world and see the train set that ran right around the shop, the buns were long and draped with white icing out of which shone a bright red cherry, so he went to the counter and pointed to the fattest and then they went and sat down by a table next to the window. A pretty girl in a uniform came and handed him a plate with a knife by the side of the bun. He looked at the knife and looked at his mum and Mum shook her head. Fingers are fine, she said.

It was on a corner, this tea shop. That's why it was called the Corner House, Mum told him. He thought it funny. Like my book? he asked, taking the book from his pocket. That's right, Mum said, just like the House at Pooh Corner, only this corner house is not in a forest but in the very middle of London with all the busy people going about their business. They do say, she said, that if you sat here for long enough you would see everyone in the world, because sooner or later everyone comes to Piccadilly

7

Circus. It seemed hard for him to believe that. What, everyone in the whole world? he asked. Even Hottentots and Red Indians? That's what they say, but we can't see any of them today because of the smog. The Red Indians would like the smog, he told her, because now they can creep about without being seen, ready to scalp us, and drew his white handkerchief over his face again and pretended to shoot them. What d'you think, Mum, are there any Indians out there today? and Mum said nothing, just looked out the window at the thick blank outside. Mum, he said, Mum, and she looked back at him. The white handkerchief had fallen round his neck and she leant over and rubbed her finger over the little triangular flap that hung round his neck before pulling it up over his mouth and nose again. We can't stay here all day, smog or no smog, and she got up to go even though he would have liked another bun.

When they got out it was worse than ever, he couldn't even see his own feet, and he started to count. He counted to fifty and then from fifty to sixty. Soon he was counting more than he had ever counted on his own, conjuring numbers that he'd barely thought possible, when suddenly Mum stopped and started to scrabble about in her handbag. Oh, God, Henry, where's my purse? You haven't got it, have you? and Henry knew then that something important had happened, because she always asked him silly questions like that when she was worried. As if he would have her purse! No, Mum, he said, but she wasn't taking any notice, she was searching her coat pockets and her handbag again. It's got all our money and tickets and everything, she was saying. And then she held her hand to her mouth, like she remembered, Oh, God, Henry, I've left it behind in that bloody cafe. She looked back and then bent down and brought him close. I'm going to have to run back, darling, as quick as I can, otherwise someone will take it, if they haven't already. I won't be a second. Stay here and don't move. And then she was gone. And it was cold and all swirly and empty and he was alone. The fog seemed to close in all around him, but he wasn't worried for he knew Mum would come back and even if she didn't right away, he still had his book with his name and where he lived in it. So he waited and waited. People would loom out of the gloom towards him and every time he thought it must be Mum and every time they hurried past. He waited but still she did not come. He started to call out to her, not loudly, but loud enough for her to hear if she was nearby, and a man came up and said, Hello, sonny Jim, lost are we, and he remembered what his mum had said and he felt for his book, where Mum had written, but it wasn't there, not in his left pocket and not in his right and then he remembered taking it out at the tea shop and putting it down on the chair next to him. He'd left it there, just like Mum and her purse. And he knew he must do what his mum had done, run as fast he could to get there before someone took it, and then he was running. It was just down the road, he knew that, more than fifty paces, more than sixty, and he counted them as he ran, but when he got to the end the tea shop wasn't there, so he counted another ten, but still he could not find it. And then he saw her coming along. He raced towards her, but she was a man with a hat and a stick who waved him away, like he was a nasty dog. And he thought that he must have missed her, so he ran back, and then, catching sight of his mum's back, threw himself upon the hem of her coat. But she wasn't his mum either, but someone else, who jumped back in fright, thinking he was trying to snatch her handbag. She cried out, he can't remember what, except he knew she was angry and he ran, ran on, stopping only when he realized he'd forgotten how many paces he'd run, whether he was back to where he had been or run the other way. How many paces had he run? It took a million trillion steps to walk the whole of London and he must have run hundreds and hundreds of them already. He ran again, running blindly, until the ground dropped away and he stumbled, rolling out onto the road. He scrambled back on the pavement, edging against the wall. There was a corner, a corner just like the one with the tea shop, but here there was no window, no lights, no door with a tinkling bell. It was the wrong corner. But which way had he come? He stepped out to look both ways, but there was nothing to see. And now he knew he was lost, lost like Hansel and Gretel in a great forest, alone and without friends, and knew too that only by shouting and running would he find a way out, and so he started to run, run as fast as he could, running and calling out the only name he knew her by, Mum! Mum!, running harder than he had ever run before, running along a street that seemed never to come to an end, looking for the corner that would shine out like a lighthouse where Mum would be waiting with a scold and a glass of fizz and a sticky bun, running smack into another boy who was carrying a box, which sprang out of his hand and smashed open on the pavement, tumbling him over again. Only he wasn't a boy at all but a small man with a bowler hat, hardly taller than the lad across the road. The man grabbed him by the sleeve and pulled him up.

'Look what you done.' He picked up the box and something glinting by his feet. 'See that? Them's bone handles, those knives. Worth a bob or two. On your hand and knees. If I don't get a full set back you'll have to pay for the lot of them.'

He hunted round, handing each one back to the man, who examined them before putting them back in the box. When they had finished he stood up, and taking hold of Henry dragged him to a doorway. There was something shining hanging down.

'You wait here,' he said. 'I've got to show them to the gentleman what's buying them. And if he don't want them no more, it's your mum and dad who'll have to cough up. Don't you run away now, or I'll set the law on you.'

Henry stood there, not daring to move. He had no idea where he was and he was shaking. The little man came out.

'I thought as much,' he said, pulling the door closed behind him, 'some of them are in a right state. He don't want them on his table no more. You owe me a few bob, I reckon. We could go to your mum and dad, but look, I don't want to get you into trouble. So, how much you got in your pocket?'

'I haven't got anything.'

'All alone in the big city with not a penny to your name, I don't think! You don't look like a boy going begging to me.'

Henry burst into tears.

'I've lost my mum,' he sobbed.

'Lost your mum?'

'I can't find her. She ran away, to get her purse.'

The little man looked around and got down on his knees.

'Now, now. Not to worry. I can't find my slippers of a morn- ing, but usually if I think careful like, I remember where I last put them. And then I go there and there they are, all warm and comforting. Where did you last put her, your mum?'

'In the tea shop.'

'The tea shop, eh? Do you remember anything about it, like where it might have been?'

Henry gulped and nodded.

'It was a house like Pooh Corner. With cakes and windows where everyone went past.'

'Did it have a name?'

'A circus, Mum said.'

'A circus?'

'Yes. Everyone goes there, Mum said. Even Red Indians.'

The little man whistled into his teeth and shook his head.

'Trouble with circuses, here one day gone the next. How long, since you lost her, then?'

'I don't know. Ever so long now. She'll be ever so cross.'

The man scratched his head.

'What's your name?'

'Henry.'

'Henry. Mine's Joe. Joe Hawkins. Eyes on the back of me head, that's me.' He held out his hand.

'I want my mum.'

'Course you do. The trouble is we don't know where your mum is. Tell you what, though.' He nodded in the direction of the road. 'See that over there? That's my lorry. Bet you've never ridden in a lorry before, all high up.'

Henry shook his head.

'You can see everything from a lorry. Like a bird in the sky, you are. Tell you what we're going to do. We're going to get in that lorry and drive around and see if we can find her. What do you say to that?'

Henry tried to stand his ground.

'Mum said I should stay where I was. She said I shouldn't move.'

'Yes, but you haven't, have you? You been running here and there, there's no telling where you was. We don't know where "was" is, do we? She'll be where you was, and you're here, where she isn't. She might never come here. But, to my way of thinking, if we drive around, we might spot her, might spot this circus before it moves off. Come on, let's be having you.'

Joe led him across the road and lifted him up to the high seat with the little window just above his head. What kind of coat was she wearing, your mum? he asked, swinging himself up behind the big wheel across on the far side, and Henry told him a brown one, with a fur collar. Proper mink, I bet, Joe said, and though Henry didn't know what Joe was talking about, he nodded in agreement. Joe started the engine. You look that side and I'll look this, he instructed. No telling how quick we might spot her. They looked and they looked but they couldn't find her. The fog was as thick as it had ever been and looking across at Joe, working the big wheel, Henry had the feeling that this would never end, that this is where he would remain for the rest of his life, riding in this lorry, looking for his mum and never finding her. He saw no possibility of another life. He was lost, trapped he knew not quite where, and he started to shake and cry again. Joe told him to be quiet, that if he carried on like that he'd have to let him out, and Henry knew that he must be miles and miles away from Mum now, and he didn't want to be left alone again any more and so he sniffed himself silent. That's better, Joe said, and handed him an oily rag from between the seats to wipe himself dry. Henry shook his head and pulled out the big white hanky that Mum had given him. Are you taking me home? he asked and Joe looked at him and patted him on the knee. That's right, Henry. I'm taking you home.

Then there was scrub and an empty road and a tiny house at the end of it, with a yard and the smell of dirty water, and a kitchen with a cat with mange on the table.

'That's Captain Hook. Stroke him if you want.'

But he didn't. The Captain had one eye and bare patches of skin on his back. A voice called.

'Joe? You're home early.'

She came through, wiping her hands on an apron, smelling of soap. She was bigger than Joe, taller and wider, with big red arms and little eyes.

'Look what I've found,' Joe said. She looked down at him, the white hanky clutched in his hand.

'What's that, then?'

'What's it look like?'

'What's he doing here?'

'He were lost.'

The woman looked at Henry, as if Joe had made it up.

'That right?'

Henry nodded. He couldn't speak. He were lost.

'How come? You run away?'

He shook his head. 'No. My mum lost her purse.'

The woman turned to Joe.

'Where was this, then?'

'Soho way. I was . . .' He held up three fingers. 'Mr P. Brokers, Esq.'

She nodded.

'So. Your mum left you?'

He nodded again.

'Can't have been a very good mum to leave a nice-looking boy like you. What's your name?'

The man prodded him.

'Go on, tell her.'

'Henry.'

'Henry!' the woman exclaimed. 'I went with a Henry once. You remember, Joe? Henry Basset?'

'I remember knocking his blasted teeth out.'

'And how old is this Henry?'

Joe pushed him again.

'Go on.'

'I'm nearly seven. Will you help me find my mum? I want to go home.'

She looked at him.

'It won't be easy, finding your mum in a big place like London. Is that where you live, London?'

He shook his head.

'Where, then?'

He tried to remember but couldn't. Mum had told him he was sure, but he couldn't.

'In a house,' he said. 'Near the train station.'

'What station?'

'The one Daddy goes to in the morning.'

'Ah, that one. Does it have a name?'

A name!

'My mum can tell.'

'Yes, but she's run off.'

'She's never! She forgot her purse. She went back to get it.'

'But didn't she come back. Funny, that.'

He tried to tell her about the fog, but she would have none of it.

'It's never too foggy to lose your own flesh and blood. Not unless you want to. What mother runs off and leaves a child in the middle of London?'

'Don't be too hard on him, Dora.'

'He's got to learn some time. I don't want him getting his hopes up.'

Joe put his arm around him and tried to reassure him.

'We'll try and find your mum, don't you worry.'

'But if she don't want to be found . . .' The woman sniffed and poured herself another cup.

'Mum said if I ever got lost I should go to the police.'

Joe bent down on his haunches again and put his hands on Henry's shoulders.

'And so we will, Henry, so we will. But in this muck we couldn't even find the police station. As soon as it clears up, I'll go and see them. Cross my heart and hope to die.'

The woman laughed.

But Joe kept his promise. He went out early the very next morning and when he came back told Henry that he'd been to the police, that he'd talked to the head of Scotland Yard, who was a very clever chap, and he had told Joe that seeing how bad the fog was, what Henry should do was to stay at Joe's house until they found his mum, otherwise he'd have to be put in an orphanage and sent out to work. And the policeman had also told Joe that while he was staying with them he needn't go to school. The best thing would be for him to stay at home with Dora so they knew where to come and get him, or if he wanted to, on some days he could ride with Joe in his van, help him carry things and look out the window to see if he could spot his mum.

Not long after, when the fog had cleared, Henry thought he remembered the name of the town and the road and he told Joe and Joe slapped his leg and wrote it down and went back to Scotland Yard straight away with the news, and Henry waited all day, expecting to see Joe's face coming through the door all lit up, but when he returned Joe's face was long and grey and he sat Henry on his knee and told him that he must have got it wrong, that the police had looked and looked but could find no such place, no such road.

'But Mum told me!'

Dora flipped the table with the edge of her apron.

'Then she told you wrong, didn't she?'

She bent down close.

'Know what I think? I think she told you wrong deliberate, just to be rid of you.'

Joe pushed her back with the flat of his hand and eased his trembling, saying that he'd probably misheard his mum, that's all, and what the man from Scotland Yard wanted him to do now was to draw a big picture of her so that he could show it to all the other policemen so that they'd know exactly what she looked like. And Joe took out a box of coloured pencils from his pocket.

'Work my fingers to the bone and you spend it on bleeding crayons,' Dora complained.

'The biddy at the house I was working at gave them to me this morning,' Joe explained. Dora gave him a look,

'I thought you were at Scotland Yard this morning,' Henry said.

'Most of the morning I was, but I had a little job to do. Removals.'

And Dora laughed again.

So Henry drew the picture and when it was finished Joe took it away and came back the next day and told him that the man at Scotland Yard thought it was a very good picture and that if she wanted to be found, they'd have no trouble in finding his mum at all.

'Shall I draw one of Daddy now?' Henry asked.

'If you like,' Joe said.

'Daddy has a funny hand.'

'There's a lot of men in London with funny hands,' Dora told him. 'Funny hands, funny fingers. Take Joe here. Don't I find your fingers funny, Joe? Don't they just tickle my fancy to death.'

Joe hushed her.

'What way are your dad's funny?' Joe asked.

'He has no fingers, here and here,' he told him, holding up his right hand and holding his middle fingers down with his left hand.

'That is funny,' Joe agreed. 'How'd he come by losing them?'

'He lost them fighting the Germans,' he said. 'If he hadn't fought the Germans we would have all been killed. My daddy was very brave.'

'He might have fought all the Germans,' Dora said, 'but how does he wipe his arse these days? Or does Mummy do it for him,' and quick as a snake Joe leant out over the table and hit her across the face.

'Don't,' he said. 'Don't no more, all right.'

'Well, get your skates on and see what you can turn up.'

And that's what Joe did, went out every day in his big van, driving round the streets, looking for her, asking if anyone had seen her, but every day he came back with the same news, that she was nowhere to be found, and every day Henry got more and more used to Joe and Dora and the cat with the twitching back, and how their little home worked.

*

He walked through the store, past a stack of grinning, faintly menacing soft toys, to the stairs and the thin grinding sound of the electric railway. Halfway up he could see the layout, three, four tracks of it, with tunnels and sidings and little stations set about fields. There were goods trains and passenger trains and the Royal Mail running round, and on the platforms stood men with brief-cases and mothers and children and porters from another time pushing suitcased luggage. An InterCity rattled by. On the road by the track, a green lorry had its bonnet up, parked in a lay-by beside a field of yellow. It was peaceful and placed, a world of clouds and false memory.

A boy stood next to him, his head pressed against the partition.

'Good, isn't it?'

He nodded, trying to avoid eye contact. The boy was persistent.

'My mum's brought me up from Cambridge.'
Henry nodded, troubled.
'Where are you from?'
He swallowed. Five years gone in an instant.
'Me?' he said. 'Nowhere special.'

TWO

So let it be now that we see Anglefield Road: not a cul-de-sac
sloping down to the steep railway embankment: not a dimly lit
street of middle-income houses with a garland of lampposts
about its lumpy, light-bulb end: not a conclave of aspirational
dwellings hidden from the noise of train doors slamming and
station whistles blowing by shrouds of ragged poplar and forgotten beech: not a maze of privet hedges and clipped front gardens:
not a row of patched paths leading to pebble-dashed walls and
half-timbered brick: not a divergence of drives upon which stand
a variety of polished saloons and mud-spattered estates: no, none
of these, but a liner, vast and twinkling, carrying the sleep
dreams of pyjamaed husbands and nightdressed wives, their unforgiving sons and daughters turning but a meagre wall away.

It is of simple geometry. From its narrow, hedge-guarded
entrance it opens out into a straight but slow descent, the slabbed
pavements illuminated by intermittent lampposts and shadowed
by thinly spaced trees. Six houses mark this stark declivity, six
houses faced off in pairs, while at the base are planted four darker
dwellings ranged around the ring of tarmac upon which the daily
milk float circles and the weekly dustcart turns, its test-tube shape
a signal that this craft carries a volatile cargo, wherein who knows
what mixture lies, half stirred. One sudden jolt, one unexpected
rise in temperature, one unforeseen ingredient and this inert and
stable compound would collide and combust and leave safe
and sturdy Anglefield Road holed below the waterline.

Beyond these four houses, beyond where the Armstrongs, the
Plimsolls, the Millens and the Roaches dwell, washing up against
the bow of their long and narrow gardens, lies the uncharted sea
of the railway embankment, that unbroken wave of wood and rail
that blocks the light and carries the trains, a forsaken water which

threatens always to engulf them, but, by the consistency of its height and the sheer incline of its escarpment, protects them from the flotsam of the town beyond.

There is no captain on this Anglefield Road, no paid-up, uniformed crew. The vessel takes volunteers as its complement and it is they who set the ship's course, polish Anglefield Road's fittings, scrape the barnacles that despoil Anglefield's pre-war hull. But even in days of rosy contemplation, when the air is fresh and the only task set before them is to lift their glass and view their domain of enclosed and billowing green, they stand there, these voyagers, looking out over their several fences, their sturdy line of birch, their accurate throw of fir, wondering where this voyage might take them; not simply the white-beached paradise they believe they might alight upon still, or the moonlit romance they assumed once was theirs for the taking, but darker imaginings, the sudden storm they might not weather, the treacherous mutiny to which they might succumb, the hidden reef that might founder them all and have them pulling away with clutched children and snatched possessions as the lights flicker and the bow lifts and Anglefield Road slips into cold oblivion. Yes, a liner then, this cul-de-sac of theirs, its blunted decks and airy recreation rooms built it was supposed for the profit to be found in pleasure, its charts mapped out to pleasing and ordered destinations, but now, requisitioned by unseen hands and with its day rooms emptied, its corridors silent, is being carried by unforeseen currents into deep and unknown waters.

So let it be now then that we see Anglefield Road, as any homecoming figure might on this April night, its long deck grey and wet and dawn-seeking, riding on the darkened swell of the town. A string of porch lights peer through a drifting rain, outlining the rise and fall of this vessel's Fallopian mould, but though a light wind ladens the leaves, stirs the branches, the road itself holds steady. Out of sight of the lights and the cold glimmer of its restless surface, a ragged cat emerges on the lapping edge of the embankment, padding down through the thick, wet bracken, a vole set firm in its damp, mould-speckled mouth. The vole does not struggle, for the skin of its soft belly has been pierced by the cat's teeth and any movement it might wish to make only brings it further discomfort. The cat has been prowling for many hours, depositing its early evening toilet under the Millens' rhododendron bushes, before moving down over the Plimsolls' back lawn and up into the reaches of the waste ground. It has hunted well, the cat, and with his stomach full, intends this vole to be his morning trophy, to lay decapitated on the back doorstep, where exclamations will be made and praise given. Thus he moves with purpose and chooses the easiest route for his return home, under the ragged hole beneath the fence that leads into the Armstrongs' garden. With the vole held high in his mouth he trots up the path, which borders first on their vegetable garden, with its two compost heaps and three cold frames and thence their lawn, cleared by Marjorie that morning of last autumn's deposit of sodden leaves, the rake's long handle leaning protectively over the oblong wooden box containing the miniature cricket set which sits, warped and unused these thirty years, on the porch of their summer house opposite. It is not the only house in the neighbourhood to have a lawn, a rake and a boxed game, but it is the only house where no curtains hang in the back bedroom which overlooks them and in which Hector and Marjorie choose to sleep. It is something they have grown to love, perhaps the only thing they love about their home, this thick veil of green hanging down over their ever-open window. In the spring small birds build their nests in the exploded strands above and they wake to the demand of relentless young mouths; in summer's height it gives them shade to their siesta; and through the winter it protects them from the wind, the snow and as on this April night, the unhurried rain. It is large, their bedroom, left deliberately cold, but the bed they inhabit is warm, bought in a London market the month they married and host to their lifetime of love and quarrel and, so Hector believes, their only child's conception. Though in their late fifties, they occupy it in the same manner as they did then, naked, but in these later years, thicker-fleshed and stomach-swollen, he lying to her right, one of Marjorie's heavy breasts resting like sunken dough in the palm of his near fingerless right hand. He holds her softly, without thought, as the cat crouches, sensing the approach of the mail train on its way up north, its brown-coated complement of men standing in regulation line, rocking trick-track on their rubber heels, their practised hands winging envelopes into their allotted box; pigeonholed letters coming home to roost. One spins through the air now, as the train thunders through, over the very postbox into which it had been dropped earlier that afternoon, the cat's shadow flickering against the distant wall, giving illusory movement to his stationary posture. Flakes of light scatter up against the hanging strands of green, the metre of the train's passing clattering into Hector's hard-fought-for sleep, that morning's telephone conversation rattling in his head.

'Is that the railway bookshop?' He couldn't remember the name.

'It is.'

'You have a *House at Pooh Corner* for sale.'

'Several, I would imagine.'

'1947. Dedication inside. Slightly torn frontispiece.'

A silence and a shuffle. He had stood by the phone, waiting. Outside Marjorie had been drawing long tooth marks on the lawn. They should have raked in the leaves months ago, but theirs was a garden where tidying, directing growth, was frowned upon. They preferred to leave their leaves floating, scattered across the grass, mulched into the paths, brought into the kitchen on any winter shoe. The woman returned. She had it in her hand.

'Could you describe it to me?'

'The condition?'

'The inscription.'

'No name, just "This book belongs to", and a couple of letters below. Maybe an "A", could be an "R". It's hard to tell.'

'If I send a cheque, when you could send it?'

'You've a trusting voice. I'll put it in the post this morning.'

He'd been trying to remember whether he had been foolish enough to fill out the stub, with the name and amount set out in that tell-tale boxed configuration, drifting away at last upon the waters of a shallow sleep by the distracting thought of it, when the train came up and knowing what it is and what it might be carrying, his hand tightens, recalling the urgency with which he had written the address, one eye on his wife outside, the pen hasty in his hand. Marjorie winces at the sudden intensity of his hold. She does not cry out or pull his hand away, but placates his grip by brushing her fingers over the freckled web of bone, imagining it was dreamt desire that fashioned the purchase, not knowing that she is stirring other, less dormant hopes. She is awake momentarily, opening her eyes to the absolute clarity of the room, shadows chasing shadows across the counterpane, staccato rhythm to her thought, her right leg chill and half-draped over the edge of the bed. They're going to war, then, those rat-a-tat-tat boys, a fresh breed sent suddenly parentless into the swirling mist of conflict. Better to lose them that way than . . . ah, who knows any more? She sighs and stretching across, spreads her own fingers over the quiescent swell of him, finding in its slumber the path back into her own sleeping realm. She turns back as his hand resumes its nightly hold, as the letter falls in its allotted box, and the lights of the train vanish into the dark spray of the night.

The cat moves forward, up the side of the darkened house and out into their open gravel drive. It is raining hard, the water running down the hill and collecting in the curve of the communal gutter, and as he picks his way across the puddled pavement he takes shelter underneath the silver saloon that sits in the open garage over which, in the master bedroom, lie Suzanne and Matty Plimsoll. No bedwear for the Armstrongs, but, twenty years their junior, polka-dot shorts for Matty and a faded *Evita* T-shirt for his younger wife, Suzanne. She has heard the train too, listening to her husband's familiar breathing, and though it is Matty who sleeps, it is she who is dreaming, thinking of the holiday priest dressed in black, sitting on the dazzling shingle in his large Catholic hat, shaking his head at her and throwing white pebbles upon the great swell of water. Every year he came, every year, dressed in the same frock, throwing the same stones into the same sea, every year, sitting alone, smiling at the waves and what he imagined lay beyond. Not a day goes by that she does not picture him, that man of God, who turned his head to find her standing there, her innocent daisy dress billowing in the breeze, yet she feels closer to him than she does to anyone. Only he has looked into her heart and seen what lay within, only that priest, who threw the stone and sent the blush rushing up over every particle of her young, indecent skin. She sees him all the time now; when she's looking out over sunbathers at the Bonito Pool, checking her uniform in the mirror, touching herself quietly in the empty cabin hours of the day. Tonight, in the dark glow of the suitcase-spilled room, she stares up at the ceiling and watches herself walking back along the shingle, dressed as she is now, finding him sitting there in his black frock and his Catholic hat, the breeze tugging at the immodest hem of her shirt, those white stones like hard-boiled eggs, rolling cold and peeled in his slow and handsome hand.

Four nights ago, Sunday the 4th of April, they had been working their way back from a world cruise. Matty was laid out in their cabin, trying to get some shut-eye before his early morning shift in the kitchens. She and Matty hadn't been getting on well this last voyage, Matty dropping heavy hints that the time might be right to consider working ashore. Ashore? He had even suggested that if it was the sea she would miss, they could always move to the south coast so she could work on the ferries. As if that could compare. Taking advantage of a fifteen-minute break, dressed in company code, Suzanne was leaning up against the railings with Dickey and Murray, looking out onto the unlikely lights of Gibraltar. Suzanne wore a dress of dark green, the tan of her deck days glowing under the loops of fairy lights; far too fetching for the evening ahead, Dickey had warned, reminding her of the pest from Cabin 24D currently stalking the Crow's Nest. Dickey, the senior bar steward, stood upright in his button-polished waistcoat, balancing a glass of tonic water in the crook of his arm, his trousers drawn high, his bow tie bobbing with the slow working of his throat, eyes level with the evening dew atop the white railings. Murray's dress suit was protected by a vaguely transparent sheath of green plastic. He suffered from the damp. The stop had been an unscheduled one. Instead of sailing by on the blast of a whistle and up along the coast of Portugal, they had turned inwards under cover of the dark and now sat in the sluggish water of the harbour. There was no call for it. No one had been taken ill, they were making no attempt to dock, and as far as they knew, the ship was secure.

Staring out to the clambering loom of the rock, they could hear the sounds of the Gibraltar night. Suzanne was tired. Only another three days to go and then Southampton docks and the drive home to Anglefield Road. Home and rest. Rest and play. Play and work. If only there wasn't all this blessed consistency in the world. If only she could put everything on a cruise, take it out, put it back whenever she felt like it. If only Anglefield Road moved once in a while, docked up against some other town.

Dickey took out a small bottle from one of his waistcoat pockets and shook a few drops of bitters into his glass.

'At least we're not visiting,' he observed, lifting the glass to his mouth. 'You get a very poor class of tourist there now, what with the bottom dropping into the package-holiday market.'

Dickey held an unchecked animosity towards Gibraltar ever since he had been bitten there by one of their monkeys. Suzanne rather liked the place, its sturdy old-fashioned ways. It was like an England she had read about but never known, only hotter. But perhaps England had been warmer in the past too.

'I don't know why you always jibe against Gib,' Murray complained. 'Personally speaking Mr Mint is very fond of it. All those harlots and handbags.'

Murray ran his hands through his hair. One of the senior stewards, he wore it half an inch longer than regulation allowed. However, the company knew a good steward when they met one. His real name was Charles. Dickey took another sip.

'That's odd.' He straightened his waistcoat and pointed to the dark launch speeding across the water. 'Unless I'm very much mistaken, that's heading our way.'

'We're not meant to be taking on any passengers, are we?'

Neither man attempted to answer Suzanne's question. They watched as the motor launch drew closer.

'Customs, perhaps. Some distinctly dodgy customers on this trip,' Murray ventured.

'It looks of military bent,' Dickey said. 'The navy, do you think?'

'The Spanish navy?'

Dickey and Murray looked at each other.

'How long has she been deep sea?' Dickey asked.

'Seven years?'

'Seven years and she still doesn't know that the Spanish navy is

the one navy never allowed into Gibraltar harbour. That, my dear, is the Royal Navy. Our very own Senior Service.'

'The one that sticks to your lip,' Murray added. Dickey spat the last of his drink over the side.

'What would the navy want with us?' she asked.

Dickey drew his arm across the panorama of the ship. 'Perhaps they've reintroduced the press gang. Perhaps our passengers are about to be treated to a life of biscuits and buggery.'

'Can anyone join?' Murray asked. 'Mr Mint is very partial to digestives.'

The motor launch drew alongside. Six crew-cutted young men, a look of authorized determination about them, stood on the deck, preparing to board. A rope ladder was lowered from the baggage port.

'Whoever they are, it's most irregular,' Dickey observed.

'Yes, and it's me that will have to find the irregular cabin space,' Murray whined. 'I've a good mind to complain. We're rushed off our pieds as it is.'

The men began to clutch at the climb. Each carried a small overnight bag. Murray leant over in the vain attempt to get a better look.

'Still, what's fluffing pillows for six bruising hulks like that to a professional like me,' he said, as one by one they disappeared into the depths of the ship. 'Do you think I should give them a wave?'

The next morning the captain called them all down to the Genoese mess. The Argentinians had invaded the Falkland Islands. A Task Force to retake the islands was being assembled. The *Canberra* was to be requisitioned, one of the Ships Taken Up From Trade, STUFT he had called it, the named irony rippling round the room. They wouldn't be going to the South Atlantic itself, only about halfway, to Ascension Island, carrying the troops needed, two thousand of them. It would be a volunteer company, sailing under Royal Navy rules. British and Irish nationals could apply, but the Genoese and the Indian crews were being flown home. Men only, the company had insisted; no women except for a few officers. The girls had kicked up such a ruckus that by the next day they relented. Any regular could apply.

That evening, when Matty came back from his shift, they had

25

sat up half the night working out on the back of a menu how much money they would make. Triple pay, the company had promised. Unlike Matty, on a normal cruise she never had to dip into her wages at all, thanks to all the tips she earned, watching the fivers peeled back as she bent down with a tray of drinks in her hand or smiling conspiratorially at that whispered bar-baked request. There wouldn't be much note-slipping on this voyage, no table-hopping charges to be made, no empty cabins to allot for those afternoon assignations, but even without them they were destined to make a tidy sum. Matty wanted to spend it on doing up the home, while she didn't know what to do with it: something special. This last trip she had gone with a party of passengers to see the Pope. It was one of the most wonderful things that had ever happened to her, seeing him close up. As he bent towards her, she could see the dent in his head where that madman had tried to shoot him. She had never seen a bullet wound before, and she wanted to reach out and touch it, to feel how it had closed up, sealed his holiness, made him more perfect, almost miraculous.

'You should have gone, Matty,' she said, scolding the top of his head with their sheet of sums. 'I'd feel safer if you had.'

Matty brushed his hair back over his bald spot.

'I was working.'

'But the Pope. You should have wangled it. Especially now.'

The Pope had given her a crucifix on a long silver chain, and she took it wherever she went, around her neck, in her handbag, in the front pocket of her uniform, sometimes even tied around her middle, underneath her shirt. At night she kissed it and placed it on the bedside table. Matty didn't like it, she could tell by the way he pushed it to the side whenever he checked the alarm on the clock. It was almost as if he felt there was someone else sharing their bed. He was right in a way; there was. Funny to think that the holiest man in the world had felt the top of her head, funny to think that as she stood there, this adventure of theirs was beginning to take shape. She had never even heard of the Falklands before the announcement, and like many there that morning, she thought that they must be somewhere near the Hebrides. The Argentinians invading Scotland! It made no sense at all. It was only slightly clearer when Matty had whispered the truth of their geography. When the Pope had bent over her and blessed her, his right arm shaking, his voice thin and papery like his hands, did he know what was going to happen? Was that why he had given them an audience? Did God tell him things? Was that how it worked? God never told her things, and yet she wanted Him to, like she had wanted that priest to open his hands and draw her close, whisper words into her wind-blown ear, words that might have unlocked her little heart. Yes, it was all beginning to start then. She should have known, standing before him, with the Catholic priest and the beach and all the wicked thoughts careering about her head, his great black cloak and what lay dormant underneath, the great unused flood of it, that the Pope would have sensed the mystery upon which she was about to embark, that the animal of history crouched before her was ready to pounce.

She brushes her stomach lightly, and as she does so discovers that the T-shirt is damp. She had worn it after her bath, while ironing a pile of shirts, and caught up in the TV had forgotten to take it off. It was Matty's fault. He'd walked in from cleaning the car, his hands red and soapy, and coming up behind her, had wound his arms about her. Suzanne wriggled out of his embrace.

'Matty, I'm trying to iron. You're all wet.'

'So?'

'Why you had to clean the car in the first place . . .'

Matty went over to the fridge, brought out the cheese they had bought on the drive home and, peeling back the cellophane, bit into it. His teeth were slightly too large for his mouth. Why couldn't he use a knife? In the early days she didn't mind, but now it irritated her. He always did it, unwrapped it like a child might a choc-ice, tucking into it as if it was his exclusive treat. If she started to eat cheese again, would he still slobber all over it like that? Not that she had any intention of abandoning her strict regime. Her figure was her passport to the *Canberra*'s top territory, opened up those wallets, kept her there.

'Have you cancelled the milk?' Matty asked. Suzanne pressed the steamer button for a hard three seconds.

'Yes.'

'What about the papers?'

'Matty.' A note of weariness crept into her voice. 'I've done the papers, I've cancelled the milk; now I'm doing the ironing.'

Matty stood there, chewing on his deficiencies.

'I'd have mown the lawn if it hadn't been for the rain. It'll be in a proper state when we get back.' He looked out of the back window. 'Of course with the money we'll be getting, we could have a patio from here to the rose bed. Tubs, tables, an umbrella or two. It could look quite Continental.'

Suzy banged the iron down on the board.

'Freddie's doing it.'

'The patio?'

'The mowing. He popped over earlier. Any excuse.'

Matty took another bite of cheese.

'I suppose I shouldn't say anything under the circs,' he said, his mouth working full, 'but why we have to put up with having that monstrosity next door – I won't grace it with the name "car" – I don't know. It completely spoils the look of the place. It's covered in orange spots, for crying out loud!'

Crumbs spilt from the crease of his mouth. He stood there, waiting for her assent. His hair was receding fast. Every day an attitude older. Suzanne sniffed.

'It was left unpainted,' she said. 'To see if it rusts.'

'And now we know it does. It's four foot higher off the ground than any other car I know.'

'It was a prototype,' she explained. 'A try-out.' She picked up the pile of shirts. 'There. You can take that lot upstairs.'

He put the cheese down on the table and held his arms out in front of him, unwilling to let go of his stick.

'That's all very well,' he said, 'but why do they have to try it out next door to us?'

'You know why. Rich Brother George gave it to him. It didn't cost them a penny.'

Suzanne folded up the ironing board and moved it into the little alcove, where the tennis racquets and badminton set lay. When she came back he was still standing there.

'Rich Brother George, Rich Brother George,' he was saying. 'What would they do without Rich Brother George.'

Suzanne added three pairs of socks to his pile.

'Don't you start. They've got enough problems with the Roaches. He's sent in a letter of complaint. Anonymously, of course.'

She broke off a wedge of cheese and, popping it into his mouth, kissed him. She shouldn't have said that.

'Go on, before you get them all creased,' she said. 'I've got a few more things to sort out down here.'

'I still don't know if we're doing the right thing, Suzy.'

'We'll be fine, you said so yourself.'

'Still. What if anything happens? What'll happen to Marcia?'

'She'll be fine. We'll all be fine. Just think of the money. Perhaps you're right. We could have a sun lounge, like on board.'

He stood there, eyes dropped.

'I'll go up, then,' he said.

'OK. I won't be long.'

'Don't. We've an early start tomorrow.'

She knew from the way he walked what he hoped lay in store. Well, if it sent him off to sleep quickly. However, by the time she joined him, Matty was sitting upright, engrossed in a late-night Western, his arms folded and wearing an expression as if he was in church, listening to a sermon. It always amazed her, grown men and Westerns, the way they believed in all those tassels, all that walking tall, all that bang-bang you're dead.

It was a big bedroom, running front to back. She'd got him to knock it through when she moved in. It marked and expanded her territory. As she climbed into bed, a cowboy was sitting on a horse shooting at a pack of mules.

'That's not very sporting of him,' she said, rubbing his calf with the crook of her instep.

'Later,' he said, frowning fiercely at the television, moving his leg away.

Later was what she didn't want. Luckily he fell asleep after twenty minutes. She leant up over the bed and switched the set off, her shirt accidentally drawn over one of the trio of framed photographs that stood to one side, knocking it back so that all three fell clack-clack-clack onto the pine veneer. She picked them up slowly, setting them back without a sound – Matty and the wedding cake; Suzy leaning bridal-laced against the long bonnet of the hired Talbot; and the third, the three of them, that first time, smiling under the Mediterranean sun, each holding a brace of skates as if they'd just shot them out of the sky. She used to skate a lot when she was younger. It was how she met Matty, going round the Promenade Deck on roller skates. He had been on one of the company cruises to the Greek Islands with his daughter, had wanted to show Marcia where her mother's family came from. They were both novices at roller skating, could hardly stand up straight, though Marcia had a good sense of balance and would have got on fine if her father hadn't insisted on holding on to her. So, true to her vocation, Suzanne found herself taking the two of them around, not for just the once, but every morning on the way out, and discovered as she took his arm and held him steady that she looked forward to it, indeed missed it that morning when Marcia had an upset stomach. 'You should have come by yourself,' she had told him the next day as they sat having coffee, Marcia pounding the circuit one more time, and Matty had looked at her, surprised. 'But she wasn't well,' he said, 'I couldn't have left her,' and it flashed through her mind then, not simply that the exchange revealed that she knew nothing about being a parent, but more importantly that it was quite possible there had been nothing wrong with Marcia at all, that she was more than likely simply jealous of the attention Suzanne was receiving. Marcia wasn't stupid. She could see how Suzanne showed off to her father at the end of every session with her twirling curtsey, her pleated skirt riding high above her waist, Matty trying hard not to look at her legs. She had good legs then. She raises them up and feels the back of her calves. She has good legs now. 'Well, I felt like an abandoned bride,' she had replied, and it was in the saying of it, while Matty protested, that she saw the priest shaking his Catholic hat at what had crept into her mind as sharp as a turn on ice; that this man would be good enough, would give her the degree of protection that she needed, widower, divorcee or whatever, and she was right. No one would have imagined that he would have come back to Anglefield Road with a young woman in tow, a wife not dead a full year and a daughter half her age, but that's what he had done. By the time they got to Paxos all he had eyes for was Suzanne and the way she stood on that rock above the taverna in her white one-piece bathing suit, feet together, arms raised, smiling down at him, as the Catholic priest threw his hat upon the water and she dived into the perfect blue.

She settles back in bed. Matty murmurs and presses himself against her. He will wake this morning, she thinks, wake with all that willed upon me, and now, weary of the prospect, leans over and sets the radio alarm for an quarter of an hour later, determined to be hurried out of bed before he has time to draw her close. She swings her feet out and sits upright. Matty moves, half searching for her form. She waits a few minutes, then pads downstairs through to the kitchen, taking out the white linen bag tucked into the flour tin. She sits at the table and rolls herself a three-paper joint before putting the rest of the package in her raincoat pocket. Stepping into her wellington boots she unlocks the back door and hastens down the length of the garden, threading her arms through the flapping coat as she walks. The rain falls lightly on her face and legs, but once at their boundary fence the embankment gives her shelter. The old gate at the end has to be pushed hard, for the ground has swollen under the rotting frame, but she works with practised ease, raising it up, two hands on the handle, pushing with body and shoulder. As it scrapes open, it describes its movement on the embankment floor, reminding her of the marks she used to make at school with the sharp stub of her pencil screwed tight into her Woolworth's compass, criss-crossed circles and lines of intersection, and knowing that this too reveals the presence of a meeting, she scuffs the ground as best she can. Leaving the gate open and moving forward with one hand held in front of her face, the other trailing along the fence, she notices by the dim light of the railway station above that the frequency of her passage is becoming increasingly distinct, even though she hasn't used it for three months. Clumsier than a cat's, wider than a fox's, no one could mistake this path for anything else but one made by a human, and moreover, by the manner of its geography – its worn beginnings, its seemingly arbitrary end, the furtive manner with which it hugs the perimeter, unwilling to venture into the hinterland – a path conceived for private purpose, tamped firm by stealth, fashioned for the night.

As she reaches the spot where she must climb, another train

approaches the station, a passenger train, and though she knows that no one can see her, she steps forward into the screen of tangle and bush, stilled. Doors open, voices break the air, coughs and chatters, the mutter of a night-out couple arguing their way home, a quartet of fans singing of some football victory, and then, above them all, a clearer, stronger voice.

'Richard?' it cries. 'Are you sure?'

Looking up through the narrow gap between the station fence and the platform, though she can see a blur of legs and shoes moving towards the tunnel exit, above her one set stands still, black and polished on the puddled platform. The voice repeats the name, and then adds to his question.

'Richard?' he calls. 'Richard? Are you sure it isn't you?' but before Richard or whoever it might be can give a reply, the whistle blows and the contact is lost. She hears the man curse, the word itself indistinct but the sentiment clear enough, one of impatience and irritation, with the hint of a perceived and unsubstantiated affront. The whistle sounds again, urgency in the blast, and from the back, a warning. 'Close the doors! Close the doors!' The shoes disappear. The door is pulled shut and Suzanne waits for the train to leave, waits for all their journeys to resume, but as the wheels begin to turn she hears the shoes jump down again, metal-capped, stumbling for a moment as an unseen hand catches the flapping door and hurls it back hard against its frame. The guard shouts in disapproval, his impotent splutterings travelling the length of the platform. As quickly as it came, the train is gone and the station falls silent, empty of feet and shoes, save for this one stranded pair. They stand motionless for a moment, glinting in the orange-coloured dark, before following the rest, slowly at first, but then, like the vanished train, gathering momentum, as if more sure of their purpose. She holds her breath until the hollow haste of their hurrying vanishes in the echo of the tunnel, then moves herself to the place in the fence where the upended log stands.

When she had first started coming, the night after the Christmas bonfire, she'd had great difficulty climbing into their garden for they had no gate leading onto the scrubland, and along that stretch of fence the bank fell away steeply. The first time she had done it her top had snagged on a nail and the 9.40 had come in just as she had lifted it half away from her body, trying to work it free. Anyone looking down from the station would have seen her caught halfway across, Hector Armstrong, Freddie Millen, Mark's father, anyone. She was reminded of the times when she and her best friend used to stand in the allotments and lift their school jerseys up over their heads when the trains trundled past, remembering too the beating she took the afternoon one of the passengers happened to be her father. 'I only it did for a laugh, Dad,' she protested but he took his belt to her just the same. Sixteen she was and she accepted it. And this, was this for a laugh, scrambling through the undergrowth to see a boy seventeen years her junior? Well, in a manner of speaking, yes. A serious laugh.

After that first visit she returned the following day and rolled up against the fence one of the logs that Matty had sawn up that winter. That and the overhanging branch makes the hurdle easier now, easier too now that she knows what she's doing, knows what's on the other side, knows how to get back. She never thought of that either, the first time, how to get back, standing in their rusty wheelbarrow, holding her precarious balance, until it tipped her into Mark's flailing arms. 'How did you get that bruise?' Matty asked her a couple of days later, walking into the bathroom as she stood drying herself, and Suzanne, turning round to examine on her upper thigh what she had not noticed, had told him quite truthfully what type of object had produced such an intimate discoloration. 'Never thought I'd see you and a wheelbarrow within fifteen feet of each other,' he had joked, cupping his hand over it before moving across to brush his teeth. 'What were you doing? Burying someone?' and that night she lay awake, tracing the tender outline of the tumble and the stifled laughter, imagining the unmapped route of conspiracy on which she was embarking, the bodies she might have to hide. Since then, like the approach, her exit is now catered for, a pile of unwanted bricks surreptitiously removed from the back of the Roaches' shed and leant up against the other side, a flight of unsuspected steps.

Suzanne climbs up onto the log and reaching up, hauls herself over. She lands softly on the other side, conscious of her breath and her body and the quiet surround. The rain has stopped; the trees are still. She stands for a moment, collecting herself, listening to the water running off the branches, checking that no one else is about, then, wrapping the raincoat about her, walks up.

In the halfway depth of the garden a light glows from the high window in the shed, Mark's radio probably, or the small lamp that his father keeps by his workbench. He comes most nights now, after supper, after the formalities of familial existence have been observed, to sit in the little snug he has made at the far end, smoke the marijuana he bought round the back of the school music block, drink from the half-bottle of vodka he has stolen from the nearby supermarket, and tonight, against all promises to the contrary, has taken his father's unwanted heirloom out of its casing and holding it across his lap has spent the last hour of this solitary evening oiling the barrel, squeezing the cloth hard in his hand, marvelling at the pressure he can apply, how the sweet-smelling droplets run over his wrist, infecting the cuffs of his checked shirt with their sweet perfume. There may come a time when he will position the dull glinting barrel to the ivory of his hesitant teeth, and, God willing, obliterate the world and the fault it has found with him. He could have executed the course of action tonight, loaded it up and have done with it, but the thought of disturbing everyone's sleep worries him. It is an unwanted conse-quence of his intended action he has yet to resolve. He is an Anglefield boy and knows the importance of being a good neighbour.

He places the gun back in the rack and takes another pull of vodka. The door creaks open. He pushes the bottle down in between the cushions, quickly.

'Anyone at home?'

'Suze!' Mark looks up. 'I thought you weren't coming.'

Suzanne steps in and pulls the door behind her. He looks ridicu-lously young, but then, he is ridiculously young. She wonders how she looks in comparison. Not as young as he. But there is a glow to her that has long fled his skin.

'He took a bit of a while to get to sleep.'

'You make him sound like a baby.'

'That's what he is sometimes.'

'And what if baby wakes?'

34

'Then down will come Suzy, cradle and all.' She pulls out the package and drops it into his lap. 'That enough?'

Mark unwraps the silver foil and turns the sticky brown block in his hand. 'Sure,' he says.

'You can have more.'

'No, this is fine. What do I owe you?'

'Are you trying to be funny?' She reaches back into her pocket. 'I brought a ready made sampler.'

She lights it and taking a deep breath holds her lungs steady. Her head swims. It feels like she is back on board, floating in that strangely ordered world of work and freedom. The floor rises under her feet and she leans against the workbench to steady her balance. He looks lovely in this light.

'How's it going?' she says.

'Oh, you know.' Mark shrugs his shoulders. 'I had to go for a chat and a check up, yesterday.'

'And?'

'He told me I should get out more.'

'He's probably right.'

'Asked me if I had a girlfriend.'

'And what did you say?'

'Said they were lining up.'

She smiles and blowing the sweet scent into the air, hands the joint over.

'Doesn't your dad ever say anything about the smell in here?'

'He pretends not to notice. They both pretend not to notice, carry on as if everything's normal. It's not normal. It's me.'

'I know.'

She does know, that's the strange part. But why does she know, how does she know? That's what she can't figure out. Mark is in the same quandary.

'Show me something normal, Suzy.'

She opens her raincoat.

'There, that make you feel better?' she had said, and looking at his smile, she knows it has. He feigns disappointment.

'I thought you might have nothing on underneath.'

'In this weather? It's this or nothing.'

'I'll have to make do, then.'

He has a certain confidence about him these days, she is pleased to note. He would never have said something like that when they started. She feels no qualms about showing herself. His need to look erases any trace of embarrassment she might have felt. She is still uncertain how it happened last Christmas Eve, all she can remember is Anglefield Road in its pedantic celebrations, the unlit bonfire standing in the middle of the road, Hector ladling out the spiced punch, Freddie and Matty dressed in women's clothing riding the twins' presents in uncertain circles, Patsy imploring them to be careful, while beyond the rim of the hub sits Mark, the outcast, scowling in the chair his father had brought out for him. Feeling what, bored, sympathetic, impatient, the urge for *Canberra* excess to spill out onto the road, she had walked over, sat next to him and without warning taken his head in her hand and pushed him down into the water tub, dipping her head alongside, both snapping at the elusive fruit. They rose, half gasping, fighting over the same bobbing apple, water running down their necks, the food of contempt pressed close between their mouths. They both bit once, and flinging his head back, he had pulled the little vodka bottle from his jacket pocket and handed it to her quickly, the back of his hand sheltering the act from a prying parent's eyes. She drank it willingly, the best drink she had had all night, passing it back unseen, a confederate now; back and forth it went until emptied.

'Care for a drive?' he said. She laid her hand on his.

'Mark.'

'She had hair just like yours. Don't know about the rest of her. Never got the chance.' He flung the bottle back in the bushes, his dark hair flopped over his face. 'God, this is fucking boring. Got any dope? You look the sort.'

Her mouth hung open, as if she'd pushed back into the cold water. She was the sort, her immediate stash tucked into the bag in the flour tin and another, altogether larger, lodged behind the sheets in the airing cupboard. It was risky, bringing stuff in from the ship, but sometimes the opportunity was too good to pass by. Anyway it was fun, smuggling it in under their noses, making a few extra quid, selling it to a couple of the younger couples she knew in town. None of this lot, though.

'Well?'

'Well what?'

'Do you have any or not?'

A shriek went up. Freddie had fallen off his scooter. Suzanne looked down at the bitten apple in her lap. Matty would have a fit if he knew.

'I'm sure your parents wouldn't approve.'

'Fuck my parents.' He got up, resting his weight on his good leg. 'I'm off to the hut. Why don't you come round and roll us a smoke, when all these good Christians are asleep.'

Which is what she did hours later, Matty out cold on the living-room couch, moved furtively down the garden, feeling her way along the embankment, the dark corridor rolling underfoot. Over the fence and there he was, in this shed singing loudly to the radio. She sat on the arm of his brown leather chair and fashioned one of her elaborate dove-tail extravaganzas, and with that first inhalation felt Anglefield Road float away. Here were intimacies to be orchestrated. She ruffled his hair, sensing the man that lay within the child. How erotic she had found it, those first hesitant caresses of this furious, impotent boy, unable to do any more than bite his lip in uncertainty.

He stares at her hard, like the first time, like Matty does.

'I don't know why you do this,' he says.

She draws the coat round her.

''Cause I like catching my death of cold, that's why.'

''Cause you feel sorry for me.'

It cannot be denied. She does feel sorry for him. Doesn't everybody?

'So what? I feel sorry for lots of people. I feel sorry for Hector, I feel sorry for Freddie. I don't hop across their fence half naked at the dead of night.'

'They're not completely fucked.'

'Yes, they are.' She jumps to her feet and puts her arms around his head. 'We all are,' she says. 'Every one of us.'

She stands there, feeling him tremble against her. She presses his head against her breasts, feels his hands gather themselves underneath her shirt. She can hear him mouth the single syllable of her name, feel his lips' whispered imprint, realizing how much has

37

changed since that first evening. She holds him close, waiting for him to subside. Afterwards she squats down on her haunches and rolls another joint on his lap. She can taste the night air as it rises from the concrete floor.

'I can't stay long,' she says. The muscles in her leg are tense. It's hard holding herself steady. Her voice trembles with the effort. 'We're off early tomorrow.'

He nods.

'I wish I was going with you.'

She lightly cuffs his head and lights the joint.

'Tell you what. I'll bring you back a souvenir.' She stands up, passing it over, anxious to leave. 'You wouldn't see much of me, anyway. I'll be working.'

Mark looks down at his knees.

'There'd be moments.'

She smiles. There'd be moments. Mark holds his hands in his lap and works his fingers together.

'Will you come and see me when you get back?'

'Course I will.'

'I bet you don't.'

'Why d'you say that?'

'I don't know. Maybe deep down I don't want you to.'

'It's not a very nice thing to say, Mark, after all I've done.'

'You don't understand, Suze. You've given me a taste of what life could be like. Sometimes I wish I'd never known.'

'Are you telling me you'd rather I hadn't come?'

'I'm saying you're selfish like me. I'm saying that you've made it worse as well as better.'

'I'd better go, then.'

'No, it isn't that I don't—'

She holds her hand over his mouth.

'I'd better anyway.'

She bends down and kisses him and with a whispered 'see you', his outstretched fingers trailing down her turning back, falling by his side like a discarded rope freed of its mooring, she slips back out into the night. It is a sour end to the meeting, and hurrying back she wishes she had known how to sweeten the departure, worries too that she has stayed too long, scrambling over the fencing, legs slapped by the clinging wet of fern, ducking under the branches, half running, head bent, across the lawn until she sees the unexpected pool of light and Marcia standing in the doorway, small and dark, her arms folded in a stern, interrogative pose. Suzanne slows down, brushing the leaves from her coat, wondering if Marcia has woken Matty, wondering if she is going to have to face the two of them. How long has she been back, waiting like this? She moves forward, softly calling.

'Marcia! Didn't expect to see you!'

'So I see.' Marcia looks back into the house. 'I thought you must have gone to bed early.'

'We did. I couldn't sleep. You know your father, though, sleep through anything.'

'Not quite anything.'

Six years on and still the prurient innuendo. Irritated, Suzanne moves abruptly, pushing past, closing the door, dampening the sound of the wind.

Marcia follows her into the kitchen.

'What were you doing out there?'

What was she doing out there? Suzanne crosses to the fridge and pulls out a carton of orange juice.

'Just having a bit of a think. Strange times, these.' She lifts the carton, tilting the question. Marcia shakes her head. Suzanne takes a swift gulp, swallowing her disquiet.

'We weren't expecting you,' she says.

'I've got some time off. I came down on the ten thirty.'

One of the pairs of shoes, then. Suzanne looks down, but she doesn't recognize them. Great big clodhoppers they are, quite unsuitable for Marcia's short legs.

Marcia is reminded of her earlier observation.

'You've been out over half an hour. Your lips are quite blue. Are you wearing anything under that?'

'Marcy, Marcy. What sort of question is that? If you must know, I felt like a joint. Your father doesn't approve. Not in the house, anyway. But he'll be thrilled to see you, though you should have rung. Or brought someone down. We don't like you walking alone at night.'

'Brought someone down?'

'A friend. Girlfriend, boyfriend, whatever.'

Suzanne leans back against the washing machine, still warm from its final cycle. That would be the day, Marcia fucking someone in the basement with Daddy and the interloper similarly engaged upstairs. She used to have the bedroom at the back, but when Suzanne moved in it didn't seem quite right. So Matty did up the basement and moved her down there. Though she kicked up a fuss at the time, she likes it, away from Suzanne, away from her new father. Not that she's here that much these days. Suzanne prefers it too. His past buried.

'So, you've come to see us off.'

'Not exactly.' She points to the transistor radio stuck on the windowsill. 'Have you been listening to the news recently? There's no knowing what's going to happen.' She pats the pockets of her jeans. 'I don't suppose you've got any dope left?'

Suzanne shakes her head, although there is a good half-ounce upstairs.

'We're only going down halfway. It's not as if we're going to be part of some D-Day landing. We didn't think you minded.'

Marcia turns her back on her, scrabbled in her shoulder bag, and pulled out a packet of cigarettes.

'Well, I do,' she says. She lights the cigarette and inhales with a practised necessity. Suzanne is surprised.

'I thought you told Matty you'd given up. He hates you smoking.'

Marcia pulls on it fiercely. Twenty a day, Suzanne thinks, if not more.

'I don't see why he had to go to sea in the first place. He was quite happy where he was, with his own business.'

'Marcia. Why do you think? He wanted my company. I wanted his.' Wanted him to keep her on the straight and narrow too. It was so easy, to stray once out of sight of land.

'He says he hardly ever sees you.'

It was true. Their paths rarely crossed. A few cross-over hours of sleep, a shared breakfast, an occasional unbalanced bout of love-making, one exhausted, battered by machine or weary from the demands of relentless sociability, the other fresh from sleep or insistent through brandy and beer. They moved in different circles, drank in different bars, but whereas Suzanne could be escorted below, sit on a bar-stool and joke with the cooks and boilermen, it was harder for Matty to settle comfortably up top. There was a level of sophistication working there which only the initiates could appreciate. Marcia was right. They saw each other seldom: but it served its purpose.

'We work different shifts,' she explains, picking up the cigarette packet. 'Not the most social of arrangements, I agree, but we do the best we can. May I?'

'I just don't see why you can't miss this one,' Marcia persists, shrugging away the request.

'The money's too good to turn down. We won't be in any danger.'

'But he'll be . . .' She points to the floor.

'Below deck. I know.'

'If anything does happen . . .'

'Nothing will. He's probably safer there than where I'm going to be.'

'I'm not bothered about . . .' She stops. Suzanne finishes her sentence for her.

'About me.'

'No, I didn't mean . . .'

'Yes, you did. I don't blame you, Marcia. He's your father. I'm – well, I'm nothing to you, really.'

There is a pause. Suzanne looks her cleanly in the eye, stepdaughter and stepmother, united by the house and a sleeping man and their shared suspicions. It would be me that's half dressed, she thinks, wondering if Marcia has yet scurried along at night, trying not to her drop her secrets along the trail. Suddenly she can't bear the sight of her.

'I'm off upstairs. Talk to him in the morning if you feel that strongly about it.'

Suzanne hangs her coat over the banisters and climbs the stairs. Going into the bathroom she sits down on the lavatory, lights the cigarette and rubs her hair dry with a towel. She drops the cigarette in the bowl and watches it swirl away. Back in the bedroom she shivers. She is colder than she thought. She should have changed before she went out. Crossing her arms she pulls the damp T-shirt up over her head, throwing it into a corner before moving across to the walk-in cupboard and taking out another. A sudden spatter of rain rattles the window. She opens the blind and looks across. The lamppost throws a dour light over the circle and onto the window across the road. A movement below catches her eye, the Roaches' cat coming out from underneath their car, carrying its latest victim. Kill anything, that bloody animal. She bangs on the window in the hope of frightening it into letting the creature go, but all she does in succeed in disturbing Matty.

'Suzy?'

She crosses back quickly. 'Go back to sleep,' she whispers. 'We'll make love in the morning.'

Reassured, Matty settles. Pulling on the dry shirt, she stands by the bed and looks down. He's not so bad. He works hard enough, does his best. If he wants to make love in the morning, why not? She turns to the dark mirror, touching the slight swell of her stomach before climbing back into bed. She kisses the back of his neck as Mark presses his head against her breasts and the black-skirted priest shakes his Catholic hat at her and throws another stone.

Trotting out along the road, the cat is disturbed by another, more distant movement, a falling shadow where there should be light, turning quickly into the Millens' dense shrubbery, coming up against the inert form of their tortoise. Of all the pets and creatures that inhabit Anglefield Road this tortoise is the most widely travelled, inching his way day on day through the secrets of their gardens, taking winter refuge in any number of comfortable hideaways, the Armstrongs' rotting compost, the upended sheet-stuffed cardboard box inside the Plimsolls' garage, and last season under the Millens' long and heavily padlocked shed, from which seeped an imperceptible flow of engine oil which dripped upon his shell and thus accounts for its brilliant gloss and his peculiarly mechanical smell. The cat drops the crippled vole for a moment and investigates with a curious paw, but this tortoise knows him well and remains secure within his keep. Mindful of its purpose the cat takes up its prey once more, scratching his back against the 'For Sale' post stuck into the flowerbed, before moving on.

They had gone to bed early the Millens, as they did most

evenings, nine, nine thirty, for they both tire quickly these days. Patsy sleeps in a high-necked white gown with embroidered flowers down the front, her long grey hair tied in a knot, her angular face made soft and heavy by aromatic sedation, her pillow infused with drops of lavender essence, which Marjorie had advised would help her to sleep and which helps dispel the smell of engines that seems to invade the very house.

Patsy is unable to sleep, puffing up the pillows, turning this way and that, waiting for the twins to wake, counting bills, subtracting money, coming up with nothing. If only Freddie would take a grip. Tonight as she sat on the edge of the bed combing her hair, he had come in from the bathroom wearing those baggy underpants she hated, sat down beside her and taken her free hand in his. He usually did that when the news was unsettling, like last July when he'd been fired, or that Tuesday, five years ago, when she'd walked into the waiting room with the news that she was carrying twins. Forty-three years old and carrying twins! He looked as if he was going to sink back into the walls, his colour drained so. Twins, he had said. You mean two of them? and had plumped down, felled, seeking out her reassuring grasp. Still, he hadn't looked as if he was the bearer of bad news this evening. He had simply patted her hand and said:

'I thought we might go for a drive this weekend.'

'In the Rommel?'

'Patsy!'

'Well, it should be on Salisbury Plain, rumbling about on manoeuvres, not parked on a residential drive. Every time I get into it I feel I should be invading Poland.'

'Rich Brother George says they're the car of the future, these four-wheel-drives.'

'Who's future would that be, Freddie? Yours, mine, Field Marshal Keitel's?'

'We needn't go far. Just round the estate. You might find it interesting.'

'What, like Venice is interesting? I'll bring my Baedeker, shall I? Come on, Freddie, what's all this about?'

She started to work the hairbrush down the back of her head in earnest. She had worn her hair long since she was eleven. Last time

Suzanne was back on leave, she had told Patsy she should go to the new salon in the High Street and 'see what they could do with it'. She meant well enough, but Patsy had found the suggestion intrusive, almost rude. It was her hair. Why would anyone else think about it?

Freddy stuck out his lanky legs, looked at his toes and wiggled them about.

'I want you to answer me a question, Patsy.'

'It's not a trick question, is it, Freddie?' she said, brushing with increased vigour. 'I'm too tired for silly games.'

'No. It's a very serious question.'

'At this time of night?'

'It's not that sort of serious.'

'What is it, then?'

He got up and started patrolling the three sides of the bed.

'Imagine you're driving around the neighbourhood on a Sunday morning.'

'I'd rather not.'

'Just pretend, Patsy. It's Sunday morning; the sun is shining, the papers have been read, the breakfast things put away . . .'

'Yes, come on, Freddie, get on with it.'

'As you're driving along, looking out your side window, what do you see?'

'What do you mean, what do I see?'

'As you drive by, what do you see?'

'What I usually see. Houses.'

'And outside the houses?'

'Drives, gardens, "For Sale" signs that have failed to find a buyer for six months. What am I looking for here, Freddie? Penguins, polar bears, the lost wreck of the *Hesperus*?'

Freddie ignored her.

'Stop there. If there are men in these drives, in these gardens, what do you imagine they'll be doing?'

'Most likely they'll be washing their cars, the great baboons.'

'And if they're not washing their cars?'

'They're probably mowing the—' She stopped short and threw the hairbrush at him, hitting him on the head. It made a disturbingly hollow sound. 'Freddie, you promised.'

Freddie rubbed his scalp. It was not unexpected, her reaction.

'It's not what you think, Patsy. I've had this idea. A business venture. Something Rich Brother George might be willing to invest in.'

Patsy said nothing.

'It came to me while locking up the collection. Do you realize that of all the magazines devoted to gardening there is not one that concentrates solely on lawns and the means of their subjugation?'

He stepped out of his underpants. Patsy tried not to look.

'Means of subjugation?' she said.

'Yes, you know.' Making a whirring noise with his lips he walked up and down with his hands held out in front of him. Patsy buried her face in the duvet.

'So you are talking about lawnmowers.'

'I am.' He picked his pyjamas up from the pillow and pulled the bottoms up over his hairless hindquarters. 'But not in the way you think.'

Patsy lifted her face from the refuge of the bed.

'Freddie, you promised me you would never mention that word in this house again. And Freddie . . .' She pointed to the errant organ.

'What? Oh, sorry.' He put his hands inside his pyjama trousers and rearranged himself. 'That is why I used the phrase "means of subjugation". I am trying to keep to my word.'

Patsy slipped the rubber band from her wrist and wound it round her thick clump of hair.

'I meant what I said, Freddie,' she warned. 'One more two-stroke taken apart on the kitchen table, one more lecture as to the perfidy of the Flymo, one more wedding anniversary spent watching them mow Trent Bridge and you're out on your ear.'

Freddie sat down beside her again. Patsy was watching him carefully.

'Forget the forbidden word for a moment, Patsy, and concentrate on the idea as a cold-blooded business proposition. A monthly magazine devoted solely to the lawn. After all, the lawn is central to all gardens, and – ' he lowered his voice as if approaching a subject of infinite delicacy – 'is one of the most problematic areas for your committed gardener.'

'And I thought it was just grass.'

A rhyme came into her head, a song she had heard at a Christmas pantomime. 'Why does a brown cow give white milk if it only eats green grass?' A man in tights had hopped about pointing to the words written on a huge sheet of cardboard. And what was Freddie doing if not dancing to some sort of ridiculous pantomime?

'Freddie. I haven't said this before, but you need to get a proper grip. All this day-dreaming isn't going to get us anywhere.'

'That's where you're wrong.'

He swallowed and held back for a moment. He took her hand again.

'The lawn is an absolute minefield of problems, Patsy, an absolute minefield. Let's say you had just moved house and were considering laying down a new lawn. Think of the difficulties that lie before you.' He started to count them off with his fingers. 'For a start, do you go for turf or sowing? The great benefit of turfing is that it saves time, an advantage considerably discounted by the difficulty in obtaining turf free from weeds. Seeds, on the other hand . . .'

'Yes, Freddie, can we move on.'

'And even after you've decided, there are so many other unanswered questions. What type of seeds? How do you prepare the soil? When is the best time? And that's just the beginning, Patsy. Aeration, propagation, dressing, drainage, the problems of moss and couch grass, how to deal with drought; all are subjects which warrant intense discussion.'

'Water.'

'What?'

'How to deal with drought. Water. Even I could write that one.'

'Then of course there are the diseases. Lawns are very prone to disease.'

'So is my aunt, Freddie, but I don't expect they're queuing up outside W. H. Smith's to buy a magazine on her.'

Freddie battled on.

'It would have to come out monthly so you could follow the lawn through the seasons. There'd be articles on fertilizers, specialist equipment, handy maintenance tips, test drives, lawnmowers of the rich and famous.' His voice was beginning to rise. Patsy could feel him getting carried away. 'And of course I could write a series on the you-know-whats of old; the first machine with a double-edge cutting barrel, the demise of the horse and pony mowers, those lovely old-fashioned hand jobs of the twenties.'

He patted the top of her leg

'Well, you're not getting any lovely old-fashioned hand jobs from me.'

'What?'

She pointed down at his pyjamas. It was peering out again.

'Oh, sorry.' He tucked it away with a vigour that implied he was more irritated by its intrusion than she. 'And think of the potential revenue, Patsy. We'd cover the costs of production by the advertising alone, I'm convinced of it.'

'Just sounds like an excuse to me. If I had my way I'd concrete over every lawn in England.'

'Patsy! The twins were conceived on our lawn.'

'I know that, Freddie. I was there, remember.'

'If I hadn't been out there you-know-whatting that after-noon . . .'

'Freddie, I do not want to talk about it.'

'And if the Atco's chain hadn't broken and I hadn't asked you to come and hold the spanner . . .'

'Freddie! That's enough.'

'I'm just pointing out that a healthy interest in keeping a good lawn need not be an exclusively male pastime. Under the right circumstances it can be something that can benefit the whole family.'

There was a pause. She leant across and unscrewed the lid of the jar of face cream. 'The point is, you promised not have any-thing to do with them at all this year.'

Freddie broke back eagerly.

'And I haven't, but the more I thought about this, the more plausible it became! You can't stop a man from thinking, Patsy.'

Yes you can, she thought, working the cream into her face, masking the thought by saying, 'Anyway, what would you call it? No, don't tell me.'

Freddie waited until the shine on her forehead had subsided. It made her look a little less combative.

'Well, do you want to hear the name or not?' he asked. 'I have to use the word, you understand.' Patsy wiped her eyebrows clean.

'Yes, yes. Get on with it.'

He took a deep breath. 'I would call it *Lawn-Mowing Monthly*.'

'I thought you might.'

'Or *Lawns and Lawn-Mowing*. What do you think?'

'I think I might have to polish off this bottle of Chanel. Is it in the slightest degree alcoholic, do you think?'

'I'm serious, Patsy. The first step in setting up any new business is to identify your market. And that's exactly what I've done.'

'Identified a lot of crackpots, you mean. Anyway not all men are obsessed by the bloody things. Look at next door. Their front lawn looks like your pubic hair. Horrible and scraggy.'

Freddie fed his hand into his pyjamas and scratched himself.

'I can't help my pubic hair, Patsy, but after a year's subscription of *Lawn-Mowing Monthly* Richard Roach could have a lawn Capability Brown would be proud of,' and with that he jumped into bed, turned his back on her, and fell asleep.

Lawn-Mowing Monthly; *Lawns and Lawn-Mowing*. Irritatingly, like Freddie, now that the idea was in her head, she couldn't stop thinking about it. *Lawns and Lawn-Mowing* sounded better. Price £3.50. Editor, Freddie Millen. If it took off they could get rid of that fuel-guzzling monster RBG had foisted upon them.

A sudden cry brings her to her feet. Christine, not Christopher; she recognizes the lower register of her voice; her son sleeps on. Will this be how it is in later life, Christine the one who demands, impatient for the ten minutes her brother left her for the world outside? Is that what her life will be, always racing to catch up? Patsy is caught by the sudden stab that has taken to striking her behind the eyes the past two months. Worry, that's the cause of it, worry about money, worry about Freddie, worry about the twins and their sedentary parents' voyage into the treacherous waters of middle-aged health. Christine cries again and though she knows she must go, Patsy steadies herself, holding on to the expensive orange drapes that smother the window and trail along the carpet like an abandoned wedding dress, another unwanted gift courtesy of Rich Brother George. Rich Brother George, Rich Brother George, who lives in every part of the house, from the photographs of him receiving the MBE to the bottles of wine that he brings over on his brief visits. Rich Brother George, Rich Brother George. Everything has gone right for Rich Brother George, the younger brother, the less clever, the less good-looking. Why, he was not even good at games, like Freddie had been once. Long ago, Patsy could have thrown Freddie over and married Rich Brother George and flown away on a cloud of impulse. He'd even suggested it on the eve of their engagement party, that she choose him instead of Freddie, run away with him there and then and pick up the family pieces later, and though it was said jokingly, if she had said yes he'd have had her out that pub before the barman had sliced the lemon for her G and T. He was going places, she could tell, and up till then she'd quite liked him, despite his overconfidence, his artless self-promotion. But that turned her, and she was angry with him, and had remained angry with him ever since, trying to ruin their party, the idea of them, careless in his desire. And she doesn't regret it either. To regret it would be to deny life, deny Freddie, deny the twins, the future the world holds for them. All she regrets is that the division between the two brothers is not greater, that RBG is not a whole lot richer, too busy or too ashamed to bother with them. But he isn't. He's just rich enough to need to show the difference.

Through the unsteady gap she can see Anglefield Road bathed in the blustery light of night, the houses firm and stationary, the road so dependably Anglefield. And yet how it moves away from her! How it seems to be slipping from her grasp before her very eyes! It seems so distant now, so alien! When it was time to leave the hospital and Freddie had driven them back here, she had lain the twins side by side in their cots, and looked out of this same window and thought: This is where it will all happen, where they see their first horizons, where they will absorb the world. Below is the path upon which they will skip and run and greet their daddy and turn from one small excitement to the next. Beyond it is the circle around which they will ride their bikes, and from there the pavement that will lead them to the great adventure of school.

And I will watch them, from this window, from the door below, and see them grow.

Below, the battered 'For Sale' sign twists in the wind, cold corkscrew to her heart, while the smear of something living moves quickly from under its shadow. Looking up she sees a figure come scuttling down, head bent, one hand holding together a half-opened raincoat. The Cockroach. She holds an alarmed hand to her mouth as he slips turning onto his path, stumbling towards the front porch, reaching out, seeking stability on the treacherous deck. The door opens and Richard Roach disappears inside. No lifting of brass knocker, no pressing for rhyming chime, no drink-fuddled fumble with front-door key for the Cockroach; just the matrimonial hand primed to an unseen accuracy; the opened door and the scuttle inside. Christine's cries blossom. Patsy steps away and hurries to their bedroom. Whatever the pros and cons of the magazine, Freddie was wrong. Richard Roach wouldn't read *Lawns and Lawn-Mowing*, not in a hundred years.

Yes, theirs is a scraggy stretch of grass, tufted and bare-patched like the skin of the soaked tom moving towards its backyard conclusion, his spare frame made more skeletal by the falling of the rain, the vole, awakened to its plight, struggling in the lock of its tormentor's mouth. Scraggy grass for the Roaches, then, the back as well as the front, but then the whole demeanour of their domain has an abandoned look, bloodless dung-coloured brick on the lower frontage of the house, dirty white clapboard on the upper, stark metal-framed windows staring out like neglected off-spring. They do not venture outside much, the Roaches. There was a time when they would sit outside, play family badminton on the back lawn, wheel the barbecue out and feed themselves burnt chicken wings and split sausages, but no longer. Nature has dealt them a hard blow and they love her not. They would be hard pressed to name a day when either of them had been outside for any length of time these last few years, either alone or together. Theirs is a garden viewed as intrusive spectacle, into which they must, by dint of duty, make the occasional sortie, hacking away at errant hedges, tearing out fistfuls of unwanted growth, scouring the lawn bare with blatant disregard for its disfigurement. It is their cat who rules their garden, who suns himself on their patch of ragged green in the summer, who prowls amongst the weed-snagged bushes in the winter and who, whatever the season, marks out these barren paving stones as his everyday killing ground. Day and night they observe him, his head held high, pacing out the semicircle once, twice before setting his prey down, to tease out what little life is left. Let nature take its course, Ellen says and they stand side by side before the closed windows, witness to the crippled flutterings, the brief excursions to wounded freedom, before the busy work of death descends. When the killing comes, foretold by the sudden arch of his back and the upraised look he gives to his mistress, Roach turns away, a hand held to his anxious, nail-biting mouth, while Ellen steps forward, the breath of her arousal distilled upon the tell-tale glass. It is a command performance she is vouchsafed, full of ritual, warm with blood, a pornographic gift, wrapped in feather and fur, and she places her fingertips upon the pane as if to absorb the rhythms of this libidinous death through the pores of her unconsummated skin. There are times, in the dead calm of their captured days, when they hear cries of such intensity, the thought comes to them that the glass might shatter and let the bloody world burst in upon them, but though it is Richard who reaches out and pulls her back, it is Ellen who is the more affected, imagining that this violent and unequal struggle might be a precursor to an unequal struggle of their own, namely a quick and violent intercourse, but which instead leads to their immediate separation, him to the sheltered harbour of his upstairs box room, and she to the walnut-faced sideboard, bequeathed to her by her grandmother, the only piece of furniture in the house worth a damn and on which stands the cut-glass decanter from which she pours with a shaking and bloodless hand the first of a series of large whiskies into one of the six crystal glasses that her husband, Home Counties sales manager for Liberty Shoes, was awarded seven years ago for best salesman of the year.

The cat halts at the entrance to the path, adjusting the cruel hang of his prey. He is about to set out along the cracked pattern of his territorial bricks, when the solitude of Anglefield Road is disturbed, the looming of a figure at the rising top, a figure in a hat and a billowing coat, dark and tall, set in stark relief against the illuminated equilibrium of the road. The cat clamps his jaws down tight as he hurries into the safety of the dark. High above, Richard Roach stands in the unlit bedroom and lifting his eyes looks up to his right, the curtain edge clenched in his hand. The light from the lamp opposite illuminates his open white shirt and his shorts. He was in the midst of changing when, sensing a presence, he pulled back the curtain and saw the figure standing there on the lip of the road, the limpid tide of lamplight washing over him.

'Ellen,' he calls softly. 'Come and look.'

He'd gone up to London that morning for his quarterly sales meeting at head office. It was going to be difficult, this time around. Sales in his area were down five per cent. Most of the others were up three or four. Kevin was going to jump all over him, Roach knew it. Three years ago, when Kevin had joined the firm, they had given Roach the job of showing him the ropes. Roach wet-nursed him for a good month, filling him in on the history of the firm, introducing him to key accounts, instructing him in the tricks of the trade, even going so far as advising him on a different haircut and a decent-looking suit. He felt sorry for the young man, his father dying in a London nursing home, mother buried in some Highland graveyard, an only child all alone in the world. He knew what that was like. He'd even brought Kevin back to the house, to make him feel more at home. Ellen got some steaks and chicken legs in, fished out the bag of charcoal. Mark shut himself up in his room. Kevin turned up as Roach was wheeling out the rusting barbecue onto the patio.

'You're not ones for the entertaining, then,' he joked. Ellen drained her glass and confirmed the observation. No, they were not ones for entertaining. And was it any wonder, the hours it took him to light the thing; screwed-up *Daily Mail*s, crumbled firelighters, bits of twig, nothing worked, Kevin calling out facetious advice. Ellen knocked over his glass in pursuit of their mirth, the red wine spilling onto his trousers and into the pile of their new carpet.

'Nice lad,' Roach said, waving him off four hours later, 'if a little rough round the edges.' Ellen hung onto his arm, quite drunk.

'He can twinkle his eyes, did you notice?' she said.

'Can't say I did.'

'You better watch yourself, Richard. He's pure terrier. One moment he'll be licking your hand, the next he'll have torn your throat out.'

A week later Kevin sent them an oversized rubber plant with a note tied round the trunk. 'Thanks for everything', he wrote. 'Tell Ellen, I hope the stain comes out!' They were there to this day, the spot covered by an ornamental rug that Suzanne had given them, the plant stuck out on the patio, its rapid growth an unwelcome reminder of what had passed since then, him in the same job and Kevin head of UK sales, on first names with Sir Douglas and about to censure him for another disappointing quarter.

The train up to London had been full of the Falklands. Everybody was talking about how they expected the Task Force to give the Argentinians a good walloping. Roach wasn't so sure. He had looked up the islands on a map. They were a long way away. Just to get there in one piece would take some doing. At the office the atmosphere was much the same. Kevin had bought a Falklands T-shirt which read DON'T CRY FOR US, ARGENTINA, WE'RE GOING TO KNOCK THE F*CK OUT OF YOU, and pinned it to his door. The girls all laughed. Wendy from marketing took it down, crouched down behind her desk and re-emerged wearing it, the asterisk made three-dimensional by the blunted nipple of her left breast. Roach thought it in very bad taste. He spent the morning processing last week's orders and trying to dream up reasons why his figures were down. He couldn't think of many, apart from the obvious fact that no one had much liked their summer collection. Just before twelve Ellen rang. Hector had had the idea of giving Suzanne and Matty a send-off tomorrow morning and could he buy some flags.

'Flags?' he said, waving away Sandy, who was champing at the bit for a lunch-time pint. 'What sort of flags?'

'What sort do you think?' she shouted. 'White ones for when we surrender!' and banged down the phone. He was sure everyone must have heard. He carried on talking to the empty line for another minute before putting the receiver back on the cradle. Sandy was looking at him sympathetically. The scourge of East Anglia, Sandy was also expecting a rocket. He was down fifteen per cent.

'Shall we go forth and liquefy, O Roach of dainty feet?' he asked hopefully. Roach lifted up a sheaf of print-outs.

'Not today. Too much on. Got to be sharp for the meeting.'

'It won't do you any good, old boy. You're not young and thrusting enough. Unless you can thrust thrice daily you might as well come and get pissed. Leave the delights of our chairman's backside to others.'

Roach shook his head in protest, but Sandy was gone. Roach walked down a damp, traffic-spattered Kingsway, passed the corner pub where Sandy would be looking at his second pint of Bass. Down on the Strand he found a souvenir shop full of hair-plastered sightseers sheltering amongst the Towers of London and plastic bowlers, Houses of Parliament sweatshirts, Carnaby St underwear, Beefeater aprons hanging from the ceiling. At the back he found clumps of Union Jacks tied together like bunches of daffodils. He bought thirty-six, rather too many considering how many people were likely to turn up.

'What do you want all these for?' the girl at the counter asked. 'You going down to see them off or something?'

It was then that he had his idea. He'd read somewhere that everyone had one great idea in their lifetime, not necessarily a revolutionary idea, like Edison or the man who invented catseyes, but an idea that signalled a turning point in one's life, the route to a new, untapped territory. The test was whether you seized the moment or fell back onto the complicity of your old ways. He hurried back to the office, made a couple of phone calls and arrived at the boardroom early.

The meeting went better than he expected. Although Kevin made a few lunges in his direction it was nothing to what Sandy had to suffer. Kevin walked him into the arena with the precision of a bullfighter, seemingly without malice or a single wasted word. Breathing heavily through his nostrils, his eyes half closed, the impenetrable state of his breath drifting across the table, Sandy trembled at every indignant cut. The younger salesmen looked on, captured by the fearful beauty of it, the destruction of this worn-out colossus. There was a short break for coffee, when, stimulated by the scent of freshly spilt blood, the subject turned to the South Atlantic. Sir Douglas, who had served in the Royal

Navy, gave a languid account of the generic shortcomings of the Argentinian forces.

'All braid and no bottle,' he said. 'I was down there a couple of years ago, negotiating one of our leather contracts, and went to a trade reception on the pride of their fleet. *Belgrano*, big bugger, covered in rust, not much good for anything except firing off a couple of salvoes on their latest dictator's birthday. I've seen better vessels crossing the Serpentine. As for their average soldier, they're mostly conscripts, barely out from underneath their mother's skirts. We'll send them back in little pieces. I wouldn't be eating too much corned beef for a while, if I were you.'

Roach stood at the back eating his way through a plate of biscuits. He could barely keep his mouth shut for the waiting. Though the subject matter was apposite the tone was all wrong. Timing was of the essence here: introduced now and his idea would be dismissed as frivolous; too late and it would be swamped in the rush to suck up to Sir Douglas and thence the first round of the evening. Twenty minutes later they reassembled round the table to listen to the main item on the agenda, Kevin's presentation of the Bronco, their new line in tough, outdoor sneaker wear, the fastest-growing section of the leisure market. In the long, dormitory days of Roach's youth, Bronco had been the name of a particularly greasy lavatory paper, but no one seemed old enough to remember such a thing, or concerned enough to care. Roach tried to concentrate on the Bronco's salient selling points, its ankle-gripping upper, its rugged durability, its unique 'walk-on-water' air-cushioned sole, but the trouble was, sitting there in the middle of the table with its high bulbous back and its sturdy slightly pointed toe, the Bronco looked very much like one of those clapped-out Argentinian battleships Sir Douglas had dismissed so contemptuously; why, its very colour scheme, grey on grey, suggested some cold, ice-bound conflict.

The presentation ran its course. Launch date was confirmed: targets were set; Wendy from marketing came in to demonstrate how to assemble the Bronco display unit, but like everyone else in the room, Roach found it difficult to follow the intricacies of its erection while Wendy's own exhibits moved so vigorously inside Kevin's T-shirt. Bending the ribbed cardboard this way and that, squashing the swinging overhang of her rudely lettered chest against its reluctant folds, she wrestled with it for several minutes, before placing the construction on the table. The sneaker now rested on what looked like a dollop of dried dung. Wendy left to dazed applause. In her wake rep after area rep confessed to their adoration of the Bronco. Ray of the south-east was struck by its unique ability to appeal to both town and country, Ray of the north-west by its sheer forthright conviction, while Jamie of the Borders saw the Bronco's uncompromising shape capturing the mood of today's youth. Sandy placed his lips close to Roach's right ear and breathed four pints and twelve Rothman's down his sweat-soaked collar.

'Personally I have my doubts about this particular pump,' he whispered. 'I mean can you see your average lesser-spotted teenager forking out his hard-mugged cash for something that resembles his aunt's bedroom slippers minus the bum-fluff?'

'Sorry, Sandy? I didn't quite catch that.' Kevin tapped his teeth with his silver propelling pencil. Sandy swivelled, unabashed.

'I was just remarking to Richard, Kevin, that here we have a product of rare distinction. Rare distinction.' He leant back on his chair and put his hands behind his head. 'A racehorse which looks like a cart-horse. A first I think for the firm.'

Roach shifted in his chair putting an extra four inches between him and his old friend. Kevin leant across and pushed the stand to within a foot of Sandy's boiled face.

'I'm not a gambling man, Sandy, but I wouldn't mind betting your commission that in three months' time this little thorough-bred will be leading the field by several lengths. I'm predicting something like twenty per cent of the home market. In all territories. I hope I make myself clear. Which leaves export. Any thoughts, Brian? Twenty thousand in the first six months?'

'Twenty?' Brian blinked.

'Any problem with that?'

'No, but it's an ambitious target.' Brian tried to hide his nervousness with a little joke. 'We could always try flogging them to the Argies by telling them that with these on their feet they could run away a whole lot faster.'

A weary mutter of amusement washed around the table. Kevin

shuffled his papers, signifying the meeting's close. Roach's leg started to jiggle underneath the table, rocking the jug of dust laden water in front of him. His time had come.

'Why don't we send our troops some?' he said.

'What?' Kevin voice was sharp, annoyed. The others looked up, surprised. It wasn't like Richard Roach to clog up the proceedings so close to opening time.

'The marines,' Roach amplified. 'Why don't we send them some?'

'Send them some? I don't follow you.' Kevin glanced quickly at Sir Douglas, trying to gauge the degree of Roach's folly.

'My neighbour works on the *Canberra*,' Roach explained. 'She's a stewardess, in the cabins. According to her, the troops will be doing a lot of running on board.'

Kevin straightened up out of his overconfident slouch and sucked his stomach in. He'd gained a couple of stone since those earlier hungrier years.

'They're not going in for egg and spoon races, you know, Richard,' he observed. 'They're going to kill the little bastards.'

The table laughed. Sir Douglas's face broke into a thin smile. Roach took a deep breath. There was nothing for it now.

'I know, but the thing is, it'll take them at least four or five weeks just to get down there, all cooped up on that ship. They'll have to do a lot of training to keep fit, otherwise they'll be no use.'

Kevin gave a contemptuous snort.

'Jogging round the paddling pool, I suppose.'

'Have you seen the *Canberra*?' It was Sandy who spoke up. 'She's huge. Took the wife on a cruise there once. She displaces a fair tonnage of water herself. Hated every minute of it. Kept on getting lost. And found unfortunately. Still, plenty of room for running on the Promenade Deck if that's your thing. Personally I preferred putting my foot on the bar rail up top, sizing up the talent.'

'Wherever they do it, they'll do it in regulation footwear, not running shoes. Haven't you noticed, Richard, it's what soldiers prefer to go to war in, boots.'

Kevin passed his smirk round the room. Richard smiled back. He was on firmer ground than Kevin thought.

'Yes, but apparently P&O are worried that the soldiers' boots might damage the decks. They weren't built for that sort of wear and tear. They're already having to strengthen them for all the equipment that's going on board. So they'll have to do much of their training in shoes like this. So I thought, what if we sent them a consignment of Broncos, free of charge, as a gesture of support?'

'A pretty generous gesture. How many troops are we talking about?'

'About two and a half thousand.'

'Two and a half thousand!' Kevin pulled the display back towards him, as if protecting it from Roach's profligacy. 'You're suggesting that we hand over two and a half thousand pairs of our brand-new product and not get a penny in return? Accounts will love that.'

'Not two and a half thousand, no, but a fair proportion.' Roach reached out and took the Bronco from the stand. He tested the pliancy of its sole, felt the strength of its uppers; he held it out in the palm of his hand, as one might hold a dove, fluttering for flight. It was his shoe now: he could feel it carrying him to greatness.

'I know it would cost us revenue,' he said, 'but think of the publicity it would bring. "The Bronco! The trainers in which our boys prepared for war." '

At the mention of the word 'publicity' a holy silence descended on the room. You did not mock or speak ill of publicity. It was a sacred word. Publicity was both corrupt and pure, both whore and virgin. You sacrificed mothers and small children on its profligate altar.

'How many pairs were you thinking of?' Sir Douglas spoke quietly. The room became smaller, more intense. Matters were afoot that suddenly affected the sales force's whole pecking order. Jamie of the Borders could see six months of letting Kevin win at squash coming to naught.

'I was thinking of something in the region of two or three hundred, Sir Douglas. They won't all be front-line troops.'

'What about sizes? I know the army likes to do things by the book, but even they can't regulate the size of a chap's feet.' Kevin was fighting a rearguard action, but to an unappreciative audience. All eyes were on Roach. He turned the shoe upside down, ran his hand over the rubber soul.

'Yes, I've thought of that. Obviously we couldn't cater for everybody but we do know the demographics. So we send say equal amounts of nines, tens and elevens.' He bent the trainer in half, letting it spring back to shape. 'Throw in some twelves and eights. That would cover most, and if a few were in excess . . .'

Roach placed the Bronco back carefully on its stand, adjusted its position, its blunt snub poised to strike at Kevin's heart.

'What does it matter, yes.' Sir Douglas nodded. 'Better make it five hundred, though. We don't want to appear mean. We do have sufficient range in stock, I take it Kevin?'

'Five hundred. Absolutely. Five hundred puts a completely different perspective on it.' Kevin looked over at Roach, his fists laid out on the table. Roach pressed his knees together. He had the most enormous erection.

'I had a further idea,' he said.

'Oh?' Sir Douglas leant across the table, staring hard. Roach could feel him sizing him up.

'The thing is, we don't have much time. The *Canberra*'s due to sail tomorrow evening. We could arrange for them to be flown out, but I thought . . .' Richard swallowed. His leg was working like a jack-hammer. Wait until Ellen got to hear of this. What would she say if he returned that night and told her that he'd beaten Kevin at his own game, that single-handedly he had landed the firm its biggest slice of free publicity in its one-hundred-year history and that he was going to be a part of it! She'd only met Kevin once and yet she'd got the measure of him right away.

'I thought if I picked the stock up myself this evening, I could have them on Southampton dock first thing in the morning. If publicity got their skates on, we could have the press and TV all primed and waiting. And it wouldn't just be the local media. Not a story like this.'

Sir Douglas nodded. 'You're right. It's a great idea, Richard, well done.' He looked round the table. 'That's what's missing in this country. A bit of unashamed patriotism. Kevin, see that it's all set up. Give him all the help he needs.'

Kevin banged the end of his papers on the table and laid them flat.

'No problem. Just one thing, though. No disrespect to Richard, Douglas, but, if we're going to do this, let's not run it at half-cock. It's costing us money, remember. Let's do it properly and professionally, so we maximize the coverage. Richard might like to get his picture in the papers, but really we owe it to ourselves to aim a little higher, to get someone better known.'

Sir Douglas stroked his lip. 'You mean like a celebrity?' he said. 'A TV star. A page-three girl?'

Kevin shook his head. 'I was thinking of you, Douglas.'

'Me?' Sir Douglas looked round the table. 'I don't think my tits are big enough.'

Everyone laughed. He had such a sense of humour. Kevin shook his head, smiling.

'We'd get a lot more publicity if you made the delivery personally. Drove down with the Bentley stuffed to the gills. Photos, national press, TV interviews, what you're doing, why you're there, patriotism before profit. They'd be queuing up.'

'Yes, yes I see.' Sir Douglas tamped down his silver-grey locks. He was already in front of the camera. 'Richard, you wouldn't mind, would you, if we hijacked your little jaunt?'

He pressed his hands together, a monarch in prayer. He had long tapering fingers, tanned and picked clean. His gold cufflinks were fashioned in the shape of buttoned boots. They were going to take it away from him!

'Richard?' Sir Douglas opened his palms, waiting for his gift.

'No, Sir Douglas, though if you wanted I could always come along to help.'

'No need for that.' Kevin was re-establishing the order fast. 'That's where Sir Douglas's page-three girls come in. We'll hire a couple of busty blondes, put them in bikinis and have them handing over a presentation pair to some randy quartermaster. He'll love it, the press will love it and we'll have a picture of the Bronco in every tabloid in the country.' He rocked forward. 'Sorry to land you with this one, Douglas, but it makes better sense this way. Anyone can have ideas. The skill comes in taking full advantage of them.'

Kevin stared round the table in triumph. He had stolen Roach's brainchild in front of the whole team. Roach busied himself with his papers, not daring to look up, while the rest had racked their brains to see if there was any way they could attach themselves to this piece of unexpected glory. Sandy, uneasily aware of how close he was to foundering on the rocks of his employment, tried to steer himself clear of danger.

'I was wondering,' he announced loudly, trying hard to think of what he was saying, 'in the light of this, if whether we shouldn't be looking at the name again.'

'The name?' Sir Douglas was immediately suspicious. His mistress had suggested the name Bronco. It was what she called him in moments of sexual extremis, her bucking Bronco. He'd worn a trial pair of these trainers once, when they were together in his private gym, told her how they were looking for a name, one that represented its rugged, durable quality. 'Why don't you call them the Bronco after you,' she had said. 'You're rugged, you never wear out.' He had pushed her down on the judo mat and fucked her in them straight away. The Bronco it was.

Oblivious to the warning, Sandy sailed into the muddled current of his thought.

'I mean perhaps we should be looking at ways of linking the name and the troops symbolically.'

'Symbolically!' Sir Douglas moved the word in his mouth as if he had bitten into a bad oyster. 'In what way symbolically?'

Sandy drew rapid circles on his presentation sheet, a whirlpool of despair. The others stared down at their presentation documents, consigning Sandy to oblivion. He was going down fast.

'Well, I haven't given it very much thought. Maybe something on the lines of the Troop Trainer, or, or, the Port Stanley Plimsoll.'

There comes a time to us all, Roach knew, when, by the sum of your failings and the inevitable inadequacies of your age, it is revealed to your peers that despite your previous accomplishments, your earlier prowess, your time is up. It is not your long-suffering employer who vouchsafes this pronouncement, nor your trustworthy colleagues (though they might wish to), but your own reckless self, prompted by the emergence of a long-suppressed disdain for the corporate and goaded by a bubbling self-loathing that you can no longer contain. Your dress becomes ill informed and a mite ragged, the tie no longer quite straight, the collar just that little bit loose about the neck; the shine on your shoes is as the shave on your face, a blotched affair, small areas of mud and whiskers announcing your resignation from the smooth swim of success. You fall behind, drift away from the vigour of the pack, and once thus distanced, out in the open, you are transformed from being a senior member of the herd to the status of a wounded or enfeebled stag. Younger men seek to lock horns with you, chase you from your stamping ground; the virility that once unleashed a smile across a hundred typewriters is ridiculed, ignored: marooned on some arid brushland, banished from the lush feeding grounds, you are viewed dispassionately through the culling glass while other, less proficient executioners prepare to tear you limb from limb. It is only a matter of time. On how many occasions had Roach stood in the bar and heard the refrain 'So-and-so just isn't up to it any more'? Listening to Sandy's clutched falterings he knows that should he join Ray of the south-east and Ray of the north-west in the snug on the corner, he would hear through the froth of smacked lips and the click of cigarette lighters that particular epithet draped over Sandy's absent frame. And yet he can remember when he joined Liberty Shoes, when the firm led the field in women's evening wear, Sandy Knowles was cock of the walk. Sandy carried a cane in those days, a cane with a top-hat head and a stopper inside filled with brandy; always kept a clean shirt and set of ironed underwear in his desk at head office in case he was sent out to troubleshoot. And as for women! Sandy used to go through them like Harpo Marx let loose upon a chorus line: salesgirls, manageresses, and any number of customers. 'You trot along home, madam. I'll be glad to give you a private fitting.' That was his line. A private filling, more like. 'Once you've got them by the ankles,' he used to say, 'it slips in as easy as a foot on a greased shoe horn.' Thirteen he was reputed to have had one week, one landlady, two barmaids, three shop assistants, two manageresses, four customers and a blind woman frying bacon and eggs in a Southwold beach hut. Half the week with his trousers round his ankles and still he brought back the best sales figures in the country. Now look at him! Of course, Roach had to admit, Sandy had brought most of his troubles on himself. He hadn't changed with the times like he had. Sandy was uncomfortable with the very idea of the modern trainer. He still called them gym shoes.

'I know,' Sandy cried, 'the Para Sneaker!'

'The Para Sneaker!' Sir Douglas shuddered. 'Getting some favourable publicity by doing something for one's country is one thing. Cynical exploitation on the back of our lads' bravery is quite another.' He got up and pushed his chair back against the wall. The meeting was closed.

Sandy was fired ten minutes later. Half an hour to clear his desk, car keys confiscated, company credit card cut up and thrown into Kevin's wastepaper basket. Roach had felt obliged to attend the one-man wake, warning Ellen that he would be home late. He travelled back with an upset stomach and a scalded heart, wondering where he had gone wrong. And just when he thought the day could not get any worse, there was a cough and a tap on his shoulder. He looked up. A man was staring down at him, smiling in a disconcertingly familiar manner.

'Excuse me,' the man said, 'but aren't you Richard Roach?'

Roach looked around. 'Yes?' His voice was uncertain.

'You might not remember me,' the man continued, in a voice which suggested he anticipated quite the contrary reaction, 'but we were,' there came a slight hesitation, the hint of a conspiratorial smile, 'boys together.'

He didn't say school, Roach thought, because it hadn't been a school. He didn't say home because it hadn't been a home. Roach looked him in the eye, willing his face to betray nothing. If the man expected to see a flicker of recognition he was in for a disappointment.

'Sorry?'

'Yes. Henry. Henry Hawkins?' The man shuffled on his feet. Good shoes, expensive, Italian probably, though could be American. They often imitated Italian styles, the Americans.

'I was next to you?' he was saying. 'Nigel Ellison on the other side?'

Ah, now he had him. Soapsuds. The day after he arrived there they found him down in the basement, feeding wet sheets through the rollers.

'I'm sorry, I don't seem to . . .' Roach's voice faded.

'Nigel Ellison? Buck teeth, glasses?' The man was becoming insistent. Roach shook his head. Of course he remembered Nigel. It would be difficult to forget the boy who had kicked matron's cat to death.

'Mickey Trent?'

'Who?'

'The tall lad from Wolverhampton. The one that kept fainting all the time.'

To Roach's recollection it had happened only twice. Mickey had been standing there at the back of the tennis court as they'd been trained to, legs apart, arms folded, when he'd just crumpled to the ground. The players had had to stop the match while the St John's Ambulance men took him away on a stretcher. Wasn't surprising, really, considering the heat that day. Mickey had been lain on a bench in the men's changing room, rested for half an hour, then sent back out, only to do it all over again twenty minutes later. Not enough barley water, they'd been told. Barley water! No one had ever given them barley water.

Seeing Roach's expression of studied bewilderment, the man began to get impatient.

'What about the semi-final, when you ran into me?'

Roach decided to grow indignant.

'Ran into you?'

'Yes. Surely you remember that!'

'I've never run into anyone in my life!'

The passengers opposite were beginning to take notice. One had lain down his paper. The last thing he wanted was this sort of tittle-tattle getting about. It was time to bring it to an end.

'I'm sorry. I don't remember you at all.'

'Not at all?'

'No.'

The man had stood back, unsure of what to do next. Roach looked down to the floor and then back, willing him to go away. He was pleased he'd put on his best suit that morning. At least he hadn't been caught wearing the one with the shiny seat. The train began to slow down. It occurred to Roach that he should let the train carry him beyond his station, so that the man wouldn't know where he lived. He could travel on to the next stop and take a taxi home. But a taxi, at this time of night! He got up and pulled his raincoat down from the luggage rack and busied himself with his briefcase. Soapsuds was staring at him, his face less than a foot away. He'd changed, Roach thought. There was a measure of hard distance to his eyes, a fleshy muscularity in the way he stood that hadn't been there before. He'd been a strong but skinny lad. And I ran into him, did I? Roach felt like punching him in the face.

'This is where I get off,' he said.

The man bent down and looked through the window. He seemed surprised.

'Here?'

'Yes. Now, if you'll excuse me . . .'

He pushed his way towards the carriage door, and jumping down onto the platform, scurried his way towards the tunnel. He could sense the man watching him.

Outside the night was thick with a wet vapour. He plunged into it, thankful for its enveloping gloom. He wanted to be home but was afraid of the walk, its dangerous familiarity, as if someone else might be waiting en route, ready to pluck him out of his setting. Soapsuds on his own train, near his own house! He felt endangered, insecure, as if his very life was under threat. Instead of taking the usual road home, he turned left, down along the main road and then along the canal towpath towards the new footbridge; the long way round. He walked faster than normal, his briefcase banging awkwardly against his legs, his breasts jiggling uncomfortably under his shirt, working his way up along the black puddled path, over the bridge and up through the brash ranks of the new housing estate, towards its garish summit and the road leading back to the junction where it met the dwellings of the older town. The journey took longer than he had imagined, the glare of the street lights illuminating his unease. He heard footsteps behind, but dared not look. He was caught in the glare of strange territory and he wished he hadn't come. He ducked his head down, increased his speed, as if afraid of someone calling out his name, accusing him of trespass, arresting his progress. Oh, Anglefield Road, how he longed for it. Then the road widened and the houses settled back. The lights faded, the trees grew older, the ground more husbanded, and there it lay, Anglefield Road branching off serenely to the left. It was dark again, dark and clear and quiet, pools of Anglefield light stepping stones to his front door. Above the close of the cul-de-sac he could see the high embankment ridge and the hidden lights of the empty railway station. Below stirred the calm of Anglefield Road, moored up against it. He was safe; just the swift descent and the duck down the path. He stood, stilled, conscious of the silence and the bulk of Anglefield's shape and the complete emptiness of everything around him. Anglefield Road, so familiar, so strange, his foreign homeland. He was nearly home.

*

He calls again.

'Ellen. Ellen. Come here.'

She appears in the doorway.

'Close the door,' he says.

She closes the door and moves towards him.

'What is it?' she asks, anticipating that the reason he has called her into their bedroom at such an hour is her proximity in the bathroom and with the drink inside him a dormant memory awakened and if not named for fear of stumbling in the calling of it then laid out on the smoothness of the counterpane, to be touched and unfolded and brought to the succour of their skin, but as she moves towards him, she realizes that his back is turned towards her and that he is looking, not at her entrance, but out the window, standing in his shirt tails, with the light off. Something has halted his process of getting changed, though why he changed every night on his return she can never fathom, for nothing is done that would add wear and tear on his suit, nothing embarked upon which would have been inappropriate in such dress, but change he does and she, peculiarly, copies him, exchanging one set of clothes for another before he arrives home. And here lies the equation of their living, for while he dresses down, appearing at the head of the stairs in his tasselled casuals and a pair of clean cords, pulling a V-neck jumper over his growing paunch, invariably she has greeted him a quarter of an hour earlier in something smarter than her day wear; a pair of ironed slacks, a neat top, nothing formal, but clothes acknowledging the fact that her husband has returned and that the momentum of her day, its balance and perimeters, are changed. But tonight he was late and their routine disturbed. She had opened the door to a breathless, charging figure, an unlikely smell of drink invading the hall, a look of anguish on his face, the price he paid, so she believed, for an evening spent with a vanquished peer. Minutes later, in the bathroom, preparing for bed, she had seen their cat on the patio below, the wet fruit of the night wriggling in his mouth. She was holding her stomach, watching his busy work, when Roach called and thus she came to him and here he is, half undressed like herself, standing quite still, his hands by his side. She repeats herself.

'What is it?'

He beckons her forward. Edging between Richard and their bed, she stretches up on tiptoe and looks over his shoulder. In the middle of the circle a man stands, dressed in an overcoat, the two folds unbuttoned, flapping in the wind. He turns, looking first at one house and then another.

'Who's that?' she says. 'Someone you know.'

'You don't know the half of it. That's Henry.'

'Henry?'

'You know. The one that knocked me over.'

Below the man turns in their direction. His gaze runs straight to their house, to the window and the room in which they are standing. Roach takes a step backwards, pushing the back of her bare legs against their bed.

'He followed me here.'

'Followed you? Do you want me to call the police?'

'No.' He steps forward again and stands before the darkened window. 'Look at him!'

Ellen moves up behind him and puts her arms around his middle. He is sweating, his shirt sticking to the swell of his stomach. She presses it slightly.

'He doesn't look like much,' she says.

'I hate him.'

'It was a long time ago, Richard.'

She looks up at him. Though his cheeks are pale in this light, his lips are quivering, gorged with blood. For the first time in many months she kisses his neck. Roach seems hardly to notice.

'I still hate him,' he says. 'And he followed me here. After I tried so hard.'

'Followed you?'

He tells her of the encounter on the train.

'Perhaps you shouldn't have tried to fob him off like that.'

'I didn't want him to know where I lived. I didn't want to have anything to do with him.'

'Well, he's here now. Why don't we call the police?'

'And say what?'

'Say he's pestering you. Say you don't like it.'

'I don't like it.'

'Well, then.'

They look to the road. The man stands there still, but there is a restless, diffuse quality to him now. The fog from the canal has spilled down over the embankment and, carried by the wind, is moving slowly up the hill. All movement is stealth, all looks complicit, hooded, whatever their direction.

'He ruined that day for me.'

'I know he did.'

'Ruined it and I was the one they blamed. She passed me by because of it.'

'I know.'

'Passed me by and looked the other way.'

'I'm sure she didn't mean to, Richard.'

'She meant it. I was never asked back. Not even for the ceremony. All the others were, but not me. Oh no. I had to stay behind. And it was all his fault. Why doesn't he go away?'

'He will in time.'

'What if he knocks on the door?'

'Don't answer it.'

'He might have seen me come in.'

'Then I'll answer it. I'll tell him you've gone to bed.'

'That won't do any good.'

'Yes, it will, especially if you have.'

She turns and pulls him towards her. The room is dark, dark

and luminous, the waves of white counterpane illuminating its vastness. She looks down upon the overcoated man, her stomach churning. She can feel Roach trembling, see the muscles on his neck and his hands bunched by his side. She wants to claw him open.

'What, gone to bed, with him out there?' he says, not taking his eyes off the road.

'I will if you will.'

'Ellen!'

'Why not?' she whispers, emboldened by the thought of them in bed together with him standing outside their window. She kisses Roach again, on his lips this time. They are unbearably soft.

'What about . . .?'

They didn't even mention his name these days. A blank page their son.

'He's in his shed.'

'In his shed. It's not right, Ellen, his shed.'

'Ssh.'

She breathes deeply, feels her ribs crush the swell of her against his shirt. He pulls back, fearful of its charge.

'I don't know, Ellen. I don't want to . . . to disappoint you.'

'Then don't.'

He nods to the spectre outside.

'And what if he comes hammering on the door.'

'You'll be too busy to notice.'

She moves across to the other side of the bed, to face him and the window beyond. She crosses her hands and lifts the black hem of her shift. He looks back across his shoulder, imagining the man raised up, looking in. He cannot remember her behaving like this for years. There is blood-filled spectacle here. He recognizes the patio choreography, the deliberate manner in which she stretches the shroud over the shape of her face, how her mouth is revealed, as if something alive hung in the balance of her lips.

He pulls off his shirt, feeling awkward and bulky, as she sinks back upon the bed, the thump of her body resounding in the emptiness of their room. She lies across the width of it upended, her mouth inverted, her knees raised, the shapes and symmetry of her expectant and pliant but somehow wrong. There are quicksands on this bed, he can sense their liquid treachery, see himself caught and suffocated, engulfed in their embrace. He walks around and takes her outstretched foot, not daring to look further along the brazen line. She has good feet, a high instep, a narrow arch, flat toes, painted vein-blood red, a reminder of long-abandoned times. 'What's your husband good at?' Suzanne had asked her jokingly at that bonfire party, and with him standing there, everyone waiting for some humorous reply, Ellen had wiggled her foot and said, 'He keeps me in shoes, I suppose.' How he had taken that remark to their bed that night, lain awake with it wedged between them. 'He keeps me in shoes, I suppose.' There had been a time when he would come back from a fortnight on the road and present her with something from their latest line, when she would paint her toes and hold her ankle out gracefully as he eased them on. On one occasion she had even made love to him on the carpet, such was her gratitude, her legs wrapped around the soft white flesh of his back, her new black heels clicking together like some persistent metronome sprung to erotic life, but she shows no interest in his offerings now, pulls them on indifferently, as often as not saying, 'I don't know why you do this, Richard, I've nowhere to wear them.'

'Is he still there?' she asks and looking out he nods.

'Good. I'm glad,' she says. 'There he is and here am I. And there you are, Richard, caught in the middle, see?' She moves her hips. Her dark tangle rises and falls like floating sea-grass riding upon an ocean swell.

He lowers himself upon her, conscious of how the bed moves under his growing weight. Where she is bone, he is fat; where he is soft, she is hard; where she is sure, he is hesitant. She has lain this way deliberately, so that he might look out upon his anger, to the memory stood below, ignoring the terrain onto which he must descend. He grips her wrists, his arms quivering as he holds himself aloft. He is not here, above his wife, he is there on that July afternoon, with the heat and the crowd and Soapsuds looking towards him across the marked width of green. Legs and arms blur before him. He can smell their perspiration, how they work to ensnare him. There is rhythm to their play, urgency in their striving. He is crouched and waiting, his fingers pressed upon the ground, straining for the moment when he is called. It is a race he must run, and he the only runner. He can feel the coming of it, hear the gasps and cries as the contest nears its rapid close. Hands batter the air like trapped birds against a pane of glass. He pushes her forward, her head hanging down, her neck taut. His body slaps up against hers, like waves against a boat. Something dreadful is about to happen.

'I hate him!' His voice cracks.

'I know you do!' she cries. 'I know you do!'

'Hate him and hate him and hate him!'

He starts forward, feet pounding, body bent, racing towards it. He is so close. So close. All he has to do is to run at it, to scoop it up, hold it to his chest, and reach the other side. It is his for the taking! He stretches tendon-taut, his hand and eye closing round its perfect shape, but in the finger-splayed grasp of it, he misses his footing. His body collides with an unseen other, is sent sprawling, one hand clutching at the thread of some infernal material, the other scrabbling below for desperate restoration.

Later he lies beached, belly up on the bed, the wind knocked out of him. Ellen is stretched out beside him. He knew it was wrong to trust her. Without turning her head, she speaks, not of his past nor his future nor the slick of deceit upon which he has slipped, but of Anglefield Road. She says,

'Did you get the flags?'

The flags! The day pokes at him, like a stick jabbed between the bars of a cage.

'Thirty-six.'

'Thirty-six!' Now she turns. 'You didn't have to buy for the whole town. Anyway, they're not needed now. They're leaving early.'

She settles back, places her hands behind her head.

'So, how did Sandy what's-his-name take it.'

She knows his name perfectly well, but this way she gathers distance. She is asking one thing and thinking of another.

'Pretty well, considering.'

She is struck by a sudden thought.

'Kevin wouldn't do that to you, would he, not after what you did for him.'

'Kevin would do it to anybody.'

'Do you think we should invite him down again?'

He props himself up on his elbow. His wife's body is unmerciful and quite empty of him. He traces the lonely bone of her shoulder, casts his eyes onto the landscape of her near breast, the nub at its centre, a half-submerged stone upon a dark and fathomless pond. Any tale he casts upon these waters is true.

'Not after today. You should have seen me at the sales meeting, Ellen. I really put one over on him.'

His hand brushes the limpid surface of her breast in soothing, undulating waves. He tells her of his inspiration, of the Bronco and the parachuters and the great ship waiting by the dock. He tells her of his cunning, how he outwitted Kevin and played to Sir Douglas's gathering regard. Ripples radiate, balm to their bruised disappointments. He tells her of the waiting press, the television cameras, the opportunities he now has for self-advancement. He tells her that his time is coming, that he can feel it. She hardens beneath his flickering hand. He tells her he is going.

'But it's Bank Holiday tomorrow. And what about Trout Night?'

The second Friday of every quarter he and three other reps that cover the Home Counties meet up in Stevenage for fish curry. Ken Walgrove in surgical supplies, Phil Gregory, tiles and wallpaper, and H.B., kitchenware, who since his operation had managed to offload as much unwanted crockery as his new voicebox could describe. Trout Night. Roach had forgotten.

'I can still get there. It's only two of us this time.'

'You won't be here to see yourself on TV with me, then. Easter Friday on my own.'

A stroke of luck, Trout Night. He couldn't have sat with her. She would have seen the lie on his face. Better to be far away. His hand resumed its sweep.

'You said you didn't mind.'

She held his hand still.

'I could come with you if you wanted.'

'To Trout Night?'

'Southampton.'

A night away from Anglefield Road with Ellen. Not a fort-night's holiday, or a day trip to London, but a night in a hotel: checking in at the desk, unpacking in a strange room; the bath deep, the towels soft, lying on the covered bed, watching television in their underclothes, acting as if this was normal; an early gin and tonic downstairs, the barman replenishing the bowl of free crisps, Ellen flirting bright and small on her stool; then dinner with a bottle of wine, their talk quiet, punctuated by glissandos of laughter and afterwards another drink back at the bar, Ellen's shoulders bare, her lips full and red; then the lift to the bedroom, hearts pounding, speech silent, bodies apart; unlocking the dark-ened room to the strictures of the white line of the sheet, marking out the dimensions of their unconquered territorial bed.

'Better not. There's no telling how we long we might be, hanging around. I'll shoot off to Stevenage when it's over. There won't be much open on Friday, though there might be some buyers working Saturday. Good time to call, after all the publicity. Fame at last, Ellen. Who knows, you might even see me sandwiched between a couple of page-three girls!'

Ellen stirs at the thought. She wouldn't mind, her husband trapped between a couple of page-three girls; the terror he would feel.

'We should tell everyone,' she says.

'It'll probably only be on the local news.'

'Still.' She takes his hand and leads it to where she is slippery and wet. 'This is turning out to be quite a night. You should be followed more often.'

Roach sits up.

'You don't think he's still there?'

'Who cares.'

'I do. We can't have a complete stranger wandering outside our house in the dead of night. Listen. Did you hear that?'

She tries to pull him down.

'Forget him.'

'He'll wake the neighbours.'

'Fuck the neighbours.' Exasperated, she swings herself off the bed. 'Fuck the neighbours, fuck Kevin and fuck Henry what's-his-name.' She walks over and bangs on the window. 'Oi! You! Bugger off, before I call the police.'

But the road is empty. He is gone.

*

Henry hurries back to the station. He thought but to anchor himself just this once, before he sets out, but now he feels lost and imprudent. Seeing his old friend, remembering those times, the glow of fag ends on the dormitory roof, the ragged spy-hole penknifed into the girls' changing room, the loose drainpipe down to market thieving, he thought that it had happened thus so that he might secure himself briefly to someone's life before he disappeared for good, someone who would remember him when it was all over. He'd been drinking in one bar or another for most of the day, listening to beer-soaked declarations of ill-informed patriotism before catching a late train to his digs to collect his car and his pair of handmade boots. He'd need them, where he was going. And then he'd seen Roach sitting not five rows away, dressed in an ill-fitting suit, staring out of a darkened, rain-spattered window; Baby Faced Roach, with his plump cherubic face, his ruddy cheeks shining like a boy out snowballing on a winter's day. It confirmed what he'd known the moment he'd got the call. He wasn't coming back this time. Roach's presence was a sort of a benediction, a way of rounding off his life, preparing him for only God knew what; otherwise he'd never have got up, never chain-walked his way from seat to seat, never introduced himself. All he had wanted was for Roach to grip his hand and wish him luck, maybe remember him after it was all over. And the man pretended he didn't even know him, pretended he didn't remember running into him! Everybody remembered Roach running into him. They'd even had their picture in the nationals because of it. He hadn't known what to say next, and then before he knew it the train was slowing down and Roach was off, pushing his way through the queue in his desperation to escape. Was he ashamed of his past, or did he have something greater to hide? On impulse Henry had snatched up his overcoat and jumped out, just in time to see Roach duck into the service tunnel. And he'd followed, not knowing why, not thinking of how he was going to get back to his unit or what he would do when Roach arrived home, followed him blindly, stealth and curiosity in his heart. He'd kept twenty, thirty yards behind, walking as much as he could on the grass verges planted between path and road, concerned that he might give himself away. He need not have worried. Roach seemed too preoccupied with his own journey to notice another's. It was a long walk for a man in Roach's condition to undertake, and towards the end he could hear Roach panting, breathing hard. Is this what he did every night, subjected himself to this awkward hasty lumber? Surely not. Then, stepping out into the middle of the road, Roach had come to a uneasy standstill. Henry had taken quick refuge behind a tree, feeling foolishly exposed, waiting for Roach to move off. But there he had remained, motionless, hands hanging at his side. Ten minutes he stood, impervious to the flurries of wind and rain skipping around both their collars. Henry was beginning to regret ever having followed him when, without warning, Roach had fallen to his knees and kissed the damp tarmac before him. No wonder his suit was in such a state. Then he was off again. Henry had moved cautiously towards the spot, half expecting to see a plaque to some ancient hero set down, something to give him a clue to Roach's behaviour, but there was nothing, only the fitful light of the road down which Roach had disappeared. And without knowing why he'd walked down into its hollow, drawn into an uneasy unknown, had stood captured in its circle, the wind blowing cold, the road stirring beneath him as if he were already afloat, his whole life heaving under the tumult of unmapped destinations. He swayed from side to side, telling himself it was the drink that was doing this, knowing that it was a different sea on which he was cast, a sudden fog rolling out through the trees, snuffing out the lights of the road above, leaving him wrapped in cloying wreaths. He had been in many fogs in his life, rising out of the Norwegian fjords, closing down over San Francisco, curling up like serpents' heads from the milky waters of the Nile, but it was the English ones that carried real malignancy; he could taste that age-old mixture of sulphur and dead water on his tongue again, smell the sour bubble of boiling sheets, hear the ratchet and rumble of the rollers, the ache hanging heavy in his arms. So he ran, head down, scared of what he had lost and what he might become.

Back at the station he walks back up the tunnel. The platform is long and empty and lit by cough-drop-coloured lamps. He paces up and down, cursing at his foolishness. He hears the distant cry of something, something pained, something hunted, something leaving the world. Looking out he sees a horseshoe cluster of darkened houses and shrouded gardens, the lip of an unseen road, recognizing it to be the road from whence he came. So near! All that walking and yet, so near! He clutches at the high tarred fencing, peering closer, knowing that in one of those houses Richard Roach now lies. How many times has he sat on a train and passed Roach's house, looked out upon his garden, seen his autumn bonfire, his summer lawn? How many times has he sat opposite Roach's wife, helped her with her luggage, smiled at Roach's children. He wonders what Roach is doing at this moment? Is he lying awake thinking of him, reliving his lie, making plans for his escape? In the distance an outside light suddenly illuminates an area of grey; at its centre the black crouch of a cat. A figure steps out and stands before it: a woman he guesses from the hang of her dressing gown, but at this distance he cannot be sure. Moving forward she crouches down and pats her knees. The cat approaches, then stops. She holds out her hand in encouragement. The creature nears, and as it does, the woman gathers it up, holding it close, murmuring into its tickled ear. She rises and turns, raising her arms high into the air, lifting the cat up in a gesture of celebratory pride disappearing back into the house. Henry stares in astonishment. Now he is certain he will not return. Unbelted or unbuttoned he does not know, but what he is sure of is it is the last time he will see the revealed body of a woman. He looks along the parallel lines of rail from where his foreshortened future will come. There will be one more train this night, he is sure of it.

76

THREE

Light came early to Anglefield Road, drifting in through the dark outline of the station, the sun rising behind the waiting room's wooden white-boarded edifice, the shadows of its Wild West, tooth-jagged edges raking down over the sodden embankment, down towards the cul-de-sac's homestead paths. A front garden, a back garden, yes they shared these simple configurations; the difference was in the making of them, how they were walked and worked upon. Front gardens; back gardens; they denote a different purpose: the front an arena of intent, a demonstration of the occupants' industry, their offered state of mind; the rear the grave reality of such pretensions. Any simple soul, set down upon any similar bulbous end, would be able to gauge the variant aspects, not simply by the choice of shrub or the varying dexterity of the guiding hands, but rather how unwittingly each plot records publicly the contrasting affirmations of private faiths. Thus it was with the Plimsolls, the Armstrongs, the Millens and the Roaches.

Calf-high brick walls topped with loops of insignificant chain marked the onset of the Plimsolls' domain, though whether it signalled a beginning or an end was hard to say, for its function was not to procure or prevent, but rather to invite a stance, as one might affect behind any roped-off area, to view not the flag-stone desert that ran towards the oasis of their home, but rather the mirage beyond, behind the windows, which allowed the suppl-icant exotic visions of the Plimsolls' mock interior life; the wicker furniture, the gaudy rugs, the man-size pots and explicit ebony nudes, *Canberra* cruise booty brought ashore, scattered over the open-plan drawing room and newly mastered bedroom, dis-placing the native decor of yesteryear. One lone bare-headed poplar was all the protection such a warehouse was afforded, standing deformed sentry by their bank-loaned, year-old saloon, which Matty cleaned and Suzanne drove mostly, his birthday-present ankle-bracelet slinky down the smooth of her shaved right leg, its delicate links, like the chains atop the wall, signifying nothing as much as the strength of hold which this residential road had on her.

Not so the Armstrongs. Their roots drank from Anglefield's deepest water, knotted and curled around their brick foundations, fanning out towards the loam-laden embankment and the hard-core base of Anglefield's bitumen surface. There were hedges high in front, two of them, dark like the house's unpainted interior, well maintained, bird-nest friendly, an occasional trailing sucker the only impediment to the Armstrongs' infrequent guests. Sandwiched between them hung a reluctant gate of wrought iron, and beyond a neat brick pathway which ran between a pair of unruly oval flowerbeds, the strangle of old rose bushes surrounded by a grassy frame of green. There was an air of suspended balance about this frontage, something present and yet absent, a garden tended and yet not tended, as if the plants and shrubs that enveloped them had grown up in a manner that they had not wished for, but about which they could do nothing. It was not neglect nor incompetence which brought this about, but rather a resigned acceptance of what was. The hedges had grown, too high for Hector's ladder, out of reach of Marjorie's shears, but there it was. The roses had spread, their stems too thick for Marjorie's secateurs, blocking the light to Hector's study, but there it was. Why counter consistency? Only when one reached the porch was order restored, the brass letter box brightly polished, the crate for the milkman set permanently to one, both lit night and day by the green-hued lantern, illuminating a presence which had always been there, but which had never materialized. It bathed too, tangentially, the closed doors of their garage, another example of objective stasis, for though the Humber Snipe inside was well maintained, waxed and polished four times a year, it was rarely brought out. Marjorie preferred her bicycle. Hector used his legs.

A padlocked garage for the Armstrongs, the car black and wrapped in tarpaulin: no such shroud for the Millens. As might be expected, given its provenance, their garage was unable to contain the fiction that was their family car. It stood upon the

78

mud-packed surface, an amalgam of ugly experiments. When it was parked there, heavy and flat-footed, it dominated the road like no other car; when it was absent, no one imagined that such a vehicle could exist in such an ordinary street. Patsy had been right to call it the Rommel, with its gun-grey exterior and slit-eyed windscreen, the filthy choking stutter that came spluttering out of its exhaust. And yet, though the wheels were too large, the windows too small, the seats too narrow, the bonnet too wide, petrol consumption too high, manoeuvrability too low, there was something inspiring about this oversized lump, with its fearsome radiator and staring headlights ready to spring out through the jungle of rhododendron bushes, that compelled admiration; a predatory stance both awesome and ridiculous, given the land it stood alongside, for of all the four front gardens it was the Millens who displayed a lawn as it was written, clipped to absurdity like a toy poodle, watered and combed and fed by hand to within an inch of its pampered life; a winning exhibit no doubt, though but a miniature of the full-grown pedigree round the back. A showman's garden, then, governed by rules of engagement and plans of campaign; not a garden of dirt or delicacy, but of order and outrage, and unashamed to say so.

And to their right, divided by a schizophrenic hedge of yew (split down the centre, trim on the Millens' side, once hacked, twice forgotten, on the other), separated from the road by a half-hearted structure of brick and fence, lay the Roaches' patch, a plot of utter indifference, a no-man's-land, which one passed on the way to their front door (itself a bland portal), looking neither left nor right. That was all one could do. There was nothing to look at. There was grass, yes, but none you would have wished to walk upon. There were plants, to be sure, but none you could have admired, plucked, held to the nose. Their front garden bore neither the qualities of approach, nor of repose; it simply fell away from vision, its deficiencies not strong enough to provoke suburban ire, but sufficient for neighbourly ostracism; the Roaches as they did not want to be seen. And yet one glance was all that it took to reveal what it was, what they were. For their house was the outpost and the Roaches the sentinels, the land between them and the subjects of their scrutiny cleared, freed of obstacles; a no-man's-land over which to monitor the ever-present threat outside – of that most particular vice, encroachment.

Richard Roach was back at the bedroom window the following morning, the curtain wrapped togalike around the upper half of his flabby form. Outside Suzanne was swinging an expensive-looking shoulder bag into the boot of her car.

'I thought you said they were leaving early,' he complained to the huddled form of his wife. 'I don't call this early, do you?'

Ellen pulled the counterpane up over her head.

'I don't call it anything,' she mumbled. 'I'm trying to sleep.'

*

Suzanne had woken before first light. Matty lay on his back, his large hands clasping the duvet to his chin. She had always liked his hands, the thick spread of them, the way they could manipulate her. It had been so unexpected. Perhaps it was all that meat he handled that instilled in them such surprising knowledge; how her flesh moved over the bone, the hang and lie of it all. She turned towards him, remembering her promise. In an hour or so they could be on their way.

'Matty?'

He edged away, clinging to last vestiges of slumber. Suzanne lay back, impatient to set off for Southampton, to watch *Canberra*'s history unfold. Matty thought they had signed up for the money, what they might do with it, what it might do with them, but that wasn't why she had joined. She wanted to be part of the ship at the time of its greatest adventure. She was the ship, same as Dickey and Tina were the ship. That's what Matty would never understand. To him the *Canberra* was the workbench, the clock-in, the place where he earned his wage and counted out the squashed hours of his working life. It was only on land he felt the constrictions loosen. It was the opposite for Suzanne. It was the opposite for most of them. When she had first suggested that he join her, she knew the moment the words had slipped out that it would be a mistake, that Matty wouldn't understand what it meant to work deep sea, wouldn't appreciate how different a nation it was from the one he would leave behind, how foreign were its people, how strange their customs, how amoral their laws. Only she had returned from a long and sinfully pleasurable two-month absence and with Matty dispirited by the prospect of another three such turns in the next nine months, her guilt-wrapped presents lying unopened, she had coaxed him into acquiescence with the enticing possibilities of it, pantomiming the excitement of such entrapment, caught like this, intimate like this, with pay and perks and portholes to cap it all, and in truth, they always needed men with Matty's skills, just as she needed him there to get her back on the straight and narrow. One more trip like the last and Anglefield Road would be closed off for good, she knew that. So she had sold him the territory and his mastery of it, driving him down to the office the week following. Matty had cashed in his share of his business, paid off the mortgage, and became a master butcher at sea. And she, what had she become? A married woman, in married quarters, squeezing past a married man with the smell of dead meat in his hair. And every day she looked over the pool, watching the other girls and the drink trays and the familiar routes they took, and wished she was back with Tina in their old room, tapping into that visceral *Canberra* energy.

Matty coughed himself awake. Perhaps he was right. Perhaps it was the money that was the lure after all, not the sum of it, but the getting of it, throwing dice in convention's face, getting rich through risk. Wasn't that the coming thing? Money was being made again, but not by the Anglefield Roads of this world; by a different kind of street altogether. She only had to look at the type of passengers they were getting these days to know that: the brassy clothes they wore; the way they drank their champagne, gulping it down as if they were thirsty; the sudden arguments that would be conjured up; the braying laughter, the cat-fights, the way they didn't care; even the sex they pursued was different, hard, acquisitive, grabbed and fought over, like the first day of a January sale.

She leant across and pressed in.

'Matty? Time to get up soon.'

He rolled over on his back, opened one eye.

'What's the day like?' He rubbed his stomach. He was beginning to get a bit of a gut.

'I'll go and look, shall I?'

She got up and raised the blind. They were there all, her

neighbours and their houses, a light mist clinging to the gabled eaves like abandoned dreams. Soon Anglefield Road would awake; a curtain drawn, a spouse pressed into service (willing or reluctant, it would make no substantive difference), a hand descending onto a more solitary landscape; gardens surveyed all. Soon it would stir and confront the day; a cistern flushed, a radio switched, a kettle filled. And with their preparations done, then what? Embezzlement, adultery, a cup of gossip down the road? And if she never came back? What would Anglefield Road do then?

'It's murky,' she said. 'Best make an early start.'

She walked back and sat on the bed beside him. Matty shaded his eyes from the low glare and tugged at the hem of her shirt.

'Weren't you wearing *Evita* last night?'

'What? Oh.' She nodded to the corner. 'It got damp, ironing your bloody shirts.' She ran her hand through his fading hair. There was something of moment she wished to voice, some uncovered weight she wished to share, something buried, now dug up, heavy with the muck of the past, perhaps hidden in the folds of her discarded shirt: dust in the bedroom air.

'Matty, we are doing the right thing, aren't we? What if . . .' Her hand rose from his head to hers, running the fear of something absent through her hair. Was that it; what if? Matty chose to play dumb.

'What if what?'

'We never came back.'

'Best make the most of it, then.'

Sitting up, he drew the shirt over her head, kissing her blind breasts before sinking back, working his shorts off. Her mouth felt dry, *Canberra* dry. Not dead, then, but never come back. That's why the Pope had blessed her, why she had visited Mark last night, why Matty wanted to make love. She knelt over him.

'Come on, then. A quick one.'

She reached down, his mouth opening in anticipation. There was anchorage here, a holding and a letting go, a discarded rope splashing into the water, the slow churn of the engine as the ship moved away. She could feel the thrill of *Canberra* familiarity, *Canberra* uncertainty running through the length of her body. She was naked, diving into the sea of history. She held her breath and plunged, but coming up for air became aware of the smell of cooking bacon, and then, like water streaming out of waterlogged ears, heard the deliberate clump of boots break through, the clatter of knives and forks, laid out one, two, three, on the table below. She yanked herself free, her hand clamped across his lips. Matty tried to pull her back.

'What's the matter?'

'Can't you hear?' she whispered. 'Marcia. She's cooking breakfast.'

'So?'

She rolled off and stood up.

'So, we'd better go down and eat it.'

Fifteen minutes later they were sitting at the Formica table, its cramped quarters a testament to their nomadic life. Marcia was dressed in the same clothes as the night before, her boots unlaced, her face pulled tight. A rack of toast stood in the middle beside a small vase of daffodils. She must have brought the flowers down from London specially. Marcia took the pan from the stove and brought it to the table. She'd burnt the bacon.

'That pan sticks,' Suzanne said as Marcia tried to work the eggs free. 'You should have used the one hanging up.'

Broken yolk dripped through the spatula onto the table. Marcia wiped the surface clean, then sat down, disconsolate. Matty put out a hand.

'It doesn't matter. I'm not that hungry anyway.'

'Who could be?' Marcia's voice was faint and on the brink. She pushed back her chair and hung her arms around his neck.

They stayed there, immobile; statues carved in granite. It was a composition that denied Suzanne her existence; no space between the adamantine drape of limbs, their interlocked arms, their bowed heads, which allowed her entry.

'I could,' she said, scooping runny egg into her mouth. 'Nothing like a good fry-up before a journey.' Father and daughter lifted their heads, a look of disdain passing between them. Matty pushed Marcia gently back onto her chair. She pulled at her sleeves and blew her nose.

'Any news?' Matty asked her. She looked at him hard.

'There's going to be a war, Dad. You do know that, don't you?'

Matty sipped at his tea, unwilling to meet her gaze.

'Not necessarily.'

'But what if there is?'

'This is the *Canberra* we're talking about, Marcy. Not the *Ark Royal*.'

'And chock-a-block with soldiers. It'll be a target.' She looked over at Suzanne. Suzanne waved her fork in the air.

'Go ahead. Don't mind me.'

Suzy busied herself with her food, watching the two of them walk down to the bottom of the garden. She could tell by the gestures what Marcia was saying, pointing down to the danger underwater, upwards to the threat from the sky, throwing an accusatory wave back to where she was sitting. She could see Matty shake his head as Marcia held on to the gate, scuffing her feet at her father's intransigence, unaware how close she was to the evidence of Suzanne's own wayward behaviour. She swept her plate clean, feverish with hunger, then devoured the other two. When they returned she was standing in the hall, the trim of her stomach masking a still ravenous interior.

'Well?'

Marcia stepped forward and placed upon her cheek a kiss, cold and without tenderness, but a kiss all the same.

'Look after him,' she said. 'I want him back in one piece.' Suzanne held her close, feeling the strain in the younger woman, unwilling to respond.

'I will. And you too. Use the house as much as you want. Wild parties while we're away. Give the neighbours something to talk about.'

Marcia broke free, failing to smile.

'If you don't mind,' she said, turning back to her father.

Suzanne walked out to the car without another word. Anglefield Road was silent, emptied of colour, the road ending in a wisp of nothing, only the drained light of the street lamps providing the illusion of place.

'Come on, Matty,' she called out. 'We haven't got all day.'

They came out twenty minutes later. Suzanne had timed it on the dashboard clock. Matty's eyes were rubbed red.

'Are you OK? I'll drive if you're not up to it.'

A foolish question to ask a man in a crisis. He shook his head and climbed in. Marcia walked over and stood by the passenger door, her arms folded. Most daughters would have gone to their father's side, but not her. Her gaze glided over Suzanne in studied dismissal. Matty leant across and rolled down the window.

'We'll be off, then.'

Marcia moved her mouth; a prayer, a wish, a final promise? Suzanne couldn't tell. Matty inched the car out, looking up and down the road.

'I thought you said we were getting a bit of a send-off,' he sniffed, wiping the condensation from the windscreen. 'It's not every day your next-door neighbours go to war.'

'We're not going to war.' She wound the window up, hoping Marcia hadn't heard. 'Anyway I told Freddie we were leaving early. Some hope, that.'

'We're still part of the Task Force, Suzy, however you look at it.'

As they started up the road, the front door opposite was thrown open. Mark came out onto the porch and waved a tiny Union Jack in the air. Suzanne gave the thumbs-up sign.

'See?' she said, settling back into her seat. 'That was nice. Considering.'

'Considering what?'

'You know. His problems.'

The car hit the kerb, then straightened. Matty was staring into the driving mirror, lips pursed. Suzanne turned round. Mark and Marcia were talking in the middle of the road.

'Matty, she's twenty-two. She can look after herself.'

'Like that other poor girl could? See what I mean?'

Mark handed Marcia a cigarette; fat, uneven, illegal. Suzanne felt a sudden chill.

'There's nothing we can do about it now. Come on, Matty, let's get a move on.'

'All right, all right. I'll just let that milk float turn.'

Suzanne closed her eyes. It was going to be a long journey.

*

Roach dropped the curtain and hopped back into bed. He envied Matty, having a wife like Suzanne, though she wouldn't suit him,

85

he knew enough to see that. Whenever Anglefield Road got together, it was always Suzanne who pushed things close to the edge.

'Mark's out there, seeing them off,' he said. 'Never thought I'd see him up this early.'

'More than he would for us.'

'We can't give up on him, Ellen.'

Ellen pulled the cover further over her head. Roach put his hands behind his head, listening to the faint murmur of voices outside. They had given up on him long ago. They had a son once, he supposed, but when that was and where he had gone he couldn't say. Precious little son residing in Mark now, that's for sure, but when had there been? The truth was Roach had never liked him very much, even when he was first brought home, unwrapped as it were, his baby blue eyes narrowing at the sight of his mother's apprehensive breast. Her milk had puckered the boy's lips, turned his familial blood bitter. How much he had wanted a son, and oh, the disappointment of it. The mother, the son; oh, the disappointment of it all. He lay there staring at the window. One of the curtain hooks had broken loose from its mooring.

'There's a gap in the curtain,' he said. 'No wonder I couldn't sleep.'

Defects like that disturbed him: the sudden loose screw, the faulty electrical fitting, the unexplained chip on his favourite mug; by themselves small and insignificant deteriorations but which seemed to him signs that the world he knew was slipping through his fingers. Each time he returned from a week out on the road his home seemed more fragile, less substantial, than when he left, as if it were slowly fading, disappearing from view. He would lie in bed, and see himself not there with Ellen at his side, but alone, in a room above a street, with a table and a chair and a faded lamp-shade illuminating a threadbare bed, and he lying half curled with everything lost; his job, his house, his wife, his son, his whole damned purpose. It was not merely a thought, a fear of loss that momentarily assaulted every traveller; it was a portent, a vision of what was to come: the destruction of Richard Roach. He came home, placed his lips upon her wife's cheek, asked about her day, knowing all along that one day he would lose it all. Mark was just the beginning.

He sat on the end of the bed and pulled on his socks and dressing gown. Opening the cupboard he lifted out his small overnight case and began to pack, a quickly executed accomplishment made quiet from years of practice: two shirts, two ties, his favourite brown cords, his favourite red V-neck sweater, a change of underwear, his pair of good English suede. Another day of travelling, another night away from home. Sometimes he was so tired of waiting, so exhausted by the inevitability of his demise, he wanted it to happen soon. What might it be? The manner in which he parked his car, the spilt bowl of sugar at the guest-house breakfast, Soapsuds springing out of nowhere on his monthly trip to London? Or would that other encounter be his undoing, the salesman's wet dream; the solitary slimline woman at a lonely table, the blowsy bar-fly nursing her second gin, the randy student nurse momentarily intrigued by his world-weary wit and pigskin loafers? For wherever he went, the wine bars, the curry houses, the public houses, he could not take his eyes off them, the women, however hard he tried: their dress, the shape and colour of their lips, the depth of their eye shadow, the way they stood, the shade of stocking, the length of skirt, the outline of their breasts, how they laughed, whether their eyes looked cold or sad, how they ate, how they drank, how they smoked their cigarettes, whether they looked their age, what age that might be, whether they appeared married or single, divorced or engaged, unfaithful or faithful, how close, how awkward, how wary they were with each other; he could not take his eyes off them, not because he hoped to attract one, far from it, for Richard Roach had neither the instinct nor the ability, neither the look nor the word, to cash in on such an encounter, but because he feared that amongst them sat the catalyst of his calamity, crossing her legs, inhaling her smoke, plotting the means of his destruction with every eyelash blinked. Every week he felt it, that this would be the time, and every week it was not. And yet there it was, floating alongside his slice of lemon, bubbling up through the froth of his beer.

Downstairs he dropped a slice of bread in the toaster, made a cup of coffee, and stood by the kitchen window, sipping at the bitter warmth. On the patio outside a crow stood triumphant over some dark tangled remains, its claws planted criss-cross on the upturned belly of the broken carcass as it pulled at the spilt entrails with its beak. It was dark and immeasurably beautiful and moved with a hypnotic, iridescent cruelty. Roach could feel himself fluttering inside. He banged on the window and watched the bird flap away, an umbilical cord of death dangling from its beak. He dropped the toast, uneaten, into the bin. He never ate much before going on the road; nerves partly, the butterfly prospect of his provincial performances, but also in recognition of his forthcoming diet. 'Try not to eat too many fry-ups,' Ellen would say to him the few times she got up to see him off, and although he promised her fruit juice and cereal, as soon as he propped up his paper at the bed-and-breakfast table it was the works; bacon and eggs, sausages, fried bread, tomatoes, black pudding, toast and marmalade. It was what you expected from a guest house; it was what they were there for. There was little else to recommend them.

'Dad?'

Mark came in, sticking one of the little flags Roach had bought in his shirt pocket. Marcia followed, rubbing the morning chill from her arms. She looked as if she hadn't given a moment's thought to what she looked like, hair uncombed, shirt tail hanging out over her jeans. She hadn't even bothered to tie her bootlaces, not that Doc Marten's were suitable for a young woman's foot. They were giggling like small children.

'Morning, Mr Roach.'

'Marcy!' Roach tried to inject a degree of natural cheer into his voice. 'You saw them off, then?'

She nodded.

'How are they feeling?'

'Not much different. I think I'm more nervous than they are.'

She pronounced her 'r's with a relish that Roach found displeasing. Something to do with the provenance of the mother, he supposed. Roach had never warmed to Matty's first wife, the loudness of her laughter, the stream of unintelligible language that would burst forth, above all her complete lack of ceremony, how she would appear uninvited at their front door, when he would stand full square in front of her, willing himself to be as unhelpful as Anglefield manners permitted. There was much of her uncomfortable memory residing within Marcia, and he tried to surmount it.

'Well, it's quite an honour,' he said, 'taking part in something historic like this.'

Mark, reaching for the jar of coffee, exhaled derision, his breath thick with the smell of cigarettes. Roach turned.

'I suppose you're against the Task Force going, just like you're against most things these days,' he said.

'Self-serving patriotism, that's all it is.' Mark took the flag from his shirt pocket and waved it under Roach's nose. 'You know what I'd do? Give the sheep-shaggers half a million quid each and hand the islands over. The Falklands are dead. Long live the Malvinas!'

He lifted the lid of the waste-paper bin and, smiling, dropped the Union Jack on top of a mess of potato peelings. Roach wanted to grab him and hold his head under the cold-water tap.

'So why you were out there this morning?'

It was Marcia who spoke. Mark wriggled in momentary discomfort.

'Someone had to see them off,' he said. 'The great patriots of Anglefield Road couldn't be bothered, so I thought I would. Better than nothing.'

Roach felt the pulse of embarrassment working through his neck. Why hadn't he gone out, waved them goodbye? Because of Ellen listening to him from the length of their bed; because of Henry standing underneath their window the night before? Or was it simply the journey downstairs; the view of tidy rooms, the shed outside, the hall with its long history of silence. It took so much resolve to walk through and open the front door.

'It wasn't that we didn't want to,' he explained. 'We were asked not to. They didn't want a fuss. Isn't that right, Marcia?'

Marcia shrugged her shoulders. Mark smirked.

'Waving them goodbye is hardly a fuss, Dad.'

'Yes, well, perhaps they thought Anglefield Road has had enough of the Roaches recently. What do you think?'

A low blow.

'I try not to think at all,' Mark said, holding him with his eyes.

'Perhaps you should. Perhaps you should think of the Falk-landers too, in the hands of a brutal dictatorship.'

'And we're not, I suppose?'

Roach threw his coffee cup into the plastic bowl in the sink.

'I give up. There's no point in talking to you when you're like this.'

'Still, going off and shooting a load of grease-balls, that would be fun. Better than being stuck here. Let loose the Dagoes of War!' Mark sighted along an imaginary barrel and shot his father between the eyes. Marcia put her hand to her mouth, spluttered. Roach bit into his words.

'Don't be ridiculous, Mark. No one wants a war.'

He knew it wasn't true. There were plenty straining for Argentinian blood. He had boarded the train with them as they shook the news out of their newspapers; he had sat next to them in the boardroom as they attacked their sales targets; he had stood at the bar drinking overpriced pints of bitter with Sandy while they drank double measures of bravado. He turned to Marcia, raised his eyebrows.

'Are you like this with your parents first thing in the morning?'

The use of the plural, he realized, was a mistake.

'I'm with Mark, Mr Roach. It's not as if the Falklands mean anything to us. I wish they weren't going.'

Roach leant back on the kitchen counter. She was an unpleasantly striking young woman, her mother's dark skin, her father's livid freckles, intense mistrustful eyes, an unforgiving mouth that always seemed on guard, as if anticipating one's short-comings. It could have been her in that car with Mark next to her. Mark had sat there half the night unable to move, the girl's body sat back in the passenger seat. What must that have been like? Roach spoke carefully, concentrating on the politics.

'We'd be giving in to naked aggression, Marcia, that's what you've got to understand. It's what we did in the thirties with Hitler, and looked what happened then. First it was Czecho-slovakia and we let him have it, hoping that that would be an end to it. But then came Austria and Poland and suddenly we're looking down the wrong end of World War Two. That's the whole thing about dictators. Unless you put a stop to them first time round, there's no holding them. We have to learn from the lessons of history.'

He was pleased with that last sentence. It made a measured sense. It just went to show; he didn't mind an argument, hearing other points of view, as long as it was run on civilized lines. It was all a question of attitude.

'Actually, Dad, the Ruhr was the first.'

'What?'

Mark stuck his nose into the bottle of milk.

'Hitler. He invaded the Ruhr first. 1936.'

Roach felt himself churning. He knew all about the Ruhr. He was thirty-eight years old, for Christ's sake. His father had been in the Ruhr during the occupation, in charge of prisoners of war.

'I know when the Ruhr was, Mark, don't you worry. I was simply making the point that General Galtieri is no different. Force, or the threat of it, is the only thing he understands.'

'So, where do you think he plans to invade next?' Mark asked, his back turned, a hand rummaging carelessly in the cupboard above. 'Gibraltar? Wales? The Mull of Kintyre? Poor old Paul McCartney, eh? That dreadful dirge, all for nothing.'

He pulled out the cereal packet, and pouring from a great height began to imitate the bagpipes wailing chorus. Fingernails on a blackboard, silver paper over a filling, could not have set Roach's nerves on edge more quickly. Cornflakes bounced out of the bowl, skittering over the surface in a maddening dance. Roach snatched the packet out of his son's hand, found himself shouting.

'Can't you be serious just for once? We have to set an example. I thought even you might understand that.'

'Like fucking Ireland, you mean.' Mark wafted the milk bottle under Marcia's nose. 'Does this smell off to you?' Roach snatched it away.

'It's nothing like Ireland and watch your language! I won't have it, you hear.'

'What's my language? What's my language? The same as yours.'

The same language, the same house, the same sour milk from the same sour breast. They stood there, unable to break free. Mark picked up the bowl and began to eat dry cereal with his fingers.

Marcia bent down to tie her laces. She had a tattoo in the small of her back. Roach tried not to stare. It looked like a butterfly. She straightened up, scornfully catching the fall of his eye. Roach could feel his face redden. If she didn't want people to look, she should tuck her shirt in.

'I'd best make a move,' said Roach. 'Duty calls.'

Mark looked up. 'You working today?'

'That what comes with a job, Mark. Responsibilities.'

'To London?'

Where was he going? He couldn't spend the whole day in Stevenage. What was to stop him going to Southampton? He wasn't doing anything else. He could drive over, see the lie of the land, take a few photographs of the dock, get it all straight in his head for when Ellen cross-examined him the next day, then drive up to Stevenage in the late afternoon. No one would be any the wiser. A military exercise of his own; under cover; in and out.

'Stevenage. It's Trout Night. Though God knows what the traffic will be like with all those holiday drivers let loose.'

Silence dropped in. It was a subject uneasily broached, driving. A momentary pang of pity came over him. Mark dispelled it quick enough.

'Oh, Trout Night. You don't want to miss that.'

He walked abruptly out the back door, Marcia following after a dismissive nod. Roach could hear her laughing at something Mark said.

Upstairs in the bathroom Roach brushed his teeth. His face felt heavy; his skin old and loose. Walking into the bedroom he tucked his toilet bag down the side of the case, checking the contents one more time. Everything lay there, neat and undisturbed. A salesman lived out of his suitcase, that's what Sandy had told him when first he joined the firm, but Sandy had been wrong. Roach lived *in* his suitcase. All that there was of him resided there, clean and empty and folded flat of life.

He snapped the lid shut.

'I'm off, then.'

Ellen stirred, yawned awake.

'Let's have a look at you, then. Big day today.' She raised herself up on her arms and looked him up and down. 'You can't wear that tie, Richard. It doesn't go. Try the one I gave you for Christmas.'

He pulled the tie loose and looked for the blue silk. He didn't like it much; too flash. Would that be the magnet, the cause of his downfall, a present he had never wanted to wear; a blue silk tie to match an idling eye?

'OK?'

'It's not straight, you silly thing.'

Throwing back the covers, she knelt on the bed. 'The things I have to do for you,' she said, 'my TV star of a husband. Here, let me.'

She reached up with both arms and tightened it round his neck. 'Here let me,' she had said, taking the cloth from under that cocky stare of his, 'here, let me.' High up on the inside leg it had been, and working at the stain she saw it growing, her face not inches away, him just standing there saying nothing, Richard cursing outside, she rabbiting on about how sorry she was and how she was sure it would come out. 'Oh, it'll do that all right,' he said and put his hands over hers and led her over to the long ridge of it. She sat back on her haunches and looked at him and he just pulled the zip down and fished the thing out. 'Are you all right in there?' Richard shouted out and Kevin looked down and pushed it hard into her mouth. 'Yes, everything's fine,' he called back, and then it was out in the air again, the great fat end rubbing against her cheek and she thought what if Richard came in and did she care, and at that moment she hadn't, all she wanted was the excitement of that little bastard waving it about in broad daylight; it only took half a minute, great thick gulps, and just when she had thought he had finished and had it out again, working it up and down, her hand all greasy, a great dollop came out and spilled down on the front of her dress. And what had he done? Just put himself away and walked out without a word, while she scraped it off as best she could. By the time she went back into the room he was pouring himself another glass of wine and chatting to Richard as if nothing had happened. And nothing had really. She had opened her mouth, that's all, opened her mouth and taken something that was not hers into it, something she suspected she would never see again. He was looking so pleased with himself, but it had been she who had done all the work. He just hooked it out his trousers and stood there, the little prick. Who got the pleasure, though, that's what she still wanted to know? Pleasure? More like hatred. More like scorn.

She kissed him on the cheek. Roach put his hands to the dip of her waist, wary of the movement loose inside her nightdress. She smelt of forbidden dreams.

'I'll be watching,' she said, lying back.

He nodded and closed the door quietly behind him.

*

The drive down was slow and silent. Matty spent the journey in the middle lane, impervious to Suzanne's extended right leg as it worked upon an imaginary accelerator. The trouble with Matty's driving, blind adherence to the speed limit notwithstanding, was that he drove like a hotel doorman, letting people through, waving people on, inclining his head as they flashed their lights in some obsequious demonstration of unwarranted servility. That day it seemed as if he wanted every driver in the south-west to get the better of them. Two coachloads of old-age pensioners speeding past them at the Swindon turn-off loosened her tongue.

'What's the registration of this car, Matty? WIMP 1?'

'What?'

'Put your foot down, for Christ's sake.'

Matty sniffed and took no notice.

When they got there, Southampton was in magnificent toil, as if under siege, the streets filled with candyfloss shirts and battle-dress green; flags flying, cars hooting, orders flapping, ice-cream families aimless in a military safari park, wandering wide-eyed at the strange preoccupations of the clipped creatures on display. In every shop uniformed men stood in queue-jumping authority, determined, good humoured, appraising the intended pillage with a firm and avaricious eye. The town was being stripped naked for the fighting holds of *Canberra*, shop by shop, counter by counter, rack by rack; its fruit, its meat, its vegetables, its socks and soft drinks, its beer and cigarettes, given up to a flourished signature, passed hand over hand to the waiting lorries unbalanced on the pavement. It was a medieval process; organized plunder, the itching scurry of it infecting everyone's skin. Suzanne decided that they might need some warmer clothing. They looked for thirty minutes in a near-fruitless search. Eventually she found an outdoor clothes shop denuded of everything except a rack of bright yellow windcheaters. She held one up against Matty's chest.

'It looks your size,' she said. 'Try it on.'

Matty shook his head.

'You never know, Matty. We've got nothing if the weather turns nasty.'

Matty stood firm. 'We're only going to Ascension Island. It's like the bloody tropics there.'

'Well, I'm going to.' She pulled it over her head. 'What do you think?'

'It's a waste of money, Suzanne, that's what I think.'

Suzanne drew the zip up. If there was one thing that drove her into an implacable corner it was Matty calling her by her full name when they were arguing. He imagined it made him sound more authoritative. She turned in the mirror. The hood had a black surround. She rather liked it.

'It's my money, Matty.'

'I thought it was our money.'

'You're right. It is. But it's my wind-chill factor. OK?'

Driving out towards the docks, running against the stream of emptied lorries, they followed the tailgated back of a military truck, its thick-ribbed wheels bulging out over the mounted pavement. Fifteen or so soldiers sat underneath the hang of the green tarpaulin, bodies jolting, faces set against what they were leaving behind: more squatted inside. They didn't look anything special. When they caught sight of Suzanne they whistled, mouthing the usual range of indecent suggestions. Suzanne bit her lip, privately flattered. Matty gripped the wheel, pretending not to notice.

They parked the car in the P&O car park, checked their names in, and walked down to berth 105. There had always been a sense of urgency about a coming voyage, the bustle of deliveries, the dockside spill of suitcases, the cold scent of a distant sea immense and out of reach, but even as they began the short walk down, they could sense the change. Ranks of army transport lined the parking bays; Land-Rovers, tracked vehicles, guns and trailers draped with camouflage nets. Above the ordinary shouts and clatter came a rhythm of massed hammers beating the air, and with it the smell of metal burning. Sudden dazzles of light stabbed at their eyes. They picked their way through a maze of strange stores: coils of ropes, lengths of freshly cut timber, grey metal cases with unsettling names stencilled on the side: bombs, mortar: grenades, fragmentation: rockets, Milan. And then they saw her. She rose, like she always rose, high above them, stretching up out along the dock, shining and white, with ropes and gangways holding her fast. But even at a distance there seemed a strange imbalance to her, an unexplained tilt to her geometry, a sudden convulsion that had seized her lines. Drawing nearer they could see why. Great chunks of the ship's frame lay discarded on the dockside; guard rails and wind shields that had been cut off to make way for the coming machinery of war. Fountains of sparks cascaded down the clambered cliffs of her sides. Above a helicopter was lowering a huge metal plate on the observation deck aft of the bridge: a crane swung steel girders amidships. She was a Gulliver of a ship, trussed and tied and swarmed upon by men determined to effect a terrible change. Suzanne dropped her bags.

'Oh, Matty. What have they done to my *Canberra*?'

He stepped over her bags and walked on ahead.

'They've cut the pleasure out of her,' he called out. 'And she's not yours any more.'

He sounded almost pleased.

They signed on and were assigned to their quarters. Thanks to the spare crew accommodation, Matty and Suzanne had been given an unexpectedly generous billet on D Deck. Most cruises they were two levels down, sandwiched in some bolt hole next to the Genoese mess. Now they had a pair of decent-sized bunks, a small table, proper cupboard space, even a tiny shower. Usually they had to wash with everyone else.

'This is nice, I must say,' Matty said, throwing his case onto the lower bunk. 'Lording it up in petty officers' digs. Little settee and everything. Quite the little billet doux.'

He sat down and patted the seat beside him. Suzanne, ignoring the gesture, moved to the window, staring at the bustle outside; laden soldiers lining up on the quayside waiting to board; blocks of provisions moving hand to hand up into the ship; overhead a clattering helicopter, trailing empty hooks. Not long now. She turned back.

'I'd rather be with the others.'

'In that rabbit warren? All on top of each other.'

He got up and lifted his bag onto the chest of drawers, letting it drop hard, a measure of his distaste.

'That's how us rabbits like it, Matty. Perhaps now more than ever.'

Matty began unpacking his shirts. She took the crucifix from around her neck and hung it over the mirror on the low dressing table. Later, when she was alone, she'd light a candle and say a prayer with the Pope, remembering his frail bent head and trembling hands. She had his picture tucked in her vanity case. She'd go to services too. The padre would be busy this trip, no doubt of that.

There was a knock on the door. Tina stood with a half-drunk bottle of champagne in her hand. Her face was flushed with anticipated pleasure as much as drink.

'Da-daa!'

She twirled into the room, admiring the surroundings.

'You lucky people. What I couldn't get up to in this. Don't fancy moving out and letting me share with Suzy again, do you, Matty?'

Matty threw out an irritated look.

'Perhaps not,' Tina said. She crossed over and throwing her arms around Suzanne, span her round. 'Talk about Christmas coming early,' she confided. 'Suzy, they're *gorgeous*.'

'You haven't wasted much time, then.' Suzanne threw a placatory wink in Matty's direction. 'When did you get here?'

'Yesterday afternoon. We're due on in just over an hour. You missed the briefing yesterday. Eames was furious. Here, do you know what those bastards in laundry have done? You don't mind, do you, Matty?'

Tina worked her skirt up over her thigh and turned the hem inside out.

'See that? "TART" they've written, in indelible ink. I only asked them to clean my stuff as a favour. I didn't have the time in the turn-round, what with having to drive over to see Mum. Picked it up this morning and what do I find. "TART" plastered everywhere. Skirts, jackets, blouses, you name it, it's got "TART" written on it. It's not on, is it, even as a joke. I'm not one for getting people into trouble, but I've a good mind to report this.'

Suzanne laughed.

'It's your name, you klutz.'

'It most certainly is not.'

'That's what they do in the laundry. They mark each garment with the first letter of your Christian name and the first three letters of your surname. That way they can keep track of it. So, Tina Arthurson, "Tart".'

'Well, I'm buggered. I never knew that.'

'You've never worked cabins.'

'I will on this voyage. We're all doubling up. Bars, restaurants, cabin duty, washing, ironing, we're doing everything but the steering. And get this. According to our lords and masters, social contact is to be kept at a minimum. Be pleasant, be helpful, but no intimate chit-chat. Well, guess what? Who wants to talk?'

Matty left for his first shift. Suzanne and Tina passed the bottle back and forth, drinking from the neck. It was good to be back with Tina again. Above all others it had been Tina who had inducted her into the *Canberra* way of life, Tina who had become her best friend, Tina who according to Matty disgraced herself on every voyage. Suzanne couldn't have cared less what she got up to. But that was the whole point. Tina was Suzanne's past, writ large. If ever Matty decided to chuck it in and step ashore, she'd have to hand in her cards as well. He wouldn't stand for her working deep sea on her own, now that he knew what the rest of them got up to. It had been a shock to her too, that first January seven years ago, when she had joined the ship, fleeing from an oppressive father, sharing a cabin with someone who the purser had described as one of *Canberra*'s 'most experienced' hands. She noted the smirk behind that remark, but could hardly believe it when Tina brought that girl into their cabin. Three days out, Suzanne had just come back from her first shift of the day, and taking Tina's advice she had stepped out of her uniform and had settled down onto her bunk with aching legs and blistered feet to get some rest before the long haul of the evening, when the door was flung open and Tina propelled in a tipsy twenty-three-year-old clutching a table-tennis bat and proceeded to undress the young woman and herself with a frank and expert haste that Suzanne could only sense through her tightly shut eyes. 'Perhaps she doesn't know I'm here,' she told herself, 'perhaps she thinks I'm still on duty,' only to be disillusioned when, following the girl up, Tina whispered a hasty 'sorry' as she trod on her arm. Suzanne was left to stare at the dangerously sagging mattress and the not so muffled sounds above, until after what seemed like hours later, Tina jumped down, stuffed the girl back into her sporting gear, and with a towel wrapped round her own body, hurried her off down the corridor. She came back a couple of minutes later, humming to herself. Suzanne had lain rigid with a whirl of burning embarrassment, her sheet tight over her head, hardly daring to breathe. She could hear the door being closed, then water in the little sink being run. A hand touched her on the shoulder. She pulled her sheet back. Tina stood there, rubbing her face dry.

'Oh, hello,' Suzanne said, as if surprised to see her.

'Hope you didn't mind,' Tina said. 'Needs must.'

'Mind?' Suzanne's face was glowing like a blast furnace. 'No! Not at all!'

Tina lifted her dressing gown from the back of the door and threw it round her shoulders.

'Privacy is a rare luxury on board ship,' she said. 'Everybody not only knows what you're doing but most likely has been offered a ringside seat too. That's rule number one. Rule number two is "Don't hang about". I know I should have waited until we were better acquainted but . . . Oh, look.' She bent down and picked up the table-tennis bat from the floor. 'They all do that. Gives them an excuse to return.'

She tapped the hard edge of the bunk with the rim of the bat and said, 'Are you at all interested in this sort of activity?'

Suzanne looked at the bat in her hand.

'At school I was,' she said.

'Were you?' There was an element of welcome surprise in her room-mate's voice that Suzanne found easy to embrace.

'Yes. Me and my friend Holly, we made quite a name for ourselves. Of course I'm out of practice now.'

Tina had looked at her firmly. 'What made you give it up? Boys, I suppose.'

'It was just a phase we went through.' Suzanne sat up, dragging the bedclothes around her. She was beginning to rather like this girl. 'Do you think it would help me get on if I took it up again?' she asked.

Tina had stiffened visibly. 'Well, aren't you the determined one. Screw who you like, but don't expect to get to the purser's office right away.'

'Purser's office? But I thought . . .' and she looked at the table-tennis bat in Tina's hand.

Looking back now on that stuffy afternoon, the two of them wrapped in sheets, both young and in good condition, doubled up with laughter, Tina waving the bat around, repeating the phrase, 'I was quite good at it at school,' it seemed to Suzanne that without realizing it that that had been the moment when all she had been taught in the years before, all the jeers and taunts that men and women made about their own and the other kind, dropped away. It was as if up to that time she had been some hooded bird, tied to a narrow perch, blindfolded, fed on scraps of dead thought, unable to see the brilliance of her own plumage or the shimmering colours of the living world beyond, and in that second of laughter the blindfold had been removed, the chain unlocked, and she had begun to flap her wings, to beat against the confines of that small and narrow room, ready to break out, to rise and cry and soar into the air. They were men and women all, the ship was full of them, the world was full of them, men and women and the lives they had to lead, and that was all. She had never seen it like that before, in its great simplicity, men and women and how they must cling to one another in all their crazed variety. When they had calmed down Tina asked her again.

'Not interested, then?' Her gaze was bright.

'No.' Suzanne spoke emphatically, knowing that although she was not attracted to it per se, she was interested, interested as hell.

'As long as you don't mind?'

'No!' Suzanne felt quite worldly. Tina lost no time in taking the boundaries further.

'Of course it won't always be like that,' she said. 'Men, women, Swiss maids, lost choir boys. On a cruise ship like this, it's à la carte all the way.'

Suzanne nodded and swallowed, feeling herself blush again. Tina looked her up and down, like a farmer might at market day.

'Some words of advice. You're a good-looking girl, you'll get lots of opportunity. Always remember it's you that has a job to answer to. Enjoy yourself, but don't get involved. Have your fun for a night or two, then move on, otherwise complications set in. Once they've seen the moon on the water they think they've fallen in love. That or they expect to get their leg over for the rest of the voyage. Either way it can get tedious, if not downright dangerous. Remember, there's only one of you, but there's a whole boat load of them.'

'But in your own cabin? I thought that was against the rules.'

'It's all against the rules, dear heart, but sometimes you've got no choice. Just shut the door and get on with it. But remember, if you do bring them back, don't tell them our cabin number or the deck. Keep their minds on other matters getting them here and after it's all over take them back the long way round. That way, if they try and find you again, they won't have the faintest idea how to get here. Which leads me to rule number three.'

'Which is?'

'No member of crew ever gives a passenger a crew's room number. Ever. Got it.'

'Got it.' Suzanne paused. 'You make it all sound rather like an obstacle course.'

'That's why we call it the Sack Race. It can get a little complicated at times, but mostly it's a whole lot of fun. Let's go and have a drink. All that shagging's made me thirsty.'

*

The years hadn't changed Tina, either in her easy, loose-limbed looks or her capacity for careless opportunism. The bottle finished, they went in search of Dickey up in the Crow's Nest. High up, overlooking the bow, with its grand piano, its sweeping panes of glass and circular bar, it was the queen of *Canberra*'s cocktail lounges, the torch held aloft in *Canberra*'s liberty grip. The Crow's Nest was its official name. Suzanne called it the Dovecote, in recognition of the undisputed sway Dickey held over it, fussing like a broody bird, alert and defensive, but really it was too pure, too innocent a name. The Crow's Nest hit a truer note, not simply for its giddying height and the swaying vista from a treetop observation post, but the dark predatory glow of it at night, when black-coated men would show off the sparkling trophies glittering on their arms, ready to seize some other jewelled prize from a rival's tenuous grip.

They walked through the Meridian Lounge and climbed the spiral stairs. Stripped of all its excess, the ceiling had been torn down, exposing a lattice of metalwork, now strengthened by a criss-cross of scaffolding, bolted in to take the weight of the forward flight deck being built overhead. The bar was empty, save for an electrician looping cable over the gantries. He stood on a ladder peering up into the recess, singing into the echoes of the newly opened vaults. The sun had broken through, his voice dancing upon scattering bars of light. Outside on the murky sea shone a diamond of crystal blue. She was standing on a rock, ready to dive.

Tina started to swing from upright to upright, like a girl on a seaside promenade. Suzanne stopped her in mid-flight, running her hand up one of the poles, the Pope's touch upon her.

'Don't.'

'What?'

'Can't you feel it, Tina? It's like a cathedral under restoration, everything reaching up, as if this is how it was, before, before us.' She could see the priest watching her, white stones in his hand. 'This is how *Canberra* is meant to be, the real *Canberra*; the cruises were just . . .' She stumbled for words, her voice rising in the difficulty she found. No wonder his hands trembled. 'You know, like the moneychangers in the temple.'

'You sure it's a Bloody Mary and not a Hail Mary you're after?' A small head emerged from behind the counter.

'Dickey!'

'Either way the Crow's Nest is closed. Welcome to the Officers'

Mess. It would be a war, wouldn't it, that brought back the class barrier.'

He rose, laying out bowls of nuts; as ever, neat and economical in movement. Suzanne crossed the floor, leant over with a kiss.

'I hope you've brought your iron with you, Suzy,' he said, wiping it away. 'Given our new stature, I'm not sure I trust our regular laundry for such a task.'

Tina lifted her skirt and told her tale again. Dickey looked on with interest. He had once tried to render Tina on one of his embroidered cushions. Most members of the crew had something that Dickey had laboured over hanging in their cabins. Murray had one of Capri, Tina the Copacabana, Suzanne had been given one entitled *Night Time at the Acropolis*, the location of Matty's first hesitant attempt at a proposal, but though he could do locations well enough, mountains, harbours, buildings of note, the human body had defeated him, even one as consummate as Tina's. She had come out looking like a blancmange on pipe cleaners and had refused to hang it. As retribution it now had pride of place in the staff bar, the Pig and Whistle, where after hours Dickey would sit, feet up in his requisitioned dentist's chair, while trainee stewards ran back and forth to place his pink gin upon the swivel table where the implements once lay, and his cocktail onions in the bowl where the mouthwash used to run. Suzanne took a handful of nuts and turned the subject back to the matter in hand.

'What are they like, then, our new guests?' she asked him. 'You met any?'

'One or two rather scruffy looking individuals tried to wheedle their way to a drink about half an hour ago. Journalists, I presumed, so I sent them away with a *Canberra* pencil set each. They were not in the best of tempers. Apparently the navy has put them in some very sweaty quarters down in the bilges; their punishment for having the temerity for coming along at all.'

'The soldiers, Dickey.'

'A mixed bunch, all rather firm and polite and needling each other in the most courteous of ways, a few mad medical staff, and lastly, and most definitely lastly, the Royal Navy.'

'They've done something to upset you?'

'Just because we're on a boat they think we have to do

everything the Royal Navy way. They didn't want this called the Officers' Mess, told me in future it must be referred to as the Wardroom. Even put up a notice to the effect. An hour later the army comes by and tears it down. Round and round we went, Wardroom, Officers' Mess, Wardroom, Officers' Mess, until a major from the Marines, a very fiery little fellow, told his opposite number that in the interests of his personal safety it was better not to interfere with officers of the Royal Marines and Parachute Regiment. So, Officers' Mess it is. As far as the army is concerned, the navy is a watery sort of taxi service, a bit like the gondoliers in Venice, only without the tunes. You admire their braided costumes, smile politely at their flowery lingo but after it's all over and you're back on dry land, you're rather glad it's all over.'

*

Tina left to put on her most attractive face. Though she risked a fine for being in public out of uniform, Suzanne decided to take a look around before reporting for the first shift. Matty was right. It was not only the Falklands that had been invaded, the *Canberra* had too. Like an occupied town, the invading forces were much in evidence, requisitioning private holdings, installing equipment, probing the nerves of their newly conquered domain; the natives had fled, the staff bars and social rooms she visited bare, the chairs half stacked, the drink guards down, dried cigarette stubs lying dead in unwashed ashtrays. Though the normal complement of officers and engineers were in evidence, all the entertainment staff and cruise specialists had disappeared. The outside world that the *Canberra* had taken such pains to keep at bay had come alongside and sunk its grappling hooks in her, her decks overrun, the lounges and libraries and writing rooms occupied by telex machines and wireless sets, their windows masked, the new occupants working under a red glow that reminded her of a live sex show she had once seen in Mexico City. Peering in, striving to read the expressions on their half-hidden faces, a young soldier, hands clamped over headphones, two older men bent double over the awkward spread of a map, their bare short-sleeved arms brushing against each other as they reached and smoothed down the folds, she experienced the same uncomfortable excitement she had felt then, thinking herself in their place, trying to read their movements, a ringside seat to such ordinary intimacy. One of them saw her and, nudging his companion, straightened up with a mock salute. Blushing, she walked on.

All along the corridors thick coils of wire snaked alongside her, bunched together, looped up on the ceiling, taped to the walls, some as thick as her wrist. They were like veins, those wires. The ship had been opened up, operated on, bits and pieces snatched from God knew where, smuggled in under cover of the night, new arms, new lungs, fresh blood brought in by the bucketful, a floating Frankenstein's monster, fixed up by mad science, straining to be set loose upon the sea with a new and terrible power. Suzanne was reminded of a picture she had seen many years back in one of the Sunday colour supplements of a car all squashed up, pressed into an oblong block and stuck in the corner of some millionaire's playroom, squat and ugly, the grille, the headlamps, even the registration plate still plain to see. Though she had known it could no longer move, it would not have surprised her if it had sprung to sudden life and devoured the room. Shape had changed it, changed the direction of its power, changed its desire, its cause, its effect. And had not the *Canberra* been similarly transmuted? Those original lines, her decks and divisions, her swirls of glass, her curves of railing, the echo they sounded, ripples of a stone thrown, a body vanished, a present freed and unrecorded, had been distorted, her purpose thus transformed. The ship had never seemed smaller, the corridors never more impassable, steaming bowels pressed up against decks of light and promenade; contortions to be made, unfamiliar routes to be taken, unexpected encounters along on the way. And she, what would she do in this new configuration? For the first time a tremor of uncertainty flickered through her. She knew where shape could lead her. Would she have pressed Mark's head to her breast had it not been for Anglefield Road's form, if there had been no circle of houses to gaze upon, no embankment to mask her passage, no branches to hinder it, no thundering train to quicken her heart? A straight road to cross and in at the back door. Would she have done it then?

In the lower decks, cabins that were usually filling up with retired couples, penny-conscious honeymooners and middle-aged families were now jammed with young men, high-jinksed, larking about like kids on their first trip away from home, the smell of their sweat spilling out into the passageways as they threw pillows and fought over bunks, falling silent as she neared. She knew the drill well enough, the adolescent nudges, the straightened faces, how they flattened themselves against the walls as she passed, knew too the gestures, the stifled laughter, that engulfed them in her wake, but where in former times the jibes had been spasmodic, a pair of adolescent brothers here, a couple of furtively married men there, here she ran the full building-site gauntlet, cabin after cabin, cat-call after cat-call. That's when it hit her. Out of a complement of nearly three thousand, there were at most fifteen women. This was a man's ship now, sailing into a man's world.

And then she was alone, edging past a stack of stretchers down on B Deck, wondering what was coming next. In the opposite direction a solitary soldier came hurrying along, a case, black and bulbous, stuck awkwardly under his arm, a scrap of paper scrumpled in his hand. A doctor's bag, she thought, thinking momentarily of what little she knew of war and its obvious consequence; either something English and noble, long wards with beatific nuns nursing broken bodies, or something American and sexy, full of blood and breasts, like that film *M*A*S*H*. He looked lost. She knew the signs so well, the unsure steps, the hasty look back, the fruitless examination of every passing sign. Drawing close she saw that he was pale and sweating, a trapped look on his face.

'Something wrong?' she said.

He stopped short, noticing her for the first time, surprised to be faced by a woman. She spoke again.

'Can I help at all?'

He lowered the case to the floor and smoothed out the sheet of paper.

'I'm trying to find my unit but I seem to have mislaid my bearings.' Despite the uniform he didn't look like a soldier.

'That's the whole point of ships like this,' she said. 'That's when you know the cruise has really begun. People do it all the time.'

She locked him with a smile and interested eyes. It was what she did best, teasing the passengers gently, taking their mind of uncertainties, their underlying fear of the unknown. Liners did that to some people; war too probably. And it was true. Getting lost was the passport to a whole variety of otherwise unexplainable absences; it kept you at the bar for a couple more whiskies after you promised to be back in half an hour; it allowed you four more hands at the poker game you got suckered into after dinner; it gave you time for that quick fuck with the passenger from A Deck who you'd been eyeing up all afternoon. It was how she and Tina had found any number of willing victims.

He tapped his epaulettes. He was breathing evenly now; forgetting if not the cause, the fact of his distress.

'Not in the marines. We're not meant to get lost. The trouble is this.' He waved the note at her. 'You know the saying, don't you? What's the most dangerous thing known to man?'

Suzanne felt the flush of a flirt coming. She took a pace back, starting the dance.

'That's easy,' she said. 'A woman.'

'No, no, something much worse. An officer with a map.'

There was a simplicity about the man, receiving all that went before him with an equanimity that was barely adult.

'What do they call this lost man of the army?'

'Henry,' he said, 'they call him Henry.'

'Well, Henry, I'd better take you to where you belong. Where do you belong?'

'I don't know if I'm allowed to tell you that.'

'Tell me anyway.'

'I'm with the band. The Royal Marines.'

'Not a proper soldier, then.'

It was an unnecessary comment but she said it all the same.

'Not a proper anything, really.'

It was an odd thing to say, and again it was spoken simply.

'Where are you meant to be?'

'The ladies' toilets,' he said, not daring to look up.

'You and the rest.'

'No, no. Look. That's where we're billeted to practise.'

He handed the note over. She examined it, trying to keep a straight face.

'I hardly dare ask on what.'

'The trumpet and violin.'

'I never thought of a paratrooper playing the violin.'

He stiffened visibly. 'I told you. I'm not a paratrooper. I'm a marine.'

'There's a difference, then?'

'Just a bit.'

'You seem the same to me.'

'You must never say that to a marine. Or to a Para, for that matter. We don't mix.'

She laid it on a little more.

'I never imagined violins in a military band. When would you do that? Not while you're marching, surely? You'd poke each other's eyes out.'

He took the question seriously.

'We play quartets, chamber music and such, when we're asked. Officers' balls and the like. We're quite versatile, not just oompah-oompah, like everyone thinks we are.'

She held her face steady.

'And you're here for the whole . . .' She didn't know what word to use. Cruise? Journey? Conflict?

'Oh, yes. We have other duties besides the band. Stretcher-bearing, supply loading, first aid. We're soldiers, too, you know.'

'Well, seeing as you're so indispensable, I'd better get you there. We don't want them to start without you.'

She brushed past him, smiling down at her deliberate flirtation, and in that fleeting touch, found herself wishing that Matty had stayed home. She tried to banish the thought but the fact that it had come to her was enough. She walked slightly ahead of him now, knowing that he would be looking at her legs.

'Must be very strange for you,' she heard him call out, 'having us lot on board.'

'Not especially,' she lied. 'You're all passengers to us.'

He followed her back through the decks, their passage impeded by the incoming tide of soldiers carrying their kit.

'You all seem very keen,' she said, 'considering.'

'It'll never happen. A couple of weeks' cruise in the sun and then back to barracks and Belfast. It'll be a nice change.'

'A fuss over nothing.'

'Let's hope so, yes.'

He fell silent, her frivolity suddenly misplaced. She was grateful to see the sign. They stood outside the door. Suzanne could hear the stutter of a trumpet coming from the other side. She couldn't help herself.

'There's a mirror in there, you know, for us girls to do our make-up. If you keep the door open you can watch yourself playing.'

He blushed, not knowing what to say. She spoke unexpectedly, the drink driving her thought.

'What if you're wrong? What if it does happen? Are we going to be all right?'

Now it was his turn to reassure. He jerked his head back.

'With that lot? You're sailing with the best soldiers in the world.' He lowered his voice. 'Paras included, but don't tell anyone I said so.'

They stood there.

'I better get going. I'm expected too.'

'If I've got you into trouble . . .'

'You won't have. It's what we're here for.'

He held out his hand.

'You won't tell anyone, will you?' he said.

Suzanne took it, conscious of the delicious smell of conspiracy cooking. She leant a fraction forward, put her other hand on his outstretched arm.

'About the Paras?'

'That I got lost.'

'Who am I going to tell?' she asked, opening her hand to the question, turning on her heel, skating on the ice of her triumph. Tina, that's who she'd tell. Not quite Tina's type, but perfectly acceptable for a day or two. She hurried back. She was going to be late, not a good start. Opening the door to their cabin she was surprised to see Matty, sitting on the sofa, dressed in the clothes he drove down in, his butcher's apron in a heap on the floor, the outline of his bag hidden underneath. She bent down and lifted the overalls up, slowly, like an unveiling. The bag was packed, zipped up tight, like his mouth. She knew what he was going to do. Perhaps she had known all along. She pushed it towards him with her foot. He moved his legs away.

'You're not coming, are you?' she said.

Still, it shocked her, to hear herself give body to her suppressed suspicions. How long had she known? That first night in the cabin? At breakfast, this morning? Now for the first time she felt afraid, as if it were not the *Canberra* but her life that he was abandoning. Matty was her ship-to-shore, the rope tied to the harbour. Matty reeled her in, threw her into the net. Yes she longed to be free, but now . . .

'Matty, you can't.'

He got up, put his arms round her. She pushed him away.

'It's Marcia, isn't it.'

'No!'

'Of course it is. The daughter over the wife.'

Matty couldn't answer. All that bloody ironing.

'When was all this decided?'

'A bit ago.'

'A bit ago? Like when I wanted to buy that windcheater.'

A coded silence invaded the room. She was right. Before that.

'On the motorway, then, driving like a funeral at a hearse? What were you doing, hoping to miss the boat?'

He shifted further into the refuge of the wordless, not attempting to correct her.

'What about earlier, trying to fuck me with Marcia all ears downstairs? Was that why you were so keen? Because it was going to be your last chance for a while?'

She saw the hesitation in his denial.

'It was. Jesus!'

Matty held his hands out.

'It was in the back of my mind, yes.'

'And something else in the forefront.'

'I don't belong here, Suzy. I never have. This Falkland business has just put it all into perspective.'

'But what about our plans? We had it all worked out, triple time, the patio, everything.'

'The patio! You don't want a patio. You don't even want the money. Suzy, you'd go if the pay was *less*.'

Now it was her turn to falter. She turned, her arm half stretched out, as if seeking help from the mirror and the absent picture. The crucifix had slipped down onto the cheap veneered surface. She felt her strength ebbing. Matty pushed his bag out into the centre of the floor; stood behind it.

'That night, after all this was announced, it was like I'd never seen you before. All night, you were up and down, scrabbling on bits of paper, drinking anything that came to hand. Couldn't leave me alone either.'

'Didn't hear you complaining.'

'I thought it might be me, Suzy, me and the money and what it might mean to us, but I should have known. It wasn't me or our home. It wasn't anything to do with us. It was the *Canberra* and Tina and all the rest of them. I've tried to come with you, but I can't. Even if I did, I'd be on my own.'

Now she wanted him, wanted him asleep last night and awake this morning, wanted his balding head and his burgeoning stomach, wanted the crumbs falling from his mouth and his impotent Anglefield asides, wanted his careful driving and his feeble Westerns, wanted his arms and his bruised love wrapped around her in their patio. Too late.

'When are you leaving?' she said.

'Right away. They want me off quickly, before the infection spreads.' His face was soft with reproach. 'You can always come too, Suzy. They'd understand.'

He moved the bag again, towards the door, a barrier withdrawn, a gate opening for her to walk through, adhere to this departure. But she could not. She stood unable to move. Underneath she could feel the tremble of an idling turbine running through the decks, its great suspended power waiting for the dark and coming hour. She could hear the unseen waves slapping to its rhythm, feel the fresh wind on her face, see England falling far behind. The ship gave a slight, almost secretive dip, as if some giant hand had just pressed its weight upon her. She was certain now. She felt huge and open and alone.

'Matty, I can't. What if I don't go? What have I got to look forward to? Another ten years serving frozen daiquiris to overweight couples in Bermuda shorts? Sunbathing the cruises away until I wind up looking like a flayed horse with skin cancer? Whatever happens, the *Canberra* is going to be a part of England's history, Matty, and I, I want to be a part of it too. It's the only part I'll ever get to play. I know I'll have to leave this sometime, but for what? Something secretarial in the High Street, Marcia checking in to see if I've run off with the boss?'

'She doesn't . . .'

'Of course she does and I don't blame her. I would do the same in her shoes. That's not the point. This is my life, Matty, it's given me everything, and now it's time to give something back. The *Canberra*'s taking these lads who knows where, and I'm going with them, Ascension Island, the Falklands, even the bottom of the South Atlantic, if that's what God wills. I am the *Canberra*, just like Tina is and all the rest of us. Without us she'd be lost. She needs us as much as we need her, and these soldiers need us both. That's all there is to it. And you know what? I'm glad you're not coming. I would have worried about you, with you not seeing the Pope, getting his blessing. Now I don't have to. Take your shirt off.'

'What?'

'Your shirt.' She caught his look. 'Not that. Put it under my pillow. I want to smell you at night.'

A little later, they went up on top. The day was still long in the making. Along towards the stern, cranes were stacking the Sun Deck with rust-coloured containers. Down on the dock, the press were gathered around the polished gleam of a dark green Bentley. Directly below them a line of men were hauling themselves up the gangway, bent under the weight of their bergens. She took his hand and pressed it against the rail.

'You should have learnt to love her too, Matty. We'd have never got together without her.'

'I know it.' He looked around. 'It seems like a film ending, me leaving you on the spot where we met.'

'I'm coming back, Matty.'

'Safe and sound.' He turned to face her, his hands out on her hips. She could get a written warning for that.

'Will you watch us?' she asked.

Matty looked nonplussed.

'Tonight, when we sail. Take the car up to the park. Flash your lights.'

She saw him hesitate. He had been planning on driving back right away. The return of the prodigal father, Marcia gloating in the kitchen, opening up a bottle of wine, basting the fatted calf, sucking on greedy figures.

'Do something special so I know it's you. You remember that first dance we had, in the Bonito. Slow, slow, quick quick, slow.'

'I wasn't very good, was I?'

'Hopeless.'

A commotion at the gate caused them to look back. Up by the barrier a man was scuffling with a military policeman. Suzanne pulled on Matty's sleeve.

'Look, Matty, someone else doesn't want to go.'

She kissed him.

'Don't worry about me.'

'Of course I'll worry about you.'

He hovered.

'Go on, then.'

'Yes.'

He ducked down and trotted down the gangway.

'Love you, Matty,' she called out, and she did.

*

'All right, darling?'

Richard Roach nodded, hand trembling. The waitress emptied the ashtray and moved on. Roach lit another cigarette. He should never have gone. Matters ethereal, matters tangible, all seemed intent on assaulting his sense of direction. It had all started off so well, cruising down the motorway at a steady eighty, tailing into the bank holiday traffic, weaving his way through the choke of the town before parking down by one of the red-bricked hotels near the docks. They were so busy checking in supplies he'd ambled through the barrier without any bother, carefully picking his way amongst the flotsam and jetsam, snapping off as many pictures of the *Canberra* as he could. Knots of soldiers stood around, smoking cigarettes, joking amongst themselves in displays of forced bravura. He moved as close as he dared, soaking in their brazen vitality, wishing them 'good luck' before moving on. They were Mark's age mostly, perhaps a couple of years older, but still boys rather than men. He should have brought Mark with him. It would have done him good, to see them shouldering their responsibilities.

It was bigger than he expected, the *Canberra*, longer, taller, much whiter. Its bulk seemed to shrink his idea into insignificance. As if five hundred pairs of trainers were going to make any difference. What was it about his son? Was he still finding it difficult, physically, or was it worse than that, something slipped inside his head? It must be, surely, with all that unexplained activity, his aimlessly wandering, his petty thieving, sudden acts of reckless desperation, driving on the wrong side of the road. An accident, Mark had told him, but he knew better. He'd done it deliberately, testing youth's immortal nerve, the girl raw with terror, the humpback bridge, the vast coal lorry parked overnight, waiting for the gates to open, Mark wrenching the wheel for her to take the impact, the side swipe and the career down. Didn't eat meat, wouldn't drink pasteurized milk, wouldn't talk to friends or anybody who tried to help, refused to stay in the house, spent most of his days in the shed doing goodness knows what. If he wasn't their son, he'd have him evicted.

Here, moving among unknown men, nodding to the soldiers, his camera slung round his neck, there came a sort of liberation for Richard Roach. He felt almost fatherly; exalted and tearful, closer to them than they could ever imagine. One soldier leant up against a pallet wall, dark hair, dark eyes, a touch of cruel mischief in his mouth, asked him to take a photograph of him and his mates. Roach held the Instamatic, trembling, eight of them crowding round.

'If I can take one for my scrapbook,' Roach asked, handing it back.

'You a poof or something?' the young man said. A mate smacked him on the side of the head.

'Come on, Stanley, don't be such a cunt.'

Roach stepped back.

'If you could just move, so I can get the stern in the background.'

The men's boots shuffled over, scuffling on the tarmac. Roach bent his knees, examining the composition; the men, the dockyard, the name of the *Canberra* high up in the right-hand corner; this would pass Ellen's inspection. As they moved off he raised the camera again, for a more uninhibited shot. The young Stanley was bending his bottom at him as he walked away, the others laughing at the raucous taunt. Then the green caught his eye, moving into the frame, up towards the ship, brighter than any army green, deeper too, a chauffeur-time of wax polishing glinting in the strengthening sun, Sir Douglas's Daimler with the shock of Sir Douglas's white hair fluorescent behind the half-tinted glass. Kevin's saloon followed. Roach ducked down behind the pallets, waited a moment, then inched his head up. The Bentley had pulled up near one of the gangways. Sir Douglas had emerged, dipping one hand into a Savile Row pocket, like a royal prince on walka-bout. A man with a microphone was chatting to a short-skirted young woman, one of the page-three girls, no doubt, the back of her white-booted legs jiggling in the keen salt air. Kevin was standing behind his car, surreptitiously scratching his bottom.

Roach felt a shadow draw over him.

'Who the fuck are you? Little Bo Peep?'

A squat moustachioed man in uniform was looking down at him through the peak of his cap. A sergeant of some sort. Roach wasn't sure.

'Sorry?'

'I said who the fuck are you and what the fuck is that?' He pointed with his stick.

'My camera. My son's, actually.'

'Heavy is it?'

'I'm sorry?'

'Is that why we are crouching behind a crate of tinned ordnance?'

'No, no . . . I.' Roach stood up, his back towards the dock. 'I just wanted to take some pictures.'

'Pay well do they, the Argies?'

'No, no, I'm just here to . . .'

'To fuck me about, yes I know, fuck me about in a restricted area when I've got better things to do. See that?'

He twisted Roach's arm and span him around. Sir Douglas was talking to the man with the microphone. Kevin was taking a delivery box from out the boot of his car. The page-three girl was sitting in the Bentley, doing her hair.

'That's where I'm meant to be, up there with the last piece of skirt I'm going to see till Christmas. But no, I got to fuck around with a prat like you.'

He started to propel Roach towards the sentry gate. Roach tried to shake him off. A sudden pain in his stomach doubled him up. Then he was run half backwards, towards the barricade, stumbling into oncoming soldiers and vehicles as the sergeant pushed him ahead as if he were an unwanted rubber ball. They reached a small cabin set to one side. The sergeant threw open the door and pushed him inside. Two men in peaked caps were playing cards.

'Meet Mata Hari,' the sergeant said. 'Shoot him if he moves. Call the Ministry. Let them sort him out.'

They held him for three hours. They tapped their pencils on the table and looked askance. They walked him to his car, drove it round the back and took the seats apart. They pulled the film out the camera. They made him undress. They asked him why he was there. He told them he was a shoe salesmen taking pictures for posterity. He said nothing about the Broncos. They had no sense of humour, and treated him with irritated contempt. Before they let him go they told him they just might prosecute.

He pushed ten pence under the saucer, and crossed over to the washroom. It was empty, save for a man coughing in one of the stalls. Roach's footsteps echoed all the way to the washbasin, a low and fateful sound. He ran the tap and splashed his face with water. He searched in his inside pocket and pulled out his comb, holding it under the flow, brushing his hair forward before teasing out the line of skin that bisected his head; the white line. That's how he did it now, comb and water and the palm of his hand; that's how he had done it then, in the changing room, Henry standing next to him, Lofty telling them to get their skates on. Next year, Lofty had promised them, holding the knot of his association tie between his nicotined fingers as if he were making a solemn pledge, next year, if things went right this time, they'd be up for one of the finals; the men's double, perhaps the women's single. Imagine that! He and Henry, amongst the top ball boys in Wimbledon! He had run the comb under the tap one last time, easing the broad teeth through his dark, curly hair. He wanted to use the Brylcreem, his scented hair gleaming like a cinema-foyer photograph, but when it came to lawn tennis, such creams weren't allowed. 'Imagine,' Lofty had said, confiscating the small jar that Roach had brought with him, 'if, forgetting yourself, you ran your fingers through your hair and then a minute later picked up the next stray shot. You know what that would result in? Slippery balls.' It had been the joke of the week in the changing room, Roach and his slippery balls.

One last careful tamp and he and Henry had hurried out through the frosted-glass door, down the corridor, and out into the half-covered glare. There was a short walk up before the court opened out, which gave them a fleeting moment to gather themselves, and it was there, as he took a deep breath, inhaling the hidden hum of the crowd, that Henry had reached out and ruffled Roach's hair before trotting out into the full scrutiny of the crowd. Perhaps if he'd restored the parting, nothing would have happened; the balance that was necessary for that momentous hour would have been reclaimed. As it was Roach had patted his hair down as best he could and followed Henry out. It was hot that day, hotter than any day he could remember. The sun bared down upon him, but he absorbed it, drew strength from its intensity, his arms and legs alert to the long greening distance ahead. His hair dried hard, a protective shell, his feet pressing securely against the impacted ground; his eyes like a desert hawk's, his body poised, his fingers spread, his neck stretched, ready to swoop. He listened, he watched, he floated above himself, his hands curled, his fingers talons for the loosened prey; he ran with the sweep of his billowing shirt brushing the tension of the net. He swooped, he scooped, he returned breathless to his summoned authority. He felt the eyes of the world upon him, a mother's milky tear, a father's proud grin writ upon every face, the court illuminated in a blaze of crystal clarity that seemed to presage a future he had never imagined possible; to be released into a clean and brightly lit universe, bordered by clear parameters, and within its protection, a place for him. And what had he come away with? Ridicule and disgrace; accusations.

He dried his hands and crossed over to the news-stand. He bought a large bar of fruit and nut and a copy of the *Sun*. Back in his car he turned over the front page and, looking at the impudent picture, sat eating. It took him three hours to reach Stevenage. He would have liked to pick up a hitchhiker, but the way they stood, thumbs out, feckless, insolent, reminded him of his son. There was a girl he liked the look of, foolishly alone, but feared the unspoken thoughts passing between them. At Stevenage, Mrs Dixon, the landlady, was waiting for him in the hall.

'Mr Roach. Quite a week we're having.'

Roach nodded.

'You've had a busy day, I hear.'

Mrs Dixon pointed to the phone.

'What?'

'Your wife rang. Going to be famous, she says.'

'Rang?' He put his hand to his mouth, the taste rising. 'When was this?'

At two, and then at three, Mrs Dixon told him. She'd ring again, after the news. Roach's face closed round the prospect. He could imagine the conversation. Ellen was expecting to see him handing over one of those bloody shoes, and who was she going to see now? Kevin, that's who. Without him there would be any number of perfectly sound explanations for his exclusion. Why would anyone want him when they had parachuters and models to look at? He had been behind the scenes, making sure it all ran smoothly, impressing Sir Douglas with his efficiency. Kevin changed all that, Kevin with Sir Douglas and the page-three girls and not a whisker of Richard Roach in sight. Perhaps he could brazen it out, claim that he was simply out of shot, blame it on rogue technology. But wouldn't that be as bad an admission? If Kevin had managed to stick his pock-marked grin in front of the camera, why couldn't he, isn't that what she would say? He wished he'd never had the idea in the first place, never tried to play the little bastard at his own game. Then none of this would have happened. No sales-meeting humiliation, no Sandy being handed his cards, no late-night train journey, no Soapsuds, no desperate

Southampton untruth. If Kevin had been an honourable man, it would have been a different story. Roach would have gone down, he would have stood next to a page-three girl, he would have been on television. Kevin had stolen it from him, Kevin, the young man for whom he had once felt an unaffected kinship.

'All that way for such a smudge of a place,' Mrs Dixon was saying. 'Not even British, are they?'

Roach frowned in the affirmative.

'Are they? Are you sure?'

He nodded quickly, looking to the stairs for refuge. He could hear murmuring in the lounge, a pontificating cough.

'Well, that's different. Throw the buggers out, that's what I say.'

She opened the visitors' book, turning it towards him. Many people objected to signing guest-house books, but he was not one of them. He understood the significance of records. He had a similar book for work. He took it with him everywhere. He was proud of that book, the name of every buyer, every manager, logged in, indexed by town and underneath the names of the individual shops, read the ten minutes before he walked into the store and reopened immediately after every visit, adding what fresh information he had learnt; a wife's operation, a daughter's graduation, the time they were nearly mugged in Miami, in they would go, to be called upon before the next time he drove into that town and checked his tie, his flies and the state of his shoes. 'How's the new car, Jim,' he would say, or 'Your Tony recovered from that knee injury?' and they would answer, inwardly pleased that he had remembered, the seasoned traveller giving a worldly importance to the grey wash of their own anchored lives. It was, in the main, how he kept his order book so full, how he beat his targets, kept ahead of his rivals, these little recorded histories, learning too never to reciprocate, never to burden them with his own misfortunes. That was not what they wanted to hear, nor what he came for, and thus to their perfunctory enquiries he would deliver a brief but positive response. His house was fine, his house was dandy. The patio he laid was fine, never prone to flooding, the wife was fine, never prone to sudden, malignant tears. He owned a perfectly normal house, and amongst its normal furniture wandered his family, the wife, the son, the pet. When they asked him about them he coughed and made them all a little more exciting, a little more attractive than they really were. As if they cared one fig for his real life.

He set the bag down and wrote his name under the rest of the day's entries. They were all there. Mrs Dixon swivelled the book back, examining his signature for signs of change. A shade of disappointment ran across her face.

'Still, such brave lads,' she said, 'fighting for their country. How's your boy doing?'

A pointed remark, for Mrs Dixon was one of the few people who knew of his son's catastrophe, Mrs Dixon who had taken the call a year back. Roach had had to work hard, to turn such disaster to his advantage. He had been so careful with his family. Confessional was the key.

'A full recovery, much better spirits, thank you for asking. This may sound harsh but it's taught him a lesson they all need to learn.'

Mrs Dixon nodded. Who didn't have problems when it came to offspring. She might as well have said it out loud.

'And Joanna's little one, Mrs Dixon? Still keeping you up all the hours God sends?'

Her unmarried daughter, struggling with her new responsibilities in the converted basement, without the company of the father. Mrs Dixon raised her eyes.

'HB is in the lounge already.'

'I thought I heard him. I'll get changed.'

'Sherry at six, as per usual.'

Roach nodded, and began to climb the stairs.

'Or maybe it should be champagne,' she called out.

'Bit early for that, I fear.'

Upstairs he surveyed the bulky familiarity of his second-floor occupancy; the double-doored wardrobe, the clanking claw-footed bed, the heavy, broad-beamed television sitting in the corner like an aunt from another age. Not the best room in the house, but quiet. He knew from long experience how to work it to its best advantage, how to ease the sticking lock, how to flush the lavatory with an extra twist of the wrist, how, if he opened the wardrobe doors wide, he could lie in the bath and watch the television in the reflection of its tall inside mirror.

He lifted his suitcase and his presentation show box onto the wicker chair, and switched on the electric log fire with a careful stretch of his foot. He moved about the room, reassured: the chipped mantelpiece, the whistling radiator, the decorations without meaning, all gave a strange comfort to him. Outside, in the parking lot at the back, a couple were leant up against his car, oblivious in embrace. He thought about banging on the window but decided against it. They weren't doing any harm. He watched them for a while, the slow turning of their bodies like driftwood on the tide, then drew the curtains. He took the newspaper out of his raincoat pocket and flattening it out on the floor, tore out the second page. He took the small ornamental vase from the mantelpiece, placed it on top of the television and leant the folded picture against it. He placed the Broncos alongside. Often, when showing a new line, opening the box, unwrapping the tissue paper, holding the mirror of their unblemished countenance up for inspection, he imagined that in the freshness of their scent and untouched skin lay some unspoken promise for him; that if he were to wear them himself he might change into something extraordinary, become wonderful; but these said nothing to him. Sandy was right. They were an ugly shoe. He took off his shirt, crossed the room and positioned the wardrobe door, swinging it back as far as it would go. Walking back he could see the page-three girl, the trainers and himself drawn up in an uneven line. She was a pert eighteen-year-old. He was faceless. He stood there, imagining the photograph that might have been taken, the joke they might have shared, the kiss she might have bestowed upon him afterwards. He wondered what accent she spoke with. Her smile never faded, all the time it took. He worked the mess into the carpet.

He sat on the edge of the bed, exhausted, unable to move. He could not bear to go down. He waited until the clock below chimed six, then leant across and turned on the television.

The Falklands swam into view; the Ministry of Defence announcer, a map or two, some battalion or other marching off. He waited. More maps, a couple of retired generals, but no sign of the *Canberra*. Impatiently he switched channels and there he was,

Sir Douglas, self-importance oozing out of his strangely livid tan. Roach could hardly bear to look.

'Patriotism,' he was saying. 'Pure and simple. It's not often that a man in my position can do something at a time like this, so when the chance came I fair leapt at it. And not just me. The whole firm swung into action.'

The camera moved across to reveal Wendy holding out a pair of Broncos to the moustachioed sergeant who had frog-marched him to the barrier. Kevin's foul-mouthed top had been replaced by a less belligerent garment which read 'Bronco Busters'.

'Sergeant Major,' the reporter was saying, 'what do you think of all this?'

'I don't know about the trainers, but I wish all our mail was delivered by postmen this good-looking. It's a great morale-booster for the lads.'

At the sound of Wendy's giggles Roach leapt up and kicked one of the television's legs hard. It fell sideways onto the floor fizzling, then went silent. Scorched electricity filled the room. The news-paper floated down onto the electric fire and began to burn over one of the deposed trainers. Not even a page-three girl, but Wendy, the cheapskates! He stamped on her savagely, tearing her dis-figured body in half. No sign of Kevin, though; that was some consolation.

Both Broncos had been slightly marked. He took them to the sink in the adjoining bathroom and cleaned them up as best he could, placing them on a chair by the radiator to dry. He put on a fresh shirt, smoothed out the creases of his jumper and reasserted the strict white parting. Downstairs he could hear the lounge jabbering away; task force, General Galtieri, arctic conditions, one holy mess if you ask me. If only he'd been on television. That would have shut them up. He slipped out the front door and ducked out into the spring night.

It was a young crowd's bar he found, well away from his normal haunts, sawdust on the floor, a great looming television hanging off the wall, loud thumping music. In the centre stood a pool table, and playing on it, a young woman and her leather-jacketed boyfriend, other friends looking on. Roach ordered a beer and turned his back to the bar, sipping his drink, watching her play. She was what, nineteen, twenty, her midriff bare, her plump bosom resting on the corner of the table. It was hard for him not to look, the way she leant across, the careless exposure of her white dumpy breasts, the movement they made as she lined up the cue. He stared, lifting his gaze only when she or her companion looked around. It was movement that held him, the movement of hope and youth and untroubled indifference, knowing and unknowing. There was pliancy in that life, an unbearable softness lying supple upon the shifting sands of promise; there was time, endless time, folded in the perfumed press of her flesh, time that had almost slipped out of his reach. Life was evading his grasp, but not hers. If only he could reach out, clutch it to his heart, what a race he could run then!

'What the fuck you staring at?'

'What?' Roach looked around, disorientated. The young girl, considering her shot, looked up. Her friend rapped his cue upon the floor.

'You heard me. Want a closer look?' The young man took a pace forward. The girl stood upright, her expression defiant, on the border of belligerent. Their friends stopped talking.

'No. No. Sorry. I wasn't staring, I was thinking. It's just . . .' Roach looked up. The TV behind them, its sound turned down, was playing the news. The *Canberra* was gliding out along the quayside. He nodded at the picture. 'My son's on that,' he said.

The young girl stepped out from behind her protector.

'What, that boat?' she asked

'That's right, the *Canberra*.'

'A soldier, like?'

'A marine,' he said, his eyes still raised.

'You must be very proud.'

She moved to his side. The *Canberra* was moving slowly out of Southampton Water. On board a band was playing. People were waving and cheering and holding flags. Roach looked down into his glass. He could feel tears welling up in his eyes. He sniffed and straightened his tie.

'I am,' he said. 'Very proud.'

'Shouldn't you be there, seeing him off, like?'

'I wanted to,' Roach said, 'but they wouldn't let me off work.'

'But it's bank holiday.'

'Stock taking,' he said quickly.

'Bastards.' She poked the air with her cue and turned round to her friends. 'Bastards won't even let his see his own son off. Bastards.' She turned back, renewed interest in her eyes.

'What's his name?'

His name.

'Henry. Henry Hawkins.'

'You know what our local paper's doing?'

Roach couldn't take his eyes off the screen. His son was on there, sailing over the water to uncertainty.

'No,' he said, barely listening, 'what's that?'

'Getting girls like me to write to them, give them something to look forward to while they're away.'

'That's nice.'

'I could write to your Henry, say we met. Send in my picture. Here, John.'

The tall lad came scowling over.

'What?'

'This . . .' the girl touched his arm. 'I don't know your name.'

'Richard.'

'Mine's Amy.' She turned to her companion. 'Did you hear that? Richard here's got a son going to the Falklands. On the telly there.'

'That right?' John sounded put out.

'He's a marine,' Amy told him. Her friends started to gather round, young men and young women out on the town.

'Oh?' It was clear John didn't want to believe him. 'What regiment?'

Roach hesitated for a moment. 'I'm not allowed to say,' he said. 'Not under the present circumstances.'

The girl nodded and punched her companion on the arm.

'Pillock.' She turned back to Roach. 'How old is he?'

'Eighteen.'

'Ooh, cradle snatching. I like that. Is he good-looking?'

Everyone laughed, except John. Roach joined in.

'He thinks so.' John was not impressed.

'Doesn't take after his dad, then.'

'Shut your gob, John.' She turned back again. 'Don't mind him. He's always like this.'

'I think it's a load of bollocks,' John said. 'Fighting over a lot of sheep-shaggers.'

'They're British,' Roach said. 'It's our duty.'

'It's not our duty to start a war just for Maggie's benefit.'

'He's a soldier. He's got no choice.'

'More fool him then for joining up.'

Roach banged down his glass, got off his stool and poked the lad in the chest. His heart was racing and yet he didn't feel at all afraid. It was extraordinary. He had never hit anyone in his life. When they'd been forced into boxing matches at the home, he had run round the ring trying to evade the blows.

'That's my son you're talking about,' he said. 'While you're drinking your next pint, he's preparing to fight for his country, maybe die for it.'

'You tell him, mate.' A voice came from his side. Roach looked round. To his left three men were leant up against the bar. They were watching closely. The middle one raised his glass. Roach nodded in appreciation. He pressed on.

'How would you like it if the Argies waltzed in and invaded your back garden? You wouldn't, would you? You'd be the first one to cry for help.'

'Too bloody right.' Although the voice was indistinguishable from the first, Roach sensed it came from one of the other two men. John started to back off.

'I don't agree with it, that's all. It's a free country.'

Roach swallowed the last of his beer in disgust.

'If this was Argentina,' he said, 'you'd be locked up by now.'

'If this was Argentina,' the first man said, 'he'd be floating down the River Plate with his fucking head kicked in. Care for a stroll, sweetheart, along the canal. Just you, me and my size elevens.'

They laughed. The man turned to the bar and held his glass over Roach's head.

'Arthur,' he called out, 'buy this gentleman a drink. And chuck that skinny cunt out. If you don't we will. Through the fucking window. This is a patriots' bar.'

Three more pints Roach had, three more pints and two whisky chasers. The middle man had been in the army, but not the Paras or the marines; he wasn't good enough. Not ashamed to admit it, he told Roach; the crème de la fucking crème they were. Here's to him. Here's to all of them.

'To all of them,' Roach repeated. 'To all of them.'

*

He couldn't remember the exact sequence of events. Everyone had wanted to buy him a drink, hear about Henry. The men drifted off, clapping him on the back as they departed. The skinny lad had long gone. Later at the Indian, when the bill came, it was just him and Amy left. How many others had there been? He couldn't remember, but there must have been quite a few, judging by what it cost him. He tried to focus. What did he know? He knew that he was Richard Roach and that her name was Amy and that she lived with her mum and that her breasts were white and her mouth was red with the stain of tandoori chicken and that she held her knife and fork as if they were pencils. He knew he was lonesome for his lost son and his empty wife. Now he was wiping his eyes with a paper napkin.

'I'm sorry. It's just I haven't talked like this for ages,' he said.

'Me neither. We just get pissed.'

'Ah.' He spoke slowly. 'There's more to life than getting drunk, Amy.'

He batted away Amy's look of amused tolerance, holding up his hands in admission. He had his reasons tonight, she knew that. 'What about your mum? Can't you talk to her?'

'She's too busy with her boyfriends.'

'And John?'

'John?'

'The chap in the pub. Isn't he your . . .?' He couldn't bring himself to use the word. She looked at him.

'Give me a break. It's just there's nothing to do in this poxy town. If I had a job . . .'

If only he could explain! She had her whole future before her. He could help her, tell her the truth about life, how to avoid it.

'Shoes is a good trade,' he said.

126

'People's feet all day! No, ta very much.' She stopped, realizing what she had said. 'Sorry, I didn't mean . . .'

Roach nodded. Had he told her what he did for a living? He had no recollection of it. She reached out and touched his hand. 'I wouldn't say nothing to upset you, Richard.' Richard! How long was it since anyone called him Richard, as if it meant something.

'You don't understand,' he said. 'Shoes are not just shoes. Shoes are . . . emblematic.'

'Pardon?'

He swallowed.

'A symbol. Stilettos, platform shoes, winkle-pickers. Every style sums up an era. Take today's coming trend: trainers. Might be just another shoe to you, but what does it tell you about the time we live in? That everyone's becoming obsessed with health, looking good? Partly. Back in the thirties they were keen on fitness, had clubs, not like gyms, but for outdoor activities; walking, cycling, even running around with nothing on.'

Amy laughed. Roach pretended he hadn't noticed.

'The point is, Amy, they did these activities together.'

'They could have walked by themselves.'

Roach leant forward, excited. A young girl interested in his life, his ideas!

'That's just the point! They could have, but they didn't. They didn't do it simply to get fit, but to share a love of something with their fellow men; the hills and lakes and country paths, the beauty of the natural world. It was a way of bringing people close, of sharing. That's what happens when we regard something as universal, belonging to no one. Now we don't want to belong to anyone but ourselves. Self-reliance, that's the watchword for the eighties.'

He sat back, exhausted. Amy was looking at him, disconcerted.

'And here was me thinking you took after your name.'

Roach was hurt.

'Roach?'

'Hawkins. A bit of a loner, like the bird.'

'My name's Roach.'

'I thought you said your son was called Henry. Henry Hawkins.'

Roach dabbed at his napkin, covering his confusion.

'He's taken his mother's surname.'

'You're divorced?'

He nodded.

'It was quite amicable. She stays over with us quite a lot, actually. It sounds silly, but, not wishing to be too indelicate, without, you know, the everyday intimacies getting in the way everything's a whole lot easier.'

'Everyday intimacies. They clutter up Mum's house, that's for sure.'

'Take it from me. It isn't everything.'

'Oh, I know that. We all know that. It's just that sometimes there's nothing else to do.'

'Oh, Amy. There's always something to do, even if it's only working in a shoe shop.'

'Maybe. I just hoped there might be more to my life than working behind a counter. Perhaps I could join the army, like Henry.'

Henry again. She brushed her shoulders, sat up erect.

'I'd look good in a uniform, don't you think? Fit for anything. What orders would you give me?' She saw him hesitate. 'Only kidding.'

'Kidding?'

'Never mind. Any other bloke . . . .' She leant up over the table, suddenly energized, kissed him on the forehead. Roach looked around, wondering if anyone had noticed. He was surprised to see that apart from the waiter in the corner, the restaurant was empty. Amy sat back down again.

'You know what I'm going to do tonight?' she said. 'I'm going to write to Henry, just as soon as I get home. Tell him how we met and what a great dad he's got. Who knows, we might become pen pals. More.'

A jolt of guilt broke through Roach's anaesthesia. It wasn't fair, leading her on like this. But if he hadn't . . . Oh, Amy!

'He might not even get the letter, Amy. You mustn't get your hopes up.'

'He'll get it all right. I feel it in my bones. Be funny, wouldn't it, if something came of it.'

'But Wendy.'

'Wendy?'

'Amy. I hope I haven't said anything that would lead you to believe . . .' His voice trailed off. Why shouldn't she dream?

'I'll keep up writing anyway. We could meet up when he gets back. He is coming back, Richard. I know it.'

'They're all coming back, God willing.'

'Romances like that do happen, you know. You wouldn't mind, would you?'

'Why should I mind?'

'You speaking much posher than me?'

'Mind? Oh Amy!'

Outside the wind had risen. The street was deserted, the road black and liquid, a paper bag tumbling along the line of blind-eyed shops. It was hard to focus on anything stationary. The whole world seemed to be running away from him.

'Would you do me a favour?' he said.

She looked up at him, wary.

'What.' Her voice was flat, tutored in apprehension.

He took a sudden pace forward. Amy tugged the lapels of her coat tight, preparing to ward off the expected intrusion. He willed himself steady.

'Have dinner with me again? When I come back.'

'I could do.'

'I could bring you a photograph. Of Henry.'

'After I've written to him?'

'That's what I meant.'

They stood there, the young woman, the older man, hope and age and the suspicions of their time fluttering between them. She relaxed her grip.

'When you back next?' she asked.

'Two weeks? Three. Perhaps earlier.'

'I thought you salesmen only came once a month.' She covered her mouth, instinct making a pass at impropriety. Roach was too far gone to notice.

'Area managers are not like the troops, you know,' he explained slowly. 'We're more tactical, drumming up new business, brainstorming.' He paused. 'So, how about it?'

'Yeah! That would be great.'

She wrote her name and phone number on the damp-edged paper napkin and pushed it back into his pocket. He wanted to hold her, to take the memory of her warmth and affection back to his room, but he did not know how.

'I'd better go,' she said.

'Yes.'

'It was a lovely evening, Richard.'

'Yes. Do you want me to . . .' He didn't dare say 'walk you home'. It was what teenagers did on dates. He opened out his hand. She understood and made a joke of it.

'If it's anyone who needs taking home, it's you, not me. How many brandies did you put away?'

'I'm fine.'

'That's all right, then. Bon voyage, for you and him both, eh?'

She kissed him quickly on the cheek, her feet raised, her body briefly touching his, kissed him with such unaffected honesty it was as if a red-hot iron had been pressed upon his face. Love in Stevenage, was that it, branded by searing tenderness? He watched her as she walked down the middle of the road, the determination of her staccato stride only serving to emphasize the bewildering emptiness enveloping him. He felt as if he were tumbling, rudderless like the paper bag, filled with nothing, buffeted from one closed door to another. He walked back in high, exaggerated footsteps. Once in the guest house, he hauled himself hand over hand up the stairs to the second floor, dropping his key down the inside of his shoe before finally opening the bedroom door. The broken remains of the television had been removed. Propped up on the pillow lay an irate letter from HB and a bill from Mrs Dixon for the damaged TV and carpet. He screwed them up in his hand, swaying over the blackened spot. She was a wonderful girl, Amy. Henry was so lucky, getting letters from her. Any young man would be. It would be lonely out at sea now, with the swirling dark and the bitter wind. How strange it must be for them on that great boat, their first night out, the motion of the ship their only guide as they ploughed into uncertainty. He closed his eyes and felt himself plunging. He tried to grab hold of something, but there was nothing there. He clutched his stomach and threw up against the wall. He sat down on the bed, giddy with the stink of it, and threw up onto the carpet. He wiped his mouth clean with the paper in his hand, gasping for swallowed breath. The room was being tossed about, groaning like a rowing-boat keel – caught upon the reef, the storm rising within him. He willed himself up and fought the air towards the bathroom, his head held back, his feet sticky with spattered liquid. He burst through the door just in time to throw up over the covered lavatory seat, the cistern and the pair of Broncos placed upon the chair.

*

Suzanne and Tina stood looking out. On the deck below the massed band of the marines was playing the final chorus of 'Life on the Ocean Wave'. Soldiers hung over the railings, cheering into the night. Somewhere out there was Matty, sitting alone in their car, wishing he was here or she there, just as she was wishing the same thing, but glad too to be separated from him, her ties and feelings mixed up, bumping up against each other with the slow churn of the water as the engines rumbled into life. Yes, out there was Matty, while below the violin-playing soldier she had joked with that afternoon marched and turned to the cheers of his pals. What was he thinking of as they played, the history of this crazy night, the life he must have led, the swish of her skirt as she led him across her ship, like Matty must have done all those years ago? Was that it for her, the swish of her skirt, Matty, the soldier, even poor disappointed Mark? Was Marcia with him now, watching this on television together, getting drunk or stoned, she celebrating her father's premature return, he talking of everything but her? Were they all thinking of her as she was of them? Or was there nothing to think about, just the sight and sound of the *Canberra*, lit like a burning galleon; the brilliant lunacy of now and she a light within it. What must they look like, this floating dazzle of light, this blazing departure. Was it the *Canberra* they were cheering, a restoration of British pride, or was it a mass of other things, an amalgam of all their private disappointments, the soured promise of their futures packed aboard, bound for distant glory? She remembered the riddle of that evening in Rome, standing on the bridge, looking towards the Vatican, the dome voluminous and white, as if swollen with holy milk, imagining the Pope frail in his apartment, his parchment face turned towards the open window, his skeletal hands still touched with the flesh of hers, as hers were touched with the bone of his, the mystery of all that was him mingling with the mystery of all that was her, the strange stirring she had felt, as if she had just been shown something, but knew not what. Was it this? Her destiny?

The final rope splashed. *Canberra* began to glide away. She grabbed Tina's arm.

'We're off, Tina. This is it. Did you ever see such a thing?'

'Rule, Britannia!' came booming out. The soldiers gave a roar and burst into throaty song, waving at the unseen crowd, the family, the friends, the thousand people they would never meet. For the first time Suzanne felt a peculiar affinity to this landlubber flotsam, as if they and all on board were joined to one intangible moment, everyone taking the same breath, swallowing the same thought, blinking back the same tear that rose behind her eyes. How close, how separated they all were, prayers pressing them together, prayers cleaving them apart. All the wishing in the world couldn't bind those broken ties.

Southampton Water slid slowly into darkness. Half a mile along, where the park came down to the water's edge, the waiting cars began to flash their lights and sound their horns. The ship's siren bellowed in return. She tried to make out Matty, but it was like trying to find a swallow in a swarm. Dot dash dot dash, dot dot dash. Wasn't that V for victory? Her heart was being wrenched out of her body. She could hardly feel the motion of the ship at all. It was as if the land and all that she had ever known were being pulled back by a set of invisible ropes, hauled in to the safety of some inland water, until all that was left was this ship floating into madness on the surface of a black and fearful sea.

And then she saw him, in the very thick of it; slow, slow, quick quick, slow; unhurried and constant, carrying all the spoken things he had never said, all the understanding he could never show, illuminated by the good heart that she knew to be his; slow, slow, quick quick, slow; slow, slow, quick quick, slow. It was so clear, so bright, it was as if she had been searching for a skylark on a summer's day, and, now found, marvelled at her inability to locate it before. Like the skylark's song too with its discovery, it seemed to grow stronger, the song sweeter, the rhythm more heartbreaking than she thought possible, until all the other lights had been swallowed in its firmament and there was only Matty and their past, their present, stretching ever further between them. She could hear the rhythm of the waltz again, feel the balance of the balls of her feet, see Tina winking at her as she guided him across the floor, her body pressed close, his hand nervous on her bare skin, Marcia alone at the table, swinging her legs back and forth. Slow, slow, quick quick, slow. She set her hand free and brought it to her mouth.

'Oh, Matty,' she cried. 'Was it so much to ask?'

*

'Flash your lights again.'

'They can't see anything now.'

'How do you know?'

Kevin worked the switch a couple of times.

'Southampton! I can't believe it, the little liar. I offered to come with him!'

'And I very nearly had to have dinner with Sir Douglas. It was bringing Wendy along that got me out of that one.'

'Do they . . .'

'What do you think?'

'I think you should keep the engine going,' she said, 'otherwise we'll freeze to death.'

Neither wanted for it to last for long. Halfway through, he turned on the windscreen wipers with the back of his foot.

'Like a metronome,' he said.

She laughed. 'At least you chose the right speed.'

Afterwards he sat up and flicked off the switch. She leant up against the passenger door and laid her outstretched foot on his bare leg. The ship had disappeared. All that was left was the dark and the sea and her husband's lie washing back and forth on the surface.

'Page-three girls!' she said. 'I wouldn't have thought he'd have had it in him, to deceive me like that.'

'And you're sure he's in Stevenage?'

'Second Friday of the quarter come rain or shine. Trout Night. A bunch of old farts and a fish curry.'

'On a bank holiday? Don't know about the curry, but it sounds a bit fishy to me. Do you think he's seeing someone else?'

Ellen considered for a moment. To her surprise it was an idea that had never entered her head.

'No,' she said. 'He's too busy with your blessed shoes. I have to fuck for both of us these days. Damn, I was going to ring him.' She wriggled her foot. 'Something drove it out of my mind.'

Kevin idly worked the lights, staring out into the void.

'I'm carrying him, Ellen,' he said, 'you know that, don't you?'

'I don't want to talk about it.'

'What do you want to talk about, then?'

She raised her foot and pressed. The wipers swept back and forth.

'The rhythm method,' she said.

*

Henry closed his case and shuffled his music. The others had gone to find the couple of crates of beer reputed to be waiting for them down in the newly formed mess, but he was too tired to follow, too drained to want to join in. He had not found another train, but had sat all night on the station, dozing fitfully along one of the wooden seats, turning his coat up against the damp and the noise. Any number of trains came through, sucking his body out of the wooden seat on which he lay, but he didn't mind. It was not a night for sleeping, it was a night for blinking his thoughts in the dark, for conjuring the past out of the rising mist from the canal, Richard Roach tugging at the hem of his coat.

That woman had imagined that it was him being lost that had inspired his panic, but it had nothing to do with that. It was seeing Roach again, shoved along the dock by that military policeman. Could it really have been him again? Surely that wasn't possible, not to see a man for twenty years and then to have him deny you twice in twenty-four hours. He'd been helping Ian, the two of them too weighed down with the stack of music stands to take too much notice of the sergeant major and the man coming the other way. Only as they drew closer did he register the man's protesting voice, how the sergeant major swung a camera high in the air, the man jumping at it like a dog might a stick. Even then he hadn't realized who it was, just the military clearing the area of unwanted visitors, and then, as the man tried once more, the sergeant major had given him an extra push, and stumbling back, the man had run into his left side, the music stands clattering to the ground. It was when he disengaged himself from Ian's flailing arms and started to swear at the man that he saw who it was, half kneeling on the ground, his face pale. Roach had his face in his hands, as if he was hiding, but there was no mistaking him.

'Jesus Christ!'

' 'Fraid not, son. Though it is a miracle how a pillock like this got this far.' The sergeant major lifted Roach up. Henry turned away quickly, adjusted his cap. Roach hadn't recognized him.

Roach was hustled away. Ian gathered up the music stands and manhandled them up the gangway. Henry couldn't help him. He stayed behind to watch Roach being bundled into the Portakabin down the dock. Why would he be here? To see him? But how could he know? Henry hadn't been in uniform last night. Had Roach found out somehow, spent the day trying to trace him? It was possible, he supposed, though unlikely. Coincidence, then? Henry did not trust coincidence. A freak accident? They'd had one of those before. 'I've never run into anyone in my life,' he had said. Well, that was a lie for a start. The whole nation had seen him. It had been on Pathé News, for God's sake. A week later they awoke to find his bed empty, his locker door hanging open, his name on the kitchen rota lists obliterated by a feverish black pencil. With his friend gone, Henry had felt his time had come too. Roach had not merely knocked him over, he'd pushed over the walls that held him there. He'd followed soon after, hoping that he might bump into Roach in central London, for what other direction did one take, but inwards, towards the city centre, towards prospects. He hadn't taken much (there wasn't much to take – like many in there most of his possessions had vanished over the years); a fold of clothes, the warden's hat, the three-quarter violin that Joe had given him one Christmas (a good one, he discovered later, stolen no doubt from some trusting family home), for it came to him that though he had imagined he knew not what he was going to do, it was quite obvious how he could start: he had seen buskers on the streets, hats laid at their feet, and that's what he did for six months, tucking his violin under his freshly stubbled chin, up and down the theatre queues, outside the tube stations, Leicester Square, Piccadilly, when the weather grew colder stationed through the rush-hour traffic by a warm-air vent that came up near St James'. He looked older than his age, handled himself well, fought off the arse-ambassadors, hooked up with a runaway brother and sister from Manchester, and played the tunes Joe had taught him, not modern stuff, nor bits of classical, for he knew neither, but sea shanties that Joe had sung to him: slow they were, and being of the sea, it gave the passers-by something fresh and clean to wipe their faces with after a day's work. He had his regulars too who would throw in something once a week. That was how he got stitched into the marines, Major Cunningham working for the Ministry, passing every day, asking him one evening, both of them cold and wet, stamping on the dark blocks of lampshine, where he went after this, where he came from. So he told him. A squat down in Shepherd's Bush, and before that, Dr Barnardo's.

'No family?'

'None that's knowing, sir.'

It was the sir that did it, he was sure. It wasn't intentional, something picked up from Joe. He had called everybody sir. Puts them right off their guard, he'd once said, spitting a toothsome grin.

'I know of one that's tailor made for a young man such as you,' the major had said.

'Oh?' He sounded wary. He'd only done it once, ten bob's worth, working some civil servant off when he hadn't eaten for two days. It hadn't been as bad as he thought, but he'd promised himself not to do it again.

'Come on, man, can't you guess?' The major pulled back his overcoat lapel to reveal the dull glow of a uniform.

'Best family in the world,' he said, 'the Royal Marines. Feed you, clothe you, send you out to see the world. And all they ask for is a little loyalty in return. You can't ask fairer than that, now, can you?'

136

It was the violin that got him in, how he could pick up a tune in no time at all. Didn't matter he couldn't read music. He couldn't have stood it without the playing; the barracking, the discipline, the rigidity of thought. It was how he had lived all his remembered life, what he wanted to escape from. Being in the band you were both in and out; looked up to and looked down upon; a real soldier but one who couldn't hack it, back-up support for those who could, stuck at base, moving stores, bearing stretchers, donkey work. But the sense of freedom the moment when the music hit the air! You were transformed then. You were pride and ceremony, you were unspoken memory: dream rather than drudge. The life was made for an outsider like him, wary of friendship, uncertain as to its point. The best family in the world? Certainly the biggest.

To begin with he had thought that Dora must have a big family because every day Joe would bring dirty clothes for Dora to wash. There was always washing to do, shirts and pillowcases and sheets, and every day Dora would roll up her sleeves and push them down with a long forked stick into one of the two tubs that sat on top of the coal range, and there they would bubble, a kind of grey foam floating on the top, like you got at the seaside washing at the edge of the shore. There was heat there too, a wet clinging film of it which invaded his clothes and ran down the walls and out through a ventilator on the side of the house. Sometimes there was so much washing, so much boiling, so much steam bursting out of that ventilator that it would sing like a broken ship's whistle, and Henry imagined that their house must be the source of all of London's milky woes, a kind of fog generator, like the one up the river that lit the capital's lights and which, when the wind came from the west, smudged their washing with streaks of coal dust and had him back out in the yard, rubbing his hands raw with blocks of hard grey soap. There was not a moment when there was not something boiling on the stove, when Dora wasn't carrying in buckets of cold water from the yard, her red arms stretched out like a coolie's, when the two of them weren't standing by the mangle, Dora feeding the hot sheets through the rollers, while he worked the handle. How his arms ached, but it was true what Dora had promised. It made them big. It made them strong. She taught him how to iron shirts too, whacking his legs with the forked stick when he got it wrong, showed him how to fold sheets properly, rifle-snapping them across the room, the two of them walking back and forth in some sort of skivvies' country dance until the sheets were gathered and folded and placed in one of the wicker baskets that stood by the back door. Days of steam, that's what they were, days of steam; the mangle, the cauldrons, the heavy irons lined up according to size upon the range, the bigger ones for the sheets and pillowcases, smaller ones for the collars and cuffs, to get into nooks and crannies. Crooks and nannies you mean, Joe used to say. It made Dora laugh, that.

And at the end of the day when Joe came home Henry would ask about his mum, every day Joe would shake his head and tell him that there was no news, and then one day Henry realized that he hadn't asked about his mum for some time. And then and then. And then and then. And then he didn't think about not asking about her at all. Joe would bring him presents, toys that he found, a handful of marbles, an old Dinky car; once a little watch and a waistcoat. A summer came, a winter passed. A summer passed, a winter came. He was given different clothes, not new but strangely theatrical, a brown jacket with velvet pockets, a pair of thick checked trousers with the legs cut off at the knee, voluminous shirts, scents of must and tobacco and stale pomade hanging in every fold. The best-dressed boy in Battersea, Joe would exclaim, turning him in his awkward finery. That is how he lived in those days, the wet damp smothering his thoughts, the dirt from the great chimneys blackening the windowpanes, a blindfolded house, the world outside floating from his grasp. At night he'd fall asleep in his room, with the stir of them, talking, arguing, sleeping off a night on the beer. And yet he grew to love them, Joe and Dora, the tussles they had over him. Sometimes he'd stand by the door, listening.

'You should have done something like I said.'

'Hold your tongue, woman.'

'We could have been rich if you hadn't been so gutless.'

'It were no good, Dora, I told you. Better like this.'

'Well, they'll be after us now. After all this time.'

Dora wanted to keep him at the mangle. Joe thought different.

The summer after the first summer, the kitchen a cloud of flies, Dora heating up the water for the morning's work, Joe in his vest had put his hand out, pressed it down on his head.

'How about you leaving woman's work, doing me a turn on the removals?' he said. 'Put those muscles to a man's use.'

'Joe,' Dora warned.

'He'll be all right, won't you, Hen?'

Dora pointed to the pile of tumbled sheets.

'He's needed here.'

Joe shook his head.

'He's coming with me, Dora. I'm not as fit as I used to be. Got half of Harrods to shift today. And a chap needs to get out of a woman's feet every once in a while.'

That was the third time he rode in Joe's van (he'd done it once, as a game not long after he'd arrived, hidden away in the bottom drawer of a Chesterfield, that's what Joe had called it), and after that he did it regular, once, twice a week, carting stuff from house to house, from house to shop, always something loose on the lorry floor, covered in a piece of sacking; money in hand, no-bills no-receipts kind of jobs, a fair distance some of them, quite a number at night. He got to know what to do and how to do it, how to square the corners of a wardrobe downstairs, how to take out a window, how to pack glass; he got to know the lorry too, how to crank start the engine, pausing on the fourth turn, how to lean his weight down to close the tailgate. Joe gave him a map to read. He began to recognize the streets, the back roads of London that missed the blockages, the areas that Joe liked driving around, St John's Wood, Swiss Cottage, the bare bits of the motorway they were building, the white police Jaguars that would belt past. But there were parts of London that Joe seemed to avoid, when he would take a longer route than necessary: the Strand, all round Charing Cross, Piccadilly.

'We should try it, Joe. It can't be that bad,' he said. 'Besides, there's lights in Piccadilly, isn't that so?'

Joe looked at him curious.

'Bovril, Coca-Cola, all sorts. Twenty-four hours a day. Terrible for the traffic. You know why? Everybody goes past Piccadilly once in their life.'

'I know.'

'You do?'

Henry did know, but didn't know how.

'Dora told me,' he said.

'If you say so. A woman's got to gab when she's washing. Even Dora, I suppose.'

'It was around there, I'm thinking, when you found me,' Henry said.

'When you knocked me over,' Joe corrected. 'You were that keen to be rescued. You remember that.'

'Oh yes,' said Henry and he did and he didn't.

Then it came all strange and tumbling, a feeling of restlessness, as if his very body was pushed up against the cramped walls and him desperate to burst through it and all that were in it. Suddenly he was taller than Joe, and he could lift the mangle on his own. Dora started acting odd, bumping up against him in a music hall cackle as they folded the day's sheets.

'Whoops a daisy. Any closer and we'll be washing them all over again!'

He took more notice of the outside; the life on passing pavements, snatches of radio programmes, boys his own age he'd see in playgrounds.

'I want to go to school, Dora. I don't know nothing.'

'You know what three and six add ten pence make. What more do you want?'

He started taking himself off, walking down to the river, listening to the water's hum, watching the birds peck along the mud line, raising a hand to the men on boats. He'd run out into the streets when he should be working. He'd see bicycles and hooting cars, look through the frosted glass of the public house on the corner, see men jingling money in their pockets, hear the noise of it spilling out onto the street.

One day he came back and found Joe standing in the kitchen with Dora lying on the floor and an iron in Joe's hand, with blood and hair on it and Joe breathing heavily. He looked at Henry, looked at him with his chest heaving and his arm trembling.

'Go on, vamoose, before it's too late.'

Henry shook his head, unable to comprehend where he should go.

'You weren't mine. You were someone else's. Do you remember that?'

'Yes. I remember that.'

'And now, you've got to find them, see. Leave. I'm not long here, not after this.'

Henry looked down.

'Is she dead.'

'Course she's dead. You'd be dead too if one of them irons were stuck in your head.'

He went over to the dresser and, reaching up, pulled down a brown-paper bag. He held it out to him.

A book.

'Remember it?'

'Yes. I lost it.'

'You never. Fallen down the lining, it had. Here, take it.'

He took it.

'Got your name in it.'

There was one word, Henry, and then a jagged edge where the rest should have been.

'We tore it out, see. When we tried to . . .' His voice trailed off, half in despair, half in embarrassment, then perked up again, as an explanation came to the rescue . . . 'but the writing must have got damaged 'cause we never did find out. It were no use, see.'

'Yes.'

'She was for getting rid of it, getting rid of a lot of things beside, but I wouldn't, see. I was bad, Henry, but not that bad.'

'No.'

'She didn't want you no real harm. It was her way, that's all. Getting by. But no more of that. Time to go, to the Barnardo's. You know where them is. We've driven past it often enough.'

Henry nodded.

'Tell 'em, tell 'em how your folks are gone.'

'Where are you going, Joe?'

Joe filled his pockets with the irons.

'Me? I'm taking a walk by the river. Take a trip 'cross the other side.'

Henry rushed towards him and threw his arms around him. He was all he had known this Joe and it frightened him, the little he knew. Joe pushed him away.

'Don't take on so. Barnardo's 'll look after you. Darn sight better than I ever could and that's a fact. Anyway, you'll be wanting to strike out on your own soon. Strong chap like you.'

He pulled Henry close. There was the smell of brandy on his breath. Dora didn't like him drinking brandy, said it sent him doo-lally.

'I shouldn't have done it, Henry. I shouldn't have brought you here.'

'But you found me.'

'In a manner of speaking I did, but we shouldn't have kept you. It was wrong, Henry. It was wrong.'

'But you couldn't find my . . .'

'Well, we might have tried a little harder.'

God knows he can't tell him, how they sent that note Dora wrote, telling them where the exchange would take place, where they'd bundle the boy out, and be well away. He would remember the time well enough. Joe got him to hide in the wardrobe like it was a game. That was the beauty of it. He'd touted for business nearby, had been in the area the week before, on a proper job. He turned into the road as usual, and what did he see, someone sweeping the pavement not far off, all earnest as if his life depended on it, sweeping where there were no leaves. One thing he knew about and that was the nature of unsupervised work. No workman would sweep a road when he didn't have to, not unless the foreman was breathing down his neck. He'd have a fag, read the paper or eye up someone's missus. He knew then they'd be lying in wait, so he made his delivery and drove away. Never tried again. Never, no matter what Dora said.

'There's a jail sentence waiting for us if this gets out, a long one,' he had told her.

'Only one way out of that,' she said, and he had hit her hard, to keep her from thinking of it again.

'I want him safe here, Dora. Just like you is, if you get my drift.'

That night he tore the page out of Henry's book and sent it them, that one word printed across the page. But lately, Dora had become worried again, what with Henry getting older, more inquisitive, more likely to open his mouth. She was going to do something, he was certain, sell him to a foreign freighter, pay one of her pub cronies to stick a knife in his neck upriver, far away from her doorstep.

'But what about the business, Joe?' Henry brought him back.

'What?'

Dora's eyes were bright. There was something white trickling out of her nose.

'The removals and your van?'

'I'm getting too old, Hen. You don't want to end up like me do you, with a back like mine?'

Henry said nothing.

'There you are, then. Now come on, let's skedaddle, before it's too late.'

And they walked out the house and ducked through the yard. Fresh and cold the day was, smelling of tar and bleach, wave after wave of sheets threaded across and he smelt the first time, standing in the stiff air, the water trickling down his arm, feeding the sheets into the yellow rollers, how he had to stand on tiptoe to work the handle, how once Daddy had turned the handle in the car, and how it sprang to life and Daddy had put the handle away and got in and drove off, but here the mangle never sprang to life, it was always the same, always turning.

'What about them sheets, Joe,' Henry asked. 'They should be ready for collection by tomorrow.'

'Reckon I'll deliver them in person,' Joe said, and pulling them off, wrapped them round his body. They stepped out into the back alleyway. Up the road lay the line of houses and the pub on the corner, and the Barnardo's home half a mile away. The other way led to the river. His pockets bulging and his new coats flapping, Joe began to walk down towards the water. Henry called out, the last throw.

'Joe!'

'Go on, Hen, skit, before I change my mind.'

He flapped his hands, like he did with that manky cat. Henry turned and ran, ran into the clean day, though it seemed to him that the fog was still there and he was more lost than ever.

Ian put his face round the door.

'Hen? You coming?'

Ian liked him, he could tell. What that meant he didn't know.

'Bit later.'

'Bit later there'll be no beer left.'

He folded his music stand, walked up to the Promenade Deck. There were still plenty about, mingling ranks of soldiers, officers from the P&O, cabin staff, journalists, all mixed together, looking at themselves, sizing each other up, thinking, 'We're here for the ride now, what will all make of it, this thrown-together crew?', a strength gathered in their collective uncertainty. The lights of England were strung out along an invisible black line, bunched clusters of them and roving glow-worm beams amidst the vast rolls of dark with just the hint of shape. A washing line, bits of his England hung upon it, and all the rest laid out behind like in a garden: young dark corn restless in the fields, animals curled and snuffling in their burrows, a company of trees tall to the rustle of uneasy birds; there were river banks he had sat upon, fishing lines he had thrown; there were pavements he had walked upon, towns and cities in which he had lived and left no mark; there were conversations he had had, fists he had fought, lips he had kissed. Out of the Sound *Canberra* surged forward. There was the crank of the rollers, the beat of Joe's lorry, the stamp of marching feet; there were roll-calls and name-calling and Richard Roach denying his very existence; there was Dora's great red arms and the Kent girl's thin pale ones, and the naked woman's, raising that cat to the heavens, unknowing him in her night. All that had been Henry, every footstep he had trod, every mark he had made, every breath he had taken, was rising up from this England, evaporating in the cold coming air.

He looked. A bank of fog came rolling down, lowered by the hand of a God he had never met, a curtain falling between him and all that he had been allowed to know.

England was gone. And he was alone.

FOUR

The postman parks halfway down the road, picks the mail up from the passenger seat and prepares to deliver to the final four houses. Every day he comes, save the Sundays, the bumps and indiscretions of Anglefield Road as familiar as his own, his routine varying only according to the obstacles and intrusions he might encounter along the way; coaxing the Roaches' cat out from under the post-van wheels; catching the Millen twins, as, kitted out for a morning's shopping and impervious to their mother's shrieks, they race uncertainly for the road; stepping over Marjorie's gardening implements, trowel and spade, fork and hat, left haphazard on the path; Monday to Friday diversions, orchestrated in the main by the women, maintaining the houses' momentum. Saturdays are when he sees the mechanics of masculinity on display, the garage doors swung open, power tools and boxes of spanners littering oil-stained garage floors, portable workbenches reverberating to the administrations of circular saws and sanding machines, petrol engines of various capacities spluttering into weekend life, Anglefield gutters running with the wash of soapy water, carrying away the detritus of motoring muck. Hector waxes his Humber Snipe once a month, has the bonnet up every now and again, but most weekends tends to his carpentry. He is good with his hands, works patiently beside the miniature town of labelled drawers, saws and planes and bevel gauges; bird boxes in the main, their garden is awash with them, prodigal birds coming home to roost. Richard Roach favours the car wash down the road for his Vauxhall's exterior (the firm pays) but takes the Hoover's suction attachment to the car's upholstery every week, hanging the scrubbed floor mats over the brick wall, noting the mileage on a sheet of card that he has attached to the back of his sun visor; Matty is the most regular, the sponge, the chamois leather rarely other than damp in the yellow plastic bucket that stands on the garage shelf, a job done not simply for the vehicle's sake but for the manner in which its sparkle complements the resonance of its other occupant, reflections of his good fortune both. As for Freddie, well, everyone in the road knows what Freddie is about; Saturday, Sunday, any day of the week given the chance, a mower wheeled out, an engine overhauled, a new part fitted, the machine soaped and greased and returned, with a curator's eye, to his precious fold. Lately though, unexpected inactivity has descended over the premises, as if a new law of apartheid has been enacted, man and machine forbidden their daily intercourse.

The postman's name is Tony. He has been Anglefield's postman for twelve years; watched the Roach boy grow from a cautious, silent seven-year-old into the loud and reckless youth of nineteen, the currency of a community's goodwill long exhausted; delivered letters of condolence to Matty's wreath-decked door, seen the Mediterranean resolve on his daughter's face turning mordant under the sweep of a new and brasher broom; drunk a tumbler of pink champagne with a stubble-worn Mr Millen the morning of the birth of the twins, Freddie's hand shaking both in wonder and in fright; admired Hector's nesting boxes, the chalet roofs, the decorated openings, even been given one to take home. The Armstrongs remind him of the spy couple back in the late sixties he once read about, the Krogers, their resolute geniality, their complete acceptance of each other a defence against enquiry, the regular flow of books he has delivered over these past years, their secret wrapped within.

A vain man, proud of his shock of ginger hair, he eyes the mirror before getting out. Ellen Roach, her hand clutching the open collar of her coat, is turning into the road from the lip of the hill, while behind her, manoeuvring within the upper cross of intersection, a dark car pulls away, the driver flashing a passing glance in her direction. On seeing the van she straightens momentarily, then ploughs forward, the clip of her heels quickening over the slabbed pavement. Another movement catches the postman's eye, ahead of him this time, darting left to right, scuttling as if trying to avoid detection. For a moment he anticipates felony, a whole road raided, imagines too his photograph in the local newspaper, Postman Pat transformed into Dirty Harry, but then recognizes the stoop and baggy green cords of Freddie as the man fumbles with the gate leading into the Plimsolls' back garden. Across the road, through the gap of their half-opened gate, the upended rear of Marjorie is perched between her wellington boots as she kneels before a rose bed.

He opens the van door and steps out. Ellen Roach has drawn level with him. He calls out over the roof, his voice cheeky, morning bright: 'You back early, Mrs Roach, or back late?'

He is adept in the use of licensed familiarity, the degree to which he is allowed to take part in their suburban intimacy, but realizes by the way she turns on a cold and unforgiving look that he has overstepped the mark. She holds out a pale and bony hand.

'Are those all for me?'

'Not all, no.'

He walks round, sorting them through. In Anglefield Road, though they are away more than the others, it is the Plimsolls who receive the greatest amount, mail-order catalogues, fashion magazines, postcards from friends and colleagues, and the Roaches who receive the least. Today the order is inverted. Nothing for the Plimsolls, a bank statement and a letter post-marked Weybridge for the Millens, a single jiffy bag for the Armstrongs (their book deliveries starting up again, by the feel of it) and for Mr and Mrs Roach a postcard and two envelopes, one brown and bureaucratic, one classy and cream.

Ellen snatches them out of his hand. He is tempted to remon-strate, make a joke about beds and the wrong side of them, but decides against it. Marjorie Armstrong is leaning against the gate holding out what looks like a slice of cake. He taps his chest, questioning. She nods. The Roaches' front door shuts with a bang.

*

They had been amongst the last to leave, the sweet papers and cigarette packets and crushed beer cans outlining the empty rec-tangles where the cars had parked. Kevin drove to a hotel he knew outside Maidenhead, within early next morning striking distance of home. They took a room in the extension block down by the river, into which had been squeezed a fake four-poster. It gave counterfeit vigour to her deceit. She was glad of Richard's lie; to think there was deception and turmoil behind his earnest solicitude. It made the whole mess more of a challenge.

Funny how everything had slotted into place. Richard going off for his Trout Night, Mark lounging into their bedroom not half an hour after he had left, announcing that he was going up to London, to stay with Marcia for a couple of days. She might be able to get him a job at the bookshop.

'That would be great,' she said, wondering as to the girl's motives. 'Don't forget you're . . .' She couldn't bring herself to complete the sentence. 'Your appointment.'

Mark gave her a wretched look and walked out, the uneven drag of footstep wounding memory to her repose. A couple of days without him, Richard away for most of them too. She lay luxuriating in the promise of extended privacy, floating in and out of a muddy swirl of responsibility and dream, until the phone rang, and she lifted the receiver and heard the clip of his soft Scottish accent and their unspoken history worming into her brain. He was calling from Southampton. He needed to talk to Richard and wondered if she knew where he was. Her astonishment was unreserved, her body rising up out of the bed as the revelations grew, the men in her house surrounding her with secrets and hollows, leaving spaces in which to create her own. Kevin excavated her incredulity. He was worried about Richard too, how he'd been behaving recently. They needed to talk.

'Look,' he said, 'as I'm all finished here, why don't I drive over?'

'Don't be absurd.'

'Well, you come here, then? I could pick you up from the station.'

She was going to say no. Outside Mark and Marcia were walking up the road, Marcia hoisting a small backpack over her shoulders, Mark trailing a half-empty Tesco's bag, both imbued with a casual indifference to everything and everyone around them. Had she ever done that, upped and left without a semblance of ceremony?

'All that way just to talk about Richard?'

'If you like.'

She went. She stayed. The night had risen around her. She felt abandoned, friendless, adrift upon a momentous sea, nailed to the deck by a pitiless hand.

'I don't know why I'm doing this,' she announced at some dislocated point in time, 'I don't think I even like you.'

'But you like this.'

'Do I? How wonderful it must be, to be surrounded by such certainty.'

They came down early for breakfast. She picked a copy of the *Daily Mail* from the reception desk, he the *Times* and the *Sun*. She ordered toast. Kevin chose scrambled eggs. He spread the newspaper over the width of table and began to read ostentatiously, ignoring her. The waiter delivered their order with a grin. Ellen couldn't be certain but she detected a certain complicity between the two men. Was this a regular thing? The toast was cold and flabby, the eggs pale and watery; his body, her eyes.

'Look at that. That's what I call publicity.'

He turned back the tabloid and waved a photograph of a skimpy girl draped around a soldier, both holding one of those blasted shoes. All those page-three girls looked exactly the same.

Kevin leant back, beaming.

She waved it away. It had been Richard's idea, after all.

'You should give him some credit.'

'He'd have fucked it up, Ellen.'

'Yes, I want to talk to you about that.' She tapped Kevin's plate with a smeared butter knife. 'You know what you said last night?'

Kevin flipped the pages, barely raising his eyes.

'I said a lot of things last night,' he said.

'About Richard.' Now he looked at her.

'Ah.' He put the paper aside. It had been a long time coming.

'I can't alter the facts, Ellen.'

'Don't do it, Kevin, that's all.'

'That's easier said than done. It's not just me. Sir Douglas is well aware of the problem. If I can't sort it out, I'll get the chop too, believe me.' He leaned over and tipped her chin. 'Then both your admirers would be out of work.'

'But this *Canberra* thing. Surely that counts for something.'

'It all comes down to sales, Ellen. His have been falling for six months now. What possible reason can I give for keeping him on?'

'I thought you'd just slept with her. Isn't that why you called?'

'I can hardly put that on his report now, can I. Wife a terrific fuck.'

'You'll think of something. So, what's the going rate here? Once a week? Once a month?'

'You've got it all wrong, Ellen. Look, I'll fire him and then come after you. That would make my motive clear, wouldn't it?'

'Which is?'

'The capture and total occupation of Ellen Roach.' He touched her mouth.

'Don't.'

'You're always saying don't. Don't call me, don't touch me, don't do that, don't do this.'

He ran his foot up the inside of her leg. She pushed him away.

'See what I mean?'

His foot resumed its insistent patrol while she drank the last of her coffee, thin, unpleasant stuff, the touch and the taste and that half-questioning look of his precursors to the final time back in their room, something she had promised herself not to do, his face as unlovely and disorientated as hers, a kind of vacancy filling the both of them, possessed of nothing but possession. It was the idea of a rate of exchange that propelled her. It gave her a currency, a certain hunger, a certain power. She would control her husband's destiny without his knowledge, his daily diligence a baseless coin, her occasional adultery worth its duplicity in gold.

Kevin dropped her just before the turning, away from Angle-field eyes.

'You'll be seeing me,' he said.

'I will?'

'And not just Trout Night. That's not nearly enough.'

In the hallway she kicks off her shoes and walking through, sees the cat waiting patiently outside on the patio. She drops the mail on the table, unlocks the door and with one hand under his belly gathers him to her face, murmuring her failings into his soft depths. She takes him to the kitchen and pours him a saucer full of semi-skimmed, his pink tongue delicate and curling, milky droplets caught on the hairs around his mouth. She strokes his back with her bare foot, thinking of the bed upstairs, the sleep she needs, the second shower she must remember to take.

Back in the living room she picks up the mail again. Unsettlingly the postcard, a picture of Stonehenge, is from Mark, posted yesterday afternoon: *Change of plans. Up north for weekend with M visiting friends. London Monday?* His friends, her friends? Stupid question. He doesn't have any friends; the brown envelope is from his probation officer, reminding him of his appointment later in the month; it is the other envelope which attracts her attention, unusual in size and weight, uncertainly postmarked and unsealed, like a Christmas card. She pulls it open, cutting her index finger on the sharp edge of the flap. Inside lies a gold-edged invitation card. Her eyes dart from line to line. A Summer Garden Party; Ellen and Richard Roach are cordially invited; Sir Douglas and Lady Fell; Sunday 11th July. Stockwell Park, 12.00 and beyond, and written across the top left-hand corner, in a different hand, another message. *Hope this compensates for the hi-jack!*

What does this mean? That Richard's job is more secure than Kevin would have her suppose? That Kevin had used her fear to seal a bargain that had no validity and which need not be kept; his year-long siege, those hour-long phone calls, the furiously celibate meetings, reconnoitring of her territory she always felt, finally broken by timely deception, Richard's dismissal the Trojan horse rolled past her defences, Kevin scrambling out of its belly, to claim his trophy and set the terms of his treaty. She works her tongue over the cut. What should she do when he demands his next payment? Call his bluff? She knew the answer well enough. Though the agreement might be void, was she not still the prize?

She looks to the window. A summer garden party, champagne probably, important people circulating, Richard terrified of what she might learn, Kevin (if he is invited) revelling in what he would not; she the huntress, she the game, deceiving and deceived by the both of them, moving in another world. She turns her mind to the possibilities of a new dress, something defiant, un-Anglefield, un-wifely; a new pair of shoes too, and not of the firm's making; extravagant, carnivorous. She rubs her finger across the lettering.

Stockwell Park. Across the road Marjorie stands at the gate, holding her hand up, as one might to a highwayman, warding off the advances of their over familiar postman, her hair looking like it had spent the night curled up in a dog basket.

A summer garden party. Mr and Mrs Richard Roach are invited. She looks down. A smear of blood covers their name.

*

'That's never for us, is it?'

Marjorie pushes her hands out further as if to prevent him coming any closer. Her fingernails are broken, her fingers squat. They do not look capable of baking a sponge.

He bites into the slice, a wedge neatly cut, a dusting of icing sugar, a filling of raspberry jam. It is soft and sweet and slightly warm. This morning's, then.

'That's right. Another book, by the feel of it. You should do us all a favour, Mrs Armstrong, write one yourself. A cookbook. Go in my wife's stocking whether she liked it or not.'

She ignores the compliment.

'Must you pester us with this?' she says.

What is it about today? First Mrs Roach, now Marjorie. He is shocked. If there is one constant in Anglefield Road, it is the Armstrongs and their all-consuming hospitality, without prejudice and utterly democratic. Their cheerful benevolence is bestowed on anyone and everyone. The neighbours too have noticed this. He remembers once remarking on it last summer to Mr Plimsoll, as they stood bewildered by Matty's impossible car. Marjorie had come across the road with two glasses of her home-made lemonade.

'Friendly old stick,' he had said and Mr Plimsoll, looking after Marjorie's rounded rear disappearing behind her front gate, said, 'Yes, but she doesn't half beat your back with it.'

He takes another bite and discovers a thread of muddied weed. It is bitter and sticks to his teeth. It spoils the effect. He wouldn't let his wife serve up a cake covered in grass.

'How do you mean?'

'Deliver it. Couldn't you just ignore it, write "address unknown"?'

The famous song comes in his head. It had been part of his teenage record collection Red and white sleeve, black label. 65? 66?

'No can do, I'm afraid. It's the law, see. I've no choice in the matter. Of course, once it's out of my hands you can do what you like with it. If you don't want it, there's nothing to stop you writing "Return to Sender" on the front, and popping it back in the post unopened. That is, if it has a return address on it.' He turns it over. 'Which it doesn't.'

She stares at the large blue writing, her bottom lip quivering. It's not all when the boat comes in. There are any number of nasty surprises waiting in the hold. He tries to help.

'You'll notice it's addressed to Mr Armstrong. Perhaps if you got him to open it, it wouldn't be so bad.'

He swallows the final portion whole, anxious to move on.

'So, how about it? You don't want to get me into trouble, do you?'

Still she doesn't move.

'Tell you what. I'll put it on the gatepost, see? Then it's up to you.'

He wipes the trace of sugar on the back of his trousers. Just the Millens and the Plimsolls and then he's off. He only hopes she's not still there when he comes back up. He starts the short walk down to the Plimsolls. Freddie Millen is standing in front of his car, looking anxiously up and down the road. He gives him a little wave. Freddie waves back, then raises one finger in the air.

'Have you got a minute?' he calls.

*

Marjorie flings open the door and with wellingtons planted firmly on stone step throws the package across the room. It slides along the table, knocking his cup sideways. Coffee sloshes out.

'Alnwick is it now, Hector, you bloody fool. I thought we'd agreed.'

It had been a falling off rather than an agreement, the folly of the enterprise emphasized by every expectation raised, every package opened, every addition made. The further they travelled from the dark age, the more uncertain became the memory, the more unlikely the discovery, the intensity of their search rising and falling with the cycles of their age; hope, resignation, exhaustion, washing in and out, tides upon their shore. Three years it has been since he bought the last one, and then this one, staring out from one of the mailing lists he still receives. He never thought it would arrive today, otherwise he would have been at the gate.

Marjorie was right. The likelihood of this being *the* book was remote to the point of not bothering to open the package at all. That's why they had stopped. And yet books do survive the years, complete with torn pages and disfigured dedications, cleared out of attics and unwanted bookcases. Five hundred and nineteen copies they possess, the pretty blue binding, the embossed title repeated in the rising rows, some stained, some scribbled, all incomplete, all written within, none with the right message, none torn in the right shape. Even so, they cannot set them free, for that would only serve to perpetuate the numbers in circulation. Nor can they destroy them, coming as they do from the same provenance as their own. Each one of them had belonged to someone, been held close to someone's heart: a land littered with forgotten gifts. So they made a library of them, in the room next to his own, a terrible room, dark and sombre, lined with broken spines.

He picks it up, wipes the slopped coffee off with the sleeve of his shirt.

'I've just washed that.'

It's not what she's angry about.

'I wouldn't have done it normally, Marjorie, but it sounded so close, that's all.'

'Well, I'm not looking.'

'No.'

He waits until she has gone back into the garden, then tips in another spoon of sugar, before opening the bag and pulling out the battered copy. There is no need for any prolonged examination. This is not their copy. There is no jagged tear the shape of the top left of Africa as there should be. The handwriting is quite different too, the message written in ink, not pencil. He had forgotten to ask about that. That's what happens when you're out of practice.

He climbs the stairs and opens the door. Five hundred and twenty now, the oak shelves fashioned in the garage below, space left for any number more. In the centre of the room stands a table, in the centre of the table a square of glass, and under it, the torn page. They had been sent it eighteen months after the event. It has his name and address upon it, just as Marjorie had written it that day on the train. The tear is an uneven one, the remaining letters and words left broken in the book itself they presume, but over those left upon the page another word had been imposed, scrawled across in crude blue crayoned capitals. SAFE. No kidnap demand, no ransom note, just the one word, childlike, emphatic, as if there was nothing more to be said, as if nothing more could be said. Their collection started three years later, occasioned by a copy he came across on a stall in Charing Cross Road, the ripped half looking like the jigsaw sibling of their very own, and within the hour he was home examining the fit. And though it proved to be a false hope, it showed them a design by which they might track him down: seek the book; find the boy.

He sits on the one hard chair and reads, page after tear-stained page; such an English story, told in such an English language, fashioned by such supposedly English feelings; quiet homes in huge gardens, the safety in small adventures, the sanctity of boyhood. And yet, had he not been an English boy, introduced that day to the most English of events, London lights, London bus rides, guided by a sturdy English mother's hand?

He crosses into the bedroom and sticks his head through the ivy. Marjorie is standing on the summer house veranda, her arms lain on the upended rake. She looks up. She can tell by his expression. Lost in the fog, conceived in a swirl. Sometimes she wishes he had never been born.

'Well?' she says

Hector shakes his head.

She bangs her head against a wooden pillar. On the other side of the fence the Plimsolls' lawnmower starts up.

*

Freddie stands back, beaming. It took first time, a wonderful shudder of power and authority.

'See what I mean?' he says. 'Starts first time. They don't make them like that any more.'

Tony nods, anxious to be off. Not only has he had to carry the thing across the road, he's now had to listen to a potted history of its life. Found on a rubbish tip near Bletchley; took five years to restore; ninety-five new parts needed.

He wipes his hands on the inside of his jacket. First jam, now oil.

'Well, you got a lawn to mow, I got letters to deliver. Do you want me to pop these in the box or . . .?'

'Just hand them over.'

The postman leaves. Freddie stuffs the letters down his back pocket. Bending down, he adjusts the throttle and steps back, surveying the outline of the task ahead. The lawn curves slightly into the flowerbed on the left-hand side, giving it an awkward bulge. He can either level it out with a spade, or shave the band thin, like the back of a Henley blazer. The former is his preferred option, but senses that altering the shape of their garden is not strictly in his remit. He positions himself behind the mower and takes a deep breath. It has been six months since he has mowed a lawn. This should get him going.

Since first light that morning Freddie had been sitting at his desk in the shed, hoping that by the time Patsy came down to breakfast he'd have something substantial to show her. It hadn't been going well. 'Lawns and Lawn-mowing', he had written, and underneath 'Editor: Freddie Millen F.I.E.E.', the initials lending an authoritative slant to the enterprise. Below was his list of possible contents. He'd dreamt up some cracking ideas for the first issue: 'Relics of the Past', 'How to Keep your Rollers Clean' and his best one yet, 'Grassbox to Brain Box: Lawnmowers of the Future!'.

It was giving flesh to the articles that was giving him trouble. He had the energy, the scope, but writing them was proving to be a lot harder than he'd imagined. Plus he needed a business plan to show W. H. Smith. What was a business plan, exactly? He was all for asking Rich Brother George, but Patsy seemed dead set against the idea. The library might be able to suggest a book or two; or perhaps Hector could advise him. Accountancy, hadn't that been his trade?

Half an hour ago he'd put his pen down. Staring in front of a blank sheet of paper wasn't getting him anywhere. He needed to move around, get the body moving, let the mind follow.

'Patsy!'

There was no reply. She had to be out, perhaps taking the twins to the swimming pool, or gone shopping. Leaving the table, he crossed the road to examine the task before him. Although he had been in their back garden a couple of years back, he hadn't been prepared for the sight that greeted him. The Plimsolls' lawn was a good six foot longer than his, running the full length down to the embankment, had grown rank with neglect. Ragged edges hung over weed-infested flowerbeds; moss and dandelions ravaged a grass littered with wormcasts and molehills. A sodden fashion magazine and a discarded mug added patches of anaemia to the outrage. He went looking for their machine.

Their shed was full of beach umbrellas and deckchairs. No sign of an aerator or roller, or anything needed for the maintenance of a decent lawn. The lawnmower stood in a corner opposite. He pulled it out into the light. A layer of yellowing grass cuttings lay rotting in the box, while the cutters themselves were encrusted with a thick layer of mud. A further examination revealed a rusty spark plug, frayed rubber handles, and an old bird's nest on top of the engine casing. He couldn't mow with that. He looked around. A brand-new Flymo hung on the wall. He left quickly, pretending he hadn't seen it.

Back home he walked down the garden and unlocked the museum. How he loved to see them, lying dormant, waiting for his touch. He moved amongst them, caressing their handles, brushing an intruding leaf, an errant cobweb from their proud heraldry, their names a roll-call of precision engineering. Pugh, Ransome, Qualcast; in the far corner a late Ferrabee, next to it a Lloyds Paladin, then, in pride of place, the 1946 Dennis. The Dennis hadn't had a decent run for a bit, but it was too distinguished for the Plimsolls' lawn. Something a little more rugged perhaps, like the '57 Atco. The Atco would do the job, twenty-two inches of sturdy reliable blade. He took a rag to its frame, then rolled it out into the daylight, the ratcheted barrel disconcertingly loud as he manoeuvred it down the front drive. Getting it across the road was going to be a problem. Terrible for the paintwork, tarmac. Across the road the postman was stuffing his face with one of Marjorie's cakes. He beckoned him over.

After they had lifted it across he gave the Atco a final rub down. Not surprisingly, Tony had been fascinated by its history. It looked magnificent, slants of the morning sun falling on its deep green contours, the flourished emblem emblazoned on the eminent box. There was a nautical quality about it, the curve of its majestic bow, its stately stance as it lay still on the edge of the green, ready to sail forth across the swathe; something treacherous about the sea ahead too, the unknown perils that might be lie beneath the surface, icebergs of half-buried detritus ready to shatter the carefully honed corkscrewed cut.

He walks the machine forward. He starts, not on the edge, as a novice might, but selects a plumb line, a quarter in. The Atco rolls forth imperiously, blades flashing, devouring the unkempt growth that lies in confusion in its path. Now that he is alone, it comes to him that before he completes his task, he could experiment, investigate the possibilities of decorative mowing, using different blade settings to produce unusual patterns, something a tradition-alist might frown on, but certainly suitable for an unusual feature in his magazine. He could try out the idea here, before completing a more conventional finish. A simple shape to begin with; a tor-toise, an A for Anglefield, why not Anglefield Road itself? Perhaps carving its distinctive shape on the lawn would placate the gods that were trying to evict them.

He increases the throttle. The grassbox fills rapidly. He mows three-quarters of the length, turns the machine in a wide, bulbous arc, then works his way down again; apart from one submerged wine cork catching in the blades, deeply satisfying work. It isn't a perfect cut, but it's a start. By the time they come back, he'll have it looking like a lawn fit for heroes. In a way, he is mowing for the Task Force.

A voice rises high over the hedge.

'Freddie?'

Patsy! He depresses the clutch and cuts back the engine.

'I'm over here,' he cries, trying to sound as carefree as possible.

There is a scrabble through the foliage. Patsy's face appears over the top, red and a little scratched.

'Freddie, what are you doing?'

'It's not what you think, Patsy. Suzy asked me to mow their lawn while they're away.'

'She told me you volunteered.'

'I'm just trying to be good neighbour, Patsy, but . . .' He spreads his hands out in despair. 'I mean, look at it. If there was a society for the prevention of cruelty to lawns I'm afraid those two would have come to their attention years ago. Still, the Atco will give it a nice finish, don't you think?'

A wail goes up.

'Patsy?'

'And what about this?' She holds up a pad of lined paper. 'You left it on the table.'

'My plan, yes I know. It's only a rough draft. It's not as easy as it looks, Patsy, this writing lark. You shouldn't really have read it.'

'I'll say. "I am a lawnmower"? Not something the average wife hopes to discover; that she's married to someone who thinks he's a Suffolk Punch.'

'It's a mission statement, Patsy. It suddenly struck me, the brilliant simplicity of the project, how it connects to the reader, the moment they read the title. Think about it. There's magazines about horses and cars and goodness knows what. But the person who rides a horse is called a rider not called a horser, and the chap who drives a car is called a driver not a carer.' He clutched the bar of the machine firmly. 'But the person who uses a lawnmower is himself a lawn mower. Machine and man one and the same thing. It's the unique selling point, Patsy. Of course I don't think I am one.'

'You pretended to be one last night. Holding out your hands, making that funny whirring noise.'

'I wasn't pretending.'

'That's what I mean.'

'I was imitating one.'

'Perhaps you should go on stage.'

'Patsy!'

'It'd be a living. As it is . . .'

She looks at his loyal, earnest face. She sighs, a breath of resignation.

'You're finding it hard, then, the magazine.'

'Just a bit.'

'Perhaps you're right. Perhaps we should find out what RBG thinks.'

'I got a letter from him today.'

'Saying?'

'I haven't got my glasses.'

He walks over and hands it up over the hedge. Patsy reads, scowling.

'He wants to come over in the summer in a couple of weeks. Bring the Viking Queen. Lord it over us. I suppose we could sound him out then.' She waves the foolscap in the air. 'Trouble is, once he starts sticking his nose in, there'd be no stopping him. He'd roll right over you.' She folded the letter in half, then in quarters, pressing hard on the creases as if to seal her brother-in-law within. 'I'm going to put him off, get you started. We'll work on it together.'

'What about . . .' He points to his unfinished business.

'Consider this your Falklands, Freddie. You're the Argentinian navy, I'm Margaret Thatcher and I've just put an exclusion zone round this garden. If you so much as look at this lawn before we've got something down on paper, I'm going to set my best hammer loose on your fleet. Anyway, you've got plenty of time. They won't be back for weeks.'

*

Matty wakes, the noise of the ship's engine stirring his uneasy dreams. It sounds all wrong, hurried, overloud, as if under threat. He checks the clock; half eleven. They should be heading down towards the Bay of Biscay by now, if the accompanying ships haven't slowed them down.

He had got back late, well after one, a present for Marcia in the back of the car, disappointed as he parked the car in the garage and walked through into the darkened house that she hadn't stayed, that she'd assumed, wrongly, that he wouldn't consider what she'd said, of what he was to her, of what she should be to him and the woman who bound them together. He couldn't sleep. He did not want to sleep.

In the kitchen he took out the flour, puddled warm water into the dried yeast and greased one of Elena's baking tins. They hadn't been used in years. He worked the mixture well, remembering how it used to be. Sitting in the park, working the headlights, the *Canberra* had appeared to him as a magnificent illusion, a conjuring trick, an elaborate paper cut-out, lit from inside, sailing against a theatre cloth of black. Suzanne was on that stage. He waved to her as he walked away down the dock, watched her bring her hand to her eye, as if she might regret his leaving, for a moment even envisaged her running down after him, as, in those long waiting hours in Southampton, trying to phone Marcia without success, wishing that he had not given his word, toying with the idea of leaving anyway, knowing Suzanne would never know one way or the other, he imagined climbing back on board, finding her weeping inconsolably in their cabin, accepting her smothers of gratitude with the proviso of a balance redressed, but once alone in the car, doing what he had promised, he could not bring substance to this knowledge. Something had broken between them, a connection, a common link. Maybe it had never been there in the first place, the stabs of light he sent out into the dark serving only to illuminate that void. For such messages are not for the home-comers only. As often as not they illuminate the need for separation, the danger in coming too close, the likelihood of wrenching, calamitous, grief.

Then the bottle came out. He had never liked ouzo much when Elena was alive, but in the years between it brought something to him, not a memory exactly, but a hint of something elusive, barely visible in the cloudy swirl. Just opening the cap seemed to release the expectation of it into the room. He sat waiting for the dough to rise, drinking tumbler after tumbler, thinking back on what it had been like those earlier days, Elena serving behind the counter, that boy he hired running off with the first week's takings, the little Danish pastries from the shop next door she would pop in her mouth, patting her stomach as he waggled his finger at her. He knew what he was doing then, knew his whole future, his business, his wife, the time when they'd start a family, all growing under his hand. They opened the shop the same year Marcia was born, olive and sunny like her mother, like her mother too, quick to temper, strong in voice; the family and its fortune blossoming, glowing with a rising health. Just an ordinary butcher's shop until he started the side lines: raised game pies, prime-cut steak-and-kidney puddings, Elena in the back adding the memories of her own childhood, cooking up little loaves of olive bread. It grew, the shop, not in size, but in scope; they took in cheese and a little wine. They cooked their own ham, they cured their own bacon; they made savoury tarts and twelve different types of sausage: they became their own. Then, like a sudden drop in temperature, collapse, Elena gone, Marcia fifteen, a difficult time for a daughter to confide in a father, and he too felt ostracized, separated, adrift from all he had trusted, the cruise to Greece a way of realigning those links. He had seen what Suzanne was the first time she took his arm, not a gold-digger exactly, but on the lookout for a good man with prospects, a safe man, one who might temper her frivolity, thought too that her modernity would be good for breaking into Marcia's teenage defences, and recognized above all things that the other quality she offered, her determined youth, was an attraction he could not deny; and so it had proved. The *Canberra* was a part of that allure too, part of the journey to a land in which he had never lived, and which, once he been allowed entry, failed to live up to any one of its expectations, Suzy sashaying along the games deck, in her blue coat and white skirt, he eight decks below, working with knife and saw, his hands swollen in the cold, the light and the sea and her companionship an ocean away. He wouldn't care if he never saw the sea again.

By the time the loaves were cooked and he took to bed, dawn was coming up. He thought he might not be able to sleep at all, but now, looking at the bedside clock, he realizes he has slept for four and a half hours.

He draws back the curtain. There would be no patio now, he knows that, whatever Suzy might say, probably no Anglefield Road. When she got back they'd put the house up for sale, move on to somewhere fresh, some new port into which none of their ships had sailed. Some small town where he could start a new business, near the coast if she wanted. But what if there was no Suzy? What would he do then? What was keeping him here? His dead wife? Marcia? What does this house mean to him?

He looks down.

Seared into the long grass of his lawn, someone has outlined the shape of an erect penis.

*

Anglefield Road sails on; cars come, cars go, doors open, doors close, words are said or left unspoken. Yet their eyes are focused on murkier waters now, breakfast skitting across the tabloid headlines, televisions fixed upon the funereal form of the news announcer, a nation's conversation summoned by the one bell and its singular chime. The war, the war, Britain is going to war. And such a strange war at that, against a country that had always been as much friend as foe, for what little Anglefield Road knew about it, the aged capital, with its crumbling balconied buildings, the plains of grass, the leather-stitched gauchos, the tinned meat unlocked for Anglefield's austere youth. Not an enemy at all, the invitation to animosity invoked by a word that had no foundation, Spic, and which sat ill upon the tongue. Junta was the alternative, not that a braided dictator or two taking the fly-past had bothered this or any other cul-de-sac before. But we had been invaded, so up the ginger. No matter that the land was no bigger than a back garden, a thumbnail scrap of unwanted scrub perched on the outskirts of the awesome Antarctic, a *Whisky Galore* sort of entity, ludicrous, with penguins and sheep and a flying flag, denoting, like all the discarded baggage of yesteryear, a Gibraltar-like refusal to be dislodged, tenacious limpet on our outhouse doorstep. But as shuttle diplomacy faded, and late-night whisky-glass determination shone through the drawn curtains of govern-ment, the boats of Britain were pushed out to bob doggedly across the unknown water, to set battle not solely against the immoderate antagonist but the lonely perils of distance; the stretched supply line and garbled communication, the hastily packed luggage stacked higgle-piggle in their holds, the wintering weather they must overcome, the forgotten, half-mapped terrain that had to be reconnoitred, landed upon, retaken. This was no European landscape before them; no old battle plans to examine, no memoirs to read, no world war memory set in the footprints of this land. Our map was a mouse-chewed, Ealing comedy scroll, lost in the Foreign Office basement; our representative a Peter Sellers absurdity, indignant in a plumed hat and plummy voice, our navy all but broken up, its ships destined to be sold down the river, our stance a foot-stamping throwback to a time long evaporated, the people we sought to liberate long dismissed from our contemporary minds. But restore the old order we must, not simply with a submarine and a clever canoe, but a flotilla, Elizabethan in its proud conceit, twenty-eight thousand human beings waved away, fifty-one warships, twenty-one Royal Fleet Auxiliaries and most telling of all, fifty-four merchant ships snatched from their everyday trade, liners and tankers, repair ships and tugs, supply ships that serviced the North Sea oil fields, ro-ro ferries, thirty thousand tons of stores and provision to be shipped, sixty thousand tons of fuel criss-crossing the water, moving forward into patriotic uncertainty.

And for the vessels left behind? Anglefield Road's own manoeuvrings become mechanical, set to negotiate the lanes and currents on autopilot, as if these waters were safely placid and safely known. Like all of Britain, their sights are set to the fading shapes of those other ships; to the aircraft carrier *Hermes* with its crisply spoken admiral and its Harrier jump jets, to the grey anonymity of the battleships sailing to no man's sea, and to that other ship that for twenty-two years had carried Britain and its imperial dream: the *Canberra*.

FIVE

They had a month of it nearly, before the cold and the stark reality of leaving Ascension Island behind set in, that dirty scab of volcanic ash that burnt and festered in the sun; thirty days, from that Saturday, the 10th of April, when the first Sea King helicopter flew out to christen the mid-ships flight deck, to the May of that same date, four days out from Ascension Island and that hallucinatory sight, a cold sea filled with destroyers and frigates dispersing across the horizon, and this great ship of theirs, her white hull streaked with rust, guns bolted onto the railings, the plates of war grown old and discoloured like a grafted skin, ploughing into the grey Atlantic swell, already bloated with the floating dead of the two countries. A month, which, given the intensity of their surroundings, wasn't bad. Bad? Father, it was glorious.

She had always been an adventurous ship, not simply in the gleaming white bulk of her, but rather in the nature of the space she commanded, how her lines appeared to float out alongside her, as if this great vessel was as elusive and expansive as the air and water that surrounded it, a pied piper, dancing upon the waves, leading sons and daughters a world away. The ship had been an orphanage half its life, taking England's strays to Australia, uprooting brothers and sisters, their lives suitcase-packed, their passage cheap-note paid, as they counted out their captive days, pacing decks, imagining what would greet them when the ship dropped anchor in the virgin bay of their dreams. Perhaps it was this freshness of history that gave the ship its aura of lawless dependability, this combination of theft and trust, strange ballast for such a vessel, fleeing footprints imprinted on the varnished wood, ghost-breath letters on the thickened glass, a new language written, an older one erased. Yet it hadn't lasted. Planes had put a stop to that traffic, those bulbous 747s, wheeled out only nine years after the blocks had been knocked out from under the *Canberra*'s keel. Three hundred and sixty-two mortals had been air-lifted out that first day in January; no cabins, no Sun Decks, no rail to lean on, no wonder to inhale. Just a tray and a blanket and the hum of pressurized boredom to placate them: a silver-coated Trojan Pegasus, flying through the air aimed at the ship's destruction. Bombs hadn't blown a hole in her, though they'd had their scares; sandbanks hadn't broken her back, though the ship had been driven onto any number of those off-shore beaches; a fire might have done it and Suzanne remembered a bad one, arcing in the engine room, smoke flooding the tourist cabins on C and D Deck, but it was economics that had finished her off nearly. Six jumbo jets could carry as many passengers to Australia in twenty-six hours as the *Canberra* could in three weeks. Those planes and the hike in fuel prices had the owners negotiating rates at the breaker's yard. Other factors firmed up the booking. The ship's draught was unwieldy, thirty-two scraping feet of it, violating the interiors of too many available ports of call. In an attempt to drum up business she had been untimely democratized too, converted from a first-class/tourist-class vessel into a one-class catch-all, though it was an awkward sort of faith; the high and low trappings contrived for other denominations, the congregation unsure, the ministers uncomfortable. What had appeared to be swift and graceful now appeared sluggish, overweight. But unwilling to discard their property, they brought pause to their plotting. New furnishings, new orders, gave a credibility to the one class that the earlier proclamations could not; new engines reduced the ship's draught by three feet, inviting the embraces of fresh, more enticing harbours. The lure of untamed money had altered her course too, *Canberra*'s compass set to the magnet of brash coin, learning to love the newly minted rich.

And now, ten years later, another set of rules. A civilian ship no longer, the *Canberra* had to accommodate her new masters, haul in new practices; the art of evasion, the art of concealment, the sea to be viewed as not simply as occasionally hostile, but as an area of constant danger, harbouring an enemy's intentions and an enemy's hardware. Bomb the *Canberra*? Set foul torpedo to its belly? There were fresh words to add to the dictionary; 'corpens' – to alter course by wheeling in the wake of the ship ahead; RAS – to replenish at sea; and most improbable of all, Darken Ship – to render invisible what the *Canberra* was built to do, blaze its fairy-tale promise from every porthole, every deck and every railing. Rolls of black canvas were handed out, drills imposed to ensure that no chink of light escaped.

Building went on apace. Out on the Observation Deck, unused to the slippery grease of the sea, workmen worked through the storms of those early Bay of Biscay days to weld the second helicopter deck, battling against the dip of the swaying ship, risking their lives to have the job completed before being flown off to a Southampton home and a safe bed. Observation Deck vanquished, Bonito Pool drained, old familiar rooms were given new, incongruous identities. The William Fawcett shop, from which not three years before Suzy had sauntered, that predatory white swimsuit prescient under her arm, had been stripped down to accommodate the commander of the military forces; the photographic shop, where Charlie Grisewood hung tell-tale reels of cruise-induced debauchery in his darkroom for their after-hours amusement, auctioning the most grotesque to the highest bidder ('Sorry, sir, your film came out completely blank. Could there be something wrong with your camera?'), had become headquarters to one of the two Commando units aboard, while in the hairdressing salon, the men who had thrown the lasso around *Canberra*'s unbridled wanderings sat in their Royal Navy shirtsleeves, their authority set firm under rows of purple hairdryers.

*

Three days out Suzanne woke to the feeling that someone was trying to shake the cabin. Her first snatched thought was to the past, what she had known, relied upon, and heard in that befuddled reverberation an impatient Matty, locked out after his late night shift, before sitting up, the truth gnawing empty on her stomach. She was beginning to miss him, his landlubber nit-picking ways. The bunk shook again. For a moment she imagined that one of the engine turbines had seized up, but the steady motion of the ship dispelled that fear. Poking her head out of her cabin door, she could hear a pulse banging against the sides, like the muffled hammer of a blacksmith's blows. Suzanne knew all the vagaries of this vessel. Bare foot or high heeled, its floors and walls were like a second skin to her. This she did not recognize. She shook Tina awake.

'Listen,' she said. 'What the hell's that?'

Tina groaned and pulled her sheet over her head. She'd moved in an hour after Matty had gone. 'Just like old times,' she said, and though Suzanne laughed in agreement, she understood in an instant, from the manner in which Tina had thrown her bag at her, from the manner in which she had caught it, Tina trying to pass on the baton as it were, that it wasn't like the old times at all. They had been equals then, two young women set loose in a world decked out like a department store, and they with unlimited credit, buying whatever took their fancy, determined to discard it a few days later if for no other reason than the wilful need for change. The lure of that particular indulgence had never completely evaporated, but in the passing years Suzanne had become conscious of the unwanted interest that so often accrued. Tina had no such inhibitions. Late last night, true to form she had come clattering down the corridor, a pair of boots in unsteady tow. There'd been a lot of whispering, the odd lurch against the flimsy door, the prize clearly hesitant, Tina cajoling, trying to confound his doubts. Eventually Tina had put her head round.

'Tell the Major you don't mind him coming in for a bit,' Tina had pleaded.

She was having none of it. In earlier times Tina would have never asked. In earlier times she would never have refused. Now she felt put upon, repulsed, the man standing behind Tina red-faced, unsteady, pathetically anxious in his pawing, weakness leaking out of his watery eyes. Call that desire! She could just imagine him in bed, worrying at it with the pointless energy of a rodent at his wheel, driven by nothing other than the fact of its existence.

'But I do mind,' she had said, and anticipating Tina's own rejoinder the following morning, pulled her bedclothes about her, shutting off all discussion. Tina had slammed the door shut and rolled back humming and well fucked at half four, banging

168

around the room in a deliberate display of displeasure. Suzanne had revelled in every thump.

She dressed, and pulling on her new windcheater walked up one flight onto the Promenade Deck. It was early. Though she could feel the ship's motion cleanly enough, there was another rhythm sounding through the boards. Up from the stern a group of soldiers came jogging towards her. Behind them came their instructor

'Come on, lads,' he bellowed. 'Sing out for the lady.'

The chant came, half sung, half spoken; panted breaths both.

> 'We are strong,
> We are tough,
> Because we eat our Wheatipuffs.'

'She can't hear you!' he shouted. Louder it came.

> 'We are strong!
> We are tough!
> Because we eat our Wheatipuffs!'

She stepped back. They thudded past, faces held in concentration, eyes held resolutely forward, as if the deck in front was devoid of anything but their required presence. Though the instructor winked, she felt cheated. It had never happened to her before, a group of young men acting as if she wasn't there. For an instant she thought only of her gathering age, the signs that hung about her, a husband stewing in self-imposed separation at home, a disaffected comrade at arms sleeping off their once-shared glories in their cabin and she caught between the two. Another group came pounding up behind, followed by another. The ship was shaking with them.

'Four times, apparently.'

She turned round. There he was, her lost marine. She had seen him the night before, up there in the Stadium Bar with the rest of the Marine Band, caught his eye in between one of the numbers. She'd waved, a hidden kind of a greeting, fingers dancing on her hip, but like the men now rounding the corner, there had been no acknowledgement. She gave him a brisk response.

'I'm sorry?'

'Four times round equals one mile.'

'I never knew that.'

He stood there waiting. He looked lost still. Suzanne relented.

'Henry, isn't it?'

'There's a lot of things you don't know about this ship.' He nodded to the garment draped over her shoulders. 'That's a bright colour. You going to wear that all the way down?'

'Why, don't you like it?'

'Remind me not to stand too close to you when we get there. They'll appreciate a good target, the Argentinian pilots.'

'How do you mean, "there"? We're only going as far as Ascension.'

His face furrowed in disbelief, disguised incompetently by an itch he found below his eye. It was enough to raise the first flicker of alarm.

'No, really, it's been agreed.'

'I'm sure it has. Not that anything will come of it. We'll faff around for a bit then get sent home. These politicians always screw things up.'

They moved across to the railings. The ship that had accompanied them since they left Southampton, the ro-ro ferry *Elk*, was tucked in a quarter of a mile away. They were some eighty-eight miles west of Cabo Carvoeiro, the sky already a deepening shade of blue, the air warmer. It would take, what, a week to Ascension, see the men off or bring them home. Two weeks, then, at the very minimum. Two weeks of these young men, their bursting fitness, their pent-up energy.

Another group pounded past.

'You sound as if you're disappointed.'

Henry gave his back to the sea. He had a scar running along the bone of his chin and his fingers, played out on the railing, were fastidiously neat. His eyes followed the running soldiers. His voice was with them too.

'They will be. As far as they're concerned, if we're going, let's go now, and stop mucking about.'

'But they might get . . .'

He turned back to her embarrassed face, both leaning over the damp bar, a foot each on the lower rung, their faces turned in to one another.

'You're a civilian. You don't understand. The point is . . .' He stopped, held his hand out. She knew what he wanted.

'Suzy.'

He looked out again, towards their distant companion, as if he didn't want her to see what he was saying, didn't want her to see his lips form the words. She liked the way he didn't use her name, the way he put it away for future reference.

'The point is they want to fight. That's what all this jogging is about, so that when they get there they can start killing people as quickly and as efficiently as possible. That's what they are trained to do and for most of them, that's all they do, train: Norway, Arabia, Dartmoor. And for what? The back streets of Belfast? But now they've got chance of a real war, when they can finally find out just how good they are. They don't want peace. They want to get out there and kill some Spics.'

Kill some Spics. She'd seen some T-shirts to that effect, but the words, spoken so carelessly, seeded on the wind, seemed incomprehensible. The ship cut through the water.

'Think of them as catwalk models,' he said. 'They have the same arrogance, the same sense of their own unique place; the knowledge that only they can really hack it. There are many women who look like models, some even might even be models, but only the chosen make it to the top drawer. These guys are the same. They know who they are and who the rest of us are not. So they'll thank you for making their cocoa, all polite and well mannered, or cheer their band hoarse, but when it matters, we're all just an arrangement of muscle and vein and dislocated gut. Time to rock and roll.'

'They sound a bloodthirsty lot.'

'In a war, you don't want them any other way.'

'And us a pleasure liner. I saw you playing last night. You were great.'

'We were crap. We should be better when we get to Freetown. We'll be doing something special there.'

'Don't tell me. Your violins.'

He smiled.

'Serenades come later. After it's all over.'

'That's what I mean. There you are giving concerts, there we are, serving cocktails and dinner at eight; toothpicks and silver cutlery and white tablecloths, all the officers dressed in port and cigars. It's hard to believe that . . .'

A movement caught her eye.

'Look! Out there!'

Now it was his turn to look worried. She laughed, back in *Canberra* control.

'You've never seen a whale before?' she said. 'It's good luck to see a whale.'

They often kept them company, attracted by *Canberra*'s bulk, swimming alongside, playing a sort of catch-as-you-can. Sunlight dazzled the water. She drew her hand over her forehead and squinted hard at the heave of black breaking through the waves. There was something wrong. This one was heading straight towards the bow, bisecting the ship's path. *Canberra*'s sirens hooted. The whale kept coming towards them.

'Why don't we alter course?'

Was it she who spoke, or him echoing her thought? The whale drew closer. She could see the gleam on its unearthly skin, sunlight on the patches of age that spotted its side, its great tail flopping back into the water like a soft plane. Huge like *Canberra*, moving like *Canberra*, leviathans of the ocean both. It was so unnecessary, the ship and the whale converging on some arbitrary point, with all the ocean to choose from.

'Make it stop,' she shouted.

Ship and whale ploughed on, white and black, lines of intersection drawn by the hand of their creator. She thought of the white cupola set against the black Roman sky, the Pope's bended head, how he touched her, his fingertips trembling with the might of God's power. She saw the cut of *Canberra*'s hull cleaving the brimming green, the perfect curve of the whale's dome crashing towards it, the priest dancing along the shoreline of her childhood beach, his black cloak rising over the waters in the skirt-pulling breeze. A final spout and long glide and then she saw the whale no more. *Canberra* shuddered. Suzanne ran past the oncoming men to the stern. Below the sea churned a foaming red. Sections of the black body rose and fell in the twisted water. There was a whale, living like her, alone like her, cut in half without a moment's hesitation, a whale no more, just muscle and vein and dislocated gut.

She took off her windcheater and threw it over the side. It rushed away, like a snatched parachute, lifting high in the rushing updraft before floating down. She could see it settle on the bloody wake, arms flailing, body turning, before being dragged down out of sight. A hand gripped her arm.

'What did you do that for?'

She looked round. His eyes were wide, troubled. He hung on to her wrist, as if afraid she was going to jump. She swung her arm free.

'You were right,' she said. 'When we get there. It would have made a good target.'

*

And yet, despite the evidence marshalled before her eyes, it was hard to believe the reality that might lie ahead. The sun grew hotter, the wind dropped. The P&O and navy staff changed into their summer whites. Warnings went out about the dangers of excessive sunbathing. Suzanne slapped on the cream and took no notice. In the afternoon, between shifts she and Tina would take themselves up to the Monkey Island, the tiny hidden deck perched above the bridge, peel off and listen to the activity down on the Sun Deck and the newly formed landing pads below, as the Paras and marines went through their routines: jogging, martial arts classes, teams of eight lifting up huge wooden beams, other units stripping down machine guns, reassembling them, eyes closed, the instructor pacing up and down, shouting in their ear, stopwatch ticking. And when they weren't out on deck, they'd be in huddles, at the end of passageways, crouched on the stairs, listening to their NCOs' litany of combat; recognition conduct, challenges, survival procedures, communications. Boys, that's what they were, not much older than Mark, but already a lifetime away.

It didn't take Suzanne long to fall into her new routine. Tina had been correct. They were Jacks and Jills of all trades, cleaning out the cabins, changing the sheets, brewing up endless mugs of coffee in the little office they had down on D Deck, where men from the middle ranks would drop by after a hard day at the briefings and paperclips. She had never imagined that the army could be such a bureaucratic institution, so dependent on type-writers and telexes, written messages passed back and forth, stamped and dated and clutched in hurrying hands. She had thought of parades and mission-pointing blackboards, officers barking orders and men turning on salutes, not the chase of paper-work, the forms to be filled, the reports to be made, the roll-calls to be taken. Was that what an officer did, apply his scribble to everything? Was that the reason why the rank and file were so resolutely insolent, so contemptuous of their superiors? There was order here, but of a strangely dark-humoured kind. If she spoke to some of her officers like the men talked to theirs, she would have got the sack long ago. Here, it seemed part of an equation. Orders were to be obeyed as long as sufficient ridicule could be extracted. It was all so much more informal than she had expected, different-ranking officers addressing each other by their Christian names, at work as well as in their hours of leisure. They didn't stand to attention much either, nor salute, at least not when she was around. They passed a careful familiarity between them, governed by a set of unspoken but well-observed rules, the first of which was respect rank and don't be fooled by friendship. Between the men of the 3rd Battalion The Parachute Regiment and the two Royal Marines Commando units there lay a well patrolled no-man's-land, mined with barely camouflaged antipathy. Separate accommodation, separate eating times, separate drinking clubs, kept the rivalry far enough apart to prevent any lasting damage, each of them claiming good cause to distrust the other. According to the marines, the Paras were barely human, psychotic creatures good only for reckless bravado. According to the Paras, it was the marines who lost the Falklands, and the Paras who were being sent to get them back. Through the taunts it was the knowledge that each were as good as each other that rankled the most.

And all the time the running, endless, circuitous running. Every day they ran, in the early morning, in the late evening, before breakfast, after lunch, dressed in vests and shorts and ugly trainers, carrying rifles and rucksacks, one poor lad up front cradling something that looked like a large rocket in his arms, close-cropped young men in groups of six, emblazoned with tattoos to mother, to the regiment, to their wives and sweethearts, stronger messages on their vests, what they had done in Northern Ireland, what they were going to do to the Argentinians, what some of them had managed in Linda Lovelace's throat. She came to love the sound of it, lying in the cabin one deck below. Her dreams became infected with their rhythm; winter branches knocking against the porthole, priests with their jackhammers digging up Anglefield Road, Matty building his patio, banging in improbable nails with his bare fists; she woke to them all. They were getting stronger by the day.

But as the exercises grew in number and strength Suzanne began to sense a change of atmosphere. There was nothing new in that. Every voyage took on a particular character: ill feelings, high spirits, a few unguarded incidents could affect the whole cruise. Up in the Crow's Nest it was civilized enough. Dickey mixed his cocktails, Murray fussed with his napkins and made humorously queer comments to the delight of the reporters and the officers, who gently teased each other over coffee and brandy, discussing war and politics and the nature of this Lilliputian adventure. It was different below. Soldiers, civilians, off duty they were mixed all together, a new kind of crew, taking orders, Yes Sir, No Sir, morning noon and night, living in and out of each other's pockets, and with duty done, stretched out, beered up, valves ready to blow. Like all cruises, it was the body which took precedence but there was a kind of nakedness to these men she had never seen before, not simply in terms of the endless parade of their young, fit, flesh, but by the careless indifference they showed to it. She began to understand what Henry had tried to explain. Standing stark naked in the morning for the showers, reeling back along the corridors at night, loud and bravely drunk, their bodies on demand at any hour they cared to name, there was no quality to their physical life that caused them embarrassment or concern. They were both mindful and indifferent to its needs. She could see it in the way they ate their food, the plates almost licked clean, she could hear it in the cheers at the bloody war films they watched, number it by the pairs of off-duty feet jammed up under the railings, as they counted off an extra one hundred and fifty sit-ups before turning into bed; she could marvel at their determination, the ruthless expectations they imposed upon themselves and, despite the ship's reputation, which she herself had played no small part, she could blush at their shameless bravado, as, at any hour of the day, a line of fifteen, twenty would be standing outside the toilets, their intentions made clear by the breast-laden gloss of the magazines held in their hands: the tosser's *Times*.

'You know what's going to happen to us if they allow this to go unchecked?' Murray said, wandering into the crew's Pig and Whistle one evening. 'Forget this talk of Exocets and submarines. Sunk by spunk, that's likely to be our fate. Oh, Mother!'

Two days after the hit and run with the whale (for that's what it was. A civilian *Canberra* wouldn't have treated her so, the passengers would have complained, the captain forced to account to his cruel indifference. But now it was a military ship, no different in intent than a tank, determined that nothing should deflect it from its path. And mind? The troops had loved it, the birth of their *Canberra*, its baptism in blood.) they stopped off at Sierra Leone. Suzanne and Tina were in their cabin when the hooter sounded, and the engines started that slow churn that presaged the glide into docking. Suzanne always loved that feeling, the ship pushing back its power, stirring the calm quayside waters with the turbulent energy of the far-flung voyage. It seemed to her the very essence of cruising, that uneven mix, the adventurer and the domiciled. Tina was sitting on her bunk, painting her toenails green. Suzanne was at the little dressing table, finishing off a long letter to Matty. A page a day she'd managed, with surprisingly little effort. She'd never written so much in her life. They were going to send their first mail out from here, their first delivery was coming in too. Imagine that, a letter from quiet Anglefield Road, dropped in that little pillar box by the station and flown out to this state of heightened unreality. Imagine Matty writing to her, sitting at the kitchen table, holding his biro in that laboured manner of his, palm curved round, fingers facing inwards instead of outwards, proof of his slow immovable thought. Imagine what he might have written, the declarations contained within, the demands he might want to make on her eventual return. Imagine her the same! Imagine him taking control of her life, making decisions! She decorated the last page with a forest of kisses and stuffed the wad into the envelope.

'You coming to take a look?' she asked.

She'd been trying hard to put things right, Tina too. They could still be friends, accept their differences. It was simply that they weren't musketeers any more, revelling in each other's audacity, and the memory of that former conspiracy had grown upon the skin of their camaraderie like the first discoloration of a cancerous growth, fearful reminder of the excesses of the past.

Tina yawned, affecting boredom as much as weariness.

'Bognor's got more to offer than here. You go on up if you want to. I'm going to get some kip. Big date tonight.'

'Big date every night. Afternoons too, if I hear correctly.'

'Dickey's such an old woman.'

'Dickey keeps an eye on us, that's all.'

'So?'

'So, I'll go up on deck and you'll get some kip.'

Freetown lay under a sticky heat, the risk of infection and an ignominious return home, a mosquito bite away. Sleeves were to be rolled down; souvenir hunting outlawed, disembarkation forbidden. The quayside was a tin-shack, shabby affair. The concrete jetty looked flimsy and ramshackle. One knock from the *Canberra* would have it tumbling into the sea. On the other side from the jetty, in blatant disregard of orders, groups of soldiers were beginning to barter with the owners of the little boats that had paddled out, their dugout canoes laden with animal skins and hunting knives, stacks of squawking cages, packed with parrots and monkeys balanced in Babel towers at the back.

Walking over to the port side of the Promenade Deck she saw Dickey talking to one of the Para commanders, but as she made her way towards them, discovered Henry, out of uniform, leaning up against the railing and alone as usual. She always seemed to be coming across him. Was he lying in wait for her, she wondered, like she sometimes now lay in wait for him, taking the long way round past the ladies, when she knew they'd be practising. Was that what it was, the beginning of the dance? She liked standing there, busying herself in one of the storeroom cupboards, one ear listening out for P&O officers looking to be officious, one ear listening to their rehearsals. They were good, she could tell, versatile too. Most days they'd given some sort of concert, a brass band in the afternoon, a rock band in the evening; folk songs, popular classics, dance music, they could play them all. She'd sneak in and watch, move herself into a position where she could see him, where he could see her. And here he was again, another little turn. Slow, slow, quick quick, slow. Henry saw her and threw an exaggerated grimace.

'Not much of a place, is it,' he said.

'We'll not be stopping long.'

'Fuel?'

'Water, I think. You're getting through quite a lot. You're cleaner than most passengers, neater too. The purser has been given the task of going ashore and trying to secure fifty irons and ironing boards. Not that you'd think by the looks of it Sierra Leone was very hot on irons. You wouldn't think soldiers were either, for that matter.'

'That's because you've never gone out with a serviceman. There's not many men here who'd let their wives within spitting distance of their uniform.'

'Well, who'd have thought it, the armed forces, chasing women out of the washroom.' She thought of a week ago, and ironing Matty's shirts and how it had all ended. She wouldn't be doing that again. 'It's given you a thirst, too, all this laundry work. Apparently we're almost out of beer, though how you do it is a mystery to us all, considering you're only allowed two cans a night each.'

Henry smiled and held up his fingers. She felt something then. He had nice fingers, long and tapering, with funny flattened ends; delicate in touch. A man's hands could be lovely.

He crossed one first finger with the other; a counting lesson.

'That's easy. One man goes and collects his two cans, and another ten for his five mates. Half an hour later one of those mates goes and does the same, and so on and so forth until all six have gone and they've each drunk ten cans over their ration. Simple, really.'

He put his hands down, a trickle of desire washing through her, like the first rush of cool water over a dried riverbed. She could feel herself soften, swell. She kept it bright. It was what she was trained to do.

'But not difficult for the authorities to spot, you would have thought.'

He waved that finger at her again.

'They spot it, all right. It's the doing anything about it they turn a blind eye to. The men are getting away with something, and that's as it should be. It's very important in a military organization for the men to think they're putting one over their superiors.'

'What's this with "the men"? Aren't you one of them too?'

'One of them.' He looked towards a group moving towards the side. 'In a manner of speaking, I suppose I am.'

'And in another?'

Before he could answer a young man elbowed his way through and leant over the side.

'Forty thousand gallons of four star, and get your finger out!' he shouted. His mates laughed. Henry looked away.

'One of yours?' she asked.

'Can't you tell? Yes, one of ours. Quite a little talent, our Stanley. Hardest man in the regiment. Or likes to think so.'

'Doesn't look much.'

'Take my word for it. He can look a whole psychiatrist's couch worth when he's a mind to.'

He raised his arm to the shore.

'Oh dear,' he said. 'We've got visitors.'

Down below, making their way past empty petrol drums, stepping over coils of dirty rope and watery patches of oil, a family of four were approaching, their nationality proclaimed, not simply by the Union Jacks each was carrying, but by their dress and demeanour, matronly mother's ankle-deep dress, father's resolutely white legs poking out of empire-khaki shorts, the public-school parting borne on the head of the nine-year-old son, the self-conscious walk of the teenage daughter, the sun shining through the legs of her Laura Ashley dress. The marine who Henry had pointed out put his hand to his mouth and called down to the father as he led his troupe close to where the party were disembarking.

'Don't fancy yours much, mate!'

Laughter.

'Oi, mister.' The man looked up, his eyes full of wounded hope.

'How much to rent your daughter out? Half an hour would do.'

The girl shut her eyes, but he did not stop.

'Do you give a discount for block bookings?'

The girl turned to shelter behind her mother. Her brother stepped forward, and raised his flag, bearing it arm high.

'Rule, Britannia,' he shouted, his voice high pitched, quavering.

'Piss off, you little queer, and take that fat old cow with you,' the marine shouted, turning his attention back to his sister. 'Come on, sweetheart, get your kit off. Show us your tits!'

The cat-calls grew louder. What astonished Suzanne was that the officers standing by did nothing. She was about to go over when Dickey appeared at the young man's side, tapped him on the shoulder. Stanley turned, smiling, enjoying the kill.

'Joke over,' Dickey said.

The soldier bent his head close to the little man, then straightened up.

'Whatever you say, half pint,' he said and turned back to his companions. 'Come on, lads, let see what the bum boats brought.'

They ran over to the other side. Dickey walked back, raising his eyebrows as he passed, whether in regards to her, or what had just happened she wasn't sure. She gripped the rail, her knuckles white and angry. It was the first time anyone on this voyage had caused her displeasure. It meant more to her somehow that a non-paying passenger should have treated them so.

'There was no call for that,' she said, as if including him in her condemnation. 'They only came to . . .'

Below the family were making their dejected retreat back along the quayside, the girl weeping against her mother's arm.

'Only came to what?' Henry said. 'To get a bit of the glory, say they did their bit?' He nodded over to the group of young men, now yelling obscenities down to the boats. 'If this goes through, some of those lads will be dead in a couple of weeks, and they know it. The last thing they want is armchair patriots riding on their coat-tails. They've enough to carry as it is, without that.'

'They didn't deserve that, though. They weren't asking for anything.'

'No? They wanted to be a part of it, at no risk to themselves.'

'What about us, then, me and all the others stuck on this bloody boat?'

'Oh, they love you. You're here for the ride too.' A roar went up. Stanley was working one of the fire hoses onto the boats below. They could hear the angry yells and splashing in the water.

'Don't be too hard on them,' Henry warned. 'Every day they're being fired up. Every evening too. It's got to go somewhere.' He looked at his watch. 'Time I went. Rehearsal and all that. We're putting on the full show in a couple of days, Beating the Retreat. Worth watching if you're free.'

'Try and stop me.' She hesitated, then spoke again. 'You could drop round afterwards if you wanted, in the office. I've managed to wangle half a bottle of brandy.'

There was study in his eyes. She tried to keep hers open, free. Below the mail bags were being bundled out of the baggage port. Alongside it stood six or seven sacks, of incoming mail, Matty's first letter amongst them no doubt, perhaps one from Mark too, even Marcia. She'd be all gracious and concerned, now that Matty had turned in her favour. And she thought she'd won that battle years ago. Henry was speaking.

'. . . but after that I should be OK.'

'What?'

'The string quartet. We're performing for the officers while they have their dinner. An hour and a half should do it.'

An hour and a half. Give herself time to change, do herself up a bit. Just a bit. Something to look forward to. He made to leave.

'Till the band strikes up, then.'

It was too vague for her. She threw in other enticements.

'Oh, I dare say we'll bump into each other before that. The coffee's always on.'

'You make a good cup.'

'I make the *only* cup.'

Suzanne and Tina seemed to be in possession of one of the few coffee percolators aboard. It had attracted quite a crowd, officers, soldiers, dropping in at all hours, showing them photographs of their wives, their children, their girlfriends, their mum, their dad, the family dog. Despite their bravado they wanted to be reassured that there was a home, a loved one, a life after killing.

Back at her cabin she opened the door to find Tina sitting up on the lower bunk wrapped in a bed cover, the small gingery man from the couple of nights before straightening his cap in their dressing-table mirror. A strong smell of male deodorant filled the room. She could tell by the way he looked quickly back at Tina that he was peeved at being found out breaking the rules, and blamed her for the intrusion. He held out his hand, hoping that his winning smile would cover his annoyance.

'Major Osgood,' he announced.

'Who I'm pleased to say was good,' Tina added.

The Major flushed an archipelago of pink freckles.

'The Major's in charge of our area of Darken Ship,' Tina told her.

The Major nodded, pointing to the sunlit porthole.

'Very important, Darken Ship. Man in plane, he find *Canberra*, he bomb the merry effluent out of us. Me here to advise use of big blanket.'

Tina giggled. Suzanne refused to smile.

'I'm sure I can manage to cover a porthole on my own, even if Tina can't,' she said.

'Absolutely. Tina's told me all about you, the lovely Suzanne. A rare cut, so I gather.'

Though disguised there was snobbery in the inflection. She felt angry with herself, for belittling Matty's hands so recently.

'If you don't mind, I have to get changed.'

The Major fumbled with his buttons and left, muttering awkward pleasantries. Suzanne kicked the door shut. Tina got up and, sticking her leg in the sink, began to wash herself.

'You could have been a bit more friendly,' she said

'I think you're being friendly enough for the both of us, don't you?'

'Yes, well this one's special. He may be a major now, but with all this going on, he says the sky's the limit. Been waiting for this all his life, he said, and I don't think he just meant the Falklands.'

'What about you?'

'What about me?'

'The others. Does he realize there's a queue?'

'I'm operating on what they call a need-to-know basis.'

'Tina, Tina.'

Tina held up the wet flannel.

'I'm not the only one, you old prude. It's all Queen and Country on this cruise, Suzanne, Queen and Country. *Canberra*'s queens and my—'

'Yes, thank you,' Suzanne interrupted. 'I think I get your drift.'

Canberra's queens, yes, they too were making merry. There was no reason for it to be a surprise. This was, after all, a ship of men, the older men of the *Canberra*, the young men of the task force. For the old men the *Canberra* was their home, their rooms filled with a lifetime of voyage and lost love affairs. It was the land that swallowed them without a trace, not the ocean: the bedsit in Brighton, a sister's upstairs spare room, their days spent swinging half-empty shopping bags and swallowing G and Ts in their irregular bars, host to unwanted stories and feckless drinking, objects of pity and not so discreet derision: sitting under the sign of the ageing queen. Here however ran a different reign, their cabins sanctuaries of self-esteem, museums of past glories, and most profoundly, breeding grounds for new adventures, each one lovingly decorated in a manner which denoted the care and precision which is the mark of all seafarers, with a certain aptitude for fuss; for they were, all, of a party: lace curtains, damask bed covers, Persian rugs, Moroccan carpets, reproductions of Old Masters, posters of bullfighters and favourite singers, portraits of a much-loved mother, a distant father, a family that had long since cut them loose, snapshots of old boyfriends, their knowing eyes smiling to a fond abandoned past, signed publicity stills of film stars, signed photographs of politicians, taken in the days when VIPs and the wealthy took delight in the Atlantic crossing; Clark Gable, Betty Hutton, Fred Astaire (why, Murray even had one of Winston Churchill, though his arrogant and ill-mannered treatment of the staff, not to mention his insistence of bypassing customs with his crates of champagne, brandy and any other contraband that had taken his fancy had endeared him to no one, save for the waiting press); yes, this was their life, this group of men, tenure on the *Queen Mary*, another on the *Queen Elizabeth*, their accumulations rowed over from ship to ship, packed and unpacked in tissues of cherished memory, now taken root on this *Canberra*; not YMCA gays, moustaches and leather-wear, but the old-fashioned queer family, with the queer-family walk and the queer-family patter; young lovers, old acquaintances, there was fertile breeding ground here.

And yet this was not an ordinary contingent of males, and there had been many, queens among them, who had imagined that despite their obvious attractions (young, fit, away from the restraints of bed and home) these particular two thousand young men would prove highly resistant to any overtures, coming as they did, not from the tried and tested barracks of Her Majesty's Horse Guards, but from the two most ardently masculine outfits in all the armed forces. How would they react to the flicked napkin and the excuse-me corridor-squeeze, the cabin-steward eye-flutter, and that most insolent of questions, asked with pursed lips and clasped hands. 'Any other service sir requires?' A glass in the face? A boot in the groin? An old queen deposed, chucked over the side or stuffed through a porthole. But no. Opportunity came and most definitely knocked. Cabin doors opened, cabin doors closed, men with boys, men with men, but done quietly. Yes, it was Murray, not any of the girls, who made the first conquest, Murray and his fellow tribesmen who patrolled the corridors ogling the bodies, Murray who unwisely regaled the Pig and Whistle with tales of tattoos he had uncovered, of unlikely officers he had seduced, Murray who waltzed into the Pig and Whistle one lunchtime, wiping his mouth ostentatiously, saying, 'Now that's what I call replenishing at sea!'

Though everyone laughed, Dickey hushed him.

'If I were you, Murray,' he said, 'I would keep your recollections for your memoirs. And then publish them posthumously.'

*

In the days after Sierra Leone they sailed into a world of feverish gloom. The sea became heavy, a viscous fluid that seemed to cling to the sides of the ship like oil, their progress barely discernible, the sky bubbling with low sagging clouds, dirty moisture dripping down. The ship's complement suffered too; their blood turning feverish, their temperatures volatile, hot and sweaty, like the weather. It was as if the mosquitoes of Sierra Leone had infected them after all. The drinking became louder, the nights longer. Skirmishes broke out. There was nothing else but the ship and each other's bad company, harnessed in the day to be sure, but at night smouldering in the corridors like a half-burnt bonfire, ready to flare up at the slightest hint of the oxygen they needed; aggression, frustration, desire. Suzanne had been on many cruises but never one so loaded down with the weight of one raging gender. Small wonder the ship felt unbalanced, as if about to tip over into the unknown.

Tina carried on in her own sweet way. James Osgood from the marines, Mike Grimshaw from the Paras, a sergeant from neither she nor Tina knew where. She didn't use their cabin much for fear of further unwanted encounters. Instead she found a small unoccupied bathroom one level below, tucked away in a cul-de-sac amongst the laundry, and sneaked in one of the wicker chairs that used to adorn the Meridian Lounge. Lying in the small bath, her knees poking up out of the water, she would listen to the sounds of the ship, the creak and the roll of the low innards, the hum of the engines, the sudden sound of a pair of heels clacking along the corridor, unlocking a nearby door, someone humming one of the tunes the military band had played the night before, wondering what had placed her in the midst of this piece of unreal theatre. She would sit in the wicker chair and write her endless letter, though why she wrote to Matty at all she did not know. There had been no letter from him that time at Sierra Leone as she'd expected, nor from Mark, nor from anyone. It was as if she had been erased from their memory, or that they simply were indifferent to her fate and feelings. Their silence had made her realize that when it mattered she was alone, and feeling alone, she looked forward to seeing the one man on board who seemed suspended in a similar state. She began to see him regularly, nothing arranged, though she knew the hours he practised, as he knew hers. Sometimes he'd stroll by the office with a mate in tow; sometimes Tina would be there, ready to cast them into other, unwanted waters, but mostly there'd be just the two of them. There was chatter then, in amongst the box of biscuits and the asthmatic cough of the coffee machine. He told her of the improbability of it all, how he joined up and went down to the Royal Marines School of Music at Deal. He told of the regulations governing military bands, of the variations that occur, how if a ship carries an admiral the band is increased by two.

'What, a couple more trumpets?' she had asked.

'An oboist and a bassoonist.'

An oboist and a bassoonist? Who thought that one up? Did that mean they had bassoonists in the marines doing bugger-all until an admiral decided to go for a boat ride? Were their barracks like one of those Second World War Battle of Britain films, with oboists and bassoonists lounging around in armchairs, waiting for the call? She was afraid to ask.

In the evening the band were due to appear, the sky cleared, the wind blew fresher, the sunset now longer, metallic and brooding, but golden, bursting over a vast and sparkling horizon. Ascension Island was only a couple of days away, the prospect of shore leave, swimming, bars, women even, closer by the hour. The news working the rounds held that there was no news. Diplomacy continued, veiled threats crossing from shore to shore, the leaders of the various worlds talking variously to the camera, blowing hot, blowing cold; only the *Canberra* held her steadfast course. Apart from the nobs up top and the nuts-and-bolts navvies below, the whole ship's complement were on deck. They'd earned it. They were all working harder; roll-calls, action-station drills, abandon-ship rehearsals, they all had to do it. Now was the time for them to enjoy some unashamed spectacle. Dickey stood next to Suzanne holding a bowl of peanuts looking down onto new helicopter deck, the decks fly-lined with dangling legs. For the first time it seemed like an ordinary cruise: all the elements were there; an evening's entertainment for the passengers, the day's heat leaking out of the wooden decks, the flat calm of the sea with only a slight breeze to stir the thought.

As they marched out to the roll of drums, the bandleader holding his staff in his hand, like an Old Testament prophet, stern and proud, leading with utter conviction, a great cheer went up. It took her a few minutes to find Henry, although he had told her where he would be. When she saw him, halfway down, she gave a little cheer. Dickey looked at her.

'Well, why not?' she said.

'No reason,' he said.

There were names no doubt for the different manoeuvres they made, names too for the songs they played. Some she recognized but could not put title to; some she could name but had forgotten the words; sometimes her memory surprised her. 'Men of Harlech', when had she learnt that? At school, at home, or had she just absorbed it, part of her British genes? The troops' voices lusted in the breeze. She was surprised at their enthusiasm for such old-fashioned songs. She'd imagined these modern young men would have had no time for them. Yet here, under the tutelage of this band, they sang with an unassuming pride that she had never seen displayed in any other group of youths she had ever known.

She caught Dickey smiling.

'What?' she said.

'Nothing, my dear,' said, passing the peanuts. 'It's nice to see you happy again, that's all.'

As the band turned and wheeled and moved in and out of each other, the rhythm of their boots reverberating in the swimming-pool hollow underneath, it became clear to her that their very history was woven into this march, this pattern, and that this hard-booted beat was as a code, an open sesame, by which the chosen could enter their well-guarded world. Every step that they took had been taken before, every note they played had been played before, every twist and turn, every baton thrown, was but a mould from a previous cast. It was not simply tradition or ritual. It was a source, a way of learning. It was the land they marched over, the seas they sailed upon, the turf where they were buried, the flag in which they were wrapped. Here were their medals and their regimental plate, here the bayonets, the muskets, the spit on their boots. She'd learnt something of the marines' past by now, the Zeebrugge Raid, Crete, Korea. Henry had told her of the band's own role in those darker days, stuck in the bowels of warships plotting maps and marking battle boards, how in World War Two the band had one of the highest casualty rates of all their divisions, and though she had listened and nodded and asked questions in which she had little interest, it was only now, listening to the religious hum that could be heard between each number played, two thousand men utterly silent, as if captured in the grip of their own faith, that she understood. This was their Bible and their Book of Common Prayer; this drum-rolling, this weaving their service, the bandleader their priest, the tunes he led their hymns.

And then something happened. She was watching Henry, thinking of what she knew of him and why she was watching him at all, thinking of Matty at home, wondering what he was doing at this hour, whether perhaps he was writing at this very moment at that breakfast table, or more likely sitting with his feet up, munching cheese and watching television, while she! she was here experiencing history, glorious uncertainty! He would never see such a night as this, and whatever she said, however keen her description, could never appreciate the tears that were welling in her eyes, the quavering that she found lodged in her throat, the grip as she held on Dickey's arm, as they moved from song to song, her nose itching, shivers of yes, patriotism running up the very core of her, like she was in love for the very first time! Matty had abandoned not simply her, but their place in history, left her to fill it as best she could, and it was on this thought that her eyes fell on Henry, Henry who she saw almost every day, Henry who looked down at his shoes and who ironed the most perfect shirts she had ever seen, Henry whose fingers moved so beguilingly over those hard golden stops, her thoughts turning heretical, and in that revolution, with Henry here and Matty there and the priest in his great black cloak shrouding her wicked thoughts, he faltered, whether in turning or tripping over her gaze she could not tell, but falter he did, a ripple of disorder running through the band and then as they regained their equilibrium, another, one of discontent that like a stone thrown, coursed through the audience itself, two thousand hands gripped, two thousand lungs snatching at sudden intakes of breath, a group of marines nearby dipping their heads in shame, a nearby squad of Paras giggling audibly. Scowls and muttering rose up against a current of jeers, then died down as the band resumed its course.

They regrouped quickly enough. 'Hearts of Oak', 'Sailing', finishing with 'Rule, Britannia!'. Without realizing it she found herself singing alongside. Dickey was wiping his eyes with a handkerchief. He looked at her sternly.

'Salt water. It always affects me like this,' he said, shouting to make himself heard.

She nodded and cupped her mouth to his ear.

'I need some brandy, Dickey, for later this evening.'

Dickey looked askance.

'Yes, I know. Can you swing it?'

Back at the Crow's Nest the officers and news reporters were collecting, ready for the pre-prandial drinks. The band had broken through the clouds of despondency. Spirits were high, the banter loud and confident. Dickey let himself in behind the bar and made a point of rummaging.

'Quick,' he said, waggling a bottle of Rémy Martin at her.

She undid the clasp of her bag and hauled it in. A cough sounded behind her.

'Major Osborne,' she said.

'Osgood,' he corrected. 'James.'

'James.' She looked about. The bar was filling up quickly. She had no right to be here.

'Enjoy the show? I did, but I expect you've seen it all before.'

He nodded quickly, ignoring the question.

'We seem to have got off on rather the wrong foot the other day,' he said. 'I was hoping after the meal, you and Tina might like to join us in our little club down the road. We would of course have invited you to dinner, but . . .'

She finished the sentence for him, adding to his embarrassment.

'Staff aren't allowed, yes I know . . .'

'Bloody shame that,' he said.

'Well, that's as may be. Don't forget. I know the cook.'

It wasn't true. It might have been the *Canberra*'s kitchens still, but it was army personnel manning them. They stood there. A burst of laughter came from a group of journalists. One called over.

'James, listen to this.' James waved a hand away.

'Well, how about it?'

The officers' club, neutral ground for proles such as she: interesting conversation, interesting men, flirting for a few hours, on equal terms with the toffs from the P&O hierarchy.

'I'm sorry, I don't think I can.'

'Oh? Tina was sure you'd be free. She's joining us later.'

'I'm sorry, I've made other . . .' She bit her tongue. What was this, acting like some inept teenager, fresh out of school? 'I've got things to do.'

He lowered his voice.

'Well, I hope you're not intending to do them with anyone from the Parachute Regiment, that's all. They are the most frightful bunch, really.' He tapped her bag. 'And brandy is quite the worst thing you could give him. They can't take it, you know, alcohol. Something to do with jumping out of planes all the time. Thins the blood.'

He turned and shouted.

'Isn't that right, Miles? None of you lot can take your drink!'

Suzanne ducked out under the cover of a chorus of indignation. She hurried down to the hidden cabin, where on the bath she'd laid out a razor, her bottle of Chloe and hanging above it a not quite regulation blouse. She sat in the wicker chair and smoked a cigarette while the trickle of water slowly filled the bath. Lowering herself in she wiped her hands dry on her shoulder and lit another. Her hand was shaking. She inhaled deeply, the smoke enveloping the clutch of her heart. Damp from her fingers soaked the paper. The cigarette collapsed free and dropped on the bone between her breasts. Instead of ducking under water, she jumped up.

'What the fuck was that?'

A voice directly outside, the halt of a sturdy boot. She stood absolutely still, the cigarette breaking up, whale flecks sinking as the water slapped from side to side. She held her hand to her mouth, her other arm stretched out towards the door. She'd forgotten to lock it. In the stillness she could hear the echo of a train door slamming and voices on the night wind.

'A rat, you think?'

'A rat! That was water.'

'Perhaps we're sinking.'

'That's no fucking funny. I hate fucking boats.'

'That's what it would be, then. Some Para puking.'

'All right, all right. Let's get on with it.'

A cough and then footsteps, any number of them, heavy and around them laughing and whispering, the banter of aggression and beer, trudging past up to the end of the corridor.

'Right, lads,' she could hear. 'We'll soon sort this out. Marines to the left, Paras to the right. Come on, come on, sort yourselves out.'

There was a shuffling of feet and then, unaccountably the noise of belts and zips being undone. There weren't any showers here. The voice spoke again, but for a sergeant, or any in command, surprisingly softly, as if he didn't want to be overheard. Suzanne wondered whether she hadn't stumbled across some clandestine operation, something involving the SAS or Special Boat Squadron. Stepping out of the bath, she pushed the door tight against the frame, turned the handle and inched open the door. Down at the far end, two lines of men were staring grimly at each other, their trousers and underwear around their ankles. A sergeant stood on either side.

'Right, lads,' the one on the right was saying, 'now's your chance to rescue your regiment from disgrace and dishonour. A bunch of complete and utter wankers is what Sergeant McGloughlin here called us after that little cock-up tonight, and you are here to prove that he is absolutely fucking right. We may be shit at "Beating the Retreat", but as for "Beating the Meat", we have no equals, right? You know the rules. No visual stimulation, no closing of eyes and no blowing kisses to the crap hat opposite. Hold your cock firmly in your right hand and when I give the order, and not forgetting to look directly at the ugly cunt opposite, start wanking. Anybody breaking the rules will mean disqualification for the whole team. First team to complete the job wins two bottles of Scotch.'

The soldier nearest to her put up his hand, short cropped hair, vivid tattoos down his upper arms. She recognized him straight away, Stanley. He was shaped for fighting, she thought, the cockiness, the aggression, the cut of his head. His knuckles were scuffed and bruised. Funny, she thought, that she should be thinking of his fist, considering what he was holding in it.

'I'm left-handed, Sergeant,' he was saying.

'What?' The sergeant walked up to him.

'I'm left-handed,' he repeated. 'See?' He took hold of his genitals in his left hand and jiggled them about.

'Any more advance stimulation, Bembo, and I'll disqualify your whole team. All right, either hand. But not both!'

'No one wanks with both hands, Sarge.'

'How do you keep it off the floor, then? OK, lads. Spit on palms. Grip foreskins. Wanking begin!'

She watched through the crack in the door as men stared at each other with bulging eyes and bulging arms, their fists working away. She had seen a few in her time but never two rows of them. They looked uncomfortable.

'Come on, you tossers,' the sergeant was bellowing, 'let's see some spunk hit the floor.'

Their faces getting redder, the arms and fists working harder, leaning back, their legs half bent, their members jumping up and down, Suzanne was reminded of a row of battery chickens bobbing up and down for their food, oblivious of the indignity thrust upon them. It wasn't as if, in its essence, it was something she hadn't seen before, a man standing before her, performing for both their gratification, but never before had she understood it as pure mechanism, where even desire, or frustration played no part. There was no discernible difference here from all those other times she had witnessed, or indeed aided, their expressions, their urgency, the pucker of their lips. The whole act seemed not only comic but futile, a host of men in their rude, competitive element. She saw their exclusivity, their earnest preoccupation with this ugly bit of gristle, saw too in the strangled clucking sound coming from each of them, that these men, above all others, understood it too. With increasing gasps they started to come, first two side by side, then in response a man opposite, the sergeants walking up and down, ticking off the names on a sheet of paper. For all their noise they make they had very little to show for it. It was all rather like a disappointing firework display, full of exclamations and damp squibs. Then unexpectedly a young lad with a tattoo of Boadicea on his abdomen finished with a flourish, the stuff flying across and landing on his rival's boots.

'Fucking Christ,' his opposite number said, staring down at his defiled footwear, still pummelling, 'you've been saving yourself for Christmas or what?'

'Eyes to the front, Perkins!' the sergeant bellowed. 'You're letting your side down.'

The last Para delivered, and with a cheer pulled up his trousers. Stanley was the only one not yet finished. He was working hard but to no avail. His face bore of a countenance of desperate concentration.

'Come on, Stan,' one of his mates were saying, 'think of Maggie.'

'No talking,' the sergeant shouted. He stood in front of the young man and looked him squarely in the eye.

'Come on, Bembo, hurry up. We'll miss our scoff if you don't get a move on.'

'If I pull any harder, Sarge, it'll drop off,' he complained.

The sergeant bent down.

'That would be the kindest thing. That must be the ugliest penis I have ever seen. Does it have a name?'

'No, Sergeant.' He groaned and then in a frenzy of arm movement fell back against the wall. The Sergeant looked down at the floor.

'I'm sorry, Bembo, but have I missed something?'

'What?' The lad was barely conscious.

'The home produce, Bembo. All those little Bembos scrabbling about in your scrotum. Where the fuck are they?'

'What do you mean?' The boy was panting, his eyes half shut. 'They're on the fucking floor.'

'Well, I can't see anything. Can anybody else see Bembo's contribution?'

The men crowded round.

'You had the snip or what, mate?'

'Perhaps it flew out the porthole.'

'Evaporated on the way down, more like.'

The sergeant looked at Bembo.

'No petrol in the pump, Bembo, that your problem. Who's been getting your gallon of four-star, then? One of those two tarts lording it up in the petty officers' digs?'

Suzy shut the door, her breath quite taken from her. When they had gone she wrapped a towel around her and stood over the globules smeared on the floor, the smell of sperm rising. She wanted to press her sole upon it, stir the mess with her toes. She felt weak, a little sick. She laid the towel on the floor and walked back to the bathroom. She locked the door, washed and dressed. She plucked her eyebrows, rolled on the lipstick. She looked to the mirror in a daze, barely recognizing her own face.

In the cabin, she brewed up the coffee and waited. She uncorked the brandy and took the smallest sip. She checked her hair in the mirror. She busied herself with paperwork, the laundry lists; she replenished the towels in some of the cabins. She listened to the announcements over the tannoy, so-and-so to report to such-and-such an office, reminders of an evacuation exercise tomorrow morning. She chatted briefly to the Darken Ship officer who came by in search of more sticky tape for his blinds. No Henry. She drank a cup of coffee, took another sip of brandy. A party of paratroopers came by, slightly pissed, intent on trashing the nearest commando sleeping quarters. She sent them away happy, with a joke and cup of coffee each. An hour and a half and still he did not come. Perhaps the dinner was taking longer than he'd anticipated. Then a mate of his came past, three of them, kicking a tennis ball. She stuck a note on the doorway, 'Back in ten minutes,' and walked up to the rehearsal room. It was empty, music stands stacked up, like in a school, the instruments safely tucked in their cases each one labelled. She moved amongst them, lifting the labels one by one, McDonald, Combes, Trustcott, and then two together, Henry Hawkins, the trumpet, and the violin case. It was a quartet he was playing in, those others had nothing to do with it. It would be empty. She opened it. Crushed velvet inside, blue, like a lagoon and floating upon it a violin, glowing in brown and reds, like an English autumn, a touch of skin about it, of sensuality. She pushed the clasp that held its neck and held it in the air. It was heavier than she'd imagined. In the far corner of the case, lay a square of white linen handkerchief, folded three times, four times, and a mark of indentation, where he had placed it, between him and the rest of his chin. She slid the violin halfway back in, and picked up the white cloth, held it to her face. It smelt of wax and chalk and something else, Henry himself she supposed. The violin looked like a body in a bath, brown, enticing, arms leaning out over the side. She held the cloth to her cheek, rubbed it once, like she might a peach. There was an unexpected roughness there, no not a roughness, but a ridge of something, an initial. She held it by a corner and let it fall. Not his initials, and not a handkerchief, a napkin, a secret part of him that now she had seen. She folded the napkin back, as best she could, and went back to the office. The notice still hung on the door, the room empty. She sat back down and smoked a cigarette. She smoked a cigarette and had a brandy. She drank another and closed the door.

In the cabin Tina lay on her bunk in a T-shirt, trying to read a book. From her impatient expression, it didn't look like she was having much success.

'I thought you were out with Major Osgood tonight.'

Tina sighed.

'I was. The trouble is . . .' She put the book down. 'He's a bit boring, Suzy.'

'Get away.'

'Don't get me wrong. I still see the point of him. I mean I can't live here for ever, can I.' She slapped the side of her thigh with the back of the paperback. 'This won't last for ever, you know.'

'And what? The Major is your way out?'

'Why not? That's what you did with Matty, isn't it? Married him for the security. Let's face it, Suzy, Matty's a nice bloke, we can all see that, but he doesn't exactly set the world alight, nor I imagine your fire too often either.'

'Tina!'

'Anyway, where have you been? James said you had a date.'

'A date! I was just meeting that, you know, bloke from the band. Henry.'

'And?'

'He didn't show.'

'And you got a little pissed.'

'A little.'

'Any left?'

'A little.'

'Care to share it?'

They sat and nursed dirty glasses, neither saying much. After half an hour Suzanne said: 'Anyway, Tina. I thought men were, well, just an interlude.'

Tina tossed the last of her drink down her throat.

'I know, but he's away a lot on duty.'

And they went to sleep.

*

She didn't see Henry for a while after that, and because of it and the eyes she kept swivelling for one of his telltale spores, the flashed splay of his particular hands, the clearing of this throat before he spoke, his off-duty walk, looking down at his feet, barely registered what she was doing: the linen cupboards she inventoried, the drinks trays she carried, even, the very next night, playing lewd charades with an army medical contingent; all passed in a haze. The Parachute Regiment spent an afternoon shooting clay pigeons from the flight deck. The ship crossed the Equator. The runners kept on running, the telex machines kept on chattering, the paper chase continued, and all the while she walked the decks and corridors in search of a man she told herself she was not looking for, lost in the throes of that old, unwanted complaint. Man overboard was how they described it, or the anguish of the unpulled as Murray once vouchsafed. But however hard she tried, however often she chose not to hover outside the rehearsal room, not to take a short cut down the length of corridor where his quarters lay, wherever she chose not to look throughout that labyrinth of certainty, she could not find him.

And then came Ascension Island and she had no time for him at all. They approached at dawn. Suzanne hadn't slept and unwillingly took herself to the discomfort of the ghostly deck, climbing up to the protection of Monkey Island to get the better view. The gathering light threw unseen shadows across the water and she could see a smudge, something scabrous floating on the surface of the far flat sea. As they drew closer the sea became scattered with spots of indistinguishable colour. She had good eyes, used to defining the vagaries of shape that oceanic distance imparts, and soon began to interpret the blots into shapes and lines, the new world brought into focus. The blurs separated out, but not in

196

multiples as she had supposed but singly; there, stretched out, lay the cavernous length of an oil tanker; there, climbing into the sky, rose the aerial and radar steps of some lonely warship. She scoured the sea for the sweep of an aircraft carrier, the grey bulk of a destroyer, the sharper lines of a frigate, and saw only empty water. Where was the Armada they had been led to expect, the might of the Royal Navy? Where were the great destroyers and battleships that had set sail under such a fanfare? Was this all they could expect; a tanker, a tug, the straggle of a few ships left to fend for themselves?

As they steamed in she read the names on the hulls they passed; the bow-heavy assault ship HMS *Fearless* surrounded by a clutch of tiny landing craft; the half-tiered landing ship *Sir Galahad*, the ocean-going tug *Typhoon* floating on the water like an abandoned trainer; more landing ships, *Sir Geraint*, *Sir Tristram*, *Sir Lancelot*, abandoned knights around a rocky table. She stood in disbelief. Did not the *Canberra* seem bigger than all the rest of them, bigger, brighter, easier to spot? They had been brought to this?

By half seven they were at anchor, close inshore, about half a mile from a flat bit of rock that petered out into the water. There wasn't much to see. What looked like an oil depot on the point, a clutch of nondescript buildings almost dead ahead, the island nothing more than a scrape of reddish rock, a hillock of indeterminate green rising out of the middle: no port, no landing stage, no life visible.

'I never thought I'd say this, but I'd rather be in Gibraltar.'

'Dickey!' He stood there in a gaudy dressing gown, a gift from a grateful Hawaiian gangster. 'Not much, is it?'

'You mean the island or the boats?'

'Both.'

'Don't worry about the boats. There's a lot more coming our way in the next few days.'

She looked over towards the shore. 'I was expecting palm trees, beaches.'

'That's why you won't be allowed on it. To save disappointment.'

'How do you know?'

'Suzanne, please. Such wilful ignorance first thing in the

morning is more than I can bear. I run the bar, remember, where the officers and journalists drink? Where they talk?'

'Yes, we have noticed. Tina thinks you're going native. We never see you in the Pig and Whistle these days.'

'Frankly, Suzanne, their conversation is a mite more interesting than yours.'

'Thanks. So are you going to tell me what you know about . . .' she waved her hand towards the uninspiring landscape, 'this . . . disappointment.'

Dickey began to point with an air of superiority that from any other man she would have found irritating.

'Over there, hidden away from the prying eyes of the press, is an American airfield, eleven thousand feet of mostly virgin concrete. Wideawake is its name, though not normally its nature. If it has a plane upon it at all, it's a weather plane, or a supply plane, or one that got lost or ran out of fuel, or in which the pilot was taken short.'

'Yes, all right, Dickey, I get the picture.'

'However, for these purposes, it is the staging post par excellence, and now bristles with things that ought not to be there: fighters, bombers, transport planes, those funny American spy planes with what looks like the Starship *Enterprise* stuck on top.'

'Nimrods.'

'I'm impressed. Nimrods, exactly. And that's not all. If we were to go round the corner . . .'

'Dickey . . .'

'We would see tankers flying in with aviation fuel. The place is drowning in the stuff. But we are not going to go round the corner because then the journalists would see, and in their excitement might let slip what's going on. But officially nothing is going on. This is an American airfield and the Falklands is nothing to do with them. The trouble is a few snapshots of Wideawake might tell a different story.'

'So what's it to be for us, then? Offloading and then off home?'

Dickey looked at her without mercy.

'Saying it won't make it happen, Suzanne.'

'I can still say it, though. So what, then?'

'The troops are going ashore to shoot holes in the air.'

'I thought you said it was out of bounds.'

'It's out of bounds to the likes of you and me. For them, it's practice time.'

*

Dickey's reassurance quickly changed into substance. Every day new ships arrived. The sea began to feel crowded, the water churning with landing craft and lighters, pilot boats and launches, taking the talk of war, as well as its means, from ship to ship. The sky grew alive with movement, the brilliant blue broken by the gallumph of transport planes, lowering over the horizon like herds of buffalo, swarms of helicopters, their fishnet loads swinging low over the water scattering in their wake. By day the ship would empty, the troops ferried over to familiarize themselves with their weapons; the anti-tank projectiles, the mortars, the Blowpipe missiles. On board, all that had been loaded had to be restowed: stores and ammunition that had come out on other vessels, re-examined, reassessed, moved from ship to ship; stocks broken down into manageable loads. Every day the troops would come back hot and exhausted, but reeking of a hunger that they could not assuage, feeding ravenously, drinking uproariously, singing long into the night.

In the hours in between the ship was as empty as she had ever known it and there was little to do. Dickey and the other barmen would wipe down the empty bar, wash glasses, preparing everything three times over for the officers' return. Suzanne and Tina would move from deck to deck, stripping out laundry, checking cupboard stocks, their tasks similarly drained of purpose. Bored, they would drift into the Pig and Whistle and drink the hours away. Seven days in, Monday April 26th, Suzanne and Tina were sitting down with Murray to an afternoon's Asti Spumante and a game of cheat. South Georgia had been retaken the day before and they were celebrating. The ship was at anchor, the decks bare. The ashtray was full, the bottles mostly finished. Murray was in something of a temper.

'I knew you were telling the truth,' Murray was saying. 'Just knew it.'

'Then why did you accuse me?'

'Well, someone's got to do it. You've been getting away with murder all afternoon.'

The clink of bottles behind him made him turn round. Dickey stood behind him holding two bottles of champagne.

'I'm ashamed of you all,' he said, pointing to the three empty bottles. 'Drinking from the tourists' trough.'

'Dickey!' Murray leaned back on his chair. 'Not come for reinforcements, I hope?'

Dickey shook his head and shot the first cork across the room. It was an affectation he despised, but there were occasions when it seemed appropriate.

'Never seen the bar so empty,' he said. 'Two hours polishing peanuts. It's like when you're on a station platform and see a train pass without any carriages. It looks unnatural.'

He leant across, and placing the bottle on the table began to tidy up the mound of cards in the middle. The others looked at each other but said nothing. Tina had once joked that if Dickey ever gave blood it would come in pint bottles and correctly labelled.

Murray nodded.

'I know what you mean. Wandering about, doing nothing, I feel unnatural.'

'You are unnatural. Do you know the Sun Deck's sagging?'

'Really?'

'I've just seen it. We've taken so much ammunition on board the engineers have had to shore it up.'

'That's what I need,' Murray said, 'some rigid insertions from a greasy hand of toil. It atrophies without regular use otherwise, don't you find, Tina?'

'Forget about your arse, Murray, and concentrate on your hand.'

'That's what they all say.' He slapped the cards down. 'Four queens.'

'Why did I know you were going to call that. Cheat.'

Murray smiled and turned up the four queens lying on top of the pile.

'Fuck.' Tina scooped up the pile. 'I was thinking. What's preventing us from going for a swim?'

Suzanne raised her hand in the air. She could feel the afternoon running into the early hours of the morning.

'How about there's no water in the pool.'

'There's no water anywhere,' Dickey told them. 'The fleet's running out. We've had to lend them some of ours.'

'How do you lend water?' Murray asked. 'Stand waiting at the other end?'

He gripped the neck and drank swiftly from within before passing it along. Suzanne poured hers out into a plastic cup. Murray burped. Tina shuffled her cards in some sort of order.

'I mean in the sea. Go down to the gun port and take a quick dip. I've got my swimming togs on under this.' She nodded to Suzanne. 'So have you.'

'You're mad,' Murray said.

'I'm bored.'

'The guards wouldn't let you,' Dickey told her. He took the champagne back and took a glass out of his pocket. The champagne bubbled up to the top of the flute. Tina held out her glass.

'If I did it topless they would.'

'Tina.' Suzanne threw a warning voice across the table.

'Well, why not? I do anyway.'

'Not on duty, you don't.'

'I'm not on duty. Well, yes I am, but that's not the point. Anyway, I'm not saying we should go topless, only we could.'

'What's this we? Leave my tits out of it.'

'All right, then. I could. Dickey!' She waved an impatient hand. Dickey poured what was left into her glass.

'Frankly, Tina, I don't know whether your breasts would be sufficient enough of an incentive,' Murray pondered. 'I mean, most people here could draw quite an accurate map of them as it is. They'd be much more likely to give us the nod if Dickey stripped off.'

'I can't swim.'

'That's not the point, ducky,' Murray said.

Suzanne came to his rescue.

'He could play us a tune, on his trumpet. Music while you shirk.'

'You mean like he did in the old days, on the *Queen Mary*?'
Murray sighed. 'Now there was a ship.' Dickey stood firm.

'I still don't advise it.'

'And why not?'

'Because you're all drunk.'

'And your point is?'

Dickey shrugged and waved the unopened bottle.

'Careful with that,' Suzanne said. 'We'll need it afterwards.'

'Would that be after the swimming or after the court-martial?'

'Court-martial? You have gone native, Dickey.'

'No, no. It's just . . .' He aimed the bottle at the ceiling and
pressed with his thumbs. 'I've been drinking too.'

The cork shot up and bounced back into Murray's groin. Tina
slapped Murray on the back.

'Don't worry, old fruit bowl,' she said over his wail of pain.
'The water will anaesthetize it.'

They went down via the cabins: Murray's to put on some
underwear, Dickey for some medicinal brandy. Tina snuck into
Suzanne's cabin to get some towels. By the time they made their
way through the stairs and passageways to the gun-port doors
on E Deck, most of the second bottle of champagne had gone.
The door was open, the lip of the hatchway opening onto a fresh
wind, smeared with a hint of oil. Somewhere down the corridor
they could hear a convoluted joke being told. Guards probably,
slacking.

'There's no one here.' Murray sounded disappointed.

'No need for the altogether then,' Tina said.

She pulled her top off and stood defiant in a matronly blue bra.

'I thought you said you had your bikini on,' Suzanne said.

Tina blushed.

'I changed. I thought this was more appropriate, you know,
looked more a spur of the moment thing, if we got caught.'

'Well, thanks for telling me.'

Suzanne stepped out of her dress. The white swimsuit seemed
to expose every imprudent moment of her history. She turned to
Dickey.

'Do you think this is a good idea?' she asked. He opened his
coat. Inside hung the trumpet.

'Dickey, Dickey.'

Murray was shaking in his underpants, his arms wrapped around his thin white body.

'Who the fuck's that on your boxers?' Tina asked, unzipping her skirt.

Murray looked down to the face on the uneven bulge.

'Mother Teresa,' he said. 'A present from Lourdes. She doesn't look very happy, does she?'

'Looks like she's got an abscess.'

'Come on, if we're going.' Suzanne stepped out onto the platform. To her left hung a frame of thick rope trailing down into the water. The ship rode on an unexpected swell. She felt dizzy.

'Come on, Tina.'

Tina hesitated.

'I don't know if we should,' she said.

'It was your idea.'

'I know, but . . .'

Tina stepped back inside. Suzanne looked out towards Ascension Island. A plane was sinking down behind the scrub of buildings. She could hear the sea below her, the coughing chug of an overflow pipe. Tina called out again.

'Suzy. Let's go back and polish off another bottle.'

Suzanne closed her eyes. She thought of Matty's gazing up to her cliff-top pose, the priest sitting on the pebble-strewn beach, her dress flapping in the breeze. She thought of Mark and the way he stared upon her unbuttoning hands, how Henry had caught her with his steady gaze. She thought of her life in the world and the constancy of eyes upon her, wishing for a moment to be rid of them all. She jumped out into the sea. She dropped in at speed, the water closing in. She dropped through ice and waterfall, through crevice and ravine. She dropped through leafy forests and cloudless skies, her arms straight, her feet pointed, her body falling with her. She was brilliant white and cascading green. She was limitless, devoid of time, free of everything but herself. Then she broke the surface, gasping, the bubble broken. The swell took her up, then away, then back into the ropes.

'Christ.'

She turned and kicked herself free, three, four yards. The sea was deep and strong, a cradle for her power. The *Canberra* rose out of the water an iron-clad giant. She threw her head back. Dickey stood tiny, a tower block away, Tina by his side.

'Tina?'

Tina shook her head and held a towel to her mouth.

'Come on, Dickey,' she called out. 'You promised.'

Dickey took the trumpet out and lifted it to his lips. The tune floated down. Suzanne recognized it immediately. She shouted back.

'. . . to see the world,
and what did we see, we saw . . .'

She gulped down unexpected water. The sea swallowed her. She spluttered back to the surface. She felt both clear-headed and muddled. Henry had a trumpet too. Was there some significance in that? Angels blew trumpets, didn't they, looked down from on high. Was that what they were, Dickey and Henry, her guardian angels? Or had they come to worship her? The sea slapped her back and turned her about again. She was beginning to lose her sense of direction. The world was bright, but a brightness that made everything hard to see. The ship was near, but an ocean away. The water was warm, but she could feel the heat pumping out of her like blood from a severed leg. What was she doing there? Was this fun? Dickey and another man were calling out, beckoning furiously.

'What?'

'Sharks,' Dickey was shouting. 'He says there's bloody sharks about.'

Suzanne turned, looking back across the surface of the water. She could see shapes underneath, dark unspoken things that seemed to move while keeping still. She could feel the water dragging her into unknown depths, the ship leaning over her, as if about to crash down upon her, and crush her into oblivion. Tina was a blue cheerleader, holding a pompom towel, jumping for her team across the water. The voices rose in pitch. No one had said anything about sharks. She struck out for the ship. It was out there she knew, the restless fear that roamed the seas, always on the lookout, always on the prowl, in constant motion just under the surface. It was at her heels, snapping at her legs, ready to take hold of her and carry her down into the very depths. She looked up again but was too near the ship to make sense of the heights above. She was at the base of the cliff, trying to grab hold of Beachy Head. Head tucked into the water, her arms dipped in weakened curls she kicked for the rope. Five strokes later she hadn't moved. She heard the shouts and kicked again, holding her breath as she knew she mustn't, but holding it anyway, to give her the burst of desperation she needed. The sea responded. A sudden surge swept her within an arm's reach. She lunged forward but the swell knocked her away, to teach her who was child and who God. She cried out and surged forward again, her feet pushing against a tumbling landslide, her hands scrabbling at the rough ground of the hanging rope, before being dragged down again. She waited this time, letting the water bounce her on its giant knee, regaining breath, hearing a voice she thought she recognized say, 'Suzy, Suzy, is that you?' teeth tugging at the memory of dark duplicity. The ship was an iron fence and the sea the means to climb it. Another rush came up behind her and she rode upon it up to the rope's face, her face jammed against the coarse mesh. She grabbed at it, her legs slipping on what they could not find, grabbed at it with her hands and her arms, one leg kicking against the hull, the other caught in the unseen tangle. Then the water let her go and she hung there, free and battered. She stayed for a moment then placed her foot down, let it slowly take the weight.

'Come on, Suzy, you're OK.'

Dickey.

She began to climb, her head jammed to the side, as if afraid to admit to anything she had done. As she did so she felt a resistance, the sea pulling her back perhaps, or a tentacle of something fearful, and she jerked up against it and felt the string around her neck break and the crucifix slide down, caught for a moment on the divide of her breasts. Her hand went for it and feeling herself unbalanced, she threw herself back, the chain falling past her the clutch of her belly to rest on the arch of her right foot. She stared down, knowing that if she moved the chain would fall and that if she did not the sea would rise and take it from her, confiscate the Pope's gift because she no longer deserved it. He had pressed it into her hand, a sign of things to come and she had abused his trust. With the crucifix gone she would be lost; maybe not only her; perhaps Dickey, perhaps Henry, perhaps the whole ship, the whole enterprise. Who knew the damage she could cause. The chain slithered across her instep, the crucifix swinging over the deep. Carefully she lifted her left foot and placed it across her right, pressing the chain between the cold flesh. If she raised her body up slowly, using only her arms to lift herself up, as she used to in gymnastics when she was younger, she could save her crucifix. She would lift her feet together, as if they had Roman nails hammered through their bones, letting her arms take the weight as she lifted them to the next rung. She would do it slowly, without fuss or complaint. She would save them all.

'Suzy, get up here.'

Dickey sounded anxious. She gripped her hands tight and took the weight of her body to her arms. They trembled with fright. She lifted her feet off, her arms half bent, her body, her life, hanging on her hands. She pulled her knees up slowly and looking down, raised her right foot up to the next rung. She pushed slowly, rising inch by inch, until the weight had travelled down her arms and spine and back into her legs. The chain was still there.

'Stop mucking about.' Dickey sounded exasperated.

The water came and kissed the sole of her foot.

'Shut up,' she said.

She held on to the sides and counted to ten. She knew she could do it now. The fear had left her, her strength, her fitness, her innate agility returning. God had thrown a test at her, and though it had nearly slipped through her fingers, her hand was closing around it now. She hung on the length of her arms again and raised herself up. Without pausing she did it again; and again. Dickey and the other man's arm reached down to pull her up.

She spoke sharply.

'No.'

'What the bloody hell you playing at, Suzy?'

'There's something on my foot.'

Dickey looked down.

'If you think I'm going to risk my life for an ankle bracelet.'

'It's not the ankle bracelet. It's my crucifix.'

Dickey was not convinced. The man spoke.

'It's OK. Hold my feet, chum.'

He leant out and pulled himself down, his head brushing past her back and bottom.

'Hold still.'

She felt his hands run down the back of her legs and feel his way towards her feet. She felt the chain move as he wound it round his finger, then the scrape of discomfort as the crucifix was pulled free. Then he was up and they were pulling her on board.

She stood up. Murray and Tina were putting on their clothes. Dickey stood there, sweating. Henry stood next to him. In his hand lay the crucifix.

'The chain's broke,' he said, letting it curl down into her hand.

'Thanks.'

'Don't thank me. Bloody fools, the lot of you.'

He turned round to Tina, speaking sharply.

'Get one of those towels round her. She's shivering.'

Dickey snatched it from Tina's hand and wrapped it around her shoulders.

'Sorry, Dickey,' she said.

'Bang goes my pension,' he said.

'If they get to hear about it.'

They all looked at him.

'You lot bugger off quick before anyone else sees you. I'll look after her.'

He took her back to a small anteroom, four chairs and a table. Another bandsman sat by a chessboard.

'This is Ian,' he said. 'He's just going back on watch, aren't you?'

Henry waited outside while she pulled off the swimsuit and dressed. Her body was cold and clammy, strangely exhilarated. She spoke through the half-open door.

'I wasn't in any real danger, was I? Those sharks, that was just to get me back.'

'Oh, they're sharks all right, worse than the ones on board.'

'Very funny.'

She opened the door, the cigarette packet in her hand.

'I don't suppose you've got a light?'

'I don't smoke. How about a cup of sweet tea?'

He sidled in and with his back to her, fiddled with the kettle on the floor. She felt herself shaking and didn't know why.

'Thanks for . . . for saving me. Saving this, anyway.' She jiggled the crucifix in her pocket.

'Don't thank me,' he said, 'I'd be for the high jump too, if this got out.'

'No wonder you didn't turn up that night. You know when to avoid trouble.'

'It wasn't that.'

He stood up and turned. For the first time she noticed that his face was cut and blotchy, one eye nearly closed, the bruise yellowing, as if it had been there a few days.

'Jesus, what happened to you? You slip or something?'

He grinned, touching the swelling below his eye.

'I'll say. Didn't you see it? Everybody else did.'

It took a moment for her to register what he had said. Her nodded, reading her change in expression.

'They don't like it when you let the side down. Especially if it's in front of the Paras.'

She remembered young Stanley, his cock peeking through his scuffed fist.

'Does it hurt?'

'Not as much the contempt. It's my own fault. I wasn't concentrating.'

He dug into his shirt pocket and pulled out a pink envelope covered in strangely childish handwriting. There was a smile to him now, but not one brought by humour.

'Someone's trying to wind me up.'

He fished out the letter, pushed it across the table.

'Read it.'

'No, I shouldn't.'

'I'd like you to. Please. It's driving me mad.'

Dear Henry,

You don't know me, but I have just met your dad, who is ever so proud of you and I promised that I would write to you.

Him and me watched the Canberra *sail away last night. He*

was really upset that he wasn't allowed to see you off. We all
tried to make it up to him. He was really proud of you and so am
I and all my friends.

How long have you been a marine? Everyone says that they
are the best soldiers in the world. We are all so proud of you going
to save the Falkland Islands, and the islanders.

It would be great if you wrote back. Thinking of you out
there on that boat and hearing your dad, makes me think of
how lucky we are to have soldiers like you, and how lucky we all
are to be alive.

So look after yourself. When you come back we could meet if
you like. Here's a picture of me taken last year (don't laugh!) by
the seaside with my mum and her new bloke. It's the only recent
one I have. I'm the stroppy looking one! Your dad says he's
going to bring me one of you when he's next in town and I'm
going to put it up in my room. The last thing I'll see every night is
you and the last thing you will see is me!!!!

Your dad is a real poppet and never tries it on.

Amy

She handed the letter back.

'Lucky you. At least you got a letter, unlike some.'

'Oh?'

'It's not important. What's she like, the girl? Pretty, I bet.'

He shook the photograph out of the envelope. As young as her letter, way below his years.

'Well, you can't win them all.'

She handed it back. He stuffed it back in, without a glance.

'That's not the point. I don't have a father. Or mother. I'm a Barnardo's boy.'

'Really? I've never met one of you lot before.'

'Yes, you have. They just haven't told you.'

'You mean they're ashamed?'

'If you like. There's something about us that unsettles people. It's as if it's our fault, to lose both, no matter what; car crash, illness, murder and suicide; it's as if they didn't really want you, didn't like you; that death was the only way they could be shot of you. People think that being an orphan leaves you scarred. It doesn't. It leaves you tainted.'

She pointed to the letter.

'So what's all that about?'

'That's what I'd like to know. How is it she's met a father I've never known, knows my name, what I do, where I am? How could that be?'

'Write to her and find out. Arrange to meet her when you get back. That's what she wants, isn't it?'

'When I'm back.'

He looked away, towards a distant self, soon to vanish. He could have had it written on his forehead.

'Don't even think it,' she said.

'What?'

'You know. The "I'm not coming back" thing.'

'I'm not the only one,' he said, 'there's two guys in Four Two who feel the same, and it isn't because they're superstitious or they think they'll screw up. They just know. And I know too, have done the first moment I heard we were going. This is it for me.'

Was there a better line, she thought. A faded burst of gunfire sped over the water. This is it for me.

'It isn't just proper soldiers that die. We'll be going, all of us, you, me, this bloody boat.'

'Do you think it'll be dangerous, then?'

'Dangerous?' He laughed. 'On this, sticking out on the water like a floating Taj Mahal, with no cover, no armour, no guns to speak of? Dangerous? Jesus.'

'But we haven't been told anything.'

'Read the signs, Suzanne. I've spent the last week humping compo.'

'Compo.'

'Army field rations, dried this, dried that. What one needs when there isn't a first-class restaurant nearby.'

He sounded almost contemptuous, not only of her ignorance, but her status as a civilian. Military culture.

'It's hard to grasp. It's still the *Canberra*. How long do you think?'

'Not long. The weather's closing in down there.' He looked to the door. It was theatre she knew, but she moved her head a little closer just the same. She could feel his breath on her.

'You want to know the date, the exact date?'

She nodded. He started using his hands again.

'Listen out for request for blood donors. Soldiers tend to spill quite a lot of the stuff in battle, so we'll all be expected to chip in. However, they'll want to give the men time for their bodies to get back into shape. Six days is what it takes the red blood cells to replace what's gone, ten days to get the lads back into tiptop condition. So as soon as you hear the announcement, start counting. You won't be far wrong.'

He splayed his fingers out, shaking them in emphasis. The priest was right after all, the priest on the long shore, the waves breaking, her dress blowing, in his hands the rolling clatter of white stones, the blackness of his cloak, the hem of her dress, the mystery of them both and why they were there, staring at each other; what she knew of him and what he knew of her: 'Everything you do is contained within you now,' he had said. 'There is no going back on the glory of your sin,' and though she knew not what he meant, she knew it to be true, that she was what she was, and would ever be that way, her legs bared, her head full of unknowing knowledge, and knowing that she would remember him, she had turned and run away and never saw him again. There were places she had not to go, things she had not to do, it was all done for her, her life.

She touched Henry's face with her fingertips.

'It needs attention,' she said.

'There's some medication in the cupboard.'

'Not this sort.'

She led him back up to her little room and sat him on the ledge of the bath. She bent down and brought her lips to the bruise, the colour of blue plums. It tasted of brine and antiseptic; it felt both soft and rough. He blinked his eyes and took her hand, held it there calmly, like a child might. The coldness had vanished, but she was shaking still. She slid her fingers round his and brought them to her mouth then slid them back down. She leant across, the fall of her unfettered breasts brushing his face and turned on the tap, then kissing him to the sound of running water.

'Why don't you take your clothes off?' she said. 'I'm going to run us a bath.'

He looked down at his feet.

'You might think this odd, but I'm not very used to this sort of thing. Not used to it at all, really.'

'Well, just sit in the chair and think about it.'

With Mark and the priest watching, she nearly added, swirling the water with her hand, going over to him, sitting over the rough material of his uniform, unbuttoning his shirt. She touched the bruise again, ran her finger down his face, moving to the zip on the back of her dress.

'I've just remembered,' she said, pushing it from her shoulders. 'I've left my swimsuit back at your place.'

He tried to rise up, as if to get it. She pushed him back down.

'I don't need it now, silly.'

Strange that he barely looked at the uncovering of her, or rather, how his eyes seemed only interested in her own, his hands reaching out as if in the dark, unaware, not of sensitivity, but of order, location, blundering almost in his haste to hold her with his eyes. The Pope had looked into her eyes, seeing what she must bring to the conflict, warmth, peace, a woman's simple humanity, to guide the wholeness of him and the ship through times of this jagged danger. This was the clink of round pebbles and the scent of the Pope's parchment skin; this was the commuter train and her teenage dare, Mark's trembling hand and his buried words; this was the reason for the embankment walks and the hours of her bawdy cabin nights; this was why she had plunged into the sea, washed her history clean, why the sea rolled and her heart rolled with it: this tiny room and the sound of water running through her hands, the bend of her flanks, how she turned and walked towards him, strong and smiling in her purpose. He would cover the storm calmly now, even when lost, disfigured. Even if it were true that he was not going to return, he would end his life remembering these coming days, and how it started, the bathwater sloshing from side to side, the manner in which she led him to it, his knees and legs wedged down, embarrassed, remember how she knelt down, her breasts flattened on the cold enamel, her head ducking down, her mouth searching in that tub of sweet apples and how later, they lay wet on the puddled floor, lost on a swollen sea.

Wary of unknown submarines, that night was the first night

Canberra weighed anchor and set to sea, the first night the order to Darken Ship became official, Henry's shirt hooked over the meagre porthole while they lay atop a bed of blankets, the ship moving in lovely motion, nothing for them to see, only to hear and feel, a sense marvellously deprived, except for the occasional use of his flashlight for the matches she had found, the glass of water he needed to refill, Henry in her arms and she in his, a man bound for war standing guard over a boy unknown, a Henry without a future, without a name to call to the past. Henry in her arms, above and underneath, Henry uncertain, unskilled, the knowledge of his imperfections adding to his hesitancy. Such deficiencies meant nothing to her, indeed she welcomed them as proof of the worth of her cause.

'I should be getting back sometime. The lads will notice.'

'I dare say they will.'

'How about you.'

'I'll think of something.'

'If we can keep it quiet.'

She stroked his unseen face, blotting memory.

'We're safe enough here,' she said. 'This is our place now.'

'Until it's time.'

'Something like that.'

'And after?'

She sat up, felt for the light and played the beam on his face.

'I thought you said you thought you weren't coming back. Or was that just a ploy?'

'Don't be silly.'

He took the light from her and shone it round the room once, the stark walls, blank stare of the locked door, the wicker chair in which she'd first made love to him, tipped up in the bath, and they lying wedged between the bath and the outer wall. How could such a meagre setting take on such beauty, she thought, a pagan temple in the moonlight, now turned to God. Then it was dark again, and he moved upon her, the first time without prompting.

'So you still think you're not coming back,' she said, settling in.

'Now more than ever.'

'Don't say that.'

'Why not?'

'It makes me sad.'

'This, this makes you sad? Oh, that I'd had such unhappiness before!'

*

She never saw him much during the day. He was busy loading stores, exercising with trial helicopter embarkations, scrubbing out the Meridian Room in preparation for its metamorphosis into an operating theatre. Often after work he and the rest of the band would be taken off to play for other ships: *Sir Percivale* one night, HMS *Fearless* the next, but always there would be the return, the clatter of the helicopter, the warning whistle of the pilot boat. Each evening, when the men had returned and the ship was under way, as they left Ascension Island for the anonymity of the dark, she would walk the length of Sun Deck to their private room, and wait for him; the hours of their greatest safety, held when the ship was at its greatest danger, out on the dark sea of history, with nothing but her body and the Pope's crucifix to protect him. She would make up their bed, lock the door, and do the rounds, returning at ten, eleven, when all was quiet, waiting for the sound of his soft footfall coming down the corridor, she lying on their little bed, sometimes a little drunk, sometimes a little sober, listening to the tapes he had lent her on his Walkman; stuff she had never heard before, piano music, sonata something, soft and mysterious, like the touch of his flesh, like the touch of her own, music that you could almost reach out and feel it was so alive, so like an inner inexpressible you. They listened to it together sometimes, heads bent together, sharing the headphones, as it rose over them like a warm incoming tide, their bodies lighter, their thoughts erased, floating in tranquillity. It was hardly human, she thought.

Diplomacy died. The airfield at Port Stanley was bombed, their aircraft destroyed, great craters blown into the runway. A Total Exclusion Zone was placed around the Falkland Islands, the might of the British navy sent out to enforce it. They began shelling the Falkland shoreline. The war, if that's what you could call it, seemed to be going their way.

Then came the first news borne out of the sea, rising like a wraith out of the deep: the sinking of the *Belgrano*, an Argentinian battle cruiser, struck by the very thing they feared themselves, as if the sea was now redolent with a deadly organism, ready to strike unseen, without warning. To a sailor that was the worst part of it. A plane might come out of the sky, bombs falling, a battleship might loom up over the horizon, guns blazing, but a submarine would track you night and day, playing an unseen game of cat and mouse, spying on your invulnerability, letting loose your ruin without so much as a battle cry. No roar of engines, no flare of guns, whistle of bomb or air-sucking shriek of shell, just the silent ripple of water, the thread of your destruction. The news came while she was in her office. She did not know the details, that this battle cruiser had been originally an American ship, the *Phoenix*, commissioned in 1938, fought the air assault on Pearl Harbor in '41, had helped in the evacuation of Java in '43, taken part in the reconquest of the Philippines, didn't know that Peron had bought her in '51, named her *17 de Octubre*, or that after his fall her name had been changed to the *General Belgrano*, after one of the leaders of the 1810 revolution. She did not know that the ship was an old ship, destined for retirement or that the day she had been swimming, 26 April, she had sailed out of her operation base of Ushuaia in Tierra del Fuego, the ice-covered mountains capped by clouds that hung like motionless sentinels over the glacial splendour of the bay. She did not know that the crew were in the main cadets, fresh out of naval college, that the ship was well maintained, the crew keen, nor that their adversary the nuclear submarine the *Conqueror* had been following her for two days. She did not know that the *Belgrano* was ploughing along on a line parallel twenty miles outside the Exclusion Zone, that her task was to watch for any British approach from either the east or from around the Horn, nor that the weather was fiendish, the brutal chop of waves running three to four metres high, the near freezing temperature whipped up by an ice-covered wind that blew at fifty kilometres an hour, nor that the ship was in what the Argentinian navy called a *crucero de guerra*, one third of her crew at battle stations, one third working, one third resting, nor that when the attack came it came twice, the first torpedo hitting her amidships on the port side, destroying her operations centre, blasting upwards through four thick steel decks, the second striking four seconds later, fifteen metres from the prow, ripping the bows away from the hull, the men enveloped by titanic waves of heat and smoke and steam that rolled over and carried them to oblivion. She did not know the details, just the fact, delivered blandly over the tannoy, but the cheer that she could hear reverberating through the ship died away almost as soon as it was delivered. They were sailors too, now. They played cards, they sat writing letters, ate in mess halls, lined up for showers and shits, looked out onto dread beauty of the water, inhaling diesel fumes in their sleep. They trusted their ship, the familiar growl of her engines, the pitch of her hull, the living innards. They knew the implacable hostility of the sea, how it would kill you in five minutes, have you drifting to eternity on an ocean of sleep, rolling on the cold vastness of the deep. And were they not in a similar condition, large like the *Belgrano*, crammed with men of military bearing like the *Belgrano*, a symbol of nationhood like the *Belgrano*, but unlike that unlucky vessel, white, undefended, alone; a ship out of her waters?

She walked round to the rehearsal room, hovering round the half-open door. She could see him with his back to her, talking, waving those hands about. One of his mates saw her and gave him a nudge. He hadn't managed to keep it that quiet, then.

He came out and pulled the door behind him, speaking before she could say anything. It was if he was irritated by her presence.

'I can't meet you tonight,' he said. 'Not after this. We want to be together.'

'Together? Aren't you that most of the time? I thought you might . . . with me.'

He reached out a quick hand.

'It's not as clear-cut as that. I'm a part of something. This is real now. This is not going to go away.'

'You'll just get drunk.'

'With a bit of luck. It's not that I don't want to see you. It's – this is my life, my family. They need me. I need them.'

'What about later?' She despised herself for saying it. He looked around.

'Give me a couple of days. We'll be sent out a lot, to keep morale up. We have to keep our own up too.'

'I thought I might help in that department. Keeping your morale up, not to mention other things.' Oh, the paucity of Tina speak! He said nothing.

'Two days, then?'

'Two days, fine. Look, I've got to get back.'

She spent a couple of hours in the Pig and Whistle talking to no one in particular. Dickey was on duty, Murray too. Tina was nowhere to be seen. She walked back into the cabin. Tina was on the sofa with a young soldier, her eyes half closed. Two empty bottles of wine stood on the table alongside half a dozen empty cans of beer. His hand was planted firmly within her blouse. As Suzanne shut the door he leant back, burped, stretched out his legs and moved his hand slowly round Tina's right breast.

'We got company, girl,' he said.

Tina took a swig from the wine bottle she was holding and held it out.

'Say hello to Stanley,' she said. Suzanne felt herself starting to blush. It was the left-handed soldier she had seen in the competition.

'Hello to Stanley.' It was an old routine. It sounded rather tired.

'Heard the news.'

'Yes?'

Stanley tipped the bottle up.

'We're celebrating.'

'He caught my eye this morning, didn't you.'

'That I did.'

'Tell her how.'

'You tell her. I'm busy.' He smiling straight at Suzanne again, his hand slow and deliberate, as if he didn't care.

'I was standing talking to his commander, what was his name?'

'Major Osgood.'

'That's right. Major Osgood.' She looked at Suzanne firmly. 'I was passing the day you know, as one has to with the officers, and Stanley here came up with some report he had to make, all dressed up in his battle gear and beret, looking very . . . very prim and proper.' She giggled. 'And then he saluted. Go on, Stanley. Show her what you did.'

She pushed him off the sofa. The man straightened up. He had dark hair, dark eyes, a touch of cruel mischief about his mouth.

'Stanley's in a rifle company,' Tina called out. 'But he doesn't like saluting.'

'Bad place to be, then, the marines.'

'Go on, Stanley, show her!' Tina ordered.

Stanley drew himself to attention.

'Up close,' Tina ordered. 'She won't see otherwise.'

Stanley took two steps forward, and saluted. Tina put her hand in front of her mouth. Suzanne looked round, puzzled.

'His hand,' Tina told her.

Suzanne drew back. Down the length of Stanley's little finger, a scroll of tattooed letters. 'Go Fuck Yourself.'

'That's what the officers see, every time he salutes,' Tina explained. 'Isn't it a scream.'

Stanley held the salute while running his eyes up and down. It was nothing she hadn't come across before, nothing she couldn't handle and yet, there was a indifferent intensity to it that unsettled her.

'Well, it's novel,' she said, holding his gaze. 'What does Major What's-his name think of it?'

'Who cares what that prick thinks. He's a total wanker and when we get there I hope he gets his bollocks shot off.'

He lowered his hand, they hung by his sides. He swayed a little, not knowing quite what to do next. His knuckles she noticed were still grazed.

'Any more questions or can I get back to the matter in hand?'

'Feel free.'

'Care to join us?'

'I'm happy as I am, thank you.'

'Do something useful with this, then.' He threw her the empty bottle and fell back. Tina caught Suzanne's questioning look.

'He's all right really.' Her words slid into each other. 'We've just had rather a lot to drink, haven't we, sweetness? Murray should never have given us that extra wine.'

'I don't know how you stand it, with all these fucking poofs on board.'

'Stanley's in . . . machine guns, isn't it? He ran past me this afternoon with goodness knows what jiggling up and down. More than one weapon, haven't you, lover?'

She put her hand to her mouth. Stanley tipped a near empty beer can over her face.

'One 7.62 calibre SLR accurate to a range of 300 metres; one 9mm Stirling sub-machine gun, range 200 metres; one belt-fed 7.62mm General Purpose Machine Gun; one 66mm Light Anti-Tank Weapon; five L2A2 grenades; five No. 80 White Phosphorous grenades, banned by the Geneva Convention; and lastly my cock, which isn't.'

He squeezed the can flat and let it drop on the floor.

'Are we going to fuck or what? 'Cause if not, I'm going.'

He looked round.

'Tina?'

Tina was fast asleep. He prodded her, without success.

'Fuck it. She's passed out on me!'

'She's had a long day.'

'She's had half my fucking beer ration, I know that. Fuck.' He looked up. 'What's your name, then?'

'Suzy.'

'Mine's Stanley.'

'She told me.'

'Right. She's pissed.'

'Aren't we all?'

'You're not.'

'Not very, no.'

'Perhaps she thinks I'm not good enough for her.'

'I'm sure that's not true.'

'What about you?'

'I think you should get some sleep.'

'I could get another bottle.'

'Not tonight.'

'Another night, then.'

'We'll see.'

'Tomorrow?'

'Let's talk about it in the morning.'

'I don't want to talk about it in the morning. There might not be a morning.'

'I think we'll last the night, don't you?'

'I'm eighteen, you know.'

'I didn't, no.'

'My father was a hangman. Bet you didn't know that either.'

'No.'

'Hundreds he hung.' He corrected himself. 'Hanged. Hanged's the word, not hung. Did you know that?'

'Can't say I did.'

'He'd get proper riled if you said hung. Hanged, that's what they were. He never talks about it but all the time, if you see what I mean.'

'Don't think I do.'

'Always there, hanging over us.'

'Very funny.'

'True, though. He's probably killed more people than any cunt on this ship will. All except me, that is. I'm going to kill coachloads.'

She felt a sudden chill, as if the cold cut of danger was slicing into her. Bend with it, that was what she'd learnt.

'You're aiming to beat his record?'

'It's going to be a good war for me. Stands to reason, with it being my name we're taking back.'

He turned towards her.

'How about it. A quick one. Don't you think I deserve it?'

'It's not a question of you deserving. It's a question of me wanting.'

'What about me wanting. The cunt that's going to die.'

'Who says you're going to die.'

'Who says I'm not? Say that I am. Or say that I'm going to have my legs shot off. What would you do then, if you knew. Eighteen years old, bollocks blown to fuck. Wouldn't you put out for me then? If you knew this was my last night.'

She found no easy answer to that.

There was a knock on the door. Major Osgood stood outside.

'Oh, I'm sorry. I thought . . .' He stopped when he saw Stanley.

'Bembo.'

'Sir.'

'What are you doing here.'

'Just escorting the lady back to her cabin, sir. Just about to leave, sir. Goodnight, miss.'

Major Osgood stood there.

'I know it's nothing to do with me,' he said, 'but I wouldn't advise socializing too easily with the men. It could cause all sorts of tension.'

'You're right,' Suzy said. 'It is nothing to do with you.'

He nodded.

'You've heard, I presume?'

'Of course.'

'Just been listening to some bleeding-heart on the BBC wringing his hands in horror, saying we're not playing fair. What do they think war is? It's about killing people. Killing theirs before they kill yours.'

'Yes, I know that.'

'They bloody don't.'

'No, I don't think a lot of them do.'

'What they don't realize is that's it's the best thing that could have happened.'

'Oh?'

'You want to know my reading of the situation?'

'Please.'

He crossed his hands over his trousers and straightened up, like he was about to lecture to a bunch of recruits. Stanley was right, she thought. He looked a complete prick.

'They'll run for cover now. Their navy isn't up to it, their air force isn't up to it, and their army definitely isn't up to it. To my way of thinking it's all over bar the shouting. I'll tell you one thing, though. We'll have to give our chaps something to do before they return or they'll go back to Blighty and rip the place apart.'

Tina began to snore. He looked round.

'Is she all right?'

'It's been a tiring day.'

'Right.' He hovered. 'Well, I better not wake her.'

'That would be best.'

'If that young man bothers you, just let me know, all right.'

'That's very considerate.'

'He's a bloody good soldier, Corporal Bembo, though a bit

rough round the edges. Tried to get into the SAS. Did a route march on a broken ankle. They were so impressed they asked him to apply again.'

'So why's he here?'

'He punched one of their officers. Knocked him clean out.'

'You sound proud.'

'I am. I respect the men and they respect me.'

'That's how it should be, I guess.'

'That's how it has to be. Without respect you're fucked . . . pardon my French.'

'It's quite all right. I share with Tina, remember.'

He leant forward.

'Well, I'd better go, then. Good night, old thing,' and before closing the door, he bent down and kissed her. It was affectionate, a lonely man yearning for nothing more from her than a little motherly appreciation.

She sat down and laughed.

Old thing.

*

The ship grew subdued, the dining room dimmed with low voices, the sergeants' mess awkwardly formal, the Pig and Whistle half empty, the drink consumed not in celebration but in grim sympathy. On the Monday after the sinking it was confirmed that the *Belgrano* had gone down with the loss of over three hundred men. The next day Suzanne sat in the crew's bar waiting for the clock to run to six. Henry had come by that morning, promising to meet up at around then. She'd told him she'd make it as best she could. She could hardly keep still.

At five thirty she walked the length of the half-empty ship, the decks cleared, a few men perched on the containers watching her progress. The light was turning, not dark yet, but softening, and she carried a little bag with her, a bottle of good German wine, a bag of olives, some smoked-salmon hors d'oeuvres that Murray had nicked from the officers' mess for her. Though *Canberra* was due to sail soon, it was too early for Darken Ship that day, and lights still bled out from the rooms lining the Promenade Deck, the blinds not yet drawn down. Save for the distant ring of a telephone the ship was silent, the complement resting momentarily from the day's activities. Her heels click-clicked down the wooden decking and she recalled Anglefield Road and the silence of it the first time she walked down it on a summer's late afternoon, with an overnight bag in her left hand containing amongst other things a little necklace for Marcia folded in blue tissue paper and the set of principles she was about to abandon, a black calf-leather bag slung over her right shoulder, the smart two-piece she was wearing, tight, a little sexy, emphasizing her independent vigour, with the lampposts and the trees and the dip in the road, and the rise of a small wood at the end, hiding what she knew to be the station; not a pretty road, an expansive road, but a road with an anchor, a road moored alongside a steady present, its course well set, and she now the new passenger. As she walked down towards Matty's house, on the right at the very end she had been told, holding the grip, conscious of her walk and who might be watching, examining her as they might a sculpture, her front, her profile, her rear, registering the differences in the houses she would come to know, the gardens, some tidy, some spartan, some simply neglected, her observations were broken by the slowing rattle of a commuter train, she saw herself suddenly, opening that carriage door, stepping down to this certainty, walking back down this road, noting the seasonal garden changes, dropping her bag in the hall, walking through to the armchair, the garden seat she might sit upon. She had warmed to its determined seclusion, the way it came unequivocally to a halt and closed in on itself; a train station, a cul-de-sac: a railway carriage, a front door: a whole world here, a whole world beyond.

A flurry of oily smoke belched out from a ventilator. She remembered the scent of that evening, of faded gardens and late summer, the rustle of the trees, porch lights floating in the gathering dusk like little craft tucked up in the safety of their harbour. She had insisted on coming this way, not to be met at the station as if she needed a guide to be escorted into hostile territory, but to arrive in her own time, to mark herself out from the very outset as sovereign. 'Expect me sometime after late afternoon,' she had said, knowing that she was going to turn up several hours later than that, after her hair had been done and she'd bought her gift for

Marcia. She had walked down the middle of Anglefield Road as if it were an abandoned railway track, emphasizing its arterial seclusion, noting the For Sale sign where it opened out, the errant hedge that engulfed the nearside path, opposite across a barren plot, a dark-haired woman, pale, hollow, standing intent by a downstairs window, a cat reclining in her arms, like her owner staring unashamedly at the clip clip clip of her progress. 'That's right, neighbour,' she thought, 'take a good look. There's not many that come down here like me. Not to your house, not his, not any. Take a good look. A change is going to come.' Hadn't she seen the world, done outrageous things? Wasn't she set apart, ready to steer this Anglefield Road into more adventurous waters? Oh, she wanted its security, the flow of its gentle currents, but she would need to row it out to sea every now and again, set it to ride a wave or two.

'All right, darling.'

She nodded to the squatting soldier, warming, as she did then, to the challenge of his stare. It had been a short walk, from the woman's stare to Matty's front door. She had rung the doorbell, wincing at its shrill tone. She would have preferred chimes. She waited then rang again. It didn't do to be kept waiting. She had been about to ring again when the door was thrown back and there he stood, Matty a little out of breath, the first time she had seen him away from the *Canberra*, a dry-land man, master of his house. He had looked older, nervous. The land did that to you, took the sparkle out. His dress was more conservative. Gone was the gaudy holiday gear. A Marks and Spencer Vyella check tucked into green cords; suburban country. One hand hung onto the latch, the other dangled by his side, unsure of itself. She had expected him to say something but he hadn't, just beckoned her in, as he scoured the road. She stepped in, making a quick inventory. A narrow hall, carpeted stairs, the smell of paint; two water-colours of somewhere Mediterranean between two cream doors, on the wall opposite a plaque, some sort of award and a dusty brown raincoat and a poncho hanging from a set of old-fashioned hooks; heavily patterned wallpaper, a solitary shade hanging from a length of brown flex, the house darker than she'd expected, the look not as modern; disappointing but with room for improvement, space in which to make her mark. She took another step forward so that he might close the door, the push of air washing up against the back of her legs. In the nearest room she could see half an ugly three-piece suite looking out onto a decent-sized lawn. French windows would be better, she thought, French windows and garden furniture on a patio.

The door closed behind her. Something clattered in a back room, like a saucepan lid rattling under steam pressure. Now what? She had thought this over many times, how to play their reunion: the insatiable lover; the prospective wife, the sympathetic step-mother: Let's go to bed, I'd love a cup of tea, or How's Marcia? The middle route seemed safest, shown up to the spare bedroom, a wash (that's what they did, respectable people, freshened up) then a gin and chit-chat, wine over dinner, cigarettes and crushes on the sofa, raising in intensity until it was time to put him to bed eager and frustrated, the spare room door closing until later landing manoeuvres.

Then he came up behind her and placed his arms around her. He smelt of cooking.

'You came, then?'

He sounded surprised. That was good. She leant back into him a little and he hesitated, unsure whether it was accidental. He didn't know then, bless him, that with women, contact like that was never accidental. He didn't know now either.

'Hope your hands are clean,' she joked. 'I've just bought this.'

'Oh God.' He took his hands away abruptly. She turned.

'As if I care, stupid.'

She took his hand and wiped it up and down her jacket lapel.

'There, that satisfy you.' She looked down. 'My God, what's that?'

A red smear ran down the cream wove of her jacket.

'Tomato. I've made a spaghetti.'

'Jesus. Where's the kitchen?'

He bit his lip as she wiped it clean with a wet dishcloth.

'I'm so sorry. I'll pay for the cleaning.'

It couldn't have worked out better; apology, confusion, the ground taken away from him. She threw the jacket on the table and put her arms round his neck.

'Pay for the cleaning! The way you're getting me to take my clothes off, you're probably going to have to buy me a whole new outfit.'

He disengaged as diplomatically as he could, indicating the room across the passageway.

'Marcia,' he whispered.

She pulled back, trying to keep her face as open as she could.

'I thought she was coming down tomorrow.'

'She couldn't wait to see you.'

Anchored, always anchored. She had got the better of Marcia then, even though she had spent the night alone in the spare room, Marcia on guard in what was then her own room upstairs. In the morning Matty had come into her room with a savoury tomato tart, baked not an hour before in his shop, and held it warm against her cheek and broke it into her mouth with stubby trembling fingers, the pastry crumbling, the taste strange at that time of day, unsettling, and sitting upright, his fingers touching her lips, brushing the crumbs back onto her lips, she thought of the priest with his folded hands lying on his black cloak looking upon her wickedness and she could wait no longer and had taken him in her mouth there and then, before anything else, before they had hardly kissed: a sacrament of course. And he had wanted to cry out, but he could not for fear of what his daughter would hear, his hands clenched in unrealized release and even at the time, in the suppression of his gasps, the smothering of her loud intent, she realized that it was a bad start, to give licence to such imprisonment, to stifle the first moments of their physical expression, and though later they moved Marcia down into the basement, and in time she had moved away, it had never changed. There was always Marcia in the next room, inhibiting their every move. And this Henry had no Marcia, no Marcia, no mother, no father, no one but himself. Was that his great attraction, that he looked to no one, only to her, as she looked now only to him. 'Do you know,' he said once, lying on their cabin floor, his hand roaming in the dark, 'if we were to swim out now, like you did, and look back, it would be as if this ship were not here. It's like as far of the rest of the world is concerned we don't exist, all there is an empty ocean. Only here do we exist. Out there we evaporate into nothing.'

Nothing? What was Matty if not nothing? What was Anglefield Road if not nothing? Did she know it better than this ship? Apart from his habits, did she know Matty any better than this man, waiting for her now, waiting for her? Ah, let Marcia take up her station again, let them have each other and their flock-paper memories. Let them reclaim Anglefield. This was a better road.

She walked the full length. No running now, no groaning, no exhortations; no buzz of planes, no hoots, no sirens, no splash of cable. The ship was silent, recovering; the sky black-blue, the island dark, invisible, and she alone, walking with destiny on the huge and empty deck.

She knocked on the door, though why she did not know. He opened it.

'You came, then.'

'I'm late, sorry.'

He closed the door behind her. She hung her arms round his neck, tried to engage him, quickly aware of her own unrestrained pulse and the tension in his. She pulled back, trying to mask her disappointment. He looked changed.

'You OK?'

'I'm fine. Tired. We've been doing a lot. More to come.'

'Tonight?'

'Tonight. But I'll be back later. That is if . . .'

She pressed a finger to his mouth.

'I brought some nibbles. Officers' fodder.'

She laid it out on the side of the bath.

'They look good.' It was an automatic reply.

'They are.' She fed him a wedge of smoked salmon and biscuit. He ate it without interest.

'Are you sure you're all right?'

'Quite sure. It's getting close now.'

'Really?'

'Really.'

'I missed you yesterday.'

'Did you?' Again it was said almost blankly.

'Yes.'

'Three hundred, you know.'

'Yes, I know.'

'It's a fuck of a lot.'

'Yes.'

'Three hundred. More.'

'It's . . .'

'Yes, what is it? Good, bad, fate, the hand of God, an accident, a grotesque design, a tempered response. Which one would you choose. They're saying it wasn't necessary, on the radio, that it put to end to peace talks.'

'I thought the bombing had already done that.'

'Who knows. No one had been killed, had they?'

'On Georgia they had.'

'Only a few. Not . . .'

'Three hundred.'

'More than three hundred. It takes everything away from you, all the playing and practising, what we've done, bleeds it dry. Three hundred dead in the blink of an eye, their mother's sons. Everything they thought, said, did, gone. What were they doing that was so terrible?'

'They were on a battleship.'

'It was outside the Exclusion Zone. Even the military acknowledge that.'

'They were inside the General Warning Zone. Who knows, a few days' time they might have done it to us.'

'Someone still might. Now more than ever. There'll be no going back now. This is just the beginning, you understand that, don't you. It's death now, death and disfigurement. The whole bloody thing. That Schubert I've been playing you, the piano music? Chuck it away. It's all a bloody lie. What did fucking Schubert know?'

'You don't talk like a soldier.'

'I'm not a soldier. I'm a bandsman, standing on the sidelines of war, there to pick up pieces. I work under the same regulations, the same rules of engagement, trained in their basic weaponry and tactics, treated as one of them, but I'm not.'

'And if they asked you to go, to carry compo under fire, to play something on a battlefield?'

'They wouldn't ask. It's not Rorke's Drift, you know.'

'But if they asked.'

'I'd go.'

'For why?'

'I'm a marine, a bandsman.'

'Exactly.'

She moved to him again, and this time his arms responded, his hands running down her back, back up to her bare shoulders.

'We should eat,' she said.

'We should?'

'They'll curl up at the edges otherwise.'

She leant back and fed him another canapé, his lips licking her fingers, his mouth delectable with morsels of food. She took an olive, passed it to him through her mouth. Lovely flirtatious intimacy. Voices could be heard, calling down the corridors.

'Not looking for you, I hope.'

The voices grew louder, not simply from nearby but all around.

'What's going on?' she said.

They opened the door. They could hear the whole ship burbling, men running up and down, shouting.

'Come on.'

They ran up the narrow passageways towards the launderettes. There were in permanent use, in a permanent state of disrepair too. As they approached they could see a couple of engineering ratings standing amongst the guts of a broken tumble-dryer. Murray was next to them, a mess of white shirts half hanging out of a washer. None of them were talking, just staring at each other.

'Murray,' Suzanne cried out. 'What's up?'

Murray turned. He was trembling with anger.

'The bastards,' he spat the words, his mouth flecked. 'They've sunk the *Sheffield*, the bastards. Sunk the *Sheffield*! They're for it now. The bastards!'

SIX

Marjorie switched off the radio, then the television. She'd been dancing between the two all morning, in case further bulletins broke. She felt only an unresolved uncertainty, an impatience, as if there was a conspiracy amongst the Task Force and its commanders and communicators to keep the information she so needed from her, as if all the other news surrounding her was but a smokescreen, designed to obscure the picture she wanted so much to see: the *Canberra*, whereabouts unknown, fate undecided. After that first evening, when she and Hector had sat in front of the television waiting for Richard Roach to appear, she had thought about little else, and the fact that this was not the *Canberra* had both relieved and disappointed her; relieved that it was not that ship in ruins, disappointed that, yet again, there was still no word of her condition. Relief and disappointment: the two had cancelled each other out, leaving a void where her emotions should be.

She drifted back up to the bedroom, poking her head through the trail of green, hearing sounds of Hector doing something with the ladder, setting it against the side wall, intending to paint a couple of the upstairs windows. Hector had made himself scarce lately, ever since the business with the book. Starting that up again without telling her, breaking into her defences like that when she'd had her day planned out. It's what she did, how she'd survived all these years, planned her days, filled them with activities, jobs in the garden, work in the charity shop, cooking for the WI. Plan the day, plan the week, and the hours and years take care of themselves. Since seeing the *Canberra*, though, her days had become longer, full of unexpected, unfulfilled gaps, commitments falling through her hands. Last night she'd sat by the window imagining the dark surrounding the great ship and the souls aboard, how it must invade their sleep; how they would wake every day to a new uncertain dawn, the growing light not giving clear comfort but exposing them to fresh danger. Hour upon hour, it ebbed and flowed like the rise and fall of the sea, the hours of dark awash with the danger of being unable to see, the hours of daylight bright with the fear of being seen. Was her life any different, the day, the night; from where did her peace of mind come? As if in response Anglefield Road had turned restless, the cries of cats, the rumble of trains, the echo of distant thunder only adding to her sense of agitation. At some hour, an argument had broken out up the road, a whisper of hisses, a car door slamming, a clatter of feet, and then, a quiet, as if conspiracy were let loose. Only Hector's breath brought any sense of calm.

She let her dressing gown fall to the floor and sat on the edge of the bed, one hand kneading the heavy folded hang of her stomach. Like an old discarded waterskin, she thought, or one of those slack holy cows, given wide berth on the teeming pavement. She had thought of getting an extra hour's sleep now that he was outside, but conscious of her ageing body, of all the things it once was, and would never be again, she didn't want to be conscious of its discoloration, its stubborn foibles, the way it had let her down, any more, certainly didn't want to lie next to it and its vacant possession and try and persuade it to heed her resolve. She hadn't been sleeping well since the day of the parcel, the day Matty and Suzanne left for the *Canberra*. It was the ship rather than the book that had unsettled her, or so it seemed. It wasn't as if she was worried about Suzanne. She had never been close to her. As for the Roaches, she could take them or leave them. Patsy was the only one she had any time for, helping her out with the twins, trying to smooth the worry lines from her face. It didn't really matter to her who lived in Anglefield Road, as long as she was considered the glue of the community: liking any of them didn't come into it. The fact that they were there, recipients of her unflagging kindnesses, her unnecessary gifts, was enough. It was Hector who had insisted on following Ellen's diktat to watch the six o'clock news, Hector who got on with Richard, who understood his dogged determination, his primitive conservatism, Hector who would have done anything to try and dilute the bitter taste of his morning's brew. They had sat balancing their dinner on their knees, and watched

Richard's boss and some young girl being interviewed with a soldier from the marines, but with no sign of Richard, no sign of Suzy or Matty either, just the *Canberra* looming up in the background, and soldiers scurrying to and fro in the back; a group of marines aping grins for the camera, a minute later a couple of bandsmen, or so she presumed, judging by the music stands they were carrying, the whole scene one of a hurried orchestration. There was something about it that set her nerves alight. They'd been on the ship themselves, years before Suzanne had ever worked on it; Hector in his biannual attempt to make her see the world afresh had booked a Caribbean cruise without telling her. She'd have told him not to waste his money. There was nothing wrong with her figure then, but sunbathing had never appealed to her, stretching out like some errant slave, nailed to the captivity of fashion, and in truth she hadn't enjoyed it, not the sun, not the cities, nothing except for sitting in the bar up at the very top, the Crow's Nest, a glass of madeira, looking out in the endless heave of the unknown, thinking how marvellous it would be to drown, to be enveloped, become part of an eternal immeasurable life. She had sat there for hours, the little barmen trying to coax conversation out of her, Hector bundling up in dogged enthusiasm, trying get her to take part in a table-tennis tournament, or game of cards, while all she wanted to do was to float away, never come back. She began to understand how a body could watch the sea and want for nothing else; how the sea could be all things; how she was she nothing. Now, winding spaghetti on a plate, it was as if a switch had been thrown. She began to take note, not of the young woman and the soldier and the half-embarrassed conversation that was being concocted on their behalf, but beyond, towards the ever-moving backdrop of the ship. What was it that had stirred her? Memory, a soldier's wave to an unseen wife, the way another had bared his bald head to reveal a tattooed British lion, or was it simply seeing the soldiers clambering aboard, their precious lives tucked away in their kitbags, hoisted on their shoulders, marching willingly up the gangway, lives which she could only inhabit by intuition, like the life of her own, blank pages the lot of them: a ship carrying her book of dreams. Since then she had striven to bend her memory to the *Canberra*'s survival, to conjure in her mind its rooms and passageways, the noise of its engines, the pitch of its haul, above all the sight of its clean prow, cutting through the clear water. She had dug out their old photograph albums, their box of holiday souvenirs; maps, wine labels, postcards of hotels they had liked, found photographs of Hector on the deck in shorts, Hector on the deck in flannels, Hector on the deck his arm round someone she had no memory of at all. Tucked into the back lay a brochure of the *Canberra* itself, the Bonito Pool and the Cricketers' Tavern, the Observation Deck, and yes, the Crow's Nest and the wide sweep of window, through which she had foreseen her long years of internal solitude. She felt inhabited by the vessel, as if something of hers had remained there. Was that it? Had they carved their initials on some wooden balustrade, or was she remembering those who had served them on board, the little barman with his fussy waistcoat and proud ways? If she closed her eyes she could walk the length of it, find her way to the cabin, C Deck, remember the face of the lone friend she made, a young girl unhappy on her honeymoon, crying her hopeless love out in the ladies' loo, her husband mysteriously absent in the hours she had expected him to be at his most attentive. Was it simply these things or was it more than that the construction of the thing itself and the unknown lives it housed. A floating house, full of young men, suddenly parentless. Yes, that was it, boys alone, boys adrift, boys at sea. It had always been like that for her. That's why the Barnardo's box still stood on the downstairs table, with what – a few loose buttons inside. She had always known about them, Barnardo's, everybody did when she was younger, they were more visible, especially in the summer and Wimbledon fortnight. If it hadn't been for the tennis half the country would have never heard of Dr Barnardo's, but thanks to those fourteen televised days nearly everybody did. It was how she got involved, watching that match on the television. '61 it was, the men's semi-finals, the contest evenly balanced between the Czech and the Australian, the Australian lean and lanky, like a chair leant against a ranch veranda, the Czech dark and compressed, like an axe in a thick forest, both a cliché of the nation's physique. The match had been close, hard fought, the crowd equally divided, knowing that they were witnessing a battle of the mind as much as the body. The first set had gone to the Czech, the second to the Australian, Marjorie wanting the Czech to win, if for no other reason than she liked the way he buried his head in his hands in the change-overs. The third set was the most bitterly fought, the play the most dazzling, as if the players knew the worst they could do was lose brilliantly. Then in the third set a snatched serve, a double fault had led to a possible break of serve, and the Australian taking the crucial third. Love–thirty down and serving to save the set, the Czech had shot the ball straight down the centre line and into the net. Instead of one of the Barnardo boys running to pick it up, both of them charged out, heads down, racing for the ball. A roar in the crowd went up but too late for them to stop, smacking into each other like a couple of battling billy goats. They'd both been felled, one laid out flat on his back, the other sitting half dazed up at the net, rubbing his scalp. A couple of St John's Ambulance men had taken the stricken lad off on a stretcher. The Czech had walked over to the other boy, whose fault it plainly was, and cuffed him lightly in admonition, and though he did it to the accompaniment of the court's laughter, there was an edge of anger to his action. The boy had robbed him of his concentration. The match had resumed, the Czech losing his serve, the set and later the match, but she hadn't followed it much. Her mind had taken a stroll down to the one Barnardo's boy remaining, and the injustice of his solitude. There were boys without parents, then, as well as parents without boys, the wound she supposed more or less as deep, the shame of their isolation just as acute. She'd done the rounds with Barnardo's years ago, been angry with them when they'd failed to deliver up that which she knew they did not possess. Safe, the page had read, Safe. Safe how. Safe where. Safe?

The next day, with the picture of the two boys sprawled across the papers, she had written to them and asked if she could become one of their collectors, which she did unflaggingly until the methodology changed, and the little money-box houses which she used to hand over so proudly were replaced by envelopes slipped through the door. An envelope was all very well but it wasn't the same as having a house in the hallway, which a family saw every day, reminding them of what it was they were, and the good fortune that they took for granted. The heart had been taken out of it, taken out of her too. But they had kept their house. It was a difficult thing to discard, that solid detached residence to which a couple might aspire, their children safe, its little doors and windows closed, its yellow ochre walls, its brick-red roof solid and secure. Their box has not been used for years, just as Dr Barnardo's boys and girls were not used for Wimbledon any more, the same way that orphans were not visible, the same way she felt she was not visible either. What was she to everyone in Anglefield Road, to the charity shop, to the town. A woman with a trowel? A teacake? A woman of no significance, whose life was as her garden, untended by approval.

She looked at the bedside clock. Ten o'clock. She'd dropped off for half an hour, without meaning to. Dressing, she left a note for Hector and stepped out into Anglefield Road. It was going to be hot. She was already beginning to sweat. She'd have to wash under her arms when she got to the shop. There was nothing worse than knowing you smelt in a shop full of customers. She liked handling old clothes, checking the pockets, mending the wears and tears, trying to erase the fact that a life had been lived in them, a life that had slipped out of reach, that lived somewhere else, inhabited another world. She and Hector dressed almost exclusively from the shop themselves, even underwear. It was easier for her, there was greater choice, but Hector had to take what was going; one week a country squire in full tweed and brown brogues, the next a retired major, brass buttons and cavalry twill. He had even accepted the brown serge lapels of a lounge lizard. 'Here, see if this fits?' she had said and he'd put it on saying, 'Very nice, very nice, Marjorie.' There was nothing left of him really, that's what it was, nothing left at all.

The air swam with honeysuckle, drowning the sour scent of perspiration. Across the road she saw Richard Roach standing by an upstairs window, biting into a piece of toast, a cup of tea in the other hand. She waved, unsure whether she should or not, whether he would appreciate being seen. He was in a bedroom, after all. You could never tell with Richard, the hidden scuttle of his thoughts. Ellen, why Ellen was an open book, that cat of hers, the way she held it, buried her head in its fur, the long strokes she gave it, for her fingers' pleasure as much as the cat's. Single bed or double, Ellen slept alone, floating on a sea of agitation.

She waved again. Richard opened his mouth and turned away.

*

'What?'

Ellen sat up. Richard stood over her holding out a cup of tea.

'They've sunk a ship.'

'The *Belgrano*, yes I know. Richard, I was asleep.'

'No, one of ours, the *Sheffield*.'

The teacup rattled in its saucer. He was shaking with anxiety or rage, it was hard to tell which. He'd been obsessed by the Falklands, ever since he'd got back from Stevenage reading out newspaper reports over breakfast, glued to the television the moment he walked through the door, even ringing her up from some telephone kiosk in Luton the night they'd announced the retaking of South Georgia. She couldn't care less about it, not the island, not the Task Force, still less about a bunch of Argentinian sailors drowning eight thousand miles away. At least this made it more interesting.

'Sunk? You mean without a trace?'

'No, Ellen, I do not mean without a trace. But with a substantial loss of life. Least, that's what they're saying.'

Ellen took the cup of tea from him and listened to him marching back down the stairs. It wasn't just the Falklands. There was the matter of the untruth. Here was a Richard she hadn't known before, prepared to lie, to carry it through, to act upon it as if it were fact. The night he'd come back she'd watched him park the car badly, a sure sign that he was preoccupied, then sat back on the sofa, feeling sore, waiting for his entrance. She'd heard him come in, wiping his feet, the right foot twice, the left foot once, a curious always repeated discrimination, as if the foot he put forward first was more likely to be mired in the detritus of the day's difficulties, the action of a fearful man, worried for the contamination that he might bring through the front door. Then came the flap of his briefcase as he pulled out the evening paper. He brought it home every night.

'How did it go?' she had called out.

236

'Not bad.' His voice had been almost chatty, brighter than usual. Would she have noticed had she not known what he was trying to cover up? 'Did you see it?'

The resonance of that question still disturbed her, to be wrong-footed so immediately, so unexpectedly, when it was she who should have been able to anticipate all the moves. After all that, she'd forgotten to watch it. They'd been in a bar in the centre of town, playfully arguing about the importance of poetry, of all things, and she hadn't even glanced up at the television, blank up on the pub wall. Kevin had been trying to convince her that the gift of poetry was that it brought greatness to the ordinary, a sense of distilled occasion. Ellen had countered that that was exactly what she disliked about it, the funny voices people put on when reading it, *telling* her it was special. The conversation had grown animated, flirtatious. It was one of those arguments whose sole purpose was to prepare the ground for forthcoming sex. Well, Richard had repeated, voice off-stage, had she seen it? Part of her had been tempted to strike at the very heart of Richard's deception, to say that she had not only seen it, but seen him there too; let him gnaw on that little conundrum. She stuck her hand out in anticipation of his approach.

'I'm sorry I didn't ring back like I promised. Karen invited me out for a drink.'

'Karen?'

'You know, the charity shop. Nearly New? Where I got your dinner jacket.'

'Ah, yes. The Dead Man's Outfitters.'

He had stepped through the door reeking of drink and curry. She only hoped there was nothing similarly revealing on her breath. On her body lay only memory. He bent down, kissed the top of her head and dropped the paper in her lap.

'They didn't want me on the box, I'm afraid.'

She couldn't resist it.

'So I noticed. Everyone else seemed to be there. Sir Douglas, Kevin.'

'Kevin?'

His voice had turned sharp. She had stared at him, aware of the duplicity burning on both their faces, conscious too of vast areas of unknown terrain that lay before her. The conversation had suddenly taken the form of a walk across an unmapped minefield.

'Yes, he was with you, wasn't he?' she had said, looking idly at the headlines, heart hammering.

'Oh, you couldn't keep Kevin away, pulling rank, the little S.H.I.T.'

He had moved the cat off the armchair and plumped down. He could barely keep his eyes open. Like her, he had been fighting to maintain an energy level he did not possess. Bed, a good night's sleep was what they both craved, but neither could admit to it.

'What was he doing?' he said.

What was he doing? When exactly would you like to know what he was doing, lying husband of mine? What he was doing that night in his car? What he was doing under a hotel breakfast table this very morning? God, why hadn't she asked him? It would only have taken a minute. A whole bloody afternoon and night she'd had with him, a dinner and breakfast with a bed in between and she had never thought to find out. How the mind doth discard its own protection when enticed into the virgin grounds of unexplored desire. What was he doing?

'I wasn't paying much attention to Kevin, Richard. I was waiting for you to appear. He was just hovering about in the background, I think, being Kevin.'

Still, she liked speaking his name, the way it ran round the room.

'Ogling our "page-three girl", no doubt.'

Ellen took full advantage of the escape route.

'Ah yes, the model. What was she like? As thick as her make-up?'

'I thought you would have recognized her. That was no model. That was Wendy from marketing.'

'Of course! Last year's Christmas do! That's why she seemed so familiar. Tarty piece. She and Sir Douglas and Kevin. Only you left out, then.'

'I don't see why it matters so much.' He kicked the cat away from his leg. 'Being on television isn't everything, Ellen.'

'It is if you're stuck here,' she said. 'I'd told Patsy and Marjorie.

Now I've got to explain why they saw Kevin and not you. I'll look such a fool.'

'I warned you not to. What's for supper?'

'Tinned something. Tuna?'

Roach had grunted. Ellen had laid the paper down. She was looking at a wounded husband, battle-worn, nursing a great hurt. She wanted to probe the lesion, to lift its swollen folds, examine the pink of its raw depth, see it twitch to outside stimuli. She thought of Kevin and his questioning gaze, the studied attentiveness of his fingers.

'Anyway, tell me about Southampton, the *Canberra*. Was it fun?'

Roach had leant forward, his face animated by a sudden and violent vigour.

'Fun, Ellen? Fun? It was magnificent, the skill, the dedication, the ship transformed, the whole town bent to one patriotic task. It was how it must have been during the war, in the Blitz, the spirit of comradeship, good cheer.'

'And Sir Douglas. He was pleased?'

'Over the moon.' Roach started to get carried away. 'I've done myself a power of good there and no mistake. Kevin didn't like it one bit. Skulked around all morning, throwing me filthy looks. We all had a drink with Sir Douglas afterwards, a quick pub lunch, then he buggered off and I wandered about a bit, before driving up to Stevenage.'

'And Trout Night?'

'One of the best.'

'Well, you must have made a good impression. I forgot to tell you.'

She pointed to the mantelpiece and watched the face behind the face collapse.

*

He'd been worrying at that invitation ever since, picking it up, turning it in his hands, as if somehow he could discern the mechanism by which he could dismantle this particular bomb. 'Do you think it wise,' he would say, 'us going? It's not as if we would fit in,' and she would purr up to him, finger his collar with brazen admiration and tell him that thanks to the *Canberra* it looked like he was the coming man. Every evening he came back from work and fixed it with a quick stare, as if he hoped that one evening it might have vanished, the garden party erased, the bomb defused. She took pleasure in moving the card from one part of the mantelpiece to the other, from room to room; leaving it upturned by the kettle in the kitchen, propping it up against the bowl of dried flowers on the hall table, a Moss Bros telephone number scribbled on the back, listening for the intake of his breath as he discovered its ticking presence. In the evening she would bring the conversation round to the party too, wondering if they could really afford her new dress; whether, considering the drink and drive problem, they should hire a taxi, and of course, the question of her new shoes. 'Italian,' she'd told him, 'something that emphasized the huntress in me.' 'Huntress?' Richard threw the word back at her, his voice wary, guarded. 'Exactly,' she replied. 'There'll be big game out there.'

'I'll be off, then.'

Richard was back. He was off, then. He said it every day.

'Anywhere to make me envious?'

'Stevenage.'

'You were there just three weeks ago!'

'Trout Night and a couple of morning calls, that was all.'

'Back at the usual time?' God, how many people asked that question.

'No telling. Bit of trouble-shooting to do. I might stay the night, follow up some calls the next day. I'll call you.' He caught her questioning look. 'It's Kevin's idea, not mine.'

Kevin again. He'd rung her almost every other day, driven down three times to meet in a station buffet, three stops down the line. He was strangely formal, waiting for her in the corner by the window, standing up when she approached, taking her coat, laying it over the chair next to where she'd sit, stirring his cup all the while they talked. Last time he had brought her a present, a book of poems, by a man she'd never heard of before. They were a bit on the lewd side, some of them, although it was hard to pin them down exactly, what with the old-fashioned words and funny spelling; was that why he'd given them to her, to get her going, to think it was intellectually OK to open her legs in his car. Well, she hadn't done that again, and wasn't going to. She was forty, for Christ's sake.

'How's the Bronco doing?' she asked. 'Did the *Canberra* thing help?'

'I'll say.'

He retrieved his order book from the spare room, where he'd been looking at last month's figures, preparing for the journey. The sales of the Bronco hadn't being going as well as he'd expected. Every time he had tried to invoke the spirit of the *Canberra*, the image of Sir Douglas and Wendy grinning before the cameras had stuck in his throat like a goitre, the sales pitch coming out like spluttered bursts. He could see the buyers leaning back, taking shelter from the onslaught. Bedford, Luton, many of his accounts had resisted his call. For the first time in a generation of fashion lines he no longer had confidence in his ability to read the terrain, to plan his attack. Even his Bible seemed to mock him with its impotency. He hardly bothered to read it. What could he possibly say to them that was as important as a son on the *Canberra*, of boys going to war? And now Stevenage again.

Yesterday he'd been summoned into the office. Kevin had kept him waiting three-quarters of an hour before he was called in. He stood at the entrance, unwilling to cross the threshold. This was the office that he had hoped to occupy one day, with his possessions ranged around the back of the desk, his diary opened to the correct date, his ballpoint placed to one side, his jacket hanging on the back of the door. What made it worse was that Kevin seemed tailor-made for its habitation, his hair as neat and tidy as his in-tray, his shirt as white and crisp as the notepad before him, the telephone intercom buttons as bright as his cufflinks. He sat with his arms folded, rocking back and forth on his leather chair, the telephone black and sleek to one side. In pride of place, at the front of the desk, stood a Bronco. Kevin beckoned him in.

'Richard. Close the door.'

He pointed to the chair opposite. Richard sat down slowly, placed his hands on his knees. On the wall facing him hung a Bronco Busters T-shirt and next to it a large blow-up of Sir Douglas and Wendy, the sergeant who'd poked him with his stick smiling in between. Corporate victory captured in glorious black and white.

'One of the best day's work I've ever done,' Kevin had boasted, catching the direction of Roach's eye, with not a trace of shame nor irony in his voice. 'Courtesy of the *Daily Mail*, that one.'

He brought his body forward suddenly, laid his arms on the desk.

'Richard, I'm sorry to say that I've had a complaint.'

'Oh?'

'Yes. The buyer from Swan's in Stevenage.'

'Mrs Whitley?'

'Just so. You called in on her just under three weeks ago? You remember, the day after . . .' He hitched his thumb over his shoulder before picking up a handwritten letter that lay unfolded on a thin stack of papers. 'She said that when you came in that morning, your appearance was, I use her own words, "uncharacteristically dishevelled".'

That Saturday, Roach had woken with the worst headache he had ever had in his life, naked except for his socks and shoes and still a little drunk. How he'd got his trousers off over them he didn't know. The sheets were muddy and torn, his pillow discoloured and damp. For some reason his suit had lain in a heap in the bath, traces of his unseemly scuffle on the *Canberra* dockside still visible on the sleeves and knees. He'd tried to get the marks off after rinsing out the Broncos themselves but hadn't he hung it up? The empty hanger dangling from the shower attachment told its own story. Cleaning up as best he could, he'd gone downstairs, and eaten dried toast to an orchestrated silence before spending the next hour back in his room blow-drying the trainers with an anaemic hairdryer. All morning he had walked around feeling as if his head might fall off, and yet he hadn't cared. It had been a wonderful night.

Kevin was tapping the letter, waiting for a response.

'I might have forgotten to shave that morning,' Roach had said. Kevin dismissed the excuse with a flick of his fingers.

'That's not the real issue. She says that the presentational sneaker that you "waved around at her", her words not mine, was not only damp but "smelt peculiar, a mixture of soap and sick" and that when she pointed this out you said it was due to a revolutionary manufacturing technique and that it would wear off after a couple of days in the open air. She goes on.

' "When I raised some doubts as to its appearance Mr Roach informed me that if this shoe was good enough for our brave lads risking their lives on the *Canberra*, it was certainly good enough for the layabouts of Stevenage, joyriding with underage girls and smoking pot on street corners, and that it was my moral duty to promote them as a symbol of patriotism. Such was his vehemence that he insisted on re-doing our window display there and then, with the Bronco and its frankly ugly stand as the centrepiece. I was surprised by his abrupt and, I'm afraid to say boorish, approach, but considering our good relationship over the years, said nothing. He promised to return in a few days' time, to see what the reaction had been, but this he did not do. As at that point we had no stock I removed it from the display, until such time as I thought appropriate.

' "The stock came, and sales went moderately well, though not perhaps as well as Mr Roach had anticipated. However, two days ago, a customer came in requiring a size ten Bronco, this, as you know, being one of the sizes most in demand. The only Bronco in that size we had remaining was the display pair that Mr Roach had left with us. Imagine my consternation and embarrassment, when, finding an obstruction lodged in the toe of the right foot, the young man reached in and removed from the inside what appeared to be a portion of what looked like dried curry. I am returning the aforementioned Bronco and contents herewith, and await your comments. Yours, Hope Whitley."

'Well?'

Roach straightened his tie.

'Oh, Jesus . . . I thought I . . . I had an accident the night before, Kevin. Food poisoning. Both ports of call, so to speak. I was up half the night. I thought I'd cleaned it all up.'

Kevin picked the Bronco up by his fingertips, sniffed it once, then raising his arm as high as he could, dropped it into the wastepaper basket at the side of the desk.

'I could can you for this, you know.'

'It was an accident.'

243

'Right now. Send you packing.'

There was a look of long-awaited triumph on Kevin's face. In spite of the barbecues and the advice, in spite of all his hard work, the best sales award seven years ago and the Bronco idea, it had come to this. For a moment he thought of falling to his knees, begging Kevin for another chance, but with it, and the picture of his debasement, how it would be told in later, shoe-lore years, came the realization that it would do no good. He would be sacked. The more he demeaned himself the firmer would be Kevin's resolve. He would be sacked, turned out onto the street with the past twenty years of his life erased. All the meetings, all the sales targets, all the spiel, all the charm offensives, all the disappointments, all his lonely thoughts driving by, gone. He would be sacked and never press the lift for the third floor ever again. Kevin was watching him closely. That was another thing. No Kevin, no Sir Douglas, no garden party. Problem solved. He felt suddenly light, as if his arms and legs were attached to balloons. He could feel himself floating, floating above this office, above this building, above the whole city, above it all! He could be Richard Roach again, nothing less. He could go home and announce that he had been sacked and that he didn't care. He would savour the look of incomprehension on Ellen's face, the flickers of bewilderment and anxiety, field the inevitable questions, what about this, what about that, with an almost carefree aplomb, that he was Richard Roach, a good man, who would find somewhere better that appreciated his true worth. He could go into business with Sandy perhaps, or turn his hand to something else. Ellen would be made to realize that those questions as to their future were ones that only he could answer, her reliance on him for once made absolute. It was an erotic thought, the sudden manifestation of his power. He saw himself frog-marching her upstairs, ripping off all her disdain and fault-finding in one furious sweep of restored masculinity. He would rise above her, rise above it all. Roach rampant. There was a ferocity within him that he could almost taste.

'Well, why don't you?' he said.

'Sorry?' Kevin pulled back, surprised.

'Why don't you?'

It was a good question, Roach reflected. Why hadn't he? And what had been his reply? Kevin smoothed the letter back down on the desk.

'It's not as simple as that,' he said.

Not as simple? There it was, handed to him on a plate, the last of the old guard up to his neck in it. Not as simple? Kevin looked down into the wastepaper basket, avoiding his eyes.

'Why not?' Roach was persistent. 'You fired Sandy just for getting pissed.'

'There's procedures to go through. He'd had warnings.'

Kevin shuffled his papers as if to demonstrate the skill needed to negotiate the mysteries of his managerial office. Roach pressed him further.

'But you just said you could fire me.'

'I don't like acting precipitately, Richard. There are two sides to every story, you know.'

Roach could feel his balance going. He prodded again.

'A trainer full of vomit, that's my side.' Remembering Sandy he leant forward, rubbed his hands together. 'Come on, Kevin. This is the opportunity you've been waiting for. You can sack me. I'd be out of your hair for ever.'

Kevin sighed. His expression was a curious mixture of rage and patience.

'Why would I want that?'

''Cause I've done you favours, covered your early mistakes, showed you kindness. You owe me. Sandy always warned me. "He won't thank you," he used to say, "in fact he'll resent it. The ambitious always do." Ellen was the same.'

'Ellen?'

That tone in his voice, it was just like Ellen's the night he came back. 'Kevin?' she had said; the same edge to it, the same note of suspicion.

'My wife. She warned me too, that time you came around. Called you a terrier.'

Roach got to his feet. It was like that night he'd met Amy and that boy at the bar. He wanted to poke Kevin in the chest, kick his chair across the room.

'She was only half right. She should have called you a thief to boot.' He reached across and fetched the Bronco out of the wastepaper basket. 'It should have been me on the TV with this, not you. It was my idea, the *Canberra*.'

'I wasn't on television.'

'Yes, you were.'

'I was not. Did you see it?'

'See it! That's what probably made me throw up over this.' He waved the Bronco under Kevin's nose. 'Made me sick the moment it came on. I had to turn it off. But I know you were there, hovering in the background. I heard!'

He dropped the shoe back in the basket. Kevin sank back in his chair, relieved.

'I don't know who told you that, Richard, but believe me, I was not on television. It was just Sir Douglas and Wendy. That was the whole point.'

'Not on television?'

'No. It was a good idea, yours, but mine was better. That's why I'm in this chair and you're not. You'd have got us thirty seconds on regional television and a picture in the local rag. I got prime-time TV and our name in all the nationals. It's not as if I haven't recognized your contribution. Who do you think got you Sir Douglas's invitation? So let's hear no more about it.' He stretched his hands out on his desk, palms open, and looked him in the eye. 'There's no question of me wanting to fire you, whatever you and your wife think. All I want is for this mess to be cleared up, for you to go up there and sort it out. I'd even think about staying over-night, firming up some of the other orders.' He leant back on his chair, hands behind his head. 'Take a leaf out of Sandy's book. Go on a charm offensive. Take the old bat out for a drink, dinner even. Invite her back to your hotel for a nightcap. You've probably got something tucked away she hasn't seen in a long time.'

He laughed. Richard stood there panting. He didn't quite understand how, yet again, resolve had evaded him. Kevin wasn't on the television? How could that be? Ellen saw him, didn't she? Perhaps he didn't know he was being filmed. Perhaps she only caught a glimpse of him. Back in his own bare cubicle, he sat wanting to ring her, not wanting to ring her, to question her, not to question her, about what exactly she had seen. It would only serve to remind her of his failure, to prise open the clam of his dishonesty. Instead he fished out the number out of his wallet and dialled Stevenage, the first time he had dared to since their meeting. The voice at the other end was a smoker's; hard and unforgiving. Eventually Amy came on.

'Given you up a long time ago,' she said. He closed his eyes, imagining her white hand, her fluffy cupid mouth and her eyes blinking wide up at him.

'I've been all over,' he said.

'Lucky for some.'

'Have you heard the news? About the battleship.'

'Yes. He wasn't . . .'

'No, no. But I'm in the area tomorrow. I thought you might like that dinner.'

Silence. In the background a Hoover and someone singing. She said, 'I don't know.'

He came back quickly, couldn't help himself, even though he knew what he sounded like.

'Doesn't have to be dinner. I'll be finished by the afternoon.'

There was a pause, a shuffling of feet.

'I could bring you his picture.'

She laughed, not so much a laugh, as a release, the common ground found again.

'All right. There's a cafe in the leisure centre. I'll meet you there. Three o'clock.'

He'd spent the lunchtime drinking with Sandy's ghost, thinking of young girls, and what one lonely man might say to them.

*

'I'll be off, then.'

Richard was back, hovering by the bedroom door. Ellen puffed up her pillow and sat up. That was another thing. His physical presence seemed to be more in evidence. He was both aware of it and more ill at ease with it. The other night she'd caught him standing sideways in front of the bathroom mirror in his underwear, prodding his paunch with an extended forefinger. A slap would have been one thing. A slap would have denoted a sort of fateful acceptance of his condition, an affectionate reassurance of ageing contentment. A prod was quite another matter alto-gether. A prod denoted dissatisfaction, an instruction towards improvement, a desire to be more desirable. His early morning erections were getting more frequent too. Today she'd nearly fallen out of bed trying to avoid it.

He crossed to the window. When he was out of bed she imagined him in it, and when he was in she wanted him out.

'Fifteen dead, they think,' he was saying.

'In Stevenage? What was it, a poisoned boot?'

He ignored her joke. Outside, Freddie Millen was wriggling underneath his car, Patsy standing beside him holding a large spanner.

'No older than Mark, some of them,' he said.

'You don't know that.'

'Yes, I do, Ellen, I saw them, boys the same age as Mark, fighting for their country, risking their lives, while ours is galli-vanting about the country.'

'He rang yesterday, didn't I tell you?'

'No.'

'He promises to be back in time for the hearing. He's cleared it with the probation officer. He's pleased that Mark's trying to get a job. Says it'll count in his favour.'

'A job! That'll be the day. This is our son you're talking about. We've no idea what he's up to since he buggered off with that Plimsoll girl. Where is he now?'

'London, he said.'

'Do you think they're, you know, together?'

'If it's on offer it's hard to resist, don't you think, Richard?' she said, adding quickly, 'When you're that age. Got an interview in the bookshop she works in, he says.'

'Perhaps our little contretemps did some good after all.'

Below Freddie Millen had emerged blinking. It might have been the oil, but his face still looked discoloured.

'It's still there, you know,' he called back. 'Freddie's eye.'

'It's the Falklands,' she said. 'There's too much male aggression flying around. Matty punching Freddie, you rowing with Mark. Perhaps that's why he's stayed away these three weeks. I thought we'd agreed to go easy on him.'

'Well, he asked for it. Going on about the Task Force.'

'Hark who's talking.'

'As if it didn't matter, Ellen, as if our boys didn't count for anything.'

'Richard, he's eighteen. He's up for a probation report. He could still go to prison. Don't you think that's enough?'

'Our son! Our son, Ellen!'

There was a silence as they both contemplated his cry. There was nothing to be done about it, no prayer they could offer up, no counsellor who would turn it around. There was their son, whose love for them seemed as alien as their love for him, something which they neither felt at ease with nor understood. Their son who had driven them apart.

'And that's another thing. What's happened to that picture of him? The one in the spare room.'

'I took it for the office.'

'Didn't take one of me, then.'

'You'd be a distraction.'

'And Mark isn't.'

'He's a responsibility.' He saw the soldier boys embarking, Amy's tearful eyes. He saw himself standing there on the quayside, his son marching up the gangway, turning to wave goodbye. He felt the flush of pride engulf his heart, how his arm would have wound around her, his son's fiancée. 'Don't worry, son, we'll look after her,' he would have shouted. 'Don't worry, son.' He sat on the edge of the bed, squeezing Ellen's hand.

'I wish he'd seen the TV too, Ellen, all going on the boat. Might have made him think. If we'd thought about it we could have sat round, the three of us, and watched it, the *Canberra* and the young soldiers fighting for their country. It might have brought it all together for him.'

Ellen shook her hand free, reached out for her tea.

'Yes, well, he had his mind on more important matters. And you had your precious Trout Night.'

Roach nodded, choosing his next words carefully.

'And Kevin on the television too, a young man like that, it would have been a good role model for him.' Ellen spluttered his caution away with undisguised scorn.

'Kevin a role model for Mark, are you serious? Anyway, what is this?' She pushed him off the bed. 'You were banging on about it all last night. You weren't on the television, Richard. Kevin was. Get over it. The point is, it was your idea and it helped, didn't it.'

Downstairs, Richard let the cat in through the back door. The day was warming up. A nice leisurely drive up, a bunch of flowers perhaps for Mrs Whitley, a contrite confession (worry about his son, not eating properly, too much spicy food on an empty stomach) and then a lunch in one of the pubs in the town centre. He hung his jacket in the back of his car, and opened the driver's door. Kevin denying the television; the barefaced cheek of it. He didn't speak, was that what he meant? Down the road Patsy was back in attendance, Freddie's legs sticking out underneath the chassis, Radio Two coming out from the half-open door.

'It's coming along, then,' Roach observed. Patsy turned. She held the spanner like a babe in arms.

'The car?'

'The shiner.'

'Oh, that. Doesn't anybody around here talk about anything else? It'll be in the *Gazette* next.'

'It's not often we have a regular set-to on our doorstep.'

'Stick around. You might see another.'

She weighed the spanner in her hand and nodded over to where Matty was coming out of his front door, straightening his yellow jumper.

'Would it kill him, do you think, if I whacked him on the head with this?'

Uncertain what to say, Richard put his car in gear and slid away. Matty crossed the road, his hands tucked into his trouser pockets.

'How's his eye?' he asked.

'What am I, a bulletin board? It's better.'

'Good.'

'You shouldn't have hit him, Matty. There was no call for it. Freddie wouldn't harm a fly.'

'I got carried away. Me coming back, Marcy not being here, seeing that . . . that shape on the lawn.'

'If anyone is to blame it was me. I made him stop. He had more important things to do. Like putting food on the table.'

'I know. I'm so sorry.' He shuffled on his feet. 'Actually it's the lawn I've come to talk about.' He patted his bald patch. 'I need Freddie's advice.'

Patsy leant down and tapped her husband's knee with the spanner. Freddie's leg shot up, followed by a dull clunk and then a cry. Freddie eased himself out, rubbing his head. When he saw who was standing next to her he made ready to propel himself back in. Patsy caught him by the leg.

'It's OK, Freddie. He needs your help. Horticulturally speaking.'

Freddie looked. Matty nodded. Freddie got up, wiping his greasy hands. The two men stood opposite each other.

'Problems?' Matty asked, nodding towards the car.

'Oil change,' said Freddie. 'And you?'

Matty dug his hands further into his pockets.

'The fact is, Freddie, that shape you left on the back lawn is still there. I'm hoping Marcy might come down this weekend and I was wondering if you wouldn't mind giving it the once-over with your machine again. I've tried to get rid of it with my own, but however much I mow it, when I look out the bathroom window, the bloody thing's still there.'

Freddie nodded in eager anticipation.

'That's because the blade settings are totally different,' he explained. 'The Atco gives a highly individual cut. It's all to do with their rotary mechanism, you know. When Charles Pugh designed it . . .'

'Freddie.' Patsy tapped her hand with the spanner again.

'Sorry. Yes. I'll do it right away, if you like.'

'No need for that. You've got until the end of the week.'

'No, no.' Freddie looked up to a cloudless sky. 'You never know with this weather.' He handed Patsy a damp rag and a couple of bolts. 'And you don't want Marcy coming home and finding *Homo erectus* on the lawn.'

'She might,' Patsy suggested. 'I might.'

Freddy ignored her.

'I'll take the blades down a quarter of an inch. That way you'll have a completely new cut. No trace of the offending outline at all.'

Patsy sat on the edge of the bath, the twins absorbed by the flotilla of rubber ducks passing between them. Though she smiled, acknowledged their squeals of delight, trailed her hand in the bubbly water, her thoughts were with the drone she could hear coming from the Plimsolls' back lawn, picturing the expression on Freddie's face, how lost he would be in the sheer pleasure of the task before him, forgetting completely the work they had to do before they met with the bank. Though he'd spent hours trying to work out a business plan, the fact was he simply wasn't up to it. True he'd got some figures from printers regarding production costs, true he'd put down a price, but under advertising revenue he'd put *whatever we can get away with*, and under sales forecasts he'd written, *more than you might imagine*. Three times she had picked up the phone to call Rich Brother George on his private number and three times she'd put the phone down the instant she'd heard the first inflections of his deeply groomed voice. It swamped you, like too much gravy over the Sunday lunch. She'd almost prefer losing everything than to suffer the indignity of being bailed out by him again. But something needed to be done. Last week she'd read Freddie's prospective letters to the leading manufacturers, informing them of his plan, but she hadn't sent them off. There was a fatal naivety in the style, the tone overexcited, juvenile. Freddie might know a lot about lawns and lawnmowing but as far as plans and planning were concerned he was a complete washout. Nevertheless, it was a good idea. Saturday, Sunday, everywhere you looked men were busy in various states of feverish activity. It was all about territory, that's why men preferred it to proper gardening. The lawn was a battle ground, a war zone, an endless struggle against moles, ants, wormholes, plantains, grubs, moss; the lawnmower only one of the weapons in their horticultural arsenal. In essence the magazine would be nothing more than a combination of war pictorials and car magazines. The engine and the enemy. All it needed was to be firmed up. She'd already decided how. She'd go herself, talk her way into see the managing directors, the advertising managers, whoever, convince them of the opportunity.

She bent down and stirred the water one more time. The mowing had stopped. Time to get back to business. Pulling the plug, she held out a large pink towel.

'Come on, sweethearts. Let's be having you.'

*

Freddie walked back with the empty grassbox. Matty was looking out of the first-floor window. Freddie called up.

'Well?'

Matty opened up his arms.

'Perfect,' he said, smiling. 'You deserve a beer.'

They sat on the step of the kitchen door, looking out. Not bad for a first cut, Freddie thought, though the grass itself was in a terrible state, clover, earth mounds, great clumps of couch.

'It needs a thorough overhaul, of course.'

'The mower?'

'The lawn. It's in a bad state, Matty.'

'Looks OK to me.'

'Needs the works. I could write a weekly plan for you, if you like. Oversee it. Do it for you if you wanted.'

'It's great as it is, Freddie, thanks. Just a quick once-over with the Flymo is all I'm good for.'

Freddie nodded, trying to find the thread though this stubborn heresy.

'There are short cuts you can take, if you must. Soot, for instance, is an excellent stimulant. Though you can't walk on it afterwards, of course.'

Matty made no reply. Freddie went for the positive.

'Still, the phallus's gone, that's the main thing. Of course I can understand you wanting it gone, Matty, with Marcy coming. It's not the sort of thing a young woman should see on her parents' back lawn, a penis.' He looked around. 'Lots of bricks here, Matty. Building an extension?' Matty shook his head.

'Patio.'

He had decided not to wait. If he waited she would be involved and then it would only serve as a reminder of what had not passed. If he built it now, ready for her return, it would be his undertaking, his command of the land as opposed to her rule of the sea. They

253

would be equals, and she would walk on it with no other senti-ment but honoured pleasure. Freddie was still talking.

'If they had a hobby like that it wouldn't matter so much.'

'What?'

'Teenagers.' Freddie wiped beer from his chin. 'If they took up a proper hobby, something to occupy their minds, it wouldn't become so important.'

'What wouldn't?'

'You know. Erectile tissue.'

What was he talking about?

'Penises. You know, the old dribbler.'

'Ah, that. I don't think it quite works like that, Freddie.'

'No? The two-stroke was enough for me, kept me on the straight and narrow as regards teenage hanky-panky was con-cerned. That's how I met Patsy, you know. Mowing.'

'Well, I never.'

'As sure as I'm sitting here. Her father ran the local bowls team. I maintained their green for them, on a voluntary basis, of course. They had a 1927 Dennis, 500cc Blackburn engine, aluminium gear case. Of course the grassbox is the real pièce de résistance on those beauties. Rides on pivots. All you have to do is to tip it out. No lifting involved at all. Marvellous if you have a hernia. Marvellous if you don't.'

After they finished their beer they rolled the machine back over the road. The car stood on the drive, ready to pounce. Freddie ran a hand over the livid spotted bonnet.

'Looks like she's got some nasty type of skin disease, doesn't it?' he joked.

'It is a bit unsightly,' Matty agreed. Freddie patted it gently.

'I'd spray her myself, but the boffins won't let me. Still, I take care of her as best I can.' He opened the passenger door and beckoned. 'She needs a run, gets bad-tempered if she doesn't. Care for a spin?'

Matty climbed in. It was mainly metal inside and smelt of petrol. Squeezing into the seat, he found his knees were higher than his lap. Freddie leant across and worked a lever underneath. Matty rose slowly as if he was at the dentist's. He felt similarly apprehensive.

'Better?'

Matty nodded. Freddie pushed a button. The engine shuddered. Black fumes poured out of the back. Matty's seat sank abruptly back to its original setting.

'Tally ho,' Freddie shouted.

Despite the narrow windows and the overpowering smell Matty found the experience instantly seductive. Being higher than everyone else gave you an entirely different perspective on the world. Other cars were not simply lower in height, they were lowered in rank, their journeys blatantly trivial, their drivers dwarfed into glorious irrelevance. Their own progress took on greater import, the manner in which they turned into a road, stopped at traffic lights, pulled up alongside other vehicles a demonstration of unimpeachable authority. Sleek lines, personalized number plates, deep shining body wax counted for nothing. It was reassuring too to discover the further diminished stature of the pedestrian class, now reduced to an insignificance that he found strangely thrilling. With their shuffling gaits and their tawdry clothes they looked like refugees. Only the young were exempt. Passing one particularly tight-skirted, black-tighted creature, her body slipping through the crowded High Street like an eel through rank weed, he felt tempted to lean out the window and whistle. He hadn't felt like that in years. He wished he had worn his dark glasses. Freddie caught his excitement.

'It's much better from the inside, no?'

Matty gulped.

'It's great, Freddie. I never thought it would be like this. The view, well it's just great. Great.' Freddie tried to temper Matty's juvenile enthusiasm with some adult responsibility.

'A lot safer, too,' he pronounced, looking stern.

'I bet.' Hang safety, Matty thought. Power, position, that's what was blowing through the primitive air conditioning. They charged into a wheel of traffic, Freddie taking imperious command of the roundabout.

'Nasty business, this *Sheffield* thing,' he observed 'Suzanne's well clear of that, I take it. Heard from her recently?'

'Fresh delivery this morning. Eight pages, handwritten, half on one of her laundry forms. She's written more on this voyage than she has the rest of her life.'

'Lots to write about, I would imagine.'

Matty murmured, but not in agreement. Yes, there was lots to write about, and yes the letters were packed with stories and observations, sometimes messages from the lads in the kitchens scrawled down one of the sides, but though she told him about what was happening, they read more like entries in a reporter's diary than letters from an absent wife. One had even been addressed to *All At Anglefield Road*, as if she expected the neighbours to come and sit in their front room while he read out it out loud. And not a mention of Marcy in any of them. He'd lied to Marcy when she finally called in, told her Suzanne had sent her love. She hadn't at all. That was all rather a let-down too, Marcy not being here. She'd only heard he was back through Mark, when he'd phoned his mum to tell her to change some appointment. He'd imagined that she'd whoop for joy, come haring back home, but no. Marcy was busy moving round the country, having fun with that boy. Still, it did no good to make an argument of it over the phone. He made it as light as possible.

'What's it to you?' she said.

'Marcy.'

'You didn't ask my permission when it came to our home, did you?'

The line had gone dead. Time to change the subject. He turned back to Freddie.

'Patsy tells me you've an idea for a magazine.'

Freddie licked his lips in anticipation. Patsy wasn't here. He had a captive audience. He could speak the words as roundly as he liked.

'Yes,' he said. '*Lawns and Lawn-Mowing*. Basically it'll be about lawns and lawn-mowing. It's incredible to think that there isn't such a magazine on the market already. I mean what is England if it isn't lawns and lawn-mowing.'

'True.' Matty nodded, wondering why Freddie was over-enunciating.

'It has a ring to it, don't you think,' Freddie said, '*Lawns and Lawn-Mowing*?'

'Definitely. There's a lot in a name.'

'There is.' Freddie wound down the window. He spoke loudly into the air. '*Lawns and Lawn-Mowing.*' A cyclist wobbled onto a traffic island, shaking his fist. Matty pretended not to notice. 'It says it all, really,' Freddie amplified. 'There's lawns, there's lawnmowers and there's lawn-mowing. Fifty-two weeks of the year.'

Matty didn't know what to say. You mowed the lawn. That was it.

'I've an appointment coming up. Trying to raise the money. Venture capital is the technical term for it, I believe.'

'Great.' Matty nodded quickly, indicating that Freddie should direct his attention to the crowded road ahead. Freddie's driving was surprisingly cavalier.

'Trouble is I'm not very good on business plans, cash flow, start-up costs, financial what's-its.'

'Forecasts.'

'Forecasts, that's right. Might as well read tea leaves for all I know about them.'

Matty looked across. The bruising around Freddie's eye was turning yellow, the mark where his knuckles had grazed Freddie's cheekbone clearly visible. He must have been still drunk. He'd been brooding on the meaning of the grass penis for about an hour when the doorbell had rung. He'd gone downstairs to find Freddie standing with his back to him, gazing out at his lawn-mower standing in the drive. 'Ah, Marcy,' he had said, 'what do you think of my handiwork? Fancy helping me finish the job?' and beaming had turned. Matty had hit him there and then.

He closed his eyes. Marcy wouldn't be staying long. Suzanne wouldn't be back for at least two weeks. Why not? This way he could make amends, try and wipe that look of indulgent contempt from Patsy's face.

'I could help if you like,' he said. 'I know a bit about business plans, what with setting up a shop, hiring staff, et cetera.'

'You would?' Freddie swung the wheel hard. Someone hooted.

'Turn the car round, why don't you,' Matty suggested. 'Let's take a look.'

*

The sound of the klaxon distracted Ellen's attention from the two teenagers who had ducked down behind a rather flash-looking Jaguar the moment she'd walked into the station car park. Turning, Ellen waved back at the grinning man, cursing the improbability of Freddie driving by with a beaming Matty Plimsoll by his side. She walked into the hall and bought her ticket, remembering the two youths as she tucked it into her purse. Though the last thing she wanted was to draw attention to herself, she felt obliged to mention it. They had looked like they were trying to break in, steal the radio; the town was full of mischief-makers these days. The man behind the counter unlocked his door and stepped out with her. The car was there, but the two youths had gone.

The journey took longer than usual, the train sitting inexplicably on the track the moment they left the next station, the mosquito whine of the guard's intercom above her head only increasing her sense of anxiety, caught on a journey of uncertainty, trapped by her own foolishness. She found herself walking up and down the corridor, leaning out the window, rocking backwards and forwards on her seat, willing the train forward. She'd be late and he'd be there on time, occupying himself with some studied ritual until she arrived in a fluster, gathering up the lost minutes. It was part of his skill, to be in control, even when faced with the slick of the unexpected, turning into the chaos as if his life was simply a matter of coordination, the dangers up ahead rendered impotent by the proficiency of his reflexes. His call that morning had come as she knew it would not long after Richard had left, and although she had maintained throughout the conversation that under no circumstances would she meet him within the hour, they both knew that within the doubling of that time, by midday, she would.

And there he was, with his white shirt and his dark hair and his cup of tea, tapping his teeth with a pencil, looking out across the platform as if he were taking a morning cappuccino overlooking the Bay of Naples. He didn't wave or smile, merely raised his head slightly, like a man of irrepressible wealth bidding at an auction. And she of course the prize.

'You sent him to Stevenage, then.' She sat down abruptly, lit a cigarette. Kevin smiled, to the memory of it as much to her.

'Told him to stay overnight. Clever, that.'

'As if I could.'

'Why not?'

'I have a son, Kevin.'

'Not around a great deal, so I hear.'

'Do I have that to thank you for as well?' She raised her hand, answering her own question. 'No, he fucks up all by himself.'

'I was fucked up once.'

'And you're not now?'

'Oh, I'm fucked up even worse now, now that I'm bewitched and bewildered.'

'Bewitched!'

He gripped her hand.

'Did you not read the poems?'

'Yes.'

'And?'

She shrugged.

'I could barely understand them for the spelling. I didn't even know how to pronounce his name.'

'Done,' he said. 'John Donne. I thought they might have spoken to you, passion across the ages.'

'They were poems, Kevin, that's all. I read them then I turned on the washing machine, did the housework, wondering what my son was up to.'

'Probably up to what most sons are up to. Perhaps you should give them to him to read as well.'

'That'll set him right, will it, a book of bloody poems? I took you for a much more practical man than that.'

'You took me for a salesman, Ellen, that beyond the order book, the sales target, I know nothing, care for nothing, unless it's a sharp suit and a new car, and a nice bit of stuff on my arm.' She started to blush. 'You think that's all salesmen can be, just salesmen. There's nothing else in their low-grade fuel that passes for blood. Car showroom, insurance, double-glazing, we're all the same. God, I've probably read more books in a year than you and Richard have read in a lifetime. Don't you think I know that when

259

you get to the top there's nothing there? Don't you think I know that, that it's still the same sky we all stand under, or that a loaf of bread tastes the same for a millionaire as it does for a guy on the dole?'

'What's bread got to do with us?'

'That's an interesting choice of words, Ellen. Us. All that makes the difference is who to share the bread with.'

'I don't want to hear this.'

'What do you want to hear. I have a room booked? A car waiting, four hours to spare?'

'I must be mad, coming here.'

'Yes, you must be, if that's all you want. Tell me about your son.'

Her son! Always her son! It came out in a burst.

'I should never have had him, if you must know. I was too young. If Richard had been a bit more careful.'

'But you don't wish he wasn't here, do you?'

'Don't I? Bloody awful as a baby, never one good night's sleep, wilful, nasty as a child. And then,' she looked out of the window, 'his accident, his leg.'

'It happens, Ellen.'

'I could have killed him for that. It's robbed me of everything, hope, future, husband. Left me stranded, stranded on a bloody island and no chance of getting off.'

Kevin blew air out of his puckered lips.

'God, no wonder he's fucked up.'

She'd turned on him.

'It isn't all a mother's fault, you know, when things go wrong. Not always a father's too. Children can screw things up without any help from us. They can be as thoughtless and as cruel and as disappointing as any adult. Richard may have his faults but he isn't any of those. Except the last, perhaps.'

'That's almost the worst one of all.'

'Almost.'

'I suppose they're the most difficult to let go, the disappointing ones.'

'You're talking as if I'm going to leave him.'

'Well, aren't you?'

She stood up.

'I haven't come here for this.'

'What have you come for, then?' He moved towards her. She spoke through a closed mouth.

'No.'

'Don't make a scene, Ellen. You wouldn't want that.' He pressed her lips with his fingers.

'Wait outside.'

He paid up, the girl behind the counter giving him a sly wink. Across the road Ellen sat on a patch of green overlooking the canal. The water was still and flaccid, going nowhere.

'I've put on weight,' she said. 'Have you noticed?'

'Can't say that I have.'

'I've been trying on outfits for this blessed do. I'm a size larger than last year. I wish we'd never been invited.'

'You've me to blame for that. I told Sir Douglas what a stunner you were. Knowing him he'll probably try and touch you up some time in the proceedings. Just smile and bear with it.'

She pushed him away, pleased. He took her arm and they walked along the towpath. His shoes were not designed for outdoor tracks, even ones hardened by the sun. They were city shoes, made to glow in the reflection of fashionable wine bars and executive car interiors.

'Richard's terrified,' she said, pulling him into her confession. 'I can see it every time he catches sight of the invite, scared witless that I'll talk to you or Sir Douglas and find out.'

'But you won't, because whenever it arises you'll steer the conversation away from it, as will he. He doesn't know it but you're the best keeper of his secret there is.' His arm crept round her. 'He has extensive grounds there, you know, Sir Douglas, all sorts of dingly dells where a couple might lose themselves.'

'So that's the reason. You're nothing if not consistent.'

She kissed him fiercely, fluttering, like a bird against a window.

'Let's get it over with, then. Nice room you've booked?'

He covered her mouth with his hand.

'Ellen, Ellen. You're going about this the wrong way. I don't want you to act precipitately, to do something you might regret.'

'Yes, you do.'

'Well, yes I do.'

'Well, where is it, then?'

He reached into his pocket and brought out the car keys.

'About twenty minutes' drive away.' He held the keys by the leather attachment and shook them. 'But unless you catch this, they'll go in the water, and we won't be going anywhere. Eh?'

They rose high in the air, Ellen swearing, blinded by the sun, teetering on the edge of the canal. They turned and sparkled and fell towards her, Kevin laughing, her legs suddenly certain, her eye true, her body leaning back over the edge. She opened her hand to the power given her, and let it fly into the heart of her palm.

'I'm driving,' she said.

*

Matty came back from Freddie's an hour later. Freddie had been right. A packet of Brooke Bond would have done a better job. He opened the door to the smell of burnt toast. He couldn't believe it but he called out nevertheless.

'Suzy?'

Marcia appeared from the kitchen doorway. She looked pale and tired.

'Marcy!'

He ran forward and hugged her close. She held herself in, unwilling to embrace the embrace. He'd forgotten. Since her mother died she'd shied away from bodily contact.

'When did you get here?'

'Last night.'

'You didn't wake me.'

She pointed to the empty beer cans.

'You were out for the count.'

She wiped the hair from her forehead. Now he noticed the ragged state of her, the dirty clothes, the broken fingernails, the untold story behind the eyes.

'Marcy, what on earth?'

'Oh, Dad!'

She fell back into his arms sobbing.

'What is it, darling? Are you all right?'

She was shaking, spasms of fear throwing jolts into his body.

He held her head, blind conjecture careering round. He looked to the flat white ceiling, the shape of her skull so familiar to him, so rarely touched. He closed his eyes and placed an unseen kiss upon it. He couldn't bear the thought of it, how everything would change. If only Suzy was here. At least she'd know what to say.

'Is it Mark?'

'Oh, Dad.'

She fell to crying again, her reticent body now abandoned against his. He'd been right all along.

'What'd he do to you?'

'Nothing. No, nothing like that.'

'Then what?'

The words came spilling out into the pit of his shoulder, her breath unwell, fingers running up and down his arm, counting out the rhythm of her explanation.

'It was because of you, Dad. You came back and I wasn't there and I wanted to be, but wanted to be somewhere else too, and then I heard about the *Sheffield* and I thought of you, how it could have been you and I felt lonely and I couldn't get here fast enough. That was it. I couldn't get here fast enough. It was my fault.'

'What was?'

She gulped.

'He borrowed a car, Dad, Mark, without permission, to get me back, one of those posh ones, a Jaguar I think. Not to keep. Just to get me back. I wanted to come back so much, to see you and we didn't have much money, not enough for the train or a bus even. He drove all the way through the night, so I could see you. Don't be too angry with him. He did it for me.'

'Stole a car!'

'It's all right. No one knows. He left it down by the station.'

'Jesus Christ, Marcy.'

'The thing is – oh, Dad, I've been so stupid. Last night, in the rush to leave, I left my bag in the car and we can't get it back. After he left it down the station he locked it, to keep it safe from thieves, he was that careful. Chucked the keys in the canal.'

'Jesus Christ.'

'What am I going to do, Dad? We didn't mean any harm.'

Marcy bit her lip. Mark was really scary, what he did, how he just didn't care. None of her friends had liked him much, but they hadn't fallen under that spell of his utter indifference, the way he talked to his mother and father, the contempt with which he viewed everything, music, politics, other people, what they said, how they looked, how they drove their cars, ate their food, wore their sunglasses. There were other things, his slow-motion donkey laugh, making a mockery of humour itself, the tumble of his dark hair, the sudden stutter that could bring his reckless self-assurance to an abrupt close. She couldn't tell her dad everything. Take the car, for instance. Yes, he'd borrowed the car, driven it at high speed all the way down from Edinburgh, but it wasn't the first time. The first time . . .

The first time was about five minutes after they'd left Anglefield Road. They'd just walked past the station when he'd told her to wait by the humpbacked bridge, while he hobbled off back the way he came. She'd waited, thinking that he'd forgotten some-thing, wondering whether this was a good idea, when she'd seen this white car come rolling slowly towards her, the passenger door swinging open and Mark leaning across, wearing a fake toothy grin, like for a camera, and she'd got in without fully realizing what he'd done, nicked it from the station car park just down the road. Not five minutes after stepping out her front door she was riding in a stolen car and being handed an enormous joint, Mark giggling like they were a couple of fifth-formers bunking off school. She was terrified at first, pleading with him to stop the car, to let her out, but then they were out of the town, with farm buildings and fields and hedges flying by, the green of the young bracken overwhelming the tangle of old brown. It was sunny and he'd wound down his window, and she had a sense of vanishing, of becoming someone else, that it wasn't real. It was like her father leaving, the whole Falklands thing. It didn't belong anywhere. Then Mark pulled into a lay-by and fished out an enormous pair of pink sunglasses from the glove compartment.

'Where exactly are we going?' he asked, sticking them over his nose. She giggled.

'London? But you won't get a job wearing those.'

He blew on the lenses, wiping them clean on the corner of his shirt, then placed them carefully over her face.

'Fuck that. Let's go and see your dad off and then who knows. You've got some time off, haven't you?' She nodded. He took the end of the joint from out of her hand and flicked it against the sign warning against lighting fires, waiting for the reprimand. She'd said nothing.

It was quicker than they'd expected. The town was full of soldiers and people waiting to see the ship leave. There was already a crowd down by the dock. They stood next to a woman with a young baby. She had a T-shirt on which said 'SIMPLY THE BEST'. She was pale and skinny, the baby pink and suckling plump. It made Marcy wonder how.

'Seeing someone off?' Marcy had asked

'His dad. Three months old and he might never see him again. Still, he had a good send-off last night, if you know what I mean. What about you?' the woman asked, looking for the ring. 'You got anyone on board?'

'Just like him,' she replied, waggling her little finger at the infant's puckering mouth. 'My dad too.'

The woman smiled and nodded in Mark's direction. 'Least your boyfriend isn't going as well.' Marcia was indignant.

'He's not my boyfriend. He just thinks he's going to screw me while my dad's away, that's all.'

The woman laughed.

'And is he?'

'Fat chance. Tonight especially. We'll be lucky to find a park bench.'

The woman considered them for a moment.

'I shouldn't be doing this,' she said, 'but seeing as you're part of the family, you can come back and sleep on the floor if you want. Use the cushions from the sofa. I've even got a sleeping bag you could use.'

Once there Marcia seemed to lose interest in trying to see her dad. Being there was enough, being absorbed into the crowd, buoyed up by drink and enforced patriotism. There was a lot of singing, bursts of prolonged cheering as the various units were recognized clambering aboard. They were too far away to make out faces, though Shirley, the woman with the baby, swore she recognized her man, swanning down the quayside with his mates.

Towards late afternoon, a town band struck up, and the whole crowd joined in. Marcia felt embarrassed for not knowing the words. Mark's bellowed enthusiasm she took to be ironic. When it grew dark the sea breeze came in, the tang of cold uncertainty throwing a muted shroud over the brightly lit ship, coiling round their legs, seeping through their clothes. Small fires were lit, one old man weaving through the little huddles with a glowing brazier, handing out free bags of roast chestnuts. By the time the ship sailed they were all zealously drunk, infected by a corrupt effervescence, waving flags, blowing whistles, hugging their new found friends as if it they had gate-crashed a tribal New Year's Eve party. It didn't seem possible that her dad was on the boat, or that she was witnessing a moment of great change. With the *Canberra* decked out, light blazing over the black water, bands playing, sirens sounding, horns blaring, it was a just another spectacle, a Guy Fawkes, a Jubilee, bunting and beer.

The woman led them back to a battered Skoda, and drove them for an hour or more while they swigged cold red wine, back to a small semi-detached house standing in a bare regimented line. The hardboard door was dented and cracked, the hall smelt of piss. The living room was small and bare, and glowed a lurid red: one sofa, one armchair, a standard lamp, two shelves full of silver cups, and an enormous television. The excitement had worn off. They were all tired, unsure of each other. Marcia and Mark didn't even know what county they were in.

'Married quarters,' Shirley said, as they manhandled the TV to gain more room. 'Not great, are they. I'm off upstairs. See you in the morning.'

They stood in the strangeness of a strange room, each waiting for the other to move.

'If my dad ever got to hear of this he'd kill me,' Marcia said.

'I'll not be telling him.'

'You'll not be telling anyone. I don't want this going round the neighbourhood, either.'

She threw the sleeping bag to the floor. Taking off her jeans and jersey, she wriggled inside. The fluorescent light from the lamp outside shone on her bare arms. Mark sat on the sofa, playing with his boot laces.

'You've got freckles,' he said.

'All over,' she said. 'I'm getting to hate them.'

'They're nice,' he said. 'I could count them all for you, if you wanted. See how many you got.'

'I bet you could.' She pulled the bag up to her neck. 'Got any of that wine left?'

He passed her the bottle.

'Is he frightened, your dad?'

'Not by the sound of it. Thinks it'll be a bit of an adventure.'

'How do you feel?'

'All watery inside, like I want to hit someone. He left me, couldn't keep away from Sexy Suzy.'

'Is that what she is?'

'Don't you think? The stuff she wears around the house.'

He reached back for the bottle.

'I wish you would, you know, let me count them for you. You'd be quite safe.' He drank wildly, wine spilling down his chin. 'It's all I can do, look, that's all I do with . . .'

He stopped. She wasn't certain what she'd heard.

'All you do with who?'

'Nothing. Forget it.'

'No, come on, tell me! You mean, like when she's . . .'

'Maybe.'

'Who is it?'

'Marcy, I can't.'

'Someone I know?' She caught his discomfort. 'It is, isn't it! Someone from the estate? And she lets you?'

'We get stoned. She takes off her clothes, trying to jump-start a dead battery. That's all there is to it.'

'I don't understand.'

'Don't you know? I thought it was the county joke – Behold the Boy Impotent. I'm no good for it, didn't you know. Actually, I kind of like it that way. I look and think, is that it? Is that what the fuss is all about?'

Marcy, interested, forgot about the earlier confession. She was pleased that someone else felt anger about the requirements of their gender.

'You mean after the accident.'

'The leg, yeah.'

'I'm sorry.'

'Why be sorry? We're all screwed one way or another. I can't get it up. So what? What does it mean? A few less babies, three or four thousand missed fucks? Big deal.'

Marcy found herself nodding in agreement. She wasn't sure what it meant either. She didn't find the penis and its attendant concerns an attractive proposition at the best of times. She'd tried with the buyer in the bookshop, and before that a customer who worked for the BBC, episodes of elongated futility both. Recently there had been a woman in her bed, and she hadn't seen much point in that either. It was like everyone was trying to push her through a departure gate for a flight she didn't want to catch.

'Is it OK, then, the leg?'

'Yeah.' He stuck it out. 'Been all right today, hasn't it?'

She leant across and touched it.

'I've never seen a . . .'

'Prosthetic leg?'

'Yes.'

'Tell you what. I'll show you my leg if you show me your freckles. All of them.'

'Sod off!'

'Why not? Look, gentlemen first, eh?'

He took off the shoe and pulled down his trousers. The leg had been taken off at the knee. His thigh was paler than it should be, as if it had been kept under a stone, thinner too, like it hadn't been fed properly, the wispy hairs denoting fragility rather than masculinity. It looked as if it had been trapped in the wild, mistreated in captivity. It sat in a cup and around it some leather straps and then below the false leg itself. It looked healthier, more male. She reached out and ran her hand up and down the smooth surface.

'What does it feel like?' he said.

'Like a piano leg,' she said.

'You feel up piano legs often, then, do you?'

She laughed.

'Do you think it's grotesque?'

'No.'

'Do you find it attractive?'

'No.'

'Do you find me attractive?'

She laughed again. He prodded her with it.

'So how about those freckles, then.'

'Not on your life.'

'How about a kiss, then?'

'Why?'

''Cause I told you things.'

'Not everything.'

'More than anybody else. Go one, one kiss.'

'All right. But no funny business. OK?'

'OK.'

He bent over. She turned her head back.

'OK?' she asked.

'OK.' He started to tap her arm. 'One, two, three, four . . .'

She pulled her arm away.

'I said no. Nighty-night.'

And that was that. In the morning they were up before dawn, tiptoeing out of the house before the woman or her baby awoke, a half-bottle of wine and a hastily scrawled note the only evidence of their stay. She'd be glad they'd gone, they knew, no stilted conversations over breakfast, no worries about being seen, an acknowledgement that their ties were only fleeting, cast off on the new tide. They walked into the next town with dew on their feet, their faces fresh and cold. She felt like she was in a Western, going to shoot up the town. Her father had left her. Now she wanted to leave too, feel the world's plunge.

They decided to head north, see some friends of hers in Coventry and then across to Nottingham, where she had been at university. There was a logic to it now, and an interest in the geography of appropriation, the map that outlaws drew. He stole cars all the way up, whenever the mood or the petrol gauge told him to, residential area, supermarket parking bay, railway forecourt, one car left, another car taken, bouncing from town to town like they were rolling dice, driving on a Monopoly board, strangers to fate. Motorways, crowded areas, surveillance cameras, he seemed indifferent to their dangers, even once cruising past a patrol car at seventy-one miles an hour, just for the hell of it, dumping the car with a howl of glee twenty minutes later outside a local magistrates' court. Indeed, after a while she understood that caution would be their undoing, inhibit the flow of their unguarded action. It was like a prolonged weekend on drugs, the pace of their lives running at a speed wholly incommensurate with everyday life, regulated by different rules of engagement, and all the while talking talking talking, like it was coming out of their ears, bubbles of conversation, his mum, his dad, her mum, her dad, the interloper; leaning in, holding back, talking in close, stopping for leg stretches and cafe meals, convulsed in laughter, engaged in argument, driving and seeing, talking and touching, yet no invasion of privacy, no attempt to rule the spaces in between, no ground to give up, no territory to conquer. She was not interested in men, she knew that now, but in him there grew a fascination, the flash in his eyes, the look of his laugh, and the pencil drag of his right leg, drawing scurrilous cartoons across the country.

It wasn't always easy. One car they stole ran out of petrol after one mile. They'd left it by the side of the road and walked back into the residential area, acting like a couple of snogging teenagers while over her shoulder he was sizing up the next opportunity. There was no malice present, no desire to harm, just to get away, keep moving. She tried not to read the news, though it was hard to avoid the headlines, knowing that somewhere underneath, unreported, lay her father's story. Then she heard, through Mark, that he hadn't gone at all, that he'd come back, just like she asked, and for some reason which she didn't fully understand she was disappointed, thinking of him at home. And it came to her, ducking down as Mark revved the engine of another car, and they roared away, as she slung her bag on the back seat and rummaged through the collection of cassettes jammed in the glove compartment, that this was why Suzanne went to war, why she wanted Matty to go with her. She wanted to experience pure excitement, pure fear, wanted to share it with someone, uncover something they would never forget, something that was theirs alone, bring it back to Anglefield Road, plant it in their garden, settle back underneath its blossoming branch. That was why she liked being with Mark. He wanted to take her with him, to share the journey, divide the memory. Later that day, parked up across from a sports centre, the car door open, she sat on his knee feeding him cheese and pickle sandwiches she had stolen from the last service station. It was her contribution, making the money go further, though she was inept. She didn't have his natural ease, his thoughtlessness.

'How did you get so good at it?' she asked. 'Nicking cars.' Mark licked his fingers, his right leg jiggling under her.

'Belinda, the girl who . . .'

'Yes, I know.'

'Her dad was a garage owner, is a garage owner, second-hand cars mostly. He let me mess around with them a bit, showed off to me too, how to wire them, how to work the locks on some of them. We got on well, until . . .'

It was something that neither of them wanted to talk about. She had pointed across the road to a dark green affair.

'After we've finished, what about that one,' she said. 'It looks a nice colour.'

He'd stopped eating, pushed her off his knee, suddenly serious.

'I'm glad you've said that. From now on you choose. OK?'

'OK.'

'We'll go to York. See the cathedral, go to the races.'

'And after that Edinburgh. John O'Groats.'

'Bloody hell. How long have you got, then?'

She rang her boss in London, Mr Fletcher, and told him that her dad was having a hard time of it, her mum being on the *Canberra*, stifling her laughter as the good man puffed up his patriotism and told her not to worry, to come back when she could. They drove up to York, where she stole three bottles of whisky from the same shop in the space of twenty minutes. They stayed the first night in a car park near the cathedral, where Mark counted the freckles on her back by the glow of the minster floodlights. In Carlisle he enumerated the configuration found upon her arms, and in Dumfries those decorating her legs. But it wasn't until the dark stone of Edinburgh and a walk above the castle, her bare back upon the grass, the pink sunglasses, the only trophy they kept, secure upon her face, that she closed her eyes to the afternoon heat and fell asleep to the constant drone of his final counting. He never did tell her how many.

Matty was moving things around in the kitchen, opening drawers, wiping down surfaces, working the toaster up and down.

'I can't believe it, that a daughter of mine would do such a thing.'

'We only used it to get here quickly, Dad. We didn't do anything to it.'

'Thank God I changed my mind. God knows what would have happened if I hadn't come back.'

'Nothing would have happened, Dad. You should have gone.'

'What!' Matty's neck flared, outraged. 'It was you who wanted me to stay. You pleaded with me.'

'Yes, I wanted you to stay, and when I heard about the *Sheffield* I thought it could have been you and wanted to see you again, just to make sure that you were here after all, that I hadn't imagined it all, but when I came in, and saw the empty bottles and the laundry and the house all messy I knew that you should have gone. I can see that now. You left them, Dad, left them all. And now you wished you hadn't.'

Matty had tears in his eyes. He fished out the clutch of paper, waved it in front of his daughter.

'She sounds so strange, Marcy,' he said, 'as if I don't know her at all, as if she doesn't know me.'

'Perhaps she doesn't. Perhaps she doesn't want to. There's a different you back at home now, just as there's a different her out there.'

'I did it for you, Marcy.'

Marcy looked at her father, for the first time seeing him through Suzanne's eyes, what a woman might need sometimes, in the true matter of a man. Not a patio builder, not a bill payer, not even father to their mother, but as companion to the journeys each other must make.

'You did it for this, Dad, the house, the garden, Anglefield Road. It was your excuse to jump ship. It would have been better if you'd waited until it was all over.'

'I suppose you think I've been a bit of a fool.'

'Well, who do you think I take after?'

The weary smile came over him. At least she'd come home, at least she'd told him.

'Go and have a shower,' he said. 'Wash the worry off your face. I'll go and see what I can do. In the car park, you say?'

*

Marcy undressed, bundled her clothes up into an old carrier bag. She'd take them over later. She hadn't told her father everything, of course, how could she, of the argument they'd had, him wanting to leave the car at the top of the road just for a laugh, her flouncing out the door, making him promise to park it somewhere else, angry that even in irresponsibility he couldn't show some sense. Didn't tell him either of the long, dreamless sleep she fell into, exhaustion and relief her somnambulates, only to wake in the none too early morning, looking about her room for her shoulder bag for her first cigarette of the day, conjuring up on the blank white of her counterpane the all too clear image of where she had seen it last, slung on the dark green leather upholstery of a four-door saloon, how she had closed her eyes willing an alternative scene to materialize to her rescue, how none came. She had been planning to do another breakfast special, orange juice, bacon, maybe waffles and take them up to her father's bedroom, a way of knocking down the door of her neglect and selfishness, opening curtains to a new companionable dawn, but now saw a more important errand to make, five minutes later crossing the road, clad hastily in her old jeans and a sweater, the sweat of last week's travelling clinging to their folds, only to find the door to the Roaches' back garden locked, the cat coming out of nowhere to rub up against her leg as the front door opened to the sound of Roach taking in the morning milk. She had run back to her house breathless, remembering the garden gate at the back which no one used, and how, protected, she might negotiate the tangle of the embankment, get to him that way, finding Suzanne's wellington boots on the back porch, slipping them on before running quickly down the lawn, worried that at any moment her father might draw back the curtains and bring a halt to her desperate plan, conscious of the march of stripes half hidden by the morning's silvery threads that had conquered the grass, conscious too of how it wasn't stopping, this living outside herself, this overflow of uncertainty overwhelming her, running yet again towards the peculiar lad that had lived next door to her for eight, nine years, whom she had gone out with briefly, sat at the pictures with, knocked back brandies in the pub, stood immobile one night pressed up against her in the well of her parents' porch while he worked his perfunctory mouth over her, his eyes smiling at her patient indifference, shrugging it off, walking away without so much as a second glance. Why did she agree to hitch up with him, why was she pleased when he turned the trip inside out? Would her father ever realize the answer to that? The gate had eased open more easily than she had anticipated, and she was surprised too how the foliage seemed to guide her towards her destination, waves of bracken and bramble giving way to a hidden path which ran parallel to the fence, curling out once to skirt round a vicious tangle of thorn, then running down to a waiting flight of log, like something you might find on an adventure playground, upended for a children's treasure island climb, delivering her into what she recognized as the barren grotto of the Roaches' back garden and the half-hidden log cabin, and the recluse inside, recovering, like she had been from their long, shipwrecked voyage. She ran quickly up to where she knew he'd be, going up to the thick cellophane window without thinking, never imagining what she would see, him naked, sunk into an armchair with a shotgun over his legs, the long sweep of his hand oiling the barrel, his false leg lying like a discarded coat on the desk in front of him and hanging from it, by the thread of cord, a white linen bag which for a moment she thought must be hers, the one Suzanne had first given her on that first trip, the complimentary toilet bag that P&O give out to all State Room passengers, but which she knew could not be hers, lying as hers did tucked in the depths of her shoulder bag with her eyeliner and tweezers and the set of contraceptive pills which she had gone to such emotional lengths to obtain and which she had never used and never would, she knew that now, the letters on the linen twisting back and forth as the stock of the gun nudged it with every thorough preserving stroke. She stood there imagining how it would have looked, the pale stump of his thigh and Suzanne's tanned body under that coat, feet stuffed into the very boots she was wearing, how she had come back that night, clumping back over the lawn, a whiff of nakedness cutting through the heavy scent, yes of course, of the Lebanese Red that they themselves had left in all those cars, not simply by the exhaled smoke but in the neatly rolled joint they had bequeathed to each and every one: a stalling card, was how Mark had described it.

She pulled open the door. Keeping her voice still, she said, 'Have you got a licence for that?'

'Might come in handy one day, when the Argies invade,' he replied, whipping the package off its hook and stuffing it between his legs. 'Fancy a smoke?'

She shook her head.

'What's with the clothes.'

'I'm going to burn them, just in case. Give me yours and I'll burn them too.'

'You talk as if we're criminals!'

'We are.'

She told him of their misfortune. He didn't seem at all worried, just inconvenienced.

'Bad time to go cherry picking,' he said, 'what with the rush hour and all the briefcases and the fact that the fucker's locked.'

He hopped unembarrassed to get dressed, stuffing the bag into a distant drawer. Where did she stand, Marcy wondered, when she unveiled her wares? By the door, on the desk, in front of his armchair? How close, how distant? How long?

They couldn't get close immediately, commuters hurrying down, buses of schoolchildren driving past, husbands being dropped off by their wives, six or seven others parking near the station entrance. They sat by the canal, waiting, neither of them speaking much. And then, the traffic stopped and there was no one.

'Good place to nick from, though, if you can pick the time,' Mark said, brushing down his jeans. 'There's always quiet moments.'

She kept a lookout while he worked a thick band of plastic down. The lock wouldn't budge.

'Poxy fucking car,' he said. She kept on looking. Did she move, Suzanne, or was it still life? And despite what he said, what exactly was it that he saw? The past, the future, the unobtainable present?

'I know,' she said. 'I know who she is, your Lady Godiva.'

He didn't stop working, though she could see his hand tighten for a moment.

'Bet you don't.'

'Bet I do. I've just trod the same path myself, remember. And your dope bag. That's hers, isn't it?'

She looked into his eyes, thinking of what he had seen; the same view as her father.

'Don't think badly of her, Marcy. She was trying to help, that's all. Like your freckles, trying to make it all a bit more enjoyable. I never told you how many, did I. Jesus!'

He pulled her down as Ellen Roach appeared suddenly walking towards the station, the bellow of a horn flattening them against their fear. They crouched down until she disappeared inside. Another car turned in.

'Did she see us?' Marcy had asked.

'She saw something. I don't think she realized it was us. We'd better get out of here. Try later.'

And there her bag and their futures lay.

*

Matty closed the door to the hum of the downstairs shower. He wore gloves and an old jacket, in the right-hand pocket of which lay a half-brick. Outside the day looked no different than it had half an hour ago. Across the road Patsy was tidying up the undergrowth beneath the drawing-room window, the twins busy by her feet with building towers out of flowerpots, Freddie would be inside, trying to put his advice into practice. Smoke was rising from out the back of the Roaches', though the car wasn't in the drive. The Armstrongs' stucco rose dirty white and silent. What was it about houses, how they changed, these little plots of land surrounded by bricks and mortar, and the creatures locked inside them, all different, all the time. Husbands, wives, sons, daughters, mothers, fathers, uncles, aunts, friends, lovers; moving in and out, crossing thresholds, causing waves. What was it? You bought a house, you lived in it, you talked to your neighbour. You went to work. You came back. You went on holiday. You came back. All you wanted was for it be all just so, all you wanted. Was it too much to ask? Wasn't that what roads like this promised, for everything to be just so? Wasn't that why they lived there, why they had locks on the door, stripes on the lawn, why they bothered?

'Not warm enough for you?'

He looked up. Hector stood on a ladder, putty knife in hand.

'Builder's merchants,' he said. 'Thought I might try and look the part.'

'An extension, is it?'

'Patio.'

'Very nice.'

The car was still there. It stood isolated, two-thirds down, at the back of the car park, as if on display, silver, shining in the sun as if a spotlight were playing on it. He walked past it slowly, recognizing the bag lying on the back seat, the Thai scarf that he had given Marcy on her last visit jammed carelessly into the top. His daughter's bag, her expectations stuffed inside. How he wanted to clasp it safe, to take her future home, to lay it, unharmed, at her feet, to demonstrate his power as father, protector, the man she could turn to. All that stood between them was a thin sheet of glass, an invisible wall that only he could climb. He skirted round the perimeter and ambled by again, pulling the door handles, turning on his heel and testing the other side. All locked. A woman came up the road dragging a shopping basket. He crossed over, looking across the railings over to the canal. He'd never liked it, green and sluggish, enlivened only by the occasional barge and the odd dead dog. Down there lay the keys, the idiot. What if he jumped in, tried to find them? Ridiculous! A camper van passed, then coming the other way a double-decker bus. Matty bent down, pretending to tie his shoelace. Any moment now a train would be due; cars would arrive, prospective passengers, and he'd be sunk. A couple of workmen got off the bus and disappeared into the station, decorators judging by the splashes of paint on their overalls. And then, as a cloud's shadow crept across, the area fell quiet, as if the lights had dimmed and the audience had settled down, waiting for the opening scene. He weighed the half-brick in his hand. It seemed pitifully light. He should have brought a whole one. He took a deep breath and half running, crossed the road, the brick at the ready. He checked. No one. He threw it against the window. The brick bounced back at him, fierce, like a batted cricket ball and he caught it, unawares, in his hand. He looked around. No one. Standing back he hurled at the window, breaking a fingernail as the brick shot out of his hand. The window shattered, showers of glass pouring into the car, the brick punching into the lip of the bag, a common bauble set in silk. He leant in, but couldn't reach. He fumbled and released the door lock.

'Oi, you!'

A portly man in uniform, the ticket collector, was standing in the station entrance. Matty wrenched open the door. Grabbing the bag he ran across the road, jumping the fence, sliding down to the towpath. Though he could hear the man shouting, he didn't seem to be making any effort to catch him, and he'd been too far away to get a decent look at him, thank God. He knew where he was going. Half a mile away was the new pedestrian bridge that led to the estate above Anglefield. They were always causing mischief up there. He'd dump the jacket, and walk back, his duty done.

Another cry went up. One of the workmen pushed past the official and began sprinting across the road towards him, arms pumping like he was on a race track. He was shouting, the words clanging through the air like a gong being beaten at the foot of the stairs, enough to have the whole town coming out of their rooms. He couldn't believe it, someone shouting, 'Stop, thief! Stop, thief!' and he not five hundred yards away from home. And Hector, hadn't he been a magistrate?

Rounding the bend he saw the humpbacked bridge, beyond a dog of some sort, lapping at the cloudy water, front feet splayed, his owner some way off, thrashing at the long grass with a walking stick. This was bad. The workman was closing fast. He wasn't shouting any more, there was no need. He'd catch up with him soon enough. The dog looked up, his muzzle slippery with strings of green, and began to bark. Matty ducked into the arch of the bridge and took to the steps leading up to the road. He was out of breath. The man was almost on top of him. He could hear the flump flump flump of his feet and the solid determination of his breath, and then, as he neared the top, felt the lunge on his back and the grab of his coat, the exclamation of seizure driven not by a sense of public duty, but by the overwhelming compulsion of the chase, ignoring the fact that all Matty was trying to do was to save his daughter as any father might, nothing bad, and that in his pig-headed, interfering ignorance this man was jeopardizing everything he had worked for, his daughter, his reputation, his respected life, and thus cornered, blind to everything but the need for preservation he turned and clasping the dusty jewel, hit the man squarely in the face, saw him reel back, his nose somehow wrong, his fingers clutching at something bursting from his mouth, bubbled oaths spluttering forth as he lurched forward, regaining a desperate balance. Matty averted his eyes, hitting him once again, the man turning in sudden unexpected study at the wall opposite, fingertips feeling the stone as if there were hieroglyphs he wished to trace, slipping suddenly sideways like a drunk on a train. Matty stuck an unwilling hand out as his pursuer folded up, his back against the wall, legs sticking out, head lolling against his chest like a badly stuffed November guy, a paintbrush sticking out from the front pocket of his overalls, splashes of a new colour, their decoration.

He scrambled up into the road, dropping the brick into the water, wiping his hands free. Twenty minutes later he was back home. Marcy, still down in the basement, called up.

'Dad?'

He slung the bag over the banister and made for the upstairs bathroom, the picture of the Parthenon on the wall, Suzanne squinting in the sun. In the corner stood the shower unit he had put in the month before she had settled in, with P&O bathrobes and the *Canberra* engraved on its clear glass doors. He locked the door, turned on the tap and slid down the wall, fully clothed. His eyes were misting up. He wanted to sleep. Outside the sun was shining. The cold water beat upon his head. He felt nothing.

*

Richard couldn't see out of the car very well and it took him several minutes to realize that he'd run into a sudden shower. The road had appeared so different he'd barely registered the familiar landmarks by which he judged his usual progress, the food factory works, the strange Gothic house standing back, the line of suburban houses which seemed pressed, like so many caged animals, against the barrier of the road.

He knew Stevenage, but not the leisure centre. It was not what he had wanted, the crowds, the noise, the smell of cheap cooking fat and chips churned up with the chlorinated water. The cafe overlooked the swimming area a few feet below. At the far end a blue tube of intestine shat squealing children into the play area. Below in the main pool the wave machine threw swimmers up and down, some clinging on the side, unsure of the enjoyment. They talked over a Formica table, two cups of tea and two slices of cake, an unwashed sauce bottle the shape of a tomato, the decoration in between. She was wearing a skirt of dull red, and a coat of cheap black leather. She looked paler than he recollected, fatter too. But when she took the coat off, her green sweater cut short on the upper arm, the young swell of her rose up like a bird plum on the wing, fluttering memories of his recent dreams.

'Did you bring his picture?' she asked.

'Yes.'

He pushed one of Mark, taken six months ago, towards her.

'It's over a year and a half old. I couldn't find one of his uniform.'

'Not bad . . . but.'

'What?'

She smiled.

'He looks younger than I imagined, not as soldier like. Hair's quite long too.'

'That's taken when he was on leave. He always does that, when he's on leave, grows his hair. A lot of them do. When you're in the army, even out of uniform, you tend to stand out; the haircut, the bearing, so when they're on leave they like to blend in a bit. Lots of blokes try and pick fights, you know, if they think you're in the army, to prove how hard they are. Girls too, shy away, think they're just rough.'

'I'm not shying away. I've written him, like I said.'

'Any reply?' It was strange. He wouldn't have been surprised if she had said yes. Why shouldn't he have a son on the *Canberra*, a good son, the son he'd deserved?

'No. You?'

'One letter. They're treating them royally, on the ship. Best barracks he's ever had.'

'Is he scared?'

'Even if he was he wouldn't tell me. That's the sort of lad he is. He wouldn't want to worry his dad. He'll be nervous, who wouldn't be, but he's got his mates, a great bunch they are, and his sergeant and the officers. They know what they're doing.'

'Did you mention me?'

'Course I did. Told him to look out, you know, for your letter. But don't be surprised if you don't hear from him straight away, Amy. They're only allowed one letter a week, he said. So family first, naturally.'

She played with the ends of her hair, looking round to the group of young men working the fruit machines. Stale smoke hung on her breath.

'So how are you, Amy?'

'Doing OK.'

'You still with the same crowd.'

'Yeah.'

'That boy, what's his name?'

'John.'

'John, still giving you a hard time.'

'He's all right.'

'Oh? I thought you didn't like him much.'

'He's all right. For a bloke.'

They laughed. He bent down and brought up a box he'd come in with.

'Look, I brought you these.' He opened the lid.

'Shoes!'

'A new type of trainer. The point is, they're the type Henry's wearing on the boat, training. I thought you might like a pair.'

'You don't know my size.'

'Yes, I do. Just by looking. Size, width, colour of toenails.'

She pulled a face and bending down, unzipped the high-plat-formed boot that she wore. Ugly things, bad for the feet too. Released from its constricting grip, her foot spread out, blood rushing back to her toes. They were stubby, unvarnished, the outer toe crushed up against its neighbour, the others leaning sideways like a collapsed fence, a sure sign of stunted growth. She eased the trainer on, stuck her foot out, and worked the laces through the eyelets, the bend of her arms pleasantly fleshy as she pulled tight, a look of simple happiness on her face. When was the last time Mark or Ellen had appreciated such a gift, not burdened it with sour protestations concerning the colour, the style, even the very fact of being asked to put them on? The other boot came off, the other Bronco slipped on. She stood up and looked down. She had been transformed into a girl fresh out of the day's schooling.

'You perfect poppet,' she said.

He pointed to the discarded boots.

'Better for you than those things.'

'Cost me twenty quid!'

'And a pair of strained arches. I'd pay you just not to wear them. I can't bear to see ill-fitting shoes, the harm it does. Constric-tion, Amy, hinders development. It's true for feet and it's true for life.'

She sat down again, turning her feet to look at the soles and heels.

'I smell a lecture coming on.'

'I think I lectured you enough last time, don't you.'

She twisted her hair.

'I've been thinking about that. You know what you said, that you'd help me, find a job and that if I wanted, that you'd put a good word in, one of those shops you know?'

He'd said that? He had no recollection of it.

'Yes.'

'Well, I pooh-poohed it at the time, but I've been thinking, like you said, it would be a start, get me out of Mum's hair, give me a taste of independence, get me on the basement floor. What was it you said?'

Roach remembered that. He'd said it to Mark hundreds of times.

'Once you're on the basement floor you can only go up.'

'Right, and do you know what, the very next day I read an article about that actress, Glenda Jackson. She started out serving behind at Boots. So, I thought: yeah, Richard's right. Why not me?'

'That's the spirit.'

'So, would you do it?'

Richard was beginning to sweat. She was taking his advice, seeking his help. If only he'd had a son like her! How he wished he hadn't deceived her, hadn't led her on. Yet if he hadn't she'd have never talked to him, never trusted him, never looked up to him. Here he was, wanting to be fired, helping Amy to get a job. Oh, Amy!

'I wouldn't blame you if you don't want to really. I can be a right rude cow when I want to. I'd probably only fuck it up.' She put her hand to her mouth. 'Pardon me.'

Richard brushed the word away. She hadn't used it like Mark would have, to rile him, to bruise the house with his anger. She'd just said it, like it was her life. Oh, Amy, life!

'It isn't just about serving customers, Amy. There's lots of other opportunities in retail. You might find out something that you're good at, if not selling, then stock control, accounting, window-dressing even.'

'You mean like mannequins?' Roach nodded, pleased that he was breaking through.

'There's an art to that and no mistake. If you took a shine to that the world would be yours. All those big shops in London, Selfridges, Harrods, pay a prince's ransom for a top window dresser.'

'I don't know about London, all my mates being here.'

'Amy. Moping around Stevenage isn't going to do you any good.'

'I don't mope.'

'Yes, you do. Those boys at the machine, they know you, the woman behind the counter, she knows you, I dare say half the people using this building know you too.'

She leant across, took his hand.

'Yeah, but it's you they're talking about. My new fancy man.'

'Amy!' He pulled his hand away. 'Look!' He pulled his wallet out and counted out three fives. He could ill afford it. 'I meant what I said about those boots. Get rid of them. There's fifteen quid. I'll give you the other five when I next see you.'

'Mr Roach!'

'No, I mean it. Throw those medieval torture implements away. Go on. I dare you.'

It was the dare that did it. She walked up past the boys at the machine and to the rubbish bin by the door, winking at their stunned silence on the way back. There was a new energy to her step. Roach beamed, proud.

'Brought your cossie?' she joked. 'I brought mine.'

'Don't be daft.'

'Why not? I'm going to. You can hire them, you know.'

He bought another cup of tea. When she came out she stood on tiptoe and waved at him. He stirred in the sugar, hand trembling. It was flashy, the bikini, like the blouse she had worn. He couldn't imagine a young woman more intentionally unclothed for him than this, the brazen squash of her breasts exercised so matter-of-factly in familial, friendly waves, distracting attention from the unintended wobble of her thighs, how in his staring he tried to avoid the sight of that other place, barely covered, and above her baby stomach, which, despite its physical bloom, spoke of an inner under-nourishment, a pregnancy of neglect. He saw how young she was, how her body, for all its bravuraed display looked uncertain, unsure, as if only born recently into the world, required to accommodate all the things she didn't know, and before them both the waters calling her down. The warning klaxon sounded and holding her nose she jumped in, squealing. The waves began to run the length of the pool, the swimmers rising and falling, rising and falling, their bodies in a kind of suspended peace. He had never seen a wave machine in action before. There'd only been an ordinary swimming pool when Mark was little. He hadn't gone there much either. For a moment he felt like running over and joining in. Richard Roach behaving wildly! Amy had swum out to the centre of the pool, the waves increasing in pace and height. She called out, swimming towards him, but the wave carried her back. She tried again, cresting the wave and flailing furiously, only to be swept back again. He stood up, hand to his mouth as she struggled one more time, her eyes fixed upon his. He wanted to reach out, to bring her to safety. He wanted his son with his arm tattoos and his military haircut to appear, to cry in youthful joy and jump in after her, lift her up on his muscular shoulders, for them to rise out of the water before him, the burst of their appreciation streaming over all their lives. She waved once more and let herself be carried away.

She came back, her hair flattened, eyes watery and red. Her lovely smell had gone.

'I'd better go. Mum's expecting me.'

'That's OK. I'll ask around for you, about a job.'

She nodded, then reached out, turning the photograph towards her.

'Can I can keep it?'

'Course you can.'

'I'll just keep on writing, then.' She picked the picture up from the table, stuck it in the pocket of her coat. 'He's got one of me, you know. I'll be on his wall and he'll be on mine. It'll be like a story book, when we meet.' She bit a nail. 'Do you think we will?'

'If he doesn't he'll have to answer to me!' he said, tapping his chest. 'Tell you what, though. Maybe he can include a letter to you in his next letter to me, two for the price of one like, to get round the restrictions. I'll write and tell him.'

'Would you?'

'Look, I'll be back here in a couple of weeks. Why don't we meet up here again, two weeks today. May the nineteenth, no not that, I've got a sales do on. The twenty-first, how about that? Friday. I might have something for you. If you don't have anything else on, we could have that dinner.'

He had stood at the window, watching as she crossed the car park, playing half-hearted hop-scotch over the empty parking lines. He looked at his watch.

*

'What's the time?'

Ellen turned away and kneeling on the bed leant across to the foot, where her bag lay. She picked it up from the floor and started to rummage around.

'Jesus, it's half four.'

He caught her looking at herself in the mirror opposite.

'Don't move,' he said. 'Just keep looking.'

He threw back the sheet and kneeling behind her, put one hand on her shoulder, the other around her folded waist. Her skin was creased and stuck with sweat. She raised her head up and stared at the reflection. She spread her knees very slightly and straightened her arms.

'You moved.'

'Just to see a bit better.'

'All right now?'

'Yes.'

Her voice dropped.

'Oh God,' she said.

'I know.'

It was like falling down a lift shaft.

Nothing was spoken for a time. He was slow and deliberate. She might have been not there. And then, he spoke again. He seemed far away, quizzical.

'You weren't moving then, I hope?'

'No. Just looking.'

'Oh? And what can you see?'

His voice was calm, distant as if he was busy doing something mundane, like unblocking the sink or mending a fuse. What could she see, aside from the rigid set of her arms, his set of fingers gripped upon her shoulders, their bodies bent to a task that seemed to demonstrate nothing but a degeneration of appetite. What could she see? A wife in her forties cheating on her husband, a mother of nineteen years neglecting her son; an older woman being used by a younger man; a younger woman fearful of losing her looks, unhappy at gaining others; the face of a young girl's forgotten dreams; the hardened features of a woman's abandoned ones. Once there had been a bride of twenty here, revealed before her pink-faced cherub, smiling at the wonder at his initiation; once there had been a double bed and she on all fours playing horses with her infant son, his little body riding hers; earlier times too, before them both, wonderful times; Ian in his hot attic bedsit, a donkey's brays in time with the creaking seaside springs; a four-poster outside Oxford, his unkempt locks still smelling of the river; sitting up in bed with Sorren, feeding each other fish and chips, the newspaper greasy on the counterpane, Newcastle's winter rain beating against the window. What did she see here? A room with only mirrors and she the prisoner sentenced to look at herself for the rest of her life, desperate to escape; behind her who? The man come to set her free, another jailer? What was it he had said? When you get to the top there's nothing there. Wasn't that the same for this relentless pounding, this wordless parody of love-making? How many others had debased themselves before this silver-backed altar, wondered at the anguish of their expression, felt like a refugee, cast out upon an alien territory, unable to make themselves understood. What could she see? Nothing but envy and disgust. Nothing but shame and retribution. Not one good feeling except the absence of it.

He gripped his hands firmly on her hips, his body slapping up against hers, like waves against a boat. She threw her head back and looked straight at the distorted image of her self. Her mouth was open. It was dark and pink inside.

'What can I see?'

Her voice began to rise, her breath coming short. She threw an arm back and gripped him close. 'I can see you fucking me, you bastard!' she cried. 'I can see you fucking me!'

*

Anglefield blooms, the spring green turning darker on the trees, the growing light blurring the edges out of the day. For the most part Marjorie works in the garden, planting out her annuals, tying back the spring's daffodils, kneeling on the square of carpet she carries around, weeding out her thoughts, placing them alongside her geranium pots, out from the last frost into the sun. In the mornings Hector is at his part-time job, checking the accounts of a local mail-order firm, but this is the season when Marjorie cuts back on her other commitments. There's too much to do, too much at stake. A neglected week in this month and you betray a garden's promise. Besides, there is the matter of the *Canberra*. So little has been heard. Even Matty seems distressed.

Matty's lawn, however, is anything but. Freddie has seen to

that. Most early evenings he is out there, raking, spiking, fertilizing, carrying out an extensive programme of extermination. It is an invasion of sorts, but one which Matty is content to accept. It's Freddie's way of saying thank you. He works alongside, mixing cement, building the brick wall, levelling the ground for the flagstones which lie, stacked, in the garage. When Suzanne comes home she will see a transformation, not simply of the house and garden, but of the whole tenor of their life. A patio is open, expansive; the lawn speaks not of encapsulation but of movement, its lines fresh and looking outward, to a new horizon. He wouldn't mind if they upped sticks after this. The lawn as runway, the patio as apron, the house as departure lounge. He spends most mornings over at the Millens, sitting in at their dining room table, working through their financial forecasts, munching through plates of biscuits with Patty and Freddie, jugs of lemonade at the ready. It's a sound proposition, Freddie's idea. Patsy has already been to see two prospective manufacturing clients. Smiths is the next hurdle, then the bank. If he had money he'd be tempted to sink a little in himself. As a matter of fact he does have a little money, not much, but enough to pay a printing bill or two. Twice he's been on the brink of suggesting some kind of partnership, but then he looks at Freddie and thinks again.

For Richard Roach it doesn't take long for the two weeks to come around, two weeks to claw back the sales, two weeks driving up and down his patch composing the letter that a brave son of his might write. Mark is back, unable to give a good account of his absence, the permanent smirk on his face something to do with Marcy no doubt, the trip fruitless, of course, Mark still jobless, still impossible, holed up in the shed again, barely coming out for meals, the date for his next court appearance only a month away.

Roach accompanies him to see his probation officer, who impresses upon both of them the need for Mark to stay at home and find a job. Mark stares out the window.

'I'm going to blow this town,' he says, 'just as fast as my leg can carry me.'

The probation officer looks across, as if to say, 'Is this what you let him get away with?' Roach smiles thinly, hoping for a sign of understanding. He is given none.

'That was no way to talk,' he tells him, driving back.

'Shouldn't have come, Dad. I warned you. I'd have been much better on my own.'

'Seems no one's good enough for your company.'

Mark sniggers, leaning back in his seat, a pose of unexpected masculinity.

'Marcy didn't seem to object.'

'No? I suppose that's why she left in such a hurry.'

Mark falls silent. That went home.

'Freddie says she only stayed half a day, and then buggered off back to London. Couldn't wait.'

Mark shrugs his shoulders.

'You don't seem very interested. I thought you would have been, after all that time in her company.'

'It was three weeks, Dad. What do you want? For us to be secretly engaged, that we dropped off at Gretna Green and got married?'

'Your mother . . .'

'My mother what?'

'Your mother was pleased that you went, had found a friend who got you out of the house. We were both hoping she'd instil a sense of responsibility in you.'

Mark starts giggling.

'What have I said?'

The laughter grows louder. He bangs his hand on the wheel.

'What have I said?'

This is where his life fades, when he is cold and grey and alone. He is not whole, not himself. How could he be, surrounded by such deliberate misunderstandings? The man his son is talking to is not the Richard Roach he knows himself to be but another, an imitation of himself, driving as Richard Roach but not Richard Roach, talking as Richard Roach but not Richard Roach, going out to earn Richard Roach's living for him, while Richard Roach lies somewhere else, driving but not driving, talking but not talking, working but not working. The Richard Roach he knows is judicious, understanding, good with people. The Richard Roach he knows is a good father, a loving father, a good husband too, provider, rock, protector. He has feelings too, the other Richard

Roach, feelings and passion. He is a man, the Richard Roach he knows, a man. He wants to cry out, denounce the impostor.

Twelve hours later he has the same argument with Ellen, the day before he returns to Stevenage. He has come home early, to write Amy's letter out again, to get it right, and has been forced to park the car halfway up the road, thanks to another delivery at Matty's. He opens the back door and hears her talking on the phone.

'Who knows when,' she is saying. 'He's like a limpet at the moment.'

It isn't often the phone rings in his house. He doesn't like the intrusion.

'Who's that,' he calls.

'For you.' She holds out the phone. 'Kevin, I've been holding the fort.' She presses the receiver into her breast. 'God, does he ever stop?'

Roach snatches the phone from her hand, waving her away. What had she been saying? What had he been saying? He turns into the hall mirror, as he responds to Kevin's quiet questioning, his fingers working on the mouth of a worried man. He pats his hair down. Yes, orders are beginning to pick up, yes the Bronco seems to be moving out of some shops at a very creditable rate. Yes, he was offering the right incentives, yes, he's got most of his displays in, yes, he was cold calling to see if he could replenish stock. Kevin grunts approval, and then:

'Ellen tells me you've been having a bit of trouble with your son.'

'She did?'

Roach turns to register his displeasure but she has gone back into the drawing room to pour herself another a whisky. Most days now, by the time he gets home she'll have had at least one. They never understood the rules of work, wives. Bringing in your troubles is never on. It isn't simply that it serves to undermine your authority, it makes you three-dimensional. Firms like you best when you have no hinterland. Wives, babies, health crises; leave them at reception.

'Not that I'm trying to stick my nose in, you understand.'

'Yes.' Nothing about Southampton, then.

'She said what he really needed was a job.'

'Yes.'

'You should have said. I could ask around the warehouse if you like, or some of our key suppliers.'

'That's very good of you, Kevin, considering.'

'Troubles is troubles,' Kevin says. 'I was a bit of a tearaway myself. Full day tomorrow?'

'Hertford, St Albans, Leighton Buzzard.' He gulps. 'I might even pop back to Stevenage, if I have time. I've mended bridges as best I can, but I thought . . .'

'Absolutely, Richard. Good man.'

He puts the phone down, relieved. Kevin had sounded pleased. In fact since the run-in they seemed to be getting on much better. It just goes to show what standing up for yourself can do. But still. He strides into the room.

'If he rings again, tell him I'll ring back and hang up.'

'I was only passing the time of day.'

'You shouldn't have talked about our son like that.'

'Why ever not?'

'You don't understand, Ellen. Calling him a limpet. Them knowing that I have a son like that undermines my authority.'

'Your authority!'

'Yes. My authority, brought by ten years of keeping our nose clean. You know nothing about the work environment, about office politics, about how one goes about things, what I have to do to keep us going.'

'What you have to do?' Her expression is one of insolent amusement.

'I don't see what's so funny.'

'No, I don't suppose you do.' She picks the decanter from off the floor and pours herself another drink. She doesn't even bother to put the stopper back these days.

'No, and frankly, you interfering like that, opening up fissures, can only hinder my career.'

'Opening up what?'

'Fissures. Cracks.'

He stares at the laughter bouncing about the room. He has become trapped in a scene of inexplicable madness. Ellen's head is thrown back, her eyes fixed upon a point way beyond him, beyond the house, beyond Anglefield Road, as if she has been transformed from a domestic being into an wild untamed one.

There is no more to be said. He climbs up to the box room, pulls out the writing paper and tries to write the letter he has been composing these last ten days. He uses an old pen from Mark's schooldays, one with an italic nib. Not many soldiers would have one of those. He writes and listens, listens and writes; Ellen coming up the stairs, Ellen collecting the evening's washing, Ellen pausing by his door. He writes a second draft; the television news comes on. He leaves his desk, standing halfway down the stairs to listen, but there's no news worth speaking of. He returns to the final version, Ellen brushing her teeth, Ellen crossing to the bedroom, Ellen closing the door.

He sleeps in the spare room, the room that was once Mark's. In the morning he gets up, stands in the garden in his underwear. It is the beginning of summer and yet there is nothing that he can see before him that would suggest a season of nourishment, hope. Down at the far end a ragged bonfire smoulders, something of Mark's no doubt. He walks over and pisses on it. Clouds of acrid steam rise. His toes dig into warm grey ash. The shed is silent, a curtain drawn over the opaque window. He almost understands why his son would rather be out here than in with them. He would rather be here himself.

Hertford, St Albans, Leighton Buzzard go without a hitch. Stevenage looks more compact somehow, as if the town is growing around him, taking him into its folds, its streets and shop fronts more amenable to his disposition. She's sitting there, at the same table, the same slice of cake in front of her, in jeans and a T-shirt, Bronco's on her feet.

Dear Amy,

Your letter was a lovely surprise. Lots of the lads are being given letters from girls they've never met, but I'm the only one who's got one addressed to him personally. Got your picture too. Are there any more at home like you!

Dad tells me that he's trying to find you a job. You should take it if he finds one. Everyone should have a job. I can't talk about mine, but whatever it is you're doing, a job gives you a purpose, a hold on life. I'm proud to be in the marines, serving my country, but everyone who works is serving their country too, that's the way I look at it, from a girl behind a sales counter to a brain surgeon. We're all patriots whether we like it or not.

Life here is hard and a bit uncertain. If we go we'll go in guns blazing. Here on the Canberra *we do lots of training, running, karate, bayonet practice. Did Dad tell you, he got his firm to send us all a pair of trainers. He's a bit of a hero here (what a thought, my dad a hero!), because it's kept our proper boots in trim.*

It's funny, looking at your picture thinking of you meeting up with him. Bit of an old stick isn't he? But listen to him. I have all my life. And on my return, who knows.

Regards,
Mark

'Who the bloody hell's Mark?'

'What?'

'This is from someone called Mark.'

Roach takes the letter back, trying to mask his confusion.

'Oh, stupid boy.' He stutters into his explanation. 'It's what he's known as. Because of his shooting skill. Mark's the Man, they say. He wasn't thinking.'

'I prefer Henry.'

'So do I. Still, you got a nice letter.'

'Yeah, it's great. Goes on a bit about you, though. I thought he might tell me more about himself.'

'It's understandable. Being away he'll be thinking about his family a lot. Next time, he'll probably be more, you know, expansive. Here. Guess what?'

He holds up a dark red pair of trunks.

It takes some persuading for him to climb the ladder. 'I'll go first,' she says, and that is worse in a way, following her up the steps, nervous of the bodily proximity, the barely covered indecency of her rear quarters so close to his face. At the top he doesn't know where to look, terrified that his eyes might stray, betray his thoughts, his confusion. He hasn't been undressed like this, in front of people, for a long time. He feels awkward, unbalanced. They have to wait for two children to go in front of them. He grips the railings. Looking down makes him feel giddy. The attendant beckons them over.

'Go on,' she says. 'You first. If I leave you up here you might chicken out.'

Roach lowers himself in.

'Is this right?'

'Feet out, hands to your side. When he taps you on the shoulder, go.'

He sits there, staring into the light blue void. What is he doing here? What if Kevin should see him, or Ellen, what would they make of it, a grown man and this girl in the swimming pool. He feels the tap on his shoulder and he pushes off, hoping that it won't be too fast. It starts slowly, but then, as he rounds the first curve he is suddenly tipped on his back gathering speed, the descent growing steeper, his body sliding from side to side, helpless like a baby. His legs kick in the air, as he tries to sit up, he goes up and sideways, down and sideways, he feels heavy and light at the same time, frightened and safe, Richard Roach rushing past everything, his job, his son, his wife, just Richard Roach racing against himself and he the winner. He bursts out into a cradle of water and lies there gurgling. Gasping and gurgling! As he gets up he is thrown violently onto his back, a tangle of arms and legs on top of him. He thrashes his way up, choking on the water. Amy is shaking a finger at him.

'You should get out the way,' she scolds. Roach hitches up his costume.

'I'll remember next time.'

Twelve times he goes, until his legs start to give way. Each time is better than the last, faster, slicker, the ejection almost as much fun as the ride itself. He tries different positions, in a ball, lying flat, on his stomach, upside down. Amy stands and claps. After that they walk into the pool and ride the wave machine, bobbing in and out of each other's orbit. He feels as sun to her planet, bringing her warmth and sustenance. When he is near her face lights up.

Afterwards, in the shower, he washes away the smell of chlorinated water. Other men come in and out of the stalls, some pale like him, breasts like him, but most of them fitter, younger, carrying a better physique. He does not care. He pats himself dry with handfuls of tissue paper. He has forgotten to bring a towel. He stands in front of the mirror and combs his hair, accentuating the parting. He's going to stay the night, ask her out to dinner, tell her stories about his son, to make up for the letter. When he comes out she is standing in the foyer, biting her thumb.

'Oh, Richard.'

She runs across to him, kisses him on the cheek. She hugs him. He looks around wildly, afraid that they might be seen. She is so full, so uninhibited. She is hugging him, kisses on his face, an unbearable softness upon him, like he was unable to breathe.

'What is it?'

'Oh, Richard.' She takes his hand and leads him to the ticket office, where a radio station is playing pop music.

'It just came on the news,' she said. 'They've landed. Our Henry, Richard, on the Falklands, our Henry.'

SEVEN

They'd anchored off Falkland Sound just past midnight, the sky still and starry, the water inky flat, the shoreline dark, unfathomable. It seemed unbelievable that beyond that mystery, that rise of distant solitude, lay the coming cries of battle. The ship was eerie, unoccupied, silent like the land. Two days before they had cross-decked 40 Commando and 3 Para onto other, more secure ships, the murderous roll of the previous week's waves suspended for a quietly miraculous day. Now with just hours to go they were about to deliver the only unit remaining into the very heart of the invasion, the men sitting on their haunches in the Meridian Ballroom, their camouflage gear and bits of twig sticking up from their webbed helmets, their faces blackened, the room a sea of eyes, dark and watchful, waiting in the rolling gloom of time.

They had left Ascension Island two days after the *Sheffield* had been hit, on an elongated evening, made spacious by a sublime sun, the ship restocked with beer and water, the men brown and fit and ready for what lay ahead. Any doubts as to the *Canberra*'s destination had long been dispelled. They would go where the troops would go, see them through. They had a frigate for company now, HMS *Ardent*, sleek and predatory, baring its guns like teeth on a shark, and together with the ro-ro ferry *Elk* and the tanker *Tidepool* they hooted and turned, dipped their bows and set out towards a harsher clime. A day later, 7 May, the predicted call for blood donors had come. Suzanne had been sitting in the crew's canteen huddled over a bowl of yoghurt and muesli. Dickey was making a face out of breakfast, bacon for hair, fried eggs for eyes, a nose of fried bread, bee-sting mouth of tomatoes. Suzanne placed a self-satisfied spoonful in her mouth.

'That may be all right for the limpid waters of the Aegean,' Dickey said, 'but it won't do you any good where we're going.' He poked her with his fork. 'You need an extra layer of fat on you.' Suzanne pointed her spoon to the public address speaker.

'Too late,' she said 'Hear that? Ten days, and we'll be going in.' Dickey was annoyed that he hadn't said it first.

'Old news,' he complained. 'And you shouldn't speak with your mouth full.'

'That's what I tried telling the Major last night,' offered Tina, blowing smoke over her toast. 'But would he listen?'

No one laughed. The spirit of adventure was evaporating fast.

On Sunday morning, 9 May, they said goodbye to the *Canberra* they had known. A sports day was held, military unit against military unit, armed force against armed force, the military against the civilians. There were needle matches between the Paras and the marines; tugs of wars between rifle and machine-gun companies, between chefs and gun crews, between bandsmen and medics. Suzanne had stood and cheered as Henry came fourth in the two hundred yards between bandsmen and the ship's engineers. In the all-comers version Murray became an unlikely hero, surprising everyone by coming sixth out of twelve, his performance enhanced he insisted by the muscular buttocks pumping in front of him.

'His carrot to my donkey,' he said, gasping over Dickey's celebratory glass of punch, 'though I might try and persuade him to consider a reversal of roles.'

Later that morning HMS *Ardent* demonstrated its speed and firepower by charging down the *Canberra*'s flank at thirty knots, firing its 20mm Oerlikon cannon, the sea erupting fire as the shells exploded. It was beautiful in the way that fireworks are, water shooting up into star-burst patterns, falling roman candles of white and green, fountains of a brutal, sexual release; a spectacle to be viewed as both entertainment and a demonstration of a warship's primary purpose: a deliverer of destruction and violence. Suzanne put her hands over her ears and jumped up and down. She felt exhilarated, excited.

'That's what they'll be doing before we go in, to soften them up,' Henry had shouted over the splendour. 'I wouldn't want to be on the end of that, would you?'

He put his arm round her and hugged her to him. The bruising on his face had gone; the tenderness remained. She shrugged him off with flirtatious admonishment. Public displays like that were against the rules, admitting to liaisons that the powers that be had refused to acknowledge, even when waved in front of them. No one seemed to mind. No one seemed to notice. Perhaps it was because they knew it was all coming to an end.

That evening, at the back of the Stadium, she sat with Tina as Henry and the band played their last concert. The music washed over her. All that she was aware of was Henry, how he stroked his nose twice each time before he played, the way he ran his tongue over his lips when he had finished, something he did in conversation too. He played his violin as well as his trumpet, in a quartet. Henry had told her what the piece was called but she didn't try to remember; all she had time for were the arch of his hand on the bow, his fingers running up and down on the neck, the folds of that white square of linen pressed down upon on his shoulder. Could he smell her touch upon it? When it was over he placed the violin on his knee and held the cloth out by its corners, triangular, like a mask, before folding it, once, twice, replacing it the case with as much care as he took over his violin. She wondered whether in years to come these traits could be sources of irritation or would they remain what they were now, foibles of endearment.

The weather grew rougher, colder. The glass fell, the wind rose, the officers changed out of their whites and back into their blues. Suzanne wished she hadn't thrown away her yellow windcheater. The ship began the long climb to the Falklands. Ten days Suzanne had told them, ten days, and for a while ten days it remained, the time elongated by the repetition of chore and the elasticity of distance. Ten days was ten days was ten days, and then abruptly she awoke and it was four, and the next day she awoke again and it had become two, and still they had an ocean to plough. May 15th, eight hundred and ten miles east north-east of Port Stanley, the wind was so bad the bridge lookouts had to be brought under cover. On May 16th, six hundred and fifty miles short with visibility bad, Air Threat Yellow, guns locked in place, they came upon a sight that no one had ever dreamt they would see, an ocean weighed down with the panoply of British naval might, appearing out of the gloom like smudges on blotting paper, taking fearsome shape as they themselves became absorbed in their creeping spread: HMS *Antrim*, HMS *Plymouth*, RFA *Sir Lancelot*, RFA *Sir Geraint*, RFA *Sir Galahad*, RFA *Sir Tristram*, RFA *Sir Percivale*, a convoy of nineteen ships, moving in the same direction, at the same speed, sailing into a sea of threats, threats from below, threats on the surface, but supremely and most nakedly the threat ready to pop over the horizon, dropping on a flat line of ten feet, streaking across the water in the bat of an eye; the Exocet.

The *Canberra* settled into place, the once brilliant cream of its hull now grey and streaked with blood-coloured rust. Like its companions abroad, there were guns on its bridge and along its decks; the three air-raid alerts, Air Threat White, Air Threat Yellow, Air Threat Red were dished out as regularly as bread rolls, the drill enacted three, four times a day; conversation became low, matter of fact, the drinking heavier, but accompanied by a grim sobriety that precluded high-jinks and led to only argument and troubled sleep. Now Darken Ship was no longer an order to be grumbled over, it was an essential condition of survival. Even Tina, who on occasions had enlivened her off-duty hours by hanging her black nightdress over the porthole, buckled to the task: twenty-two ships with no navigation lights, joined up in the darkness, collisions a blind man's bluff away. They began to live automatically. Meals were cooked, beds were changed, tea and coffee brewed, and yet they barely noticed.

Suzanne had expected that in these days of danger she would grow closer to the man she believed she loved, that she and Henry would spend their hours imagining the world they might inhabit afterwards, despite his lonely premonition. Her own intuition offered up a different scenario altogether, where he would come out of the war unscathed, and they would return to England together, to set fresh feet ashore. When she offered it up in the shelter of their make-believe cabin, the ship wallowing in the heavy sea, the door in danger of flying open, revealing the juvenile quality of their tryst, with its nest of blankets and little hurricane lamp and box of biscuits purloined from the kitchen, she felt him draw back, as if she had transgressed upon a territory whose property rights he guarded fiercely. 'What about your marriage?' he asked, a question that should have been inscribed above every cabin doorway on every ship, and one which she did not know how to answer, for up to that point she had not demanded an answer herself, had not even formed the question. Since those Ascension Island days, it was as if Matty and Anglefield Road had been overwhelmed by a flood tide. Whatever her marriage had been, it had existed here, on this boat, and it was here that it had been thrown overboard, without so much as a lifebelt chucked in after it. Would she have taken up with Henry had Matty been here, coming back to the cabin, the smell of the kitchens on his clothes, the tired acceptance in his lot shrinking the cabin walls to the point of suffocation? Had Matty ever expanded the world for her? Had he ever made the cabin walls disappear? Or did he always want to bring her back, a trophy, to Anglefield Road, stick her on the sofa, put her out on the patio, Anglefield Road bunged up tight, a stopper at the top and the blank wall of the railway at the bottom. She could barely bring herself to think of it, talking to the neighbours, answering their questions. How could she describe this, convey the majesty, the sheer wonder of it all.

'You could leave the marines,' she suggested, imagining the train pulling in on the other side of Anglefield's embankment and her own single suitcase departure.

'Why would I want to do that?'

She'd tried to turn the idea physical, turning herself upon him.

'To take orders from me instead.'

He rolled away.

'It's all I know, Suzy. What would I do if I left?'

What would they do *together*, that was the question, and without knowing it he had asked it. Suzanne sat up, wrapping the sheet around her, changing tactics. She could make him see it all, the reinvention of their life.

'You could work here, for a start. Become an entertainer.'

'An entertainer!'

'Why not? You could set up a little combo. Play tunes you like, like that sonata.'

'I don't think your average passenger wants to hear Schubert.'

'OK, something jollier. But you could.'

Henry drew a hand over his face, wiping the idea away.

'I don't know. It's all a bit sudden.' He sounded peeved.

Suzy laughed.

'And this isn't? I'm glad of this war, Henry, glad the *Belgrano* sank, and yes the *Sheffield* too.' She put her hand across his protesting mouth. It smelt of them both. 'Yes, I know I shouldn't be but I am. It's released me, Henry, brought me to you, brought you to me. All we can do now is die or find something new.'

'And if it's something we don't like?'

Far from drawing him out, from that hour he withdrew, not from fright at her implications, but to be closer to the responsibilities she was asking him to leave behind. Though he would meet her in their cabin, he no longer stayed the night. He preferred to be back with his mates, spending the dark hours in his wallow of bunkroom, snatching sleep, dangling his stockinged feet over his bed, weighing the equations of their lot. He was a soldier and the closer they came to war the further she found herself from him. Ascension Island had been an island of fairy tales. No wonder neither had put a foot on it, tested its solidity. If they had stood on the shore, seen the swelling waters on which they'd conducted their affair, maybe they would have realized how tenuous was their grip on the wheel, in what shifting sands they had thrown their anchor, how unlikely it was that they should find the chart to their destination.

Still, she tried, determined to follow him as best she could. In her off-duty hours she had begun to attend the same medical lectures as he, to share as much as she could the tasks that lay ahead. In the darkened room, ordinary soldiers sat and watched the life they would lead reel out before them, raw footage shot live from Vietnam, the camera jerky, exposed, the language visceral, braced in shock, the images shot in a brutal colour that she had never seen before; not like a film, choreographed, not flat like the television, but pulsating on the screen, leaking out onto the floor, shredded legs, an arm stripped of flesh, loose skin flapping in the helicoptered air, blackened lumps thrown over carrying backs, barely recognizable as human beings at all. She held oranges and stuck them with syringes. She learnt the seven points of injection, how to deal with a sucking chest wound, the life-saving properties of the anal drip; no delicacy here but humanity in its most urgent form, soldiers and medics running helter-skelter, banging on the body's door.

The 16th became the 17th: three hundred and thirty nautical miles. The seas heaved, the seas rolled, the ships ploughed on and still no Falklands. Perhaps they had disappeared. Perhaps the Argentinians had spirited them away under cover of that dirty spray and all that remained was acres of empty water.

Tuesday 18th, two hundred nautical miles short, and the ship was placed on a full war footing. Below the Crow's Nest, Henry along with the other members of the band had ripped out the plush carpet in the Stadium and they were now scrubbing down the deck, sterilizing it for its new role as operating theatre. Troops who had been helping in the galleys were withdrawn, reunited with their comrades and weapons. Everybody on the upper decks had to wear foul-weather clothing, anti-flash gear, life jacket and gas mask. It became second nature to them, like turning down sheets or carrying a tray of canapés. Dickey in protest at the waft of disinfectant rising up from below entertained the officers by serving drinks in his gas mask, his enquiries and conversation rendered if not inaudible then incomprehensible.

'The things I call Major Osgood without his knowing gladdens the heart,' he confided to Suzy one night. 'If only peacetime could be like this.'

In the early hours of the 19th, a decision was relayed from Northwood. Most of the troops would have to leave. It was too risky to have the bulk of them corralled in one, vulnerable ship. One roaming Étendard, one lucky Exocet, and Britain's elite forces would be sent to the bottom of the ocean, along with Britain's military standing. Given the weather conditions, the sea moun-tainous, boat transfer was impossible. It had been decided that they would either have to be airlifted out on sticks of eight to ten, or jack-stayed from ship to ship. One thousand two hundred men, hauled laboriously over the water; fifteen hours minimum, well into the other side of darkness; an impossible task. It had begun to dawn on them that perhaps it was *all* an impossible task; the ships, the landing, fighting not just the Argentinians but the coming winter. But then came the cold grey light and with it a sea that abated, a wind that died down. By nine o'clock a line of landing craft was circling round, ready to take the men from 40 and 3 Para as they queued up in their combat gear, their rifles and bergens, weaving down through the ship, through the Promenade Deck, through D and E stairs and passageways, through to the gun-port doors where, only weeks ago, Suzanne had leapt to freedom. There was no larking now, only nerve. The sea had quietened, but the rise and fall was titanic enough, the jump awesome. Suzanne and Tina watched as each man made his act of faith, jumping out to meet the apex of the rise, the LCU slapping hard against the side of the ship then falling away sharply, as if dropped from a great height. Everything they'd seen before this had been an act of theatre, the men playing at soldiers, firing their guns at fairground targets, coming back from Ascension Island looking more like lager louts at Blackpool then men preparing for war. Now she saw them as they were to each other, cajoling and cruel, careful and indifferent, each man both relying on and testing everyone else, their responsibilities not to Britain, not the Queen, nor to the Falklands but to themselves. They belonged to no one; that was where their strength lay.

And then all the hours and all the waiting were used up and they were going in, and only one unit left. That last day they hid amongst a screen of destroyers while ahead the helicopters patrolled, sounding their sonars for submarines. A fog lay upon the world, clouds pressing down, the sea a wispy soup, the ships around them ephemeral, emphasizing the uncertainty of their enterprise. Suzanne had imagined that they would steam in fast, ducking in under this cover, but their progress seemed indeter- minate, as if a net of suspended time had been thrown over the huge spread of ships.

The day was long, nervy. Men played cards, wrote letters, checked their kit one more time. Meals were mostly silent affairs punctuated by awkward laughter, quickly suppressed. Dusk was greeted by nervous relief, knowing the worst was yet to come, the order 'Darken Ship' echoing through the corridors. Suzanne hadn't seen Tina since the morning and uncertain whose turn it was she went down to their cabin to check. As she jumped the last set of steps she could hear a hammering down the corridor. Major Osgood stood there, fists and boots on the door.

'Open up,' he was shouting. 'I know you're in there.'

'Major?' He was red-faced again, swaying. Whisky, she thought, a good malt. Not the best time to be drinking. He kicked the frame again. She pulled him back.

'Stop it.'

'She won't come out.'

'I don't blame her, you carrying on like this. Anyway, she's not there.'

'Well, where is she, then, the little tart?'

'I don't know.' She unlocked the door, pushed it open. 'See?'

He stepped inside, half-expecting to see her hiding under the bed.

'I won't be treated like one of her toy boys. I asked her to marry me, did you know that?'

'No.'

'I thought she'd have told you. We talked of doing it on the way back.'

'I haven't seen much of her lately.'

'Unlike some. To marry me. And this is how she repays me.'

'What?' As if she didn't know.

'Making a proper spectacle of herself last night in some illegal drinking club, making me the laughing stock. I won't be having it.' He began kicking the furniture.

'Major, if you don't stop I'm going to have to call the military police.'

'Yes.' He kicked a chair one more time and stopped, the anger suddenly evaporating. 'Sorry. Not long to go, you know. Bit unsettling.'

'Don't worry about it.'

'I've been looking for her all day. I wanted to give her this.' He opened up his palm; a metallic ring lay in his fleshy hand. It smelt of engine oil.

'Took it off a bit of kit, if you must know, just till we get back. Bit short of engagement rings, this vessel.'

'Actually, Major, on most voyages we've got quite a supply of them. Whether anyone should invest in them or not is a different matter, but they do. I'll be seeing her later, I'm sure. Would you like me to give it to her?'

'Like you to throw it into the bloody sea.'

He was crying.

'Major.'

'The bloody sea!' He sat down abruptly. She put her arm around his head. His left leg was shaking.

'You know what she's like.' He nodded. 'She doesn't mean it. She just got carried away. Raising morale.'

'That's not what I heard.'

He took out a handkerchief, blew his nose. Suzanne patted the back of his hand.

'If there's one thing I've learnt working on this ship, Major, it's not to trust in rumour. A ship like this runs on tittle-tattle. Best to ignore it, get on with what you're doing. She'll come through, and so will you, God willing.' She raised him to his feet, kissed him on the cheek.

She had tidied up, left Tina a note, the ring attached by a strip of Elastoplast. A few hours to go and then everyone to General Emergency Stations. The last chance to see the convoy in all its dull glory. She walked along the deck, lines of men looking out towards themselves. Henry was there in flash gear and life jacket, tired after a day's chores, the operating theatre, the casualty lift, the stretchers, all primed. She stood alongside him, before them an empty sky of silver light and below the dark mass of ships. He gripped her arm.

'Makes you proud to be British, doesn't it?'

She squeezed him back without thinking, feeling it her instinctive duty to support him, not to show him any doubt. Patriotism. Had she ever thought it possible, to be patriotic? And yet here she was, watching the grey ships and the heaving sea and her and Henry standing in the rising dark, bits of Britain, bred and raised there, kicked and grown there. Where was it now, that Britain? In Anglefield Road with Matty and that sullen daughter, Ellen and the Cockroach barely speaking to one another, Freddy without a job, Marjorie imprisoned in her garden, Mark summoning up dope-filled dreams of her flesh; all of them waiting for something to happen, for their life to change, to break free of Anglefield Road. Was that the Britain she was proud of, or was it here, on the high seas, stubborn in its challenge to the odds. He was right. She was proud, proud of this great ship, decked out in this surreal garb, moving implacably towards an unknowable history. The *Canberra* had been built for many things but never this.

And she standing in the calm of it.

Henry was restless, she could tell.

'Go on,' she said. 'Get you back now. We'll have time enough.' She could sense his relief.

'Are you sure?' She kissed him.

'Sure. I want . . .' She fumbled in her pocket. 'It's a cliché, I know, but it matters. The thing you saved.'

She held the crucifix in her hand.

'It was blessed by the Pope,' she said. 'Did I say?'

'It's a Catholic country we're fighting. I'm not so sure it would help.'

'When he gave it me, he knew,' she insisted. 'I could tell. I just didn't know what. He gave it to me, to give to you, to bring you back.'

'Suzanne. You forget. I'm not going. I'm here with you.'

'You don't know that. None of us know.'

She pressed it into his hand and ran away, standing in front of the mirror in the ladies', unsure of who she'd been crying for, herself, Henry, all the young soldiers, washing her face with cold water before going into the ballroom, to move amongst the half-wakened flock. The army chaplains were there, walking through, saying prayers if they were wanted, telling jokes if not. She wasn't Florence Nightingale, nor were they wounded, but along with all the others she nursed them through the night, one lad thanking her for the coffee, his mate apologizing for the mess he'd left his cabin in, fragile things from resilient men. At midnight, flouting all regulations, Dickey and the bar stewards appeared in full evening dress, offering non-alcoholic drinks, nuts and raisins and packets of cigarettes on silver servers, their progress greeted with muted ripples of applause.

'I'm afraid the purser is going to find a slight discrepancy in the accounts,' he said, coming up to her, the tray empty. 'Particularly in regards to tobacco.'

'Dickey Dove, the Petty Pilferer.'

'I fear so. With another locked cabinet in my sights to boot.'

306

The ship's intercom system clicked open. The voice was harsh.

'Will the occupant of Cabin 36A on C Deck return to their cabin immediately and Darken Ship. I say immediately.'

'Isn't that yours, my dear?' Dickey asked.

'But I did it before I came out.'

'That'll be such a comfort, when we're swimming for the lifeboat.'

Suzanne ran back and flung back the door. Stanley was standing on a chair, holding the blackout canvas up above the porthole.

'I thought that would get you here.' He let the curtain drop. 'Clever, eh? So, as per my last request.'

He jumped down, legs akimbo. Suzanne pushed him aside, pinning the material firmly back in place.

'You mindless idiot. We could have been blown up!'

'And I could be court-martialled. Worth the risk, though, don't you think?'

What did he do exactly? Was it coercion, blackmail, did the way he moved and closed the door, his teeth grinning out of his blackened face, offer up a violence that rooted her to the spot. Was she willing? No, but there was something in the equation that she could not gainsay, the thought of death and a young man faced with the last moments of life, remembering Mark in his chair, and the whale blown to pieces and this young man, waiting to take the smell of her onto the battlefield. Was this her penance, what the Pope had ordained, what he had foreseen in the look they had exchanged, her sacrifice? His hands, did she try and stop them, did she move away? Wasn't this what they all wanted, what they all got?

He unbuckled his trousers.

'You're not saying no, then?'

'I'm not saying anything.'

He took her hand and led her underneath.

'I've been saving it up a bit,' he said.

'Have you.' They were heavy, cold. She thought of the priest and the stones rolling in his hand. This boy had come to her, risked all their lives, the enterprise, everything, to be with her. There was a hammer on the door, the handle turned.

'Suzy?'

Henry stood there. Stanley turned, her hand burning in the air.

'What the fuck do you want?'

Henry looked from one to the other, trying to read the signs.

'I heard over the intercom, the cabin number. I thought . . .' His eyes went from image to image: the blouse half open, the smear of black cream on her shoulder, the breath torn from her. Stanley was enjoying himself, the agitated stillness filling the room.

'Suzy, what's going on?'

Stanley stepped up to him.

'What's it to you?'

'I'm a friend.'

Stanley moved quickly, pushing him hard up against the door, their faces close together, face livid with black and green and patches of pink skin, Henry pale and trembling, unable to match the clear brutality.

Henry looked to her. 'Shouldn't you be with your outfit?' he said.

Stanley, laughing, relaxed his grip. Suzanne stared down at the floor. The question was trial enough.

'You're right. Why don't you trot along, tell them I won't be long.'

He threw him out into the passageway and shut the door.

'He sweet on you or something?'

She thought of her own preservation. She thought of Henry's.

'I don't believe so,' she said.

He came back over, walked her backwards towards the sofa.

'He's not bad, you know, for a wanker. Not much cop at the snot and aggression, though.'

'I can see that.'

'Snot and aggression, that's my stock in trade.' He pushed her down.

'I think you'd better go,' she said.

'You're saying no, then.'

'I'm saying, I think you'd better go.'

'Let me get this right. I'm prepared to die for Queen and Country and you won't fuck for them?'

'I'm saying, this isn't the best memory to be taking with you.

I'm not important to you. You should have better moments to take with you, to fight towards. This would lead you into danger.'

'What, a quick knob-job?'

'Not just. A lot of other things besides. You're a soldier, risking your life. You'll be making decisions soon that'll affect you and your mates. This would be a bad start, a bad decision. It would stay there, cloud your judgement.'

'I'm eighteen, Suzy. I wanted . . . one more time, just in case.'

'I know. But it isn't if you haven't had some attention.'

He grinned.

'But it's still no?'

'It's not no, it's not yes. It's up to you.' She looked at her watch. 'Whatever, you're going to have to go soon, otherwise I'll be accused of sabotaging military manoeuvres. He was right, you know. You should be with your unit.'

They stood there, not moving.

'Well?'

He sat down.

'My wife was twenty-three yesterday.'

'Was she?'

'Twenty-three. I married an older woman. How stupid is that?'

He pulled out his wallet.

'I got a baby too, a baby girl.' He brought out a photograph; a back garden and him balancing her on his head, the grin on his face.

'A cracker or what?'

'She's lovely,' she said.

They studied the picture together.

'She might never know who her dad is.'

'Oh, she'll always know that.'

He nodded, stuffed the picture back.

'I'm a bit of a cunt, you know. My dad was a hangman, did you know?'

'No.'

'About the last we had. Funny that, him topping murderers and that, with kid gloves, not to upset them like, and me, trained to be as hard as you can be, up against ordinary lads who haven't done nothing.'

'But both serving your country.'

'Doing things the country don't want done themselves. That's the thing, see. It makes you different. He's not a violent man, my dad, but he's set apart. While me . . .'

He cracked his knuckles. Suzanne waited. He turned his face full towards her, his whole history in his eyes. For a moment she wished she had lain down, let his rage and fear loose upon her, received it as from the gift of God.

'I'll be going, then.'

'God speed.'

'Would I get a kiss?'

'Of course you would.'

'A proper one.'

'A proper one, for all of you.'

She opened her mouth and held him and let him search for what he could not find. He stood up, straightening his dress.

'See you on the journey home, then.'

'Is that a promise?'

He opened the door. The Pope's crucifix hung from the handle on its mended silver chain. He lifted it off, threaded the links through his fingers. The cross swung to and fro, a hypnotic light.

'Yours?' he asked.

She shook her head, her eyes full of tears.

'Yours.'

*

She saw nothing after that, until back in the ballroom, out of the darkness, the sky cracked, shaking her from her walking dreams, followed by a distant rattle and a sound like paper being torn. The ship's broadcast came back on. HMS *Antrim* was firing on enemy troops on the headland. Flashes of light stabbed the dark, the men caught open eyed.

Then they felt themselves moving again, the engines stirring slowly, the approaching land rising up to meet the dawn. Suzanne stepped out onto the Promenade Deck. The day was clear, the air clean like washed glass, the sun stretching the light over a sequence of low and placid hills. The ship was moving past a land spawned from an old forgotten Scotland, stubbles of rock on a heathery

310

skin, little outposts of stunted houses, a dog barking at the strange intrusion, the hills of San Carlos folded down towards the shoreline, skeins of wildfowl skimming the water. She looked at the coastline, dumbfounded. Why would anyone want this? Why not give it to them? It might be very lovely, but to *fight* over?

The bay was full of anchored ships, the silver-greys of war, the red and blues of commerce, their old friend the *Elk* livid in bold russet relief, a bunch of ro-ro ferries lined up as if waiting for the next Channel crossing. As they drew closer, the land beyond began on take on shape and sound; a long whitewashed house at the end of it, a set of angular barns, a jetty high in the water leading out. On the surrounding hills patches of men were digging in. Lower down tents were being pitched. Landing craft were heading towards the beaches, others already offloading their cargo. Through the blows of hammers and the cries of men she could hear the stutter of a throttled motorbike. Dickey tapped her on the shoulder.

'I don't think we're meant to be out here,' he said. 'It might get a bit sticky.'

He led her back in. The men were crowding round the window, trying to get a glimpse.

'That's not a very good idea too.'

The intercom clicked on.

'Take cover! Take cover!'

He pushed Suzanne under a table as a sudden chatter started up, the floor shaking to the rhythm, and a roar, like Freddie and that bloody car of his, then a thump, as if something heavy had fallen onto the floor. The ship lurched, bouncing from side to side. The air was sucked from her ears. So this was God, was it? She screamed. The stuttering guns started up again.

'Was that meant for us?' she said

'The Argentinian calling card,' Dickey said. 'The mallet approach.'

The ship reeled again.

'Jesus.' She buried her head under his arm.

'It's all right. It's just the detonation. If this goes on I could mix martinis without ever having to use a shaker.'

Another thump.

'Jesus.' Suzanne put her hand into her blouse, searching for her cross. It wasn't there. She willed herself to think of something different.

'Do you know,' Dickey said, 'to quote Vera Lynn, I don't think we'll be meeting again after this.'

'Don't say that!'

'Not unless you plan to visit Ashford. I've just made a decision. After this I'm packing it in.'

'Dickey!'

A series of explosions ran alongside. Water smashed against the glass. Suzanne buried her head deeper. Dickey was getting quite chatty.

'Well, why not,' he said. 'I've put a bit aside. I could set up a shop or something, become a maître d' in a five-star hotel. Bournemouth or Brighton. Grow goats.'

'Grow goats?'

'You know what I mean. Pack servility in, dump the bow tie, take charge.'

Take charge. That's what she would do. Make Henry see what she was offering, giving something not simply for the moment, but something greater. Time was not the question, longevity was not the proposal, but there was a depth to their embrace, in their silences, in the way her stomach lurched when he looked at her; another missile from the deep.

Another thump. Dickey stroked her head.

'No wonder I left the navy, if this is what they have to offer.'

She pulled back, surprised.

'I never knew you'd been in the navy.'

'I never told you. It was a youthful mistake. I am peculiarly adapted to a certain section of the navy.'

She pretended not to understand.

'You're very sweet, Suzy, but you know perfectly well what I mean.'

'You mean submarines?'

'Submarines, exactly. I am submariner man personified. I have the height, the even temperament, I maintain an unquenchable desire for neatness, an essential requirement for life in confined spaces. However, there was one aspect of it that did not sit easily with me.'

'Which was . . .'

'The underwater part. I don't like getting my head wet.'

'But in a submarine, Dickey, you don't have to get your head wet.'

'That's what I told myself the day of my first sea trial but of course the principle is exactly the same. You are under water, a huge hat of it lying on your head. I felt like a cork, held down, desperate to pop us as quickly as possible. So I did the only thing I could.'

'Which was?'

'I threatened to glue the mascot's beak.'

'Dickey!'

'I wouldn't have done it, of course, but they're very super-stitious about their mascots, the armed forces are. We were up top in fifteen minutes and I spent the rest of my naval career pushing pens in Portland.'

The intercom came on again.

'Well, that little lot seems to have gone away. Carry on, everyone.'

She didn't need it but Dickey helped her out before dusting his knees.

'Look what they've done to my suit.'

'Never mind your DJ, Dickey, what about that?' She started to laugh.

'What?'

'The glass table you led me under.'

'Ah.'

'You see the hold-all on top?'

'Excellent protection,' Dickey boasted.

'It's full of grenades.'

Dickey took her arm and looked about him, conspiratorially.

'I know,' he confessed. 'I was looking for the easy way out.'

*

All morning they came, Pucarás, homing in on them, like wasps on a holiday beach, twisting and turning, bullets and tracer fire rising up to greet them. Suzanne went below. They had better things to think about than a frightened woman. She restocked the store cupboard, swept out the office, changed the bed linen. The raids came and the raids went. She'd be walking down a corridor and would suddenly find herself lying down flat in passageway, on the stairs, like a children's party game, dusting herself off, to start all over again.

Towards noon there came a lull in the attacks. Lunch was served. Dickey had changed back into his combat rig. The time for gestures was over. They were tucking into a creamy rice pudding when it started up again.

'Well, it was good of them to wait,' Suzanne said. Dickey scraped his bowl clean.

'Goodness has got nothing to do with it,' he said. 'They're just quicker eaters, that's all.'

An hour later the final disembarkation order came, the last of the commandos making their way down to the waiting ferries. They all went up to stand by the door as they trooped out, Dickey, Murray, Tina, the bar stewards, the cabin crews. They'd brought them here, into the very heart of it, risked their own lives for a military cause, and not a Queen's shilling between them. Suzanne thought it was the saddest sight she had ever seen. 'Good luck, miss,' one said. 'Say a prayer for me,' another. One even handed her a poem he had written.

The attacks intensified. She went down to their secret wash-room and removed any trace of their occupation. They would have the run of the ship now. Maybe she could get the chief steward to lend her one of the keys to a stateroom, just for one night. She ran a bath and stretched out, listening to the bursts of information blurting through the speaker. An enemy plane hit. A helicopter downed. Air Threat White. Air Threat Yellow. Air Threat Red. Then the ship would lurch and she would hold on tight as the water slopped over the side. Though she could feel her apprehension growing insurmountable, she drew comfort from it, as if it were leading her to a place from which nothing could touch her, her body suspended, her mind tumbling with snatches of memory and loss. Out there was Stanley and all the other boys she had known, plunged into a world she could barely imagine. She wanted to open the door and watch them ejaculate before her, she wanted Henry to kneel down and trail his hand in the water, she wanted to run to their cabin and fling herself in Matty's arms. She had never imagined that she could be so wilfully alone, cut off not only from everyone she knew, but by the very core of her self. Who was this person hidden inside? What did it make of itself? Why were she and the *Canberra* here? The ship heaved and she was thrown in the air, falling back with a splash. The ship could be sinking and she might never know it, until the sea burst in and carried her to oblivion. Her body began to convulse, locked in fear. The ship bucked again, her body arching, the air filling with such a torn scream she thought it must be the propellers breaking or a boiler burst, or wounded men throwing themselves onto a burning sea, until, out of breath, she realized it was coming from her. She put her hand to her chest, felt the pounding of her heart, the rise and fall of her breast, the slow release of spent power. Mortality had lain upon her and she was alive.

Another squawk awoke her. The *Ardent* had been hit, the ship abandoned, the walking wounded coming here. She wrapped a towel around her and scurried back to the cabin, to change into a dry set of clothes. Tina was standing on a chair, looking out. Her eyes were red.

'Christ, Suzy, you can see it burn,' she said.

They came an hour later, dressed in baggy orange survival suits, their faces blank, their talk alternately monosyllabic and hysterical. They flopped down exhausted, like puppets with their strings cut: some cried, some talked only to themselves, some shook with anger. They smelt oddly domestic, of burnt plastic, like a kitchen implement left on a stove. Their hair was singed, their faces streaked with soot, their eyes still weeping from the poisonous fumes. She handed out cigarettes and shots of whisky. Her hands were steady now. She could hold a glass, strike a match to their shaking. A nod, a smile, a squeeze of the hand was all they wanted, was all she and the others could give. Even Tina was subdued. So this was how it ended up, the bravado, the skill, the training, slumped in an armchair, holding a trembling cigarette.

At seven in the evening, the bay quiet, it was announced that the *Canberra* had been ordered to disembark all remaining troops and stores. A furious five hours followed. Medical teams, other rear echelons, all those who'd imagined they might stay for a few

315

more days were ferried out. They upped anchor at midnight, the ship emptied of noise and purpose, riding lighter in the water as if freed of responsibility.

The day was over. They'd come and left the Falklands. As they headed out into the dark a ship could be seen burning by the headland. But they were safe now. They had done their duty and they were safe. She walked to the practice room. She could leave him a note, to start things off again.

His mate Ian was there, tidying up some papers. He looked up.

'You looking for Henry?'

She nodded. He looked embarrassed. Her stomach filled with apprehension.

'They had a bit of bother with one of the medical teams. I don't know what, it's all a bit confusing. Anyway, they needed some more orderlies. He volunteered. He left twenty minutes ago. Last boat out.'

*

He had known it was coming all along, his destination, waiting to receive him. Later there were many who tried to recapture what had happened, who wrestled with the demon of cracked memory, who wrote it down in books and letters, formed static words with which to describe its lethal pulse, but he could not recall it in any formal timetable, from the moment of his leaving to that strange floating time in another world, his body uncertain whether he was flying up to heaven, or bumping down the purgatory slide to the dark vestiges of hell, his eyes bandaged, his tongue silenced, his head turning from one side to the other as the uneasy scent of a woman hovered over him. In truth he drifted in and out of his time as if under an anaesthetic, lurid images of the past peering in at him like anxious relatives, jabs of the present shaking him awake. From bandsman to medical attendant, his duty now to accompany the fighting patrols, the transformation had taken one slow boat ride, standing sardined in wallow of the vessel, his rucksack stuffed with spare socks donated by his band mates, unable to see the approaching shore, to gauge its hostility, not simply because of the chosen hour, but thanks to the ramp walled up in front of him. Boxed in, he'd been, with a liquorice all-sorts kind of company alongside, clerks and ciphers and cooks, snatched from the cruise liner's cradle. It wasn't that they were wanted; rather they were needed. Already there had been logistical problems. In his case two of the unit's medics had been withdrawn, one suffering from hypothermia, falling into the freezing water while cross-decking from the *Canberra*, the other breaking his ankle on his leap ashore.

'You could take my place in the band, if you like,' he had joked, as the injured soldier led him through the contents of his kit, his drips and his drugs, his vacuum packs of sterilized help, but the young man merely scowled, contemptuous of the ingratiation, furious with himself and the injury that had allowed such a greenhorn to take his place.

Yes, his memory might have deserted him, but the dampness never did, jumping down into the black sea, his boots filling immediately, a blast of salt air clearing away the belch of diesel fumes, as he slithered on the shifting beach towards the corrugated-roofed barn in which he spent his first night, his bag of tricks a source of speculation to a family of inquisitive mice. Those early days were the clearest to him, the dawn on that second day rising pink over San Carlos Water, the strange calm of the land counterbalanced by the furious determination of the crawling men. As the light stretched out and settled upon the expanse of water, he walked up the hill, past the sangars and gun emplacements, aimed for the time being at a high and empty sky, and saw that out in the bay the *Canberra* alone had gone. Though he had known of her departure, seeing the gap where she had lain at anchor surprised him, as if he'd thought that out of all of them, she wouldn't have deserted them. It was the final confirmation that he would never leave.

While his unit dug in on the hillside he was posted temporarily to Ajax Bay on the other side, helping to convert the old mutton factory into a field dressing station; mobile operating theatres, generators, sterilization units. He spent a morning bringing in the blood supplies, his blood, Suzanne's, the whole ship's worth in squidgy plastic sacks, labelled and dated. In the coming days blood would water this land without restraint while here it lay stacked up, separated out into groups and types. A shipload and even that wasn't enough.

The day was frighteningly clear. Now that the Argentinians knew where they were they were expecting a doubling of attack. Yet nothing came. Stores were ferried in; armoured vehicles tracked across the beach; helicopters swung their loads high above their heads, yet the skies remained clear. Around lunchtime the first casualties were brought in, Argentinians the three of them. Henry and the others gathered round them as if they were new additions to a zoo; a pilot dark-skinned and crumpled in half, his pelvis smashed, his eyes locked in disbelief; then two conscripts captured from some nearby farmhouse, with pale eyes and unruly hair and smelling oddly of bath salts, one shot through the cheek, his unruly tongue poking out of the ragged hole, the other clutching a crumpled picture of the Virgin Mary tight against his wounded stomach, convinced that he was about to be propped up against a wall and executed. Henry shook his head and pointed to the red of the cross that flew outside. For a moment he wished he'd kept the crucifix, then remembered the leer on Stanley's face, Suzanne looking down. As it was he gripped the young man's hand until the mask went over and the gas hissed and the boy closed his frightened eyes.

How long was he there. One day, two? He had hoped that he would stay there, helping with casualties, keeping records, checking names and numbers, unobtrusive as to who he might be, hoping that fate might come to him, rather than he having to seek it out, but then the order came through. He was to rejoin his unit, marching south-east, securing the high ground overlooking the settlement, the rise of the West Falkland hills silent across the Sound. He might have known, as he dug in, improving his position with walls of peat and rock, inhaling the scent of paraffin-wax tablets as his neighbours brewed a mash of tea, that he was building a box as if in a theatre, from where he could watch a bloody Roman spectacle unfold, for they came the next day by God, with their net of bombs and the spears of missiles and for many Godless days thereafter. He could remember nothing but the noise, the violence of the moment, the sudden shouts of men, the sudden stutter of guns, ships whooping, men running as the sky was torn in shreds, the ribbons of blue and gold ripped from the heavens, the flower blossoms of shells, dark sunflowers in the sky, the soldiers on the hills leaning into the air, guns juddering in their hands as they raged against the attacking planes. They came in ones and twos, hour upon hour, swooping up over the hill, dipping in for their brave and fearful run, bolts of bombs dropping, spinning into the wall of fire, showing the naked skin of their underbellies and the silver slice of their wings. On land and in the air, there was twisting, turning movement; everywhere except on the sea and the poor ships. Plane upon plane would come, Pucarás, Mirages, three thousand pounds of explosives slung in their bellies, yet the ships sat tethered in the water, like a hunter's goat, tied down to attract the bigger game, while the men hid in the grass, armed it seemed with only toothpicks. They took so much in those early days, the ships, so much ruin falling to the left and to the right of them, so much fire stitching the water, that it came as no surprise to him when they began to explode one after the other, erupting into the sky like an awakened volcano, molten lava falling back into the water, clouds of dense and acrid smoke obliterating the sunny world outside, and the desperate figures of men running back and forth, waiting for the pigmy boats trying to rescue them. By day he could see the burnt and wounded brought in on the back of BV Bandwagons, at dusk the wink of the helicopters as they clattered out into the dark, carrying them out to where Suzanne would be, handing out her coffee, sharing her cigarettes, wheeling the walking wounded over to the Meridian, where his band would try and make measure of their time. At night he would stand, half sleeping in his shelter and read the distant shoreline by the glow of their burning hulls, ships illuminated by their own destruction, and when the morning came he would discover that another ship had turned its melted face to the sea, another broken bow was poking up from beneath the water's inscrutable depth.

The pressure grew, the days expanded, like a blown balloon. One extra puff and he half expected the whole island to explode. They couldn't take much more. But then it changed. The Seacat and Blowpipe missiles, the Bofors and Oerlikon guns, the machine guns and pistols, began to take effect, the hills ringing with whistles and sheers as another shooter found his target. The planes grew fewer, the approaching slopes scarred with the remnants of broken wings and burnt-out fuselages. The weather turned, the fine water-coloured edges of the coast turned blotting-paper smudges, the solid hills across the water melting into murky shades. The wind grew colder, the ground hardened. There was an air of hostility about the land, as if it were a landlord, preparing to evict, and in response, the troops hitched their loads and began to move out, some setting off north across the moors, others skirting south-west along the inlet of water, all of them glad to be moving at last. Only Henry's unit remained, and that only for a few days.

Unlike the others they were to be flown in, their objective a mountain of some sort, their task to hold the ridge until the troops had swept through, clearing their way towards them. Then they would move as one, taking the first ring of hills that overlooked Port Stanley, pushing the Argentinians back into one, futile pocket. The night before they left, gunfire ripped the dark apart. Come the morning the news that another settlement had been taken, fought for bitterly, won at the cost of many lives. He attended a service for those who had fallen. The bodies lay in a long muddy trench, sealed up in bags, the chaplain's words scattered on the spiteful squall. He would be lying in one like that soon, his belongings delivered to the small room at the back of the refrigeration plant, the words DEAD PERSONAL EFFECTS scratched on the wall. Where would his effects go? He hadn't thought about that. The girl that had written to him, Amy? Suzanne? No, Richard Roach, that's who, his childhood friend. Let him deny him then. A bugle sounded, the long elemental notes riding on the wind. It was what they did, the forces, and it moved him. But he wished too for the whole band to be there, making brighter music of their memory, rising above the island's implacable howl.

They approached the landing ground in darkness, the helicopter buffeted by strong winds, Henry perched like the others atop a rattling jumble of guns and bags and missile launchers, but it was not darkness that covered them in the scrambled jump out but sheets of white billowing all around them, a Himalayan figure clad in skins and hair waiting to lead them through the snow, up the rocky path to the summit. It was a long walk, long and cold, every man laden down with an excess of baggage, their bodies bent to a critical weight, each step made doubly difficult by the rivers of loose rock that lay spewn upon the slopes, as if the mountain had vomited out the contents of its stomach. They climbed for two hours or more, a hard rain lashing at their faces, the wind stealing their breath, their feet slipping on the sliding stones, their rifles balanced in their hands like a tightrope walker's, the net below them removed. Henry felt he could fall at any moment, fall and plunge into the abyss.

They sat the rest of the night out under the lee of the summit. At dawn they brewed tea. Henry chewed three chocolate bars and felt sick. The weather had opened up, and crawling up to the summit, he saw for the first time the soul of the land they were tasked with taking. Some men said that it reminded them of Scotland, others parts of Devon, but to him the similarities were only that of a variety of emptiness, and even then it seemed hardly to apply. Yes there were colours of gorse and heather, there were wildfowl skimming the water, and yes there was that old familiar scent of the ocean on the wind, its salt evident upon the plain, but he was looking on a land pressed against a block of ice, a land blown here by a mountainous sea, a land which wanted for no other than its lonely self, and which demanded a sacrificial isolation, an inhuman solitude in which the only resolution for man was death. There were some lands that should not be inhabited by human beings, which should be left virgin to their touch, and though he had never seen one before he believed he was seeing one now. Beauty barely pertained to it; the rage of the natural world did. To the north there was the shape of an ugly house, plumped down in a withering sweep of grass, and behind it glinting back as far as he could determine the silver sliver of an inlet sea, its shape like the writing on a Chinese scroll, its shape filled bright and flat, molten like a mould of liquid metal. The heather was brown, darker than in Britain, flecked with snow and small boulders, studded with jewelled rivulets that sparkled in the early morning sun. Flocks of geese waded back and forth, pecking at the hidden ground. As he turned full south the flat of the land became more agitated, rising up about itself, as if beaten in a bowl, growing in intensity and until they erupted on his far right, into a broken crockery of jagged crags and crevices. It was there, in their rising and falling, where lay the men they were destined to fight. But it was the land caught in between that held him the longest, the cheerless sight of little painted Stanley, squat and uncomfortable not five miles away, with its wedge of dirty roofs and barns, the churlish whaling station, and beyond it the pockmarks of an airfield, something slow and white moving upon it. If only it could be wiped away! How whole the land would look!

The mist came down again. Henry felt as if the land had opened up just for him, telling him to commit it to memory, as if that was all he was permitted to see, until it finally closed around him. How long were they there? He cannot remember. He can only remember the cold and the waiting and how in the daylight hours he moved barely from one hour to the next. It was wet there, the ground as much water as land, every wedge dug a hole filled, even on the highest slopes. The island had a heart. It pumped its brackish blood into every peat-bound corpuscle. There was little point in digging for shelter, though they did it anyway, scooped out freezing puddles to lie in, Henry dragging his ponchos over a length of stick, wedging the corners into reluctant rock, the rain driving in from the north and the east, the wind dragging his senses hither and thither, fanning the fear of his isolation. There were hours when he wanted to leap up to the highest rock, cup his hands and call a name, but whose he could not tell. There were hours when he wished that he had a friend here, one to whom he could unburden his last thought, who might take them home, visit them every now and again, but he was mostly friendless. Major Osgood made a passing showing, one of the mortar men had clapped him on the back, telling him not to worry, that he'd do OK. He knew what they were thinking and he agreed. He felt unequal to the task. He was not one of them and never had been. Never had been! Never been a soldier, never been a musician, never even been a proper son. Day upon day he woke to the demon of his thoughts, of what he had never known, his life running from one fog bank to another, bumping into shocks of reality like those dangling fly traps Dora had hanging in the rooms, his face brushing up against the bumpy bodies. He wondered whether he shouldn't have packed his violin, to show them who he might have been, helped them pass those twilight days with the sea shanties he knew, inviting a rhythm to their immobility.

He had no such problems in the night. Old King Cole, that was the rear echelon's game then, marched up and down the lot of them, three, four times under cover of darkness to the newly established field HQ, to hack supplies back up, stockpiling for the then and now. The morning before they finally set off he brought back a mailbag, flown in from the *Canberra*. He gave it to Major Osgood, who dipped his hand in and called each man's name out softly. He didn't bother to listen. He was thinking of the ship. They'd had news of her, which the men received with polite interest, as one might a distant cousin, confirmation that she was safe, tra-laing away to the north of them, away from the reaches of planes and periscopes, moving back and forth on the same square patch of water, looking out on the summit of the high seas, unable, unwilling to break free. Was the ship as lonely and isolated as here, shrouded in a fog of mystery, its life suspended? And Suzanne, did she change the beds still, brew the coffee, lean up on the outpost of her door, inviting smiles, offering advice. He regretted now their affair, the cul-de-sac into which he had led her, the invitation of new mornings she had promised him, their cabin idyll only a trompe l'œil of paradise.

Major Osgood was standing in front of him, flapping the letter on his knee.

'What are you trying to do, wake the dead?' He held it out.

Dear Henry,

Yesterday your dad brought me your picture, out of uniform I am sorry to say but still better than nothing. Now you have one of me and I have one of you, though I don't suppose you'll be able to look at me as often as I can look at you. Your dad says as far as he knows you are still on the Canberra *(lucky for some) but wherever you are when you read this, we all hope you come home safely. I have shown your picture to my friends and they are all dead jealous.*

Love and kisses
Amy.

He pulled out the photo he'd kept, a white-skinned girl with the baby face, calling out to his fading name. He touched the letter as if to examine its latent properties, half believing that he might be hallucinating in this swirl. Osgood, watching him, spoke.

'Your girl?'

'Can't say, sir.'

'Pretty?'

He handed him the photo. Osgood looked and gave it back.

'Not underage, I hope.'

'Can't say, sir.'

'Lucky to get a letter at all.'

'Yes, sir.'

'Mine's on the *Canberra*. You remember Tina. You knew her room-mate a bit, I hear.'

'Yes, sir.'

'She hasn't dropped you a line at all?'

'No, sir.'

'No letter from the *Canberra* direct, then?'

'Not that I know of, sir.'

'It's just, my fiancée Tina, she hasn't written to me. I would have liked a letter. Before we go in.'

That day they were called into their huddle, the whole tribe of them perched on the scraggle of rocks, listening to the battle plan, Henry up at the rear, knowing that in amongst these men lay the dead and the dying. He studied the movement of their hands, the incline of their heads, the grim chuckle of laughter, their faces grey and grizzled, unshaven, unwashed. He remembered them as they had been, sun-tanned and in shorts, pounding the decks, lifting beams, the day's aggression beads of sweat upon their bodies. Out there, not two weeks away, lay the same heat; out there Suzanne was jumping into the sea; out there her swimsuit lay wet upon a table and she shivering with a cup of tea in her hand. Out there stood the little cabin, with its door locked and the blankets thrown in a huddle against it, as they bathed in the heat of the room.

A small relief map of the operation had been made out of rocks and grass. Their objective lay to the left, a mountainous fortress bedecked with crags and castles, buttresses and crevices, the

Argentinian positions heavily defended. Ahead of them lay a long exposed plateau, and rising up from it a lower ridge, running almost parallel with their goal and bisected by a broad and steep boulder-strewn run – a perfect killing ground. To its right and on a tangent to both, climbed a lesser slope which fell back on the other side onto a marshy plain. The defences were primarily dug in to face the ridge. They would skirt round, attacking from an unexpected right flank. Other troops were committed to other Argentinian positions on other mountains. The attacks would be simultaneous, at night.

He was checking his bag when Stanley squatted down beside him. He could almost smell the muscle. He didn't look up.

'You got everything we need?'

He carried on checking.

'I think so, yes.'

'OK about it?'

'I think so, yes.'

Stanley grunted, thrust the handle of a knife towards him.

'You'll need this. We all got one, dead handy when you need it. See his stomach? Stick it in and pull it up. Head in the way? In his eye, nice and easy, and twist. *Finito*. Got it?'

He dropped it on top of the bag.

'It's a bit tough on you, I know, chucked in at the deep end, but you'll be OK, Henry. You're with us now.'

He punched him on the arm and walked away. Henry felt strangely flattered.

An hour after dark they moved out, single file, Henry at the back, the soldiers' bergens bobbing up and down without so much as a creak. They'd packed and repacked them all day, eliminating any noise. One mortar man had been left behind because of a persistent cough. The descent was steep. Henry found it hard to hold back, not to let the weight carry him forward into the back of the man ahead. He was carrying a whole hospital's worth of goods. Drips, bandages, morphine, hypodermics. Although he wore three pairs of gloves he was worried about his hands, whether they would work well enough in the cold.

He moved slowly, each step closer to the land of war. He felt fluid inside, as if his organs had turned all to liquid, that one stab to the body, one bullet wound and he would flood out, a steaming stream onto the ground. After about an hour they came to a fence and a sergeant standing by it. Four others stood with him, members of Henry's own unit. They'd fallen behind. They needed to speed up or they'd get caught when it started. The sergeant started off, the pace brisker. The mist had returned, shrouding the hills.

'Down!'

It took one step before Henry registered the command, one knee dropping to the ground, the other folded against his body, his rifle thrown down in front of him, his fingers spread taut on the spongy grass. He was abreast with the other medic in front, Parry, both poised as if waiting for the starting gun of a race. They looked at each other. He was ruddy-faced, just like Roach.

'On your marks, get set, go,' Parry whispered.

The sergeant held up his hand and they waited, hardly daring to breathe, the tension building in his arms. That day on Centre Court he'd been on his hands and knees for more than two hours when he'd seen her, the woman in the white floppy hat. Like Dora she looked, only posher. Dora couldn't be alive, could she? There was something about the woman that didn't look right, one hand resting underneath the flow of her bosom, as if nursing a lost maternity. He sensed a loneliness there, a feeling of separation that was his too. Could it really be her?

The sergeant grunted. They moved on. The match had gathered in pace, points scored, points lost, his gaze fixed upon the large woman as much as the ball, but despite his internal treaties she had eyes only for the players. If only he could make her notice him! Then the ball he prayed for came, thwacked against the rim of net, rolling along the top to land in the plumb line centre of the court. He started forward without looking, knowing that with the speed of his run, the dexterity of his scoop, the manner in which he would greet the other side, she would be bound to see him, that this could be but the beginning of their day, that matches would come and go but he and Dora would have seen each other, and she would rise up and call his name. And Roach had ruined it all, knocking him for six, the crowd rippling with laughter, Lofty standing over him in the changing room, putting his hand on his leg where his shorts met his leg, squeezing a damp towel on his face. When he re-emerged the match was over and she was gone. And Roach had blamed him!

The curtain of mist drew aside and he saw that Parry had vanished. Henry stopped for a moment, hoping to catch the sound of his breath, or the stumble of a boot, but he could hear nothing. The mist drifted back again, as quickly as it had left, the path vanishing before his eyes. He kept his head high, beating the air with one free hand, as if to push the whirl aside. He was back in the yard again, a sea of flapping sheets around him, Dora holding the corners of the fog in her great pink hands, for them to dance back and forth, folding it away until it lay in a neat pile in a tub by the ringer, while she smoked under the courtyard stars. It had changed over the years, the manner of their laundry quadrille, the timid movements of a bewildered infant, the eager rush of the scolded boy, the embarrassed intimacy of a young man with fluff upon his lip, but there had come a time before that final change, when she was obliged to acknowledge him as her equal, when his hands were as nimble as hers, when the dash of his iron matched hers as the radio played its humdrum accompaniment, *Music While You Work, Workers' Playtime*, the tunes of the drones. Despite the hours he had found satisfaction then, when she would run a testing hand, examining collar and cuff, the grudging praise the only relief in the long repetition of the days. Sunday was the only day he had off, Joe had insisted on it. Chapel he said, though they never went to one. Instead he and Dora took themselves to the Anchor, from opening time to late afternoon, hauling themselves back along the towpath to sleep it off upstairs. Sundays he did as he pleased, sat in the outside toilet, plucking at his three-stringed violin (he had no bow, not for a year or two), climbing out onto the flat roof, just like he did later with Roach and Ellison. 'I'm going to join the navy, see the world,' Nigel had once said, looking out onto the night calls of the city. 'Travel, that's the name of the game.' Roach had turned on him, defiant. 'That's just Tommy-rot, Nigs,' he had spat back. 'There's no need to see anything. When I get out of here I'm just going to get on with it, and have the world leave me alone.'

If anything the mist was thicker now, but the path seemed

wider than he had the right to hope. He quickened his pace, conscious of the soft thump of the rucksack as it bounced against his back. After five minutes he thought he heard someone. He wasn't sure from which direction it came. He stopped. Yes, he could hear it now, coming from behind. Had he walked past them in his haste? Should he simply wait?

The wind blew in, the rattle of a loose fence to his right. So that's what it was. Had there been a fence to his right on the map? He didn't think so. The fog seemed to solidify before his eyes, stifling his breath, that other fog swirling in his lost head. He could taste the old bitterness on his tongue. He couldn't see. He couldn't see. He wanted to throw his burden aside, run pell-mell into Joe's outraged exclamation, wanted to sit high in the fug of his lorry wiping the condensation free with the sleeve of his jacket, the lorry inching through the sulphurous fumes to the lonely road by the river, and the squat house, like a mud-pack Arab's, where the fire ran, day and night, winter, spring and summer.

The noise came again, quite distinct this time, the soft fall of a squelching boot, the rustle of a coat. There was no doubt in his mind. He was being followed. He froze. The moment he stopped the shuffling stopped too. He looked back, peering into the darkness, but could see nothing.

He set off again, lengthening his stride, trying to put some thinking distance between them. He appeared to be in the open now, the wind expansive. A few paces on and the footsteps started up again. How far was he behind – ten foot? Twenty? And who was he? Friend or foe?

He halted abruptly, chanced it.

'Parry,' he whispered. 'Is that you?'

Again the movement stopped. Henry listened. The wind picked at the grass.

'Parry, it's me. Hawkins.'

Nothing. Not Parry, then. Not British either. The noise grew more insistent. He quickened his pace, fearful of compromising the whole enterprise. Bandsman responsible for the death of comrades. Bandsman lets the show down. Bandsman loses the war. He was sweating, no longer cold, his heart lurching from side to side, his lips sour with fear, his foe determined to keep up with him. There came an agitated flurry, like a weapon being taken out. Any moment a flare would shoot up or he'd be cut down by machine-gun fire and then the whole works would go up.

Now was the time to abandon caution, to act like a soldier, to follow his training, do what Stanley would have done. He began to run in dragging steps, his bergen pounding his body into the ground. There seemed no end to the space in front of him, no width, no length, no depth. He could have been falling. Then, out of the white, the dark loom of an outcrop of rock: an ambusher's dream; a Wild West scenario, a hide and a jump and a felling of foe. Dropping behind it he slipped off his bergen, drew out the sheathed serrated knife. He would keep it quiet, press him to the ground, stick his throat.

He must have run faster than he'd imagined, for it took a while for his adversary to catch up. Then he heard the footsteps break out into a run, the man desperate to close him down. Henry crouched, the knife shaking in his hand. As the figure passed he ran out and leapt upon him. They fell forward, Henry nearly tumbling clean over him. Was the man that small, was he so huge? There was something terribly wrong here, rolling with his assailant, his body somehow evasive, out of kilter. He scrambled back, trying to put his hand round the man's face, the clatter of something rattling in his ear, like knives dropping on a pavement, and Joe grabbing hold of him, the small dread of his being found and of being caught welling up in his throat. The man was strong, covered in oilskin, and he could not get a grip. Henry threw himself back on top, but his opponent began to fight back, squawking in his rage, his knife coming from nowhere, ripping up into Henry's cheek, slicing at his arms and chest. Joe could have saved him, Joe could have, Joe who he loved more than anyone in the world, who could have sat him in his lorry and driven him home. Joe chose to keep him, not because of greed, or because of Dora, but because – again the blows came, glancing off his shoulder, jabbing at his windpipe – but because he loved him too and would not let him go. Joe loved him and Joe destroyed him and he loved Joe and wanted to kill him back. He reached down and stabbed the little man full in the belly, hugging him close, feeling the foul air hiss out like a tyre, feeling his body sag a little, before he threw Henry off, and attacked him with renewed strength. He smelt foreign, unwashed. He'd been eating fish, Henry could smell it on his breath, like he could Joe's in the morning after an evening out, bending over his bed, poking him awake. 'Come on, Henry. Stir your stumps, there's fish to fry,' he would joke, and he wanted to lash out, lash out for the home he once had and had no more, for the room that was his which was his no more, the little light within it and his favourite book on the floor, a figure in the darkened doorway wishing him good-night, and he rose up and began again, plunging the knife into the back and the belly and the chest, stabbing furiously into the white quilted coat, until the man was quiet and he could roll out from underneath.

He lay back exhausted. Guns were booming out at sea, the land nearby trembling. The mist cleared and the mountain looked down at his feet, a scimitar moon shining upon them. He looked across. The penguin lay on its back, looking at him with a cloudy eye, its beak softly clacking. A penguin! A neat absurd penguin. How he loved them, their ridiculous walk, the skill in their appetite, the appetite in their skill. And this is what he sailed three thousand miles for. To murder a creature who only lived for the sea and the land and his egg-bound family. He had been waddling under the mist and stars, as he did every night, curious as to his new companion, and this is how his life was ending, stabbed to death to preserve a territory that had always been his and his alone.

He knelt down and stroked his head. The penguin flapped and fluttered and died.

A voice whispered in his ear.

'Medical Athletics One, Antarctic Academicals Nil.'

He was hauled to his feet, run back. Stanley propped him against the rocks.

'I might have known it was you. What the fuck are you doing here?'

There was a sudden depression of air.

'Incoming!' he shouted.

Stanley threw himself down, pulling Henry after him. The air burst in his ears, the ground lifting. Stanley pressed his mouth against his ear.

'You should be miles back.'

'I . . .'

'Forget it, keep your head down. They haven't seen us yet.' He wiped his face with his fingers, sniffing the blood. 'You've been ripped.'

'A bit.'

'Attacked by a killer penguin.' Stanley dug into Henry's pack, pulled out one of the bandages, wrapping it round his head. He stood back, grinning.

'You look like a fucking washerwoman.'

'What did you say?'

'I said . . .'

Henry started to laugh. An explosion not fifty yards away ripped into the night. A voice came bellowing out the dark.

'They've blown my fucking leg off! I'm only twenty-two and they've blown my fucking leg off!'

Henry thought he must have laughed all the night through, after that. He wanted to stand and scream the great humour of it, tell the world of this great joke about the life and death of a waddling penguin, and certainly they all thought of him as a crazy man then, running around with an outsize bandage round his head, ducking out towards the lad's groans, chuckling at the flares that rose up, brushing aside the tracer bullets that whipped past him, as he worked the man's morphine free, jabbed the syringe in. Then the air was filled with covering fire and Stanley was by his side.

'You're fucking mad, you are,' he said, and together they dragged the man back.

Fire was coming down from the Argentinian forward defences, a ridge of rock some forty metres away. Stanley began to edge round the back, Henry following. Within five minutes they were within twenty-five metres. They could hear the sentries talking excitedly, smell the smoke of their cigarettes.

Stanley lifted his hand.

'There's a man up there,' he whispered. He pointed to the rocket launcher.

'I want you to take this, and fire it in his general direction. Then I'm going to run in after them and finish them off. All right?'

Henry nodded, wanting to laugh again. It was such a joke, hiding like this, ducking under rocks, taking shelter, playing at soldiers.

He worked his way round, the rocket awkward in his hands. He could see the sentry, standing smoking a cigarette, peering out into the darkness. Behind him he could hear the chatter of others, smell the brew of something. It's what he did when he was young, with the boy opposite, crawl through the forest on his stomach, cowboys and Indians on the steep embankment, laying rolls of gun caps on the track. He hadn't thought of that in years, the boy, the railway line, the two of them squeezing through the hole in the fence, crawling out, waiting for the rails to tremble and the wheels pounding over them. He couldn't remember if he had *ever* thought of it before. He could sense it clearly, as if it lay just behind the wall of rock, that he would only have to break through to see the cinder path wind down past the rhubarb and raspberry canes to the door at the end. Not a gate, a *door*, an entrance into another world! Why, he could even smell the burn of the exploded caps, taste the cinder smoke billowing down, feel the dry prickle of pine needles as they slid back down, a woman's voice furious for playing near the tracks, how they held their mouths, excited and frightened, brushing their knees in haste, wiping away the evidence. Where was he now, that boy from across the road. Long gone, long gone . . . The image receded. He aimed the rocket and pressed, falling back as the missile leapt out of his arms. There was a blast and a shower of rocks, and then Stanley was pushing past him running full tilt, towards the cave. Henry dropped the launcher and scrambling up, found the three men curled up in shock, hands over their ears.

'Good morning, campers!' Stanley shouted and began to bayonet them, one by one. Henry marvelled how patiently they waited, as if in a doctor's waiting room, looking up almost grate-fully as their turn came. 'Thank you, very nice, thank you,' the last one was repeating, the only English he knew perhaps, his hands clutching at the point of entry as if only when the blade left would the finality of his death be confirmed. Stanley had to stick his boot on his chest to shake the man free.

'Nice work, Henry, nice fucking work,' and Henry agreed, fascinated by the drape of the men's bodies, their lost expressions, the bright excitement in Stanley's eyes.

How they worked their way forward, whether to plan or to new orders, or whether, as it mostly seemed to him, on the arbitrary design of the moment, Henry could not tell, but that's the way it was, all through that long exhausting night, him following the young and cocky marine, sheltering from the bullets and the shells, before dashing out again into that illuminated madness. He lived in a flickering life, as if caught in an old movie with the frame slipping, figures jumping out in sudden leaps, jerking out of nowhere, hugely black, hugely white, faces split by greasepaint grins of comedy and tragedy, their shouting mouths silenced by the unseen orchestra, the clash of cymbals, the boom of drums, the conductor riotous, stirring a cauldron of strings and brass. The killings seemed so bizarre, so varied, so musically choreographed, the deaths too a multiplicity of balletic turns, sudden pirouettes, fantastical leaps, a troupe of travelling players, pancaked-faced and wild in costume, magicians disintegrating before his eyes, turning into soup or slabs of meat, heroes playing their part well, rising up in action and falling back dead with a sharp intake of staged breath, others hamming it up, rolling on the ground, calling for mother, screaming for mercy. No matter how incapacitated they might look, the wounded Argentinians they discovered on their way, Stanley would shoot or bayonet, whichever he thought more appropriate. The first time they came across one, Henry had assumed he was finished, the man half propped up against a rock, a puddle of guts in his hand, but as they passed him he reached out and grabbed Henry's ankle, pleading for help. Pulling his rucksack round Henry had begun to examine him when Stanley had poked his gun in between shouting, 'Stand back, Henry! Stand back!' and Henry, eager to please, obliged, as Stanley shot three rounds in the Argentinian's head. 'We can't leave them alive, Henry, not while we're moving through. They could get one of ours, see. You go through his belongings while I collect his body tag,' and that's what they did the whole night, Henry searching through their rucksacks and pouches while Stanley straddled their bodies, working the identity tag free with his knife. It was odd what he found in their hidey-holes and dug-outs. Some had decked their little caves like a boy's den, like the one he and that other boy (Tom! That was his name!) across the road had, under a holly bush in the embankment, rock shelves stacked with cheap cigarettes, tins of cocoa, packets of biscuits; photographs of a mother or wife or child, crosses and candles wedged in higher. Some had transistor radios, Primus stoves, a washing line of socks hanging at the back. In one he found a Walkman, the play button still depressed. Henry switched the machine off and stuck it in his pocket.

But he was conscientious in his labour too, working tirelessly over their wounded own, patching up, stitching up, dressing wounds before sending them hobbling off down from the battlefield. Under fire, out of fire, he didn't care, watching out of the corner of his eye where his Stanley was and where he would be wanted next. He was like a gun dog, following his master, eager to witness his every move, anxious for the praise of it, his high-pitched chuckle, his skip of exclamation, confirmation to the young man that on this night and with this fool by his side he was invincible. They took outrageous risks storming positions oblivious to the danger, throwing in grenades, jumping in, Henry clucking away in the background, jumping up, flapping and squawking as he patched up another soldier. 'You're fucking mad, you are.' How many times was it said that night and he would nod his head in agreement, for he was mad and it was glorious, to be mad, fucking mad, to have no sense, no sense of value, nothing that would divert him from his goal, hinder their progress, make them doubt for a moment the sanity of their ways. And in truth there was nothing extraordinary about it, considering he was hardly there. He felt changed, transformed. He worked without gloves, his fingers impervious to the cold, their writhings, the gut-leaked smell no more to him than a carrion crow pacing round his feed, always looking to find Stanley again, to share a joke, to laugh with him as they moved crazily up the mountain. They were a double act, this novice, this seasoned soldier; good guy, bad guy; funny man and foil: light to his dark; his sour to this precious sweet.

At last the night gave up and with it the mountain's resistance. Dawn fingered the sky and Henry had no more laughter. They looked across from just below the final summit. Sporadic fire came from the hill opposite, an occasional shell sinking into the land to their far left. They were not bothered. Stanley's namesake was much nearer now. They could see people running through the town, crazy jeeps zigzagging across the pock-marked tracks. Two men lay dead below them, one burnt with a phosphorous grenade, one sprawled out flat on the grass, eyes open to the sky. There was a little camp stove nearby, a canteen of water, a kettle and a dented tin mug. Stanley lit a cigarette and sat down, flicking the ash carelessly down on the unbuttoned corpse.

'What a night. What a great fucking night! We did it, Henry. You and me. We fucking did it!'

He jumped down and ambled over, measured his foot against the dead man.

'Same fucking size. Better too.'

He looked around.

'Where's his other fucking leg, then?'

It lay in a couple of feet away, naked save the boot at the end.

'Lend us your knife, mate.'

Henry watched intently as Stanley held the leg upended between his knees and sliced through the laces. He was right. It was a good boot.

Stanley went back and started to pull off the other boot. The man sat up, babbling in prayer. Stanley jumped back and shot five rounds into his chest. He hopped around on one leg, clucking like a chicken.

'Fuck me! Did you see that? Sat up while I was nicking his fucking boots! Make a brew up, why don't you. Hand us my pouch. I want his name tag.'

Henry put the water on and fished out a half-eaten packet of biscuits. Stanley snatched them out of his hand, stuffing them two at a time into his mouth.

'Don't you feel great? Don't you feel just great?'

Henry nodded. He felt something had left him, he couldn't quite say what.

'They said we couldn't do it. Too far, too risky, the Argies too dug in. Three to one, that's what it usually takes, and we did it the other way round! You and me, Henry, every one of us.'

Henry nodded again. He could feel something leaving, floating out into the air, something he would never get back.

'You wait till we get home. No one's going to fuck with us now. No one is going to say Britain is past it. Fuck the lefties. Snot and aggression, that's what's won the day. That's what it's going to be from now on. Snot and aggression.'

Henry kept his head in motion.

'Meanwhile, we got some celebrating to do. All that cunt waiting for us when we get home, heroes. Got that boat home too.'

He punched Henry's arm.

'You and me on the way back, Henry, you and me. Taking turns with that Suzy tart. You one day, me the next. She can't get enough of it that one. All the voyage over, sitting on my dick.'

Henry felt a stir. He licked his lips carefully. He felt like it might be the last thing he ever said.

'I would like not to believe that.'

'Not believe it!'

Stanley dipped into his pocket and brought out the crucifix.

'Licked me clean and hung it over it, just before we left.'

Henry closed his eyes. He believed him.

A noise made them look up. Major Osgood was coming down off the summit, walking stiffly. Stanley rose to his feet, lazily.

'Hurt your leg, sir?'

The Major stepped gingerly over the rocks.

'I'll be all right.'

'Course you will, sir.'

'There's a bit of draught, though, round the back.'

Stanley moved his head, indicating to Henry to take a look. Henry hefted his kit and turned the Major round. A splinter had torn nearly all the flesh from the Major's back. Henry could see his spine and his ribcage, the plum-coloured liver, his half-buried kidneys. He looked like one of those old-fashioned encyclopedias they had in the orphanage, with the front of engines sliced off to reveal all the workings inside. He should be labelled, he thought, stuck in the Natural History Museum.

'That's a nasty nick you got there, sir,' Stanley said. 'You got a three-foot Elastoplast, Henry?'

Henry shoved him aside and handed him the Major's gun. He worked the drip in and with Stanley's help, began walking round, wrapping the man up as tight as he dared.

'What am I, a Christmas parcel?' Osgood asked.

'Putting you on the last boat to Cairo, sir,' Stanley told him, 'floating you down the Nile.'

'The only boat I want is the bloody *Canberra*. The captain's getting us hitched, you know.'

'I didn't, sir.'

'Neither does he, actually. I dare say the Colonel will put in a good word.'

'I dare say he will, sir.'

'May I have my gun back now.'

'If you think you can carry it, sir.'

'Course I can bloody carry it.'

'Course you can, sir. Now if you care to step this way.'

Stanley handed Henry his pouch and took the Major's weight on his shoulder. The three of them began to walk slowly down, Henry holding the drip aloft. After a minute Stanley stopped, put his hand down his trousers.

'Hang on a sec. I'm all caught up.'

Henry felt the whoosh on his face. He couldn't call out.

He threw himself down, felt the suck of air as the shell screamed in. Fragments ripped the air, earth and rock falling over him.

When he looked up, Major Osgood was kneeling on the ground, as if in prayer, his body propped up by his rifle, the top of his head scooped off, like a soft-boiled egg. On the rock in front of him lay a hand with a tattoo on the little finger, and in its palm a perfect set of genitals, soft and untouched, the Major's dead eyes staring at Stanley's last salute. The rest of Stanley was nowhere to be seen.

Henry walked back up on the hillside. He was tired now. He

337

wanted to sleep, to never wake again. He could hear the sudden chatter of a machine gun and then a distant cheering, the noise being taken up across the hills. He took out the Walkman he had found the night before, put on the headphones. Schubert's sonata slipped over his head, like a hangman's shroud. His enemy had listened to the same music as he, heard it just before he died, music of utter loveliness and peace: a death song now. Bits of bodies lay all about him, like a jigsaw. How could such a work of beauty be created in the face of all of this?

The sun broke out through the cloud and across the sky he saw a flock of geese, flapping their way back over the marsh. The mist had cleared over the Falklands, and though it would return, it would not cover his corpse, as he once had thought. But although he had survived he had been right. He never would leave this island. All that he had been would be left here, along with the rest of the dead. What was left was a sculpted shell, a man bereft of senses, a man who would speak to no one, not even himself, for in truth, he had nothing to say.

The guns ceased firing. The geese had gone, the sky empty, the earth filled with one living being.

A sudden stillness filled the land.

EIGHT

'Our Henry', that's what she had said, 'Our Henry on the Falklands', and though, in those frenetic three weeks, he had devoured the images laid out before him, from the static mortuary attendant announcer to the star-burst battleship perfectly silhouetted in the atomized moment of its own destruction, it was that phrase that had pushed all else aside, clung to him as her fingers had clutched at his coat. He saw the faces of the blackened men rowing for the shore and smelt the smell of her damp hair; he listened to the voice of a rejoicing Prime Minister, triumphant before the camera's lights, and heard only Amy's simple declaration of intent. 'Our Henry', she had said, and he had slunk away under cover of parental anxiety, leaving her bereft, bewildered as to the country's destiny through the fortunes of a fictitious boy. He had spent the next three weeks hunched over the television set as if there was a son of his amongst the troops in the Falklands, gripping his wife's arm as if he could hardly bear to watch their uncertain progress, Ellen marvelling at her husband's rigidity, his barely suppressed passion. 'Our Henry', Amy had said, the phrase echoing all her silly romantic hopes that he had encouraged, hopes that were not simply hers but his too. He could picture this Henry, imagining the time when he would emerge through the cordite mists of war, a new son, tempered in battle and shining full of promise, a son to be proud of, a son to look up to. Wasn't that what every parent wanted, a child to look up to, to see in their offspring a strength of character that could have been their own, had not adverse circumstance prevailed? He rang her from work every now and again, telling her that he had no news. That was to be expected. She had written another letter, but still had no reply. He was glad that the war had come. It masked such dangerous silences. They exchanged thoughts, worries; he rang off, each time promising to

339

return. 'Our Henry', she had said and of course she was right. He was their Henry. They had made him together, a son worthy of the name for him, a boyfriend (a fiancée even), for her, but as the war progressed, from Goose Green to Mount Longford, from Tumble-down to the final run down into Port Stanley, he knew that come the victory he would have to ensure that they shared his death. With the victory the time had come. He pitched upon the waves of the problem for days; a letter, a phone call? She deserved a visit, he was sure of that.

He had gone up two days ago, under cover of Trout Night, the second Friday of the quarter, although he hadn't heard from any of the others since the debacle in April. Another tradition sunk. He checked in to the guest house in the early afternoon, Mrs Dixon grim in her clipped severity. No heart-to-heart concerning offspring, no patriotic toast of sherry over of the Task Force's success, just the time of the wake-up call and an enquiry as to the severity of the English breakfast. He was shown into the top room, all angles and low ceilings. His usual, she sniffed, was being refurbished. He had the distinct impression that if she hadn't needed the money she wouldn't have taken him in at all. He didn't mind. He could always find another. It was probably a good thing. Once he'd got this over with there was no reason why he shouldn't go on seeing Amy, point her in the right direction, slipping in and out of town as salesmen do.

He waited in a newsagent's across the road until she had finished work. She had a job now, working in a florist's. She had found it without any help from him, though he liked to think that Henry's letter had spurred her on. She came out with a new-found friend, another pasty girl like her, a little older, a little taller, both giggling at something, their Henry momentarily forgotten. He ducked back in the doorway. He was a fraudster, selling dodgy insurance, conning his way into her life's savings, stealing her emotional investment. Perhaps he should have written, left it at that, cut her loose quickly; never seen her again. Then she spotted him and forgetting herself ran across the road, giving the V-sign to a swerving car. She flung her arms around him, eager, without guile, like a year-old puppy.

'Richard! I thought I'd hear from you soon. Isn't it great. When's he coming back?'

Richard looked down. He could feel himself trembling. He had loved this son too. He cleared his throat.

'I've got some bad news for you, Amy.'

He saw the slack of her jaw and her hand go to her mouth. He nodded.

'The night before they surrendered, they say. I don't know the full details even now.'

'Richard.'

She fell into his arms. He could feel her body shaking for a boy who she had never met. Why couldn't he have brought him home! Why couldn't his own son's life mean something as important!

'He did his duty,' he said.

'Course he did.'

'He was a brave boy, a good boy. We all loved him.'

He started crying. He had sacrificed the son he had always wanted for this girl. They could have fallen in love, his son and Amy, become engaged. It would have been him who had brought them together, him to whom they would have been eternally gratefully; a loving daughter-in-law, an indulged grandson, a life respected.

She walked him to the park, sat on a bench near the water. She held his head against her dumpling breasts, one arm enfolded around the curve of his back, her breath washing over his face. He looked up. He had never felt such unadorned tenderness, such straightforwardness. He *would* look after her, see her through to a better life.

'Oh, Amy. If only he had met you.'

She looked older to him now, and he felt younger: no not younger, smaller, more vulnerable: in need.

'He did in a way. My letters.'

'Yes. Your letters. How many did you send?'

'Five.'

Five letters to his son! And he had never written one!

'They would have meant a lot to him.'

'Do you think? They were just, you know, silly most of the time.'

He sat up, his voice quavering.

'They were a lot more than that. I mean they'd have all got letters from their mums and dads, their wives and sweethearts, but yours were from someone he didn't know, and yet, they shone through, Amy, with a kindness and honesty that would have lit his very darkest hours. Who knows, it might have been the last thing he thought of, meeting up with you, seeing his old dad again.'

He started crying again. A son he had never known lying dead in the Falklands, a son he had never known wasting away in a shed at the bottom of the garden. At the bottom of the garden! A son at the bottom of the garden and Ellen, her face turned to the plate glass, looking out to the barren land where he was entombed.

'Has he been . . .' She hesitated to use the word.

'Along with his comrades, yes. We'll be holding a memorial service for him at home, of course.'

'I don't suppose . . .'

Roach sat up, wiping his eyes.

'It's just family, Amy. You understand. His mother and me.'

'Of course. It's just . . . I had a feeling, you know, that after it was over, we'd meet. I had a feeling that I'd like him, that he'd like me, that we'd hit it off. Like you and me! Thought it might of led somewhere. It's what songs are made of, isn't it. Meet a stranger, fall in love.'

'Oh, Amy. I thought it too.'

'Did you?'

'Didn't like to say, didn't want to raise your hopes, but . . .'

'Richard.'

She bent down, placed her lips upon his face.

'There, I kissed his dad instead.'

He started to shake.

'Oh, Amy. I'm so alone.'

She pressed her face against his raspy old cheek. There was dandruff on the back of his jacket, a half-moon of scalp showing through the black hair. Such a kind and gentle man. She raised his head up, firm in her hands, staring into his eyes.

'Not tonight you're not,' she said.

So it came to this at last, curled up like a baby, his head on the stomach of a young girl, his hand upon her breast, not knowing how to move or what to say while she stroked his head. Hour upon hour they lay even until sleep, until in the colder dawn he woke and she woke. Did she whisper his name, did he call hers, or was there Henry hovering on their lips between their lips. It was Henry they were calling, Henry who stood between them, unblemished as they ran headlong towards him. It was Henry they reached out to, Henry they gripped, Henry who caught them wheeling. There was no tripping up here, no failed grasp, just Henry and his open arms and a stretch of a green rushing towards them.

And then a furious banging on the door, and Mrs Dixon and her finger-points of ignominy as they got dressed and were bundled out at six o'clock in the morning. He drove Amy home in silence. Her bare legs scandalized him. How young she looked! A child! He hadn't meant to do that. That was not right. He could have been her father-in-law. She could have been his new daughter. And yet, there was such softness there, such simple unadorned tenderness. If only he could float away on it, never to return.

'Don't think bad of me, Richard.'

'Me of you!'

She patted her pockets.

'Sugar. I forgot my necklace.'

'I'll go back and get it.'

'No, you've got enough on your plate. I'll get it after work.' She opened the passenger door, then closed it again. 'Will I see you again?'

'Amy. Of course you will, but . . .' She reached out, put her fingers to his lips.

'I know. I'll be thinking of you.'

He heard her call out as she opened the front door.

He drove back, magnificent.

*

It had been Richard's idea, a street party to welcome Suzanne home, appropriately patriotic, appropriately personal. Ellen had objected, pointing out that it clashed with Sir Douglas's gathering. Richard was adamant.

343

'She won't be back here until four at the earliest,' he had pointed out. 'Surely three and a half hours with people you don't know and will never meet again is enough. We have a heroine to celebrate. Ours.'

The word stabbed at his heart, the moment it left his mouth.

They'd started at first light, Freddie collecting the trestle tables from the local Scout troop, Patsy and Marjorie baking cakes and scones, Ellen buttering piles of sliced bread for the forthcoming sandwiches. Even Mark had joined in, cutting up one of their old sheets to make a banner. Now, with the morning broadening, Anglefield Road was beginning to look festive. Freddie and Hector were arranging the tables in a semicircle at the bottom of the road. Mark was busy on Matty's forecourt, putting the finishing touches to red lettering with the stubble of an old paintbrush, Marcy perched on the wall, keeping him company. Ellen had gone into town to get the drink. Each household had put in thirty pounds. Matty had left the night before, to be there whenever the *Canberra* docked.

Roach walked up the road planting Union Jacks in his neighbours' gardens, five in the Armstrongs' hedge, a neat row of ten stuck into the Millens' pristine lawn, as many again jammed into the cracks of his half fence. On the wall over at the Plimsolls' they dangled from the links of the decorative wall chain, like little boys on a row of swings. Ellen had been forced to admit they'd come in useful after all. Turning back he began scattering the remainder on the tables. Ellen honked the horn as she backed the car into the drive, the back seat laded with booze, beckoning to her son. Mark shambled over, hands in pockets, looking everywhere but at his mother, the studied walk of ordinary youth. Roach smiled. He looked just like any other young man. Marcy must be doing him some good.

Ellen wound down the window.

'I'm going to change. Unload this lot for me.'

Mark nodded, his eyes straying to Marcia's torso as she dragged the banner over towards the Millens' For Sale sign. Not a bad little figure, she thought, though she'd go to fat in a few years.

'Are you sure you won't come?' she said. 'We're not going to be there long. You could thank Kevin in person. He's been very good to you.'

Kevin had been as good as his word, found Mark a job at one of their suppliers.

'I need to put the banner up, Mum. You can thank him for both of us, can't you?'

He slunk back. Marcy was being a real pain. She stood there now, shoulders hunched, glowering at the activity. He took the end of the rope and held it out.

'Are you going to help or not?'

'Why the bloody hell should I?' She looked down scornfully at the inscription. ' "Anglefield heroine",' she mocked. 'What kind of joke is that?'

Mark ignored her, tying one end around the pole.

'That high enough?'

'Yes, but make sure you can undo it. That way, when it's all over and everyone's gone to bed, she can pop round wearing it. That would make your evening end with a bang.'

She picked up the other end, walked across the road.

'I wish I'd never told you.'

'You won't be the only one.'

'What does that mean?'

'You're just like her. You think you're better than the rest of us, better than that girl you killed, better than my dad, better than yours.' She let the banner fall. 'Make the most of today. It could be the last time you're welcome here.'

She stomped off.

'Marcy!'

*

Ellen was glad to be back inside. Why had Mark said that about Kevin, that she'd know how to thank him? Did he suspect something? That time the three of them met, when she drove him over for the interview, Kevin had made a point of being there, to introduce him to the manager. She and Kevin had a coffee across the road while he went in, that was all. Mark had shaken Kevin's hand when it was all over, reluctantly she had noticed, as if he hadn't wanted the job, and she, all she'd done was kissed Kevin on the cheek, by way of thanks. Wouldn't any mother have done the same? The funny thing was Mark was enjoying the job. Boring as hell it sounded, sitting by the telephone all day, but he seemed to have taken to it, journeying up to North London, checking invoices and delivery dates, making phone calls to exotic corners of the world. Last week he got his first wage packet. Richard could have arranged something like that, months ago, and had he? No wonder Kevin was Sales Manager; no wonder Richard was stuck where he was. She was almost on the brink of coming to a decision.

She showered, shaved her legs and under her arms, plucked her eyebrows, chose her underwear with care. The dress hung on the back of the door and as she slipped it on over her head she felt as if a skin had been removed rather than put on.

She leant out the window, a towel wrapped round her head. Richard was helping Patsy and Freddie lay out the paper plates.

'Richard,' she called down. 'Don't you think it's time you got ready? We don't want to be late.'

Roach waved her way, turned back to the task in front of him, last-minute instructions he wanted to give out.

'You're going to need more tables up the road, Freddie,' he said. 'There's no knowing how many are going to turn up. Make sure that Marcy doesn't forget the balloons and bunting.'

'Yes, Richard.'

'Also, the beer needs to be put into those tin baths that Marjorie is cleaning out. The ice is in Matty's freezer.'

Roach patted Freddie on the back. 'Got to go. See you two later!'

He walked off whistling.

'You'd think it was his wife coming back, not Matty's,' Patsy observed.

Freddie sidled up to her conspiratorially.

'All these balloons, Patsy,' he said, 'these flags and what-nots. You don't think it's going to look too much like a street party?'

'Freddie, it is a street party.'

'Yes, I know, but we're celebrating a *military* victory, aren't we? It's not like it's a jubilee or anything. It's all a bit . . .'

Patsy tucked the plates under her arm, gazed around her. Up the road Marjorie had come out and was helping Mark raise the banner. Ellen was back at her window, her mouth moving in silent conversation. For the first time in months Anglefield looked whole again. Maybe if this thing of Freddie's got off the ground they wouldn't have to move after all.

'Come on, Freddie, what is it?'

'I was thinking, if we wanted to give it a more military aspect, whether I shouldn't bring some of my you-know-whats out of storage. Line them up on the pavement, as if on parade.'

'You mean the lawnmowers? You're allowed to say the word these days, you know.'

Freddie pounced.

'Lawnmowers, exactly. Some of them are really quite martial, you know. If you were a blade of grass . . .'

Pasty checked herself. He needed a break. Ever since Matty's involvement he'd been trying hard with the project. Next week they were going to take it to Smiths' head office down in Swindon. RBG had fixed the meeting. She'd gritted her teeth and rung him herself. And now Freddie wanted to be Freddie again, bless him. She indulged him, making a show of considering the question with care.

'It's a nice idea, Freddie, though a bit risky given the quality of machine involved.' Freddie blinked his eyes in agreement. Patsy drove forward. 'You'll get paw marks all over them, kids from the estate piffling about with the engines. Anyway, it isn't a military homecoming, is it, not unless she's taken the Queen's shilling en route. She was a civilian, on a civilian ship.'

Freddie looked disappointed.

'You could bring out one, though. That ugly brute, the one that looks like a battleship.' She picked up one of the flags from the table. 'Stick this on.'

Freddie's face grew animated.

'I could sit Suzanne on the seat, drive her down, like she was on a float, waving to the crowd. Play "Rule, Britannia!" out the window. We've got a Prom recording.'

Patsy began beating the flag on his head. Hector came running out into the road.

'She's docking!' he cried. 'On the television!'

*

347

They had been told there was no one there to greet them. They'd been told that the *Queen Elizabeth* had taken all the glory, that the country had lost interest. What did they know of the truth, of the land they had left behind? They'd had the first sighting of England at around five the previous evening. By midnight they could see Portland Bill, its thin finger poking into the black sea. Then they'd hung around, drifting up the Channel, loitering outside the Isle of Wight, the dawn light breaking over the horizon, the long flat rays illuminating a couple of inquisitive yachts, circling round the *Canberra*'s huge bulk like a wary terrier, sniffing at a larger stranger. Then the two were joined by a third and the three by another four, and soon the sea had filled like a Piccadilly Circus, a Trafalgar Square, the boats hooting and whistling, moving round in a long slow circle. As they turned into the Solent it seemed as if the ghost of old Dunkirk had returned, the nation had stepped out again into little boats, pleasure steamers and yachts, sailing dinghies, even a crowd of school-children in canoes. As they sailed up, they could hear a vast cheering. Fire boats shot rainbows of water into the air, parachute flares flowered in operatic bouquets.

'Look at that.' Tina was waving back furiously.

Below, a motor launch cruised alongside, four young women naked from the waist up, waving their T-shirts above their heads.

'Ah, I don't think they're primarily for your benefit, Tina.'

'No, but it makes me realize what I've been missing.'

It was the first but not the last boat to contain such a sight. They ran a gauntlet of such seemingly willing flesh, the men cheering wildly as the girls jumped up and down. They weren't girlfriends. They weren't wives. This wasn't streaking at a football match, or even a striptease. They were offering at a distance what the men would not have close to hand, claiming a territory of their own. We have won. We can do what we want now.

How different it was from those dark days after the landing. It had been a hard time for them, in those three weeks, wallowing up and down in the pointless sea, bare-larder days, starvation-ration nights. The ship's heart had been transplanted, and they lived suppressed, in a mental limbo, with the slack of their unused bodies their only company. It was hard to tell which was emptier:

the sea, the ship, or the people on board. There was hardly anything for them to do. Every now and again a group of officers
would be flown out for some R&R, and Suzanne and Tina would
spruce up the cabins, give them all a special sheen, buttonholing
Dickey in the Pig and Whistle for snatches of news, but those who
came weren't inclined to talk. There was too much to explain, too
many rumours running about on the world's airwaves. All they
wanted was a hot bath, a whisky, and a good night's sleep in a
fresh bed. Plying the waves under the cloak of Darken Ship even
the lights of flirtation had been extinguished. Tina checked with
the purser every day, hoping that James Osgood would appear, but
he never did, and though she tried to winkle even the most innocent of information out, no one seemed anxious to speculate as to
where he might be or what he might be doing. The days were spent
fruitlessly, playing video games, watching films, listening to the
radio, patching up the gossip into quilts of unlikely patterns.
When it came, the news of the capitulation, the march into Port
Stanley, the raising of the Union Jack, yes the victory, it was hard
for them to accept, this yawning gap of inactivity had concluded
in the restoration of Britain's pride. There had been no cheering.
They felt let down, like a reader on the closing pages of a novel,
the conclusion abruptly written, the resolution flat. They had won.
Was that it? They had won?

A day later they entered Falkland Sound again, expecting to see
some old faces, to relive some of the earlier excitement. But when
they got there, all they saw were the Welsh Guards prodding up
the gangways the ragbag army of Argentina's soldiers. They were
to take them home.

They smelled bad, their clothes choked with the soiled history
of lost battles. Their eyes did not know where to look. Many had
no idea that they had been on the Falklands. Most were convinced
that they had been overrun by an army which had overwhelmed
them by the sheer number of their troops. They had been told that
the *Canberra* had been sunk, along with the aircraft carrier HMS
Invincible. Though evidence told them differently, deep in their
hearts they still believed these things. They stood them in showers,
fed them hot soup. The first night, a large contingent locked in the

Meridian Room forced the security bars open and polished off all the drink. Dickey was furious.

'They couldn't even be bothered to use the table mats,' he complained. 'One chappy was soaking his feet in one of my ice buckets.'

So they sailed across the water to the land of the enemy. It took them two days. In the usual manner of courtesy, on entering foreign waters they raised the flag of their host country, escorted in by of one of the destroyers that days ago would have blown them out the water and cheered at the sinking. Now there was protocol and distant respect.

At the quayside stood clutches of medallioned officers; army, navy, air force. There were no families, no cheering, no flag waving. Smartly pressed sailors secured their lines. As the first prisoners clattered ashore, tin-pot salutes abounded. After ten minutes the senior officers drifted away, as if not wishing to see the extent of their humiliation. Only the men seemed glad, turning to wave the ship goodbye. They were happy to be home and the *Canberra* was happy for them too.

On the way back, amidst much grumbling, the crew cleaned the ship, imagining that there'd be another filthy load waiting for them. Then the news came through. There were no more prisoners for the *Canberra*. They were going home, taking the marines with them; all of them. They were embarking tomorrow. Suzanne and Tina set to arguing as to who should keep the room and who should move out.

'Squatters' rights,' Tina claimed. 'You were hardly here coming out. And besides, for James and me it has romantic connotations.'

A knock on the door and Dickey poked his head round. He had a little trowel in his hand.

'Can I interest you ladies in a grand tour? I have persuaded the purser to let me and a couple of chosen few to go ashore. I mean, we might as well stand on the bloody thing.'

Tina declined.

'I'm going to raid the laundry,' she said. 'Deck my room out like a Turkish harem.' Suzanne let the pronoun pass.

So Dickey and Suzanne stood on the bloody thing. They weren't allowed far. Just the jetty and a small patch of beach and an escorted hundred yards down the road. The place looked wet and dirty, strewn with discarded helmets and rifles, crashed jeeps and bits of crumpled engine left on the side of the road. There were streets there like in any other town, with fences and gardens, houses with curtains and porches and smoking chimneys, little knots of strangers, locals of course, standing in bewildered huddles, but it didn't look like anything she wanted to know. It looked so mean, so pointless. What would be the point of living here; what would be the point? A wet and dirty town with wet and dirty roads, and everyone walking around wet and dirty. She felt cheated, like at the end of a unsatisfactory affair, the high moments of euphoria replaced by a sense of abandonment and worthlessness; the world of hope and love revealed to be empty, full of nothing.

She walked back to the jetty, half hoping to see Henry loping along, hoping that she would not until she was back on the boat, her equilibrium restored. She stood near the wash of the tide, ignoring what lay behind, looking towards the ship that had carried them so far. She hadn't stood on dry land for nearly three months. She felt giddy, uncertain what exactly she was seeing, or even the reality of where she was. She sat on the pebbles, feeling her life drain away. She picked up the stones and rolled them in her hand, threw them one by one into the water. Dickey appeared, a jar of something wet and dirty in his hand.

'I thought you might like a piece,' he said. 'You could plant it in the garden, let the cat pee on it.'

'I don't have a cat.'

'Invite the neighbours' one over, then. They've got a cat, haven't they?' Suzanne nodded. 'I thought so,' said Dickey. 'A neighbour isn't a neighbour without an irritating pet.'

When Suzanne got back to the cabin, Tina was sitting on the sofa, staring at a sheet of paper, the top edges torn.

'They put it on the noticeboard just as you left,' she said. 'I suppose I shouldn't have taken it down, but . . .'

Suzanne ran her eyes down the list. At the very end, two names.

Major James Osgood killed in action June 13th
Corporal Stanley Bembo killed in action June 13th

Tina took the sheet and lit the bottom, holding it in her hand as the flames licked upwards.

'I slept with two men on this voyage,' she said, 'and both have been killed. Do you think they're trying to tell me something?'

'Tina.'

The paper dropped to the floor, curled up on itself, like a scorpion dying. Tina turned it over, the flame eating into the last remaining corner.

'There's probably lots of men on this boat who are thanking their lucky stars I didn't make it three. I didn't exactly bring them good luck, did I?'

'You brought them what you could.'

'I was going to marry him.'

'It might not have lasted, Tina, considering the circumstances.'

Tina turned on her.

'What do you know about it? It might have. Stanley was married too, did you know?'

What good would it do, to tell her what she knew.

'No, I didn't.'

'With a young baby.'

She crumbled the burnt paper, and wiped her eyes.

'He was gorgeous, Suzy. Just gorgeous.'

She tried to smile.

'I should have gone for a bandsman like you. At least your Henry's safe.'

*

He was brought in on a stretcher. His name had gone before him, how he had behaved that night, his fearless irresponsibility which had saved six or seven lives. The injury on his face had cut into the corner of his eye. Shell fragments had smashed four of his teeth. He had a bandage over his face, but the light still got through. Officers he had never met dropped by to congratulate him. He felt uneasy, uncertain as to where he was, as to what they said. Drugs, he supposed, but perhaps more to do with his transformation. He lived in a world of sounds, sounds of the foghorn and the wash of the river, sounds of barge men calling and the roll of Joe's high-sided van as he turned a corner, the squeak of the wringer as he fed the sheets, the clip clip clip of hurried heels over a fog-bound pavement.

He heard the click of the door and the conversations floating above his head.

'He hasn't spoken yet?'

'Not a word.'

'And there's nothing wrong with his throat?'

'Not that we can tell.'

'His mind, then?'

'Something like that.'

He heard the click of the door and the fall of footsteps. Footsteps came, footsteps went. Then the click of the door again and a warm spoon in his mouth and some sweet rice pudding.

'Nothing wrong with his appetite, then.'

A cradle to rock him then, and waves of damp linen rolling over him, pressing down upon his troubled sleep. Heat in the room when he wanted to be cold. Light around him when he needed darkness. Constriction in his bed when he craved unfettered movement. Then another click and an inhalation of breath, her perfume drifting down.

'Henry?'

He turned his face half away, thankful for the bandage.

'Henry?'

A pause.

'He can hear me?'

'Yes, miss.'

'Henry.'

A hand took his. Such a hand. A hand like this he could have done with years ago. And if he hadn't gone, who knows. The hand stroked his, raised it as to her lips, he could sense the breath on his knuckles and he waited, waited for the quenching kiss, his own lips puckered in anticipation. Maybe he could speak. Maybe she could drag it out of him. Maybe there was a place for him in this world, maybe he could fashion a part of it, redeem himself. Then she laid his hand down again on his chest, patting it. He was not surprised. He had killed a penguin with that hand, stabbed it to death. It hurt him to relive its little struggle. How he could ever have mistaken a penguin for a man! A mistake, or a killing lust?

353

And the cloud in its eyes as it saw the moon for the last time, the clatter of its beak as it died in his arms, the little wings flapping as he flew away leaving his broken body behind.

He shook himself free.

'Best leave it, miss, for the time being.'

A click of a door. Gone.

The bandages came off. His sight had returned. His speech had not. Mates came round, leaving packets of crisps and bottles of beer. One brought a packet of cigarettes.

'He doesn't smoke.' Ian's voice. He didn't smoke no, but that was then. He put his hand over the packet, pointed with his finger towards his broken mouth. Someone struck a match and stuck it in. It wobbled uncertainly between his lips, let the smoke drift up his nostrils. So that was smoking, was it. Why not?

Another click. A shadow of a man standing over him, hands folded in front of him. Familiar hands, he thought. Same with the voice. He had heard it long ago, before he was born. A leather pouch was produced, with a drawstring of leather. It swung to and fro in front of his face.

'You were carrying this when you were picked up. Know what we found in it?'

Henry looked away. Stanley's pouch. Stanley standing over the dead, cutting away the name tags while he searched around. Like boys' dens they were.

'Ears. Nine of them. Know anything about it?'

He should have gone back, buried the penguin, said sorry.

'Who was in charge of you that night?'

Someone coughed.

'He was with Corporal Bembo, sir.'

'Bembo. He's up for a medal, isn't he?'

'Yes, sir.'

'So would this chap if it hadn't been for these.' The shadow leant forward. 'You could be on a charge for this.'

He danced with Dora once, Joe singing a sea shanty and Dora laughing holding him by the ears as she tried to teach him the moves. He couldn't remember the name of the dance. He had stabbed a penguin and laughed as men died. He'd seen him with a knife, hadn't he? Must have, carried the little bag for him, like a caddy on a gold course.

The voice returned, straightened up, no longer talking to him, no longer thinking of him. He'd been erased.

'No privileges for this man.'

'Yes, sir.'

'And keep him away from the others.'

'Yes, sir.'

'Keep him away from everyone. We don't want this getting out. I want his discharge papers ready by the time we dock. Get rid of him, soon as decently possible.'

*

She was proud of him at first, the tales of his bravery running through the ship, but as the days passed and he remained locked away, under guard, other stories rose up, scum on the clear pond; the madcap dancing, the hysterical clucking, why, one even told Dickey that he had seen Henry licking blood from his fingers like a boy with a choc ice. And there were other men to distract her, celebratory men, flushed with the power of victory, men who stood supremely masculine, who had witnessed all their mortalities, men who desired nothing more than the moment and she understood then that this was what she wanted, perhaps all she was capable of, the priest rolling stones in his hand and her standing there, touching the lewd hem of her dress, able to offer up nothing but her own shortcomings. Seeing Henry bandaged, placing her hand on his, she had been terrified that he might return the grip, end her time on this ship, settle her down, to run a shop, or start a family, terrified that tending to his wounds would lead her there of her own accord. She put his hand down as he averted his face and withdrew, relieved.

The days grew warmer, the nights lighter, the ship re-establishing its old identity, the troops out on the decks in their shorts, sunbathing. There was no swimming pool, but they lay like lizards, basking on every available space. The coffee shop reopened, the cinemas ran new films; professional entertainers were flown out, singers, comedians, musicians, and every night there were parties, singing into the dawn. Suzanne was sailing on a cruise ship once more, and she was glad. She didn't want a life of responsibility, a life with depth, not yet, maybe not ever. There were people like that, and she was one of them, not bad people, not uncaring, just unable to do anything but float upon the surface, ride the wave. They had their place, their uses, on sea, on land. People supposed it was the prerogative of the young, but that's wasn't so; you needed age to acknowledge the depth of your own shallowness. It was nothing to celebrate but its acceptance brought a troubled peace. Three days before Ascension Island they threw off their own darkness, and the *Canberra* shone out again, like a floating chandelier. She took a man that night, wilfully and felt the sorrow burning within her. This was her life and there was little she could do about it.

The last full day at sea the Band of the Royal Marines played for the last time. Henry sat upright in his isolation room. Outside he could see the soft English hills fading into the dark. He heard the huge cheer go up as the band marched out, a cheer louder than he had ever heard in his life, two thousand men lifting their voices for the men who had played for them, humped their stores, carried their wounded, dispelled their fears, and now were adding their own exploits to the polished chimes of their history. The Royal Marines. He held his trumpet to his battered mouth, but of glissandos and crescendos, of the dancing notes of his past there came nothing. He was done with them.

*

The crew had to wait until most of the troops had disembarked before they were allowed off. That was all right. Suzanne had some work to do, visit the purser's office, say goodbye to Dickey. He was locking up for the last time, an opened bottle of champagne on the bar.

'I promised Murray once to sneak him a bottle of this. The best we've got,' he said. 'A life of petty theft. I'm getting addicted to it. Just as well, considering the job prospects in Ashford.'

'It's definite, then.'

'You won't see me again. Not unless you make a surprise visit, which I don't advise. What about you?'

She showed him the papers.

'Probably for the best.'

He held out a glass. She shook her head.

'He'll be waiting. Bye-bye, Dickey.'

*

Matty stood on the dock with his hands held out, expecting her to run into his arms, but she couldn't. She walked towards him calmly. They stood apart.

'You came back, then?'

'I came back.'

'I missed you, you know.'

Suzanne nodded, unable to echo his sentiment.

'Still, it's over now. That's the main thing. Come here.'

He hugged the breath out of her, spinning her round, and she clung back, afraid when she regained her balance he would discover that all they had possessed had been spun away.

'Marcia here?' she asked.

'No.' He caught her look of resignation. 'It's not like that. The fact is . . . they're all back home, waiting.'

'All?'

He led her towards the car, unpolished, she noticed.

'Anglefield Road, a welcome party. I tried to warn them off, but . . .'

'Warn them off?'

'I thought you might have had enough excitement to last you a lifetime. A bit of peace and quiet, glad to be home.'

There it was again. Suzanne held out her hand. She couldn't wait to get there.

'Why don't I drive,' she said.

*

Roach drifted in and out between the knotted groups, talking to no one. Three marquees, sides of salmon, lobsters, oysters, roast beef, cured ham, a man in a top hat carving slabs as thick as his thumbnail from a spit-roasted pig; one tent for puddings alone, bowls of strawberries and trifles, fruit tarts, jugs of cream, great wheels of Brie; waiters wandering around with bottles of champagne; he felt sick just looking at it, thinking of the paper plates

357

and plastic cups of beer and the sliced-bread ham sandwiches that were waiting for them back at Anglefield Road. The house was huge, Elizabethan he thought, with a swathe of gravel between it and the village they had driven through, the oaks ancient and planted in rows, the doors and mullioned windows thrown open, a string quartet playing in the rose garden, at the far end a lake with any number of rowing boats and in the middle an island with a little tower poking up through the clutch of trees. And the people! Half the faces he thought he recognized, a mixture of the glamorous and the powerful, the orange tans of TV fame offset by the pallor of all-night politicians. He'd already trod on the foot of a cabinet minister, his apology drying in his throat as he realized whom he'd inadvertently assaulted. Men in tuxedos and casual linen suits, some dressed in jeans looking smarter than he ever could, the women effortless in the knowledge of their supremacy, whatever their age, costumed seduction their second nature. Ellen was drinking too much. She had imagined that she was going to be a new star, gathering inquisitive admirers all around, but no one paid her any attention. She had spent a lot of money on that dress, more than they could afford, but compared to what others were wearing she looked ordinary. Not tawdry, or shabby, not even cheap, but plain ordinary, out of place. The quality of the cut wasn't there, the floating hang of the hem, the understated assurance of the neckline; her hair didn't fall in the same manner, her fingers could not claim the same territory of care. Even the way she smoked a cigarette or took a drink from one of the waiters wasn't quite right. She was either too polite or too dismissive. Most importantly, she couldn't hold her own with the other guests. He had stood behind her at the edge of some circle, watching as she had tried to break through the ice, watched too as the conversation was passed back and forth with never a thought to the woman standing on the sidelines. This is my wife, he wanted to say. She's as smart as you, as witty as you, give her a chance, but after ten minutes or so the circle closed in altogether or simply broke up, and they were left, drifting again without a rudder.

'I'm going to wander around a bit on my own,' she told him, after the fourth attempt, implying that it was his own lumbering presence that was the main obstacle. He did the same, ending up back at the tent, helping himself to more cake. Wendy stood there sucking on a strawberry, some man chatting her up, unable to keep his eyes off her. It seemed to annoy Richard more than her.

'Wendy,' he called out. She turned, the flap of her jacket flying open. She was wearing that T-shirt, for God's sake. 'I didn't expect to see you here.'

'Richard. Better than a sales conference, eh? Our reward for the *Canberra*.'

'That's what it said on the card. Kevin here, then?'

'I expect so. I asked him to give me a lift here but would he hell. He's never forgiven me for me being on the box and not him.' She picked another fat strawberry out of the bowl. 'It's back today, you know, the *Canberra*. I nearly went down, then I thought, no, silly that, when I can stuff my face here and get legless.'

She giggled. She looked a bit legless already.

'Don't get too carried away,' Roach warned. 'Sir Douglas wouldn't like it. He's not a forgiving man. Look what happened to Sandy.'

'Poor old Sandy. You heard from him?'

As a matter of fact he had. Sandy had been talking to some French manufacturer of specialized walking boots, unknown here, with the idea of becoming their sole agent. There were one or two shoe companies like that, ripe for development. He'd rung Richard to see if he'd be interested in joining forces.

'Think of it,' he had said, 'out on the road, your own boss. Just like old times.' Roach hadn't told Ellen of the meeting, but he was tempted.

'No,' he said. 'You know what it's like.'

She nodded, bored, turning round to see who she might approach next, his eyes momentarily dropping. She caught him square on.

'Is that the Falklands T-shirt you're wearing?' he asked trying to cover himself. She grinned and pulled back the jacket open. The wording had been changed. DON'T CRY FOR US ARGENTINA. WE KNOCKED THE F*CK OUT OF YOU. Someone behind him cheered. Richard indicated that she should button up.

'Do you think Sir Douglas would approve of that here?'

'It was his idea, Richard. Loosen up, for God's sake.'

A voice boomed in his ear.

'I say, what's a rude girl like you doing in a well-bred place like this?'

Another admirer examining Wendy's slogan with intense interest. They wandered off towards the lake, the man snatching a bottle of champagne from a passing tray, Wendy squealing with pleasure, Roach following idly in their wake. Everyone seemed to be having a good time, talking and laughter, making new friends, seeing old acquaintances. Only he seemed to be alone. And Ellen, of course, wherever she might be. Wendy and her admirer had nearly reached the water's edge when Roach saw her pulling him back, pointing to a couple standing by the boat before changing direction, hurrying off around the path on the side.

It took him a moment to recognize them, but then the man's hand brushed against the woman's, Ellen's jerking back violently as if she had just scalded herself. Roach thought he was going to faint. He had never seen her move with such fervour, as if she could not bear the electricity of Kevin's touch. Her hand went to her mouth, knuckle to lip, balm to the burn. He understood it all. He threw his plate into a bush and ran towards them.

Ellen crossed her arms, tucking her hands away. Kevin took a step towards the lake.

'It was good of you to get Mark that job,' she told him.

Kevin stared ahead.

'I was glad to help.'

'You should see the change in him. Two weeks and already they've put him in charge of something or other. He's got this way with the telephone, apparently, though where he gets it from I don't know, I hate the thing myself.'

'What did I tell you? Us tearaways always come through in the end. And the court hearing?'

'A two-year suspended sentence. Banned from driving for eight.'

'He won't be following in his father's footsteps, then.'

'Not a chance of that, thank God.'

Footfalls burst upon them.

'Richard!'

360

Roach stood there panting. There was a splodge of white cream down the front of his trousers. Her hand flew to the front of her dress.

'I was just thanking Kevin for what he did for Mark.'

'Yes.' Roach wiped his mouth with the back of his hand. 'You must come round again, so we can show our appreciation. That would be nice, wouldn't it, Ellen? Another celebration in Angle-field Road.'

A splutter of half-digested cake came from his mouth. Kevin gestured to one of the boats.

'Ellen and I thought we might explore the island.'

'She doesn't like boats.'

'The sea, that what he means, Kevin, the up-and-down stuff. Lakes I can handle. Shall we go?'

In front of him; they were going off in front of him.

'Why don't I come too?' he said. 'I'll row you both.'

He clambered in, the boat rocking, Kevin tumbling into Ellen's arms as he tried to manoeuvre across, a flurry of awkward limbs and body rearrangements as they prised themselves apart. Richard pushed off.

'What's on there, then?'

'The island? A grotto.' Kevin relaxed. 'Sir Douglas built it himself. Took him years. It's covered in shells, floor to ceiling.'

'A kind of folly, then.'

'Not exactly, no, though the thing in the middle, that ruined tower, that's a folly. Nineteenth century, I believe.'

'What makes people build follies, do you think?' Richard asked. 'Is it simply something to look at, an expression of the time and money that others don't have, or it an unwillingness to look at the real world?'

'It's what it says it is,' Ellen said. 'A folly, a piece of harmless indulgence.' Roach persisted.

'Yes, but folly implies something foolish as well, something that leads to some kind of misfortune, or in some cases outright disaster.'

'It's a word, Richard, that's all.'

'All that time and money spent on a folly, money that could be spent to a better purpose. It also makes a mockery of the land. Denies its purpose.'

'Which is?'

'To sustain us all.'

Ellen's fingers were playing on the surface of the water. Kevin's hand was dipped up to the wrist. It was as if they were holding hands. Kevin objected to his definition.

'That's not land's purpose,' he said.

'It's the use we choose for it. Of course, the other thing we do is fight over it. The land we own a measure of our power, the territory we claim. Perhaps that's a folly in itself.'

He began to pull harder. Now that they'd set the trend, other couples were loosening other boats from their moorings.

'The Falklands, for instance. Fighting over a scrap of land no one cares tuppence about, young men being killed.'

'I thought you were pro the Falklands,' Ellen said.

'What if I am? It doesn't make it any less foolish, does it?'

They landed. Richard stowed the oars. A little path led up to the sunken cave, mouth open beneath a table of moss, a boy's den made from a South Sea Island inside, the curved walls studded with the whirls of coloured conches, brightly patterned shells, and under their feet a mosaic of white and black pebble.

'It must have taken him years,' Ellen said, taking Richard's arm. 'You could never do anything like this.'

'I wouldn't want to,' Richard said. 'Buried out here, with no one to look at it.'

'You're looking at it now.'

'Not for long.'

He stepped out into the midday air. He could hear the two of them walking about, talking softly inside. Then the footsteps stopped and there was no sound at all. Kevin came out first, blinking.

'Where's this tower, then?'

They waded through the bracken, clouds of flies rising in the noonday heat, Roach leading, Ellen trailing the two men. It stood in a little clearing, a broken fence leaning around it; a white-stoned mock of a ruin with a half-exposed staircase and a turret at the top.

'It's got a great view, apparently,' Kevin said. 'Coming?'

Ellen shook her head.

'I can't stand heights. You two go. I'll wait by the boat. I'm being bitten to death here.'

It was higher than it looked, the climb steeper, longer. Richard took off his jacket and sweated his way up. They stood looking out over the tops of the trees, south towards the great house and the swarm of guests bunching like bees on the lawn. To the north lay a calmer country, fenced paddocks and stable yards, riderless horses gambolling in distant fields.

Richard walked up to Kevin and pushed him hard.

'Richard, what the . . .'

Roach pushed him again, Kevin stumbling back against the crumbled stone. His mouth was dry, his legs trembled. He felt wonderful. He walked around him, like a boxer in the ring.

'Those boys on the Falklands they killed all day long, for a possession that was never theirs. I'm twice their age, Kevin, and know every inch of mine. My son, my wife, that's my job, not yours; my territory, not yours. Man kills for his territory, Kevin, even when he's lost it. Not right away. He'll bide his time, choose his moment, launch a surprise attack, at night maybe. The consequences aren't important. The act is. Think of England, the love of its land, think of France and Germany, the bones that lie there; think of the Falklands, the blood of our boys not yet soaked into the ground. This house here, how do you think his lordship's family held on to it all these years? By holding garden parties? No, they'd have killed for it, maybe on this island here, in this tower. Can't you see it, an enemy stabbed to death, a rival suitor hurled off this parapet, buried in those thickets, weighted down, thrown in the lake. There are territories everywhere, Kevin, and great trophies to be won, but by God they come at a price.'

His speech was broken by the murmur of voices and the brush of trodden undergrowth. Below them Wendy appeared, her mouth glued to her new companion. They broke apart and he span her round, lifting her T-shirt clear above her head. He raised them up like trophies. They were not that special, Roach thought, imagining Ellen. He sprang again, clamping his hand over Kevin's face, his lips pressed hard against the younger man's ear.

'When you joined the firm you were a son to me,' he said, 'and I would have stayed a father to you. But you have betrayed me in work and now sullied my home. I have not only disowned you. I am your enemy.'

He pulled his head down, so that it hung over. Wendy was unbuttoning the man's shirt.

'That's where you should be,' he whispered, 'wallowing through the filth of this world until you find some cleaner, fresher territory. Dare I say virgin. Stake your claim on that, mark it as your own.'

He pulled him down towards the stairs.

'Anyone down there?' he called out.

By the time they reached the bottom Wendy and her man had disappeared. They walked back to where Ellen was waiting. Roach untied the boat and helped her in. Kevin moved to climb aboard. Richard stopped him with the palm of his hand.

'Kevin's not coming. Are you?'

Ellen looked at Kevin, confused.

'What?'

Kevin gestured back to the wooded undergrowth.

'That's right. I'm staying here for a bit.'

'Well, how are you going to get back?'

Roach set the oars in the rowlocks. The way he did it, they'd have thought he'd spent his life on the water.

'With Wendy, I expect,' he said brightly. 'You remember Wendy, Ellen. She was the girl you didn't recognize when Kevin wasn't on the television. He can go back with her. After she's had sexual intercourse with someone she's just met. You can wait that long, can't you, Kevin?'

He pushed off. Kevin stood on the edge of the water, then turned. Ellen looked from one to the other.

'Richard, what's going on?'

'We're going home.'

'Home?' Ellen tried to claw back some dignity. 'We've only just arrived. I've hardly met anyone yet.'

'Who's there to meet?'

'Our host, for a start. Don't you think he'd find it a bit rude if we went off without so much as saying thank you?'

Roach marched her through the crowd to where Sir Douglas and friends were gathered in the rose garden. The string quartet were taking a break. Sir Douglas's hands were busy describing some amusing story, the guests dutifully attentive. Richard pushed his way through.

'Sir Douglas. You remember my wife, Ellen.'

A flicker of annoyance chased across the fine features.

'Of course. So pleased you could come.' He bent towards them both, working his practised charm. 'There is a young man in our head office, Ellen, who is absolutely smitten with you.'

'Oh?' She could feel herself redden. Sir Douglas raised his glass, took a long sip.

'Yes. He can't believe how someone like Richard here could possibly win over such a beauty.'

Laughter ran round the circle. Ellen flushed.

'I didn't know wives were the staple talk of the office.'

'Such conundrums intrigue any red-blooded male.' Sir Douglas drew Richard in. 'So, what's your secret, Richard? How'd you manage to snag this beauty?'

More laughter. Roach waved away a proffered glass. Ellen took hers, drank it a little too fast.

'I put it down to his occupation, Sir Douglas. You must know that a woman can't resist a man who knows his shoes.'

Sir Douglas nodded in appreciation, his eyes dropping to her own. He could tell they were good, she knew. She carried on, growing in confidence.

'He has other uses, as I'm sure you're aware. You must be delighted the way things are going with the Bronco. It's sailing out the shops, Richard tells me.'

Again the flicker of impatience. She understood too late. You didn't talk about the mundane business of work at such gatherings. But he was the host and the afternoon stretched ahead. He could afford to be indulgent, to show them all the depth of his breeding. He put his arm round his employee, deciding to fashion haute couture out of this burlap sack of feed.

'Bit of a rum thinker, this one. It was his idea, the whole *Canberra* thing.'

Roach raised his head to the sky. Recognition at last.

'That woman friend of yours still on it, I suppose?' Richard nodded.

'Just off it. In fact where I live, our whole road—'

Sir Douglas interrupted. He wasn't interested in Richard's road.

'We watched it dock only this morning. You should have gone down to see it, Richard, given that you missed it first time around.' Roach panicked.

'What?' he said, not daring to look at his wife.

Sir Douglas turned to the other guests. 'According to the BBC Johnny on the box, all the young women on the boats that had come out to greet them were bare-breasted. Quite a welcome sight, I should imagine, if you've been starved of such delights for over three months.'

He patted Richard on the back.

'You could have taken your lovely lady with you. Added her to the attractions.'

Richard stiffened, seizing the way out.

'What do you mean?'

There was unmistakable aggression in his voice. Sir Douglas looked around for support.

'A pretty woman in a crowd. It's always nice.'

'Are you suggesting she should follow suit? Take her clothes off? Display herself for all and sundry?'

'Richard!' Ellen reached out.

Roach shrugged her off.

'Perhaps you'd like her to do it here?'

'Richard, believe me, I didn't mean . . .'

'And why are you going on about my wife?'

'It was just a harmless . . .'

'Folly, yes I know. I won't have it, do you hear. Talking about my wife like that.'

He poked his finger to within an inch of Sir Douglas' nose.

'Make a display of her again and I'll chuck you in your bloody lake.'

He stood there, his cherub cheeks bunched into knots of fury. Someone muttered, another giggled. Sir Douglas checked his tie.

'Ellen. I think your husband might have had a little too much to drink.'

Roach reached out and flipped the tie up into the man's face.

'I haven't had anything to drink. I'm driving.'

'Well, perhaps you should start now.'

'Yes, I will, to a proper party, with my friends and neighbours, celebrating a real-life heroine, not someone who shovels someone else's idea onto the back seat of his Roller. And you know what? I lied to my wife. They're *not* selling and you know why? Sandy was right. They're bloody ugly!'

He grabbed Ellen's elbow, marched her to the car. He skidded out onto the gravel drive, wheels spitting mud and grass, Ellen ran her hands through her hair, unable to comprehend.

'Richard, what do you think you're doing?'

He took his hands off the wheel, shouting.

'I'm packing it in, that's what I'm doing! Packing it in!' He reached back and started throwing the firm's presentation material out of the window. The car began to swerve off the road. Roach grabbed the wheel back, steadied the car. 'I'm going to do something else, set out on my own, join up with Sandy, I don't know. Something that tells me I'm me.'

He turned into the main road, sped towards the small village. Driving with his eyes ahead he began to unbutton the front of her dress.

'God, Ellen, I feel so strong. So invincible. It's my world, Ellen, mine and yours. I can just feel it.'

'Richard!'

The car came to a halt. A man crossed in front of them, then a woman pushing a buggy. He turned his left hand in, rubbed her far breast.

'Jesus, Richard. We're at a pedestrian crossing. '

'I know.' He ran his hand up and down the length of her. She was loose and rubbery. The car began to move.

'I feel almost naked in this car.'

'You are almost naked in this car.'

'What if someone looks in.'

'I don't know, what if someone looks in? Do you care?'

She said nothing but leant back in her seat. He picked up the right half of the hem and drew it back. He could hear her breathing intently. They drove on in silence. They were leaving the outskirts now, and as they passed the last row of bungalows a lay-by came into view. He swerved suddenly and turned off the engine. He walked around to the other side, pulled open the passenger door.

'Turn round,' he said. She lifted her legs and swivelled.

He pulled back both halves of her dress so that her body hung open. He unzipped his trousers. He felt the wet in her mouth and the sting of the air, saw the completeness of the light shining on her body, him standing in the lay-by, watching the traffic, her holding him by her first finger and thumb as if it were bone china she had in her hand, learnt at a Swiss finishing school. He fell on top of her, his shoes digging into the gravel, mouthing such forbidden words into her ear so insistently that neither of them heard the police car drawing up alongside.

She buttoned up, ashamed. Richard seemed unaffected, even pleased. Ellen felt the eyes of the driver upon her. His older partner walked round the car, trying to keep a straight face.

'Name?'

Richard brushed the knees of his trousers.

'Roach. Richard Roach.'

'And yours, madam?'

Ellen blushed. To be caught like that.

'I'm his wife. Ellen. We weren't doing anything wrong, Officer.'

'I'm afraid you were, madam. Gross indecency, or at a push committing a lewd act in a public place.'

Richard motioned to Ellen to step back a pace. Though he lowered his voice, she could hear every word.

'The thing is, Officer,' he said, 'I've just come back from the Falklands.'

The man looked at him sternly.

'Don't try the funny with me, sunshine, I'm not in the mood.'

Richard pressed his case. He was possessed with a kind of genius. It *was* his world.

'No, it's true. I was a steward on the *Canberra*, you know; we took the troops there and back. I've been at sea for three months. The wife's just picked me up from Southampton.'

The policeman hesitated.

'We got a bit carried away.'

The policeman turned.

'Did you hear that, Mike?'

'Bloody scary months, too, I can tell you. I was shot at twice.'

The policeman put his notebook back in his pocket.

'Why don't you take him home, love. See to his needs in the privacy of your own home.'

'Yes, Officer.'

'No more lay-bys.'

'No.'

They pulled out of the lay-by, Richard giving the thumbs-up sign as they turned back into the road, Ellen's face on fire. Richard was right, there was something extraordinary in the air, a kind of release, dare she hope it, the prospect of a new beginning. Was this what had attracted her to him in the first place, the germ of this moment, knowing that one day he would engineer this anguished flowering, this platform built from which to take off and soar?

'Richard! What is it, what's come has over you?'

'I want to be me, Ellen. I want to be me,' he said. 'And I want to reach out and find you.'

His hand travelled over her, with the mastery born of conquest.

*

They hadn't spoken much on the way back; the same as going, only a lot faster. The difference was in the way they sat, Suzanne working the controls, checking the mirror, slipping in and out of lanes, Matty hunched up in his seat, staring out of the side window. The way he was acting you'd have thought it was him who'd been through the mill, not her. He was thinner than he should be, paler, too, as if he hadn't been eating properly. That wasn't like him at all. She tried to keep the conversation going, but she didn't know where to start really, the trip out, the days at war, the trip back, it was all jumbled together inside a new kind of her. A party would be best, let things slip out in drips and drabs. She'd get to the truth of the matter later. The sheaf of papers were stuck in her pocket. She hadn't tried to hide them. If he bothered to look, he would recognize them right away.

Although Matty had warned her she hadn't expected anything

like this. The moment she turned into the road, she had to jam on the brake pedal. Anglefield Road was filled to the brim; tables and chairs, bunting and balloons and halfway down the road, signalling the entrance to the inner circle, a banner stretching across, reading WELCOME BACK SUZANNE ANGLEFIELD HEROINE, and all of them standing under it, the Millens, the Armstrongs, the Roaches, and it was like she had done it, not for England, not for the Falklands, not even for herself, but for the road. They left the car behind the Roaches'. It was impossible to drive down. Though Matty was her husband, it was Richard who took charge, Richard who raised her hand in the air, Richard who led her down the street, who stood in the centre of the circle and gave a little speech of welcome. She had never seen him sparkle so. She looked for Mark but couldn't see him. Typical of the boy, to make his own entrance in his own time.

They started drinking straight away, beer, wine, a precious few on orange juice. It was different from the voyage back, because then she'd been drinking with people who had experienced what she had, but here it was as if she was famous, with everyone excited simply by her presence. She was flattered, answered their questions, kept the smile going, but it wasn't her talking.

'Was it very bad?' Hector asked and Suzanne wanted to say, 'No, it was bloody wonderful,' but instead said:

'It got a bit hairy at times.'

Marjorie was with them. They were watching Freddie pulling some kid off his lawnmower.

'You must have been frightened,' she said, watching her closely.

'We were all frightened,' Suzanne told her and for a moment she felt the thrill of sheer terror ripping through her.

'Still, you had all those lovely men to take care of you.'

It surprised Suzanne to hear Marjorie talk like that. All those lovely men.

'Actually, it was us who took care of them.'

'I'm sure you did.'

The directness of the remark shocked her. For the first time she felt unable to respond. Matty came to her rescue.

'Will you excuse us,' he said. 'Before the celebrations get out of hand. I've something to show her.' He led her up to the house and through to the French windows.

'Do you like it?'

There were flagstones and a striped umbrella and a wooden table with four wooden chairs, a bottle of Martini on the top. She hated Martini. He picked up a scarf from the back of the chair.

'I asked her to clear up. You remember this?'

'Marcy's, yes. We got it where, Turkey?'

'Wish I'd never bloody bought it.'

'Matty?'

He stood and looked out at the grass. He'd mowed that too. His hair had receded quite noticeably in these three months. He looked stooped, battered.

'It looks good, don't you think?'

'It looks lovely, Matty.'

'Our very own Riviera, like I promised. Freddie helped. He's quite good at this sort of thing, would you believe. His plan's coming along too.'

'Plan?'

Matty told her.

'I've been advising him with the forecasts. You know, it wouldn't be a bad idea if we invested the extra money you've earned in it. It's a real goer.'

Suzanne found it hard to believe. She hadn't been here half an hour and he was already planning their future.

'Matty, are you out of your mind? I want to blow it on something wild, extravagant, not invest it.'

Matty pushed the suggestion aside with an understanding nod of the head.

'We could build that swimming pool, I suppose.'

'What, here in Anglefield Road?'

'Why not?'

Why not? A house, a patio, a swimming pool, a whole world in your front room: a garden and a car and a wife to plant, move from pot to pot. And always the embankment and the distant call of a train, always the whiff of the sea on her forgotten clothes, the look of a man she must not touch.

Matty pushed himself against her.

'Oh, Suzy. I wish we could be alone.'

Well, she knew what that meant.

A cough. Matty jumped away. Marcia appeared.

'They're calling for you,' she said.

'I'll tell them you'll be out in a minute.' Matty hurried away, barely looking at his daughter. Suzanne crossed back into the kitchen, over to the larder and pulled out the flour tin.

'I don't care who sees. I need this.'

Marcy sat on the edge of the table as Suzanne crumbled the dark block of resin.

'Three months without. Must be some kind of record.' She licked the papers. 'What's wrong with him, Marcy?'

'I can't tell you.'

'Not . . .'

'No, not your complaint.'

'My complaint?'

'Your visits to Mark.'

'Mark?'

'Yes, he told me.'

So Marcia knew after all. Who else? Suddenly, she didn't care.

'Well, I'm sure you enjoyed the listening as much as he enjoyed the telling.'

'You don't seem very worried.'

'Have you told Matty?'

'No, he's got enough to worry about.'

'But you don't want to tell me what.'

'No.'

'Not ill?'

'Sort of, yes, but not ill, no. So I can tell him, then?'

'If you like. Now if you'll excuse me, my public awaits.' She handed the joint over and put a second one in her pocket. She felt herself inexplicably warming to the girl. She stood up, kissed her. 'Look after him, Marcy. He's a good man.'

The party swirled about her. She let herself be hugged and touched by anyone who had the need. She was public property and she was used to that, detached but not aloof, together but separated, moving in and out of quick conversations, keeping an eye out for Mark. Must be glad to be back. Yes, very. What was it like? A bit hairy. Looking for a good night's sleep, I should imagine. You're telling me. And what's been happening here? A man attacked on the towpath, left unconscious, not half a mile away. Terrible, she said, as if she cared. So Mark had blabbed. Well, wouldn't you if you were that age, probably exaggerated what had happened into the bargain? Where the bloody hell was he? She wanted to see him, stick the other joint in his mouth, scandalize the lot of them.

Richard had put aside half a dozen champagne bottles for the cul-de-sac's private consumption. That was where she ended up, the centre of the circle and still no sign of him. Finally she got tired of waiting.

'Where's Mark, Richard?' Richard shrugged his shoulders, throwing off a lifetime of despair.

'No idea.' He pulled his wife close to him, ran his hand over her bottom. If anything Ellen's response was even bolder. Suzanne had never seen such a display from them before.

And then there he was, leaning out of their upstairs window, calling. She walked over. He looked wilder than usual, but it was lovely to see him again.

'I've been looking for you,' she admonished. Pointing to the banner she said, 'I believe I've you to thank for that. Marcy too, Matty tells me.'

'Kind of.'

'Been with her quite a bit, I hear.'

'Told her my life story.'

'All its sordid little secrets, so she tells me.' She opened the palm of her hand, revealed the cigarette within. 'Aren't you coming down to help me out? I've been saving it.' Mark shook his head.

'I prefer it up here. Gives me an overall perspective.'

Richard came up beside her, bunching his fists aggressively on his hips.

'Mark! There you are! What are you doing in our bedroom? And what's that thing on your head?'

'This?' His voice was light, almost far away. 'It was delivered today, just after you left. Interflora.'

'Well, if it's for Suzy, why the bloody hell have you got it?'

'It wasn't for her. It was you, Dad.'

'Me?'

'Yeah. Came with a note. Want to read it?'

An unseen hand flicked an envelope onto the lawn. Ellen came hurrying over.

'He won't come down,' Roach explained, picking the message up. Ellen made to match her husband's displeasure.

'Mark, if you don't come down this instant I'll . . .' She turned to Suzanne. 'Selfish little brat, ruining everyone's evening. Richard?'

There was a cry. He had recognized the handwriting straight away. Mark laughed.

'You should read it, Mum. It doesn't take long to memorize. "For Richard. In loving memory of his only son. From your good friend Amy." Isn't that right, Dad? I haven't left anything out, have I?'

Richard looked up. Mark was grinning down.

'Couldn't wait to get rid of me, eh, Dad?'

'Mark, I . . .' Ellen was pulling at his arm

'Richard, what is this? Who's Amy?'

'Do you know what I said, Mum?'

'What?'

'To that girl I killed.'

'Mark.'

'I knew it was going to happen, the moment we hit the bridge, the car out of control, the tree coming up to hit us square on. I turned to her, Mum, and shouted, "Sorry. It's you or me," and yanked the wheel hard over, and the car slid, so like she was facing it, Mum, and she screamed and screamed seeing the end of her rushing up, knowing that I had killed her, her friend, and her screaming my name. And we hit it her side on and she went bang, through the window, and then fell back only without a head. Can you imagine it, Mum, one moment there, and the next, gone, without even a head, and I sat there with her, her bubbling like, and her head in the ditch and the headlights shining on her looking at me, eyes open, not blinking. Staring and staring at me until the battery ran out. Five hours, Mum, and me not saying sorry once. And I wish it had been me, Mum, and not her.'

'Mark.'

'Like I was laughing when I said it. She knew she was going to die, Mum, and I killed her, 'cause I couldn't kill myself then.'

'Come down, Mark.'

'Couldn't kill myself, Mum, though I wanted to.'

'Mark, please.'

'I thought, I thought you and Dad wouldn't want me to.'

'Mark.'

'The path to glory, Mum.'

And then held up his arms and threw the wreath down at their feet and Suzanne saw why he was pale and why his hands that were held in prayer glistened in the sunlit window like a cardinal's robes, Richard pushing past her, and she and Ellen chasing after him as they careered up the stairs and shouldered down the door, Suzanne tearing into the sheets, Ellen cradling her blood-drained boy, Richard's hands slippery over the deep razor-blade cuts. Suzanne pulled his sticky thumbs away, showing him the pressure points, the three of them talking to the fading child as she wound the strips of linen round, jamming a hairbrush handle and a comb to effect a tourniquet. Outside a portable record player played 'Jerusalem'. The road was bursting with life, clinking its glasses, cheering its good fortune.

Richard carried him down the stairs, Ellen chasing, Freddie calling them over to his car. They threw themselves in, and Freddie turned it full wheel over his garden, crashing through the Roaches' hedge, horn blaring, driving up over Anglefield Road like a ship ploughing the sea, tables and chairs tumbling in their wake, men and women pulled into the turbulent undercurrent. They reached the crest of the hill and bulldozing the Roaches' car aside burst out of Anglefield Road. Richard Roach bent down close and watched as the lights in his son's eyes slowly flickered and died.

*

Matty walked into the bedroom. Suzanne was standing in front of the mirror, her case half unpacked on the bed.

'No need for that now.'

She turned, startled at his entrance. There was blood on her sleeves and down the front of her dress; it reminded him of that day when she first arrived.

'What a welcome,' he said.

She turned to him, tears down her face.

'I've signed up again. After the refit.'

Matty went to draw the curtains.

'I know, I saw the papers, Suze, in your pocket, when you walked down.' His voice was light, almost conversational.

She gestured to the suitcase.

'This is what I came with, Matty. That's what I'll leave with.' She snapped the lock shut. 'I'm going to stay with Tina, sort myself out. It's not right for me here, Matty. I can't take it.'

She came up to him, her face close to his.

'I loved it, Matty, that's what it was. I loved it. I was alive. I had a man there, Matty, don't wince, it was wrong I know, but I had a man there, who's gone now, but I would have died with him, Matty, and not regretted a moment. I can't stay here. I can't stay in Anglefield Road, and don't say we can move. We can't. We're not allowed to.'

Anglefield Road was deserted. Only the Roaches' cat was left, picking his way through the upturned tables, eating his fill. Suzanne looked at her watch. She had ten minutes. If she hurried, she'd catch the next train.

NINE

Roach travelled home, Sophie patient at his feet, the tune rolling in his head. He should have called Soapsuds by his proper name, not the catcall they spat at him when he first arrived: maybe then he would have responded, maybe then he would have come up to him, grasped him, shaken his free hand.

At the station the ticket collector gave Sophie her regular chocolate biscuit, while the two men both commented on the dirty November weather. Man and dog set off, Richard bent into the wind. It did not take long, the walk up; they both knew the way, Richard years longer than Sophie, but it was Sophie's road now, Sophie who negotiated the dark outline of the tunnel, Sophie who led him up the hill, conscious of the home-coming cars and sudden adolescent bikes. At the top they turned down, the Labrador firm in her steady intent, guiding him across the road when they reached the opening of their own front path. Once on the other side Richard ran his free hand along the brush of hedge until he grasped the pole that marked the opening into Marjorie's front path. He could hear the flap of torn material that marked the height where they had strung the victory banner across the road. He had taken his half of it down long ago.

He struggled with the latch. It had become increasingly obdurate since her husband's stroke.

He knocked. A short wait and the front door opened onto the smell of baking, Marjorie wiping her hands upon what, an apron? He dipped his hand into his overcoat pocket and brought out the folded newspaper.

'More welcome than the postman, you are,' she said. 'More regular too. Do you want to come in for a minute? I've a cake cooling.'

He ignored the invitation. He could do that, being blind.

'I was wondering if you could do me a favour. There's some-thing I need to find upstairs, for an old friend. I think I know where it is, but . . .'

Marjorie patted him on the shoulder. Richard could feel the dog stiffen. She didn't like other people touching him, even ones she knew well.

'I'll just go and give this to Hector. He gets very impatient when he knows it's arrived.'

He waited, following the sounds of her movement, the sturdy tread of her feet on the stairs, the creak of a door opening, the low mutter of voices. He hadn't spoken to Hector in months. Cool air wafted over his face. Marjorie returned. They crossed the road in silence. She started forward as he fumbled with the key. She wanted to do it for him, he could tell. He blocked her good deed with a stubborn turn of his back.

'It's upstairs,' he said stepping inside, and switched on the light.

Though filled with furniture it was empty in Richard's house. Hollow rooms, hollow stairs, and looking in as they passed, a hollow bed, the dog's indentation at the foot of the bed, clear to see.

They edged into the box room. It was small and smelt over-whelmingly of leather.

'There should be a suitcase here somewhere. Brown, been around a bit, scratched initials. It wouldn't surprise me if Ellen had thrown it out, when she went through it all.'

She found it almost straight away, half hidden underneath some kind of cardboard cut-out, beside a stack of shoe boxes, an old cracked thing, imitation leather, one catch twisted out of shape, the other secure in its rusted lock. She bent down and pulled it free.

'Do you want me to open it?'

It took a pair of nail scissors, purloined from the bathroom. She stood aside as he knelt and lifted the lid.

'This shouldn't take a minute,' he said.

He dipped his head low, his hands examining familiar objects; the embossed pattern of a presentation tie, the unintentional Braille lettering of Ellen's wedding album, the blue ribbon that bound together Mark's school certificates, and yes, in his hand the object of his search, Soapsuds' treasure, not his violin, although there had been times when he had felt like jumping up and down on it and smashing it to bits, but the other thing that Soapsuds had held dear, the thing he had stolen, lifted it because of Soapsuds' belief in its immense gravitational pull, leading him towards the heart of a mystery that could never be solved and in which he, his best friend, could play no part.

He took hold of the cover and pulled it out, the wrong way as it turned out, the book flapping open in his right hand.

'It's all right, Marjorie, you can go now.'

But Marjorie did not go, not before she had thrown herself upon him, screeching in his ear, wrestling the book from his grasp, Sophie barking as they toppled into the cardboard, clawing the air for what she had seized, the weight of her breasts pressed against his face, his hand riding along the unexpected avenues of her upended skirt as she pushed him further into the boxes, treading on stomach and shoulder in her haste to get out. He could hear the screech of Hector's name as she ran across the road, as he knelt across Sophie, calming them both, unable to imagine what it was that had projected his neighbour so, unable to imagine what took place in the minutes after the attack (for that's what it was, wasn't it, an attack?), how Marjorie had picked up her skirt and red-legged pounded up the stairs, throwing open the bedroom door where Hector sat upright, frightened by the coming fury he could sense approaching, nor could Roach envisage how she flung the book on the bed before running out again, to their small room that overlooked the street, their library, where stood the table and the plate of glass upon it and the sheet of paper lying flat underneath, nor how she picked the glass square up and holding it in both hands hurled it against the wall of books, crying a name, as if she were launching a ship of war.

Hector looked down at the book. It was a book he had seen many times before.

Then Marjorie was sitting beside him on the bed.

'Do you remember what it should say?' she asked, and without waiting for a reply, mouthed the words, fingering the torn page.

This book belongs t
He
and I liv

His eyes followed quickly, his breath suddenly uneven. He tried to raise himself up as the words that wanted to spill out filled his body. Marjorie took his hand, kissed his fingers, laid it where it always lay.

'That's right, Hector. That's right.'

From her other hand she brought down the sheet of protected paper and held it jigsaw like up against the front page. Though the colour was different, the fit was perfect. She read again.

This book belongs to
Henry Armstrong
and I liv . . .

Marjorie choked. The words she thought she would never speak. Hector formed his question with difficulty.

'And I live?'

Marjorie took a deep breath. It would come clean now, like a dam bursting, like the flush of clear fresh water.

'And I live in Anglefield Road.'

*

The following day Richard and Marjorie sat in a railway carriage on their way to King's Cross, exhausted both, from talk and the burn of memory, the uncovered bones of the country turned to wintry skeleton town, fading suburban order merging into sprawling city shapes. The time of conversation had passed. Marjorie had wanted to go straight away, to stand on the wet Wild West platform and board the milk train, call her son's name, scour the unwashed streets, but Richard persuaded her as to the futility of the exercise. The movements of these men are as regulated as the inner workings of a timepiece, the players shuffling in and out of their segmented hours with the precision of carved figures on an Austrian clock tower. With the right key turned, and the spring primed he would be there, at the rush hour, working his King's

Cross patch. And if not. Then the next evening, and the next, until the finality of it.

They had talked the night, more him than her, and though it was but a brief and ancient history, she seized upon it as if the freshest meat upon the table, the dormant dormitory years of their shared youth awoken, even those favoured days at Wimbledon and the calamity that split them apart. 'You and him?' she said, her body bent double at the stab of recollection; 'Yes, me and him,' he told her, 'me where I should have been and him running pell mell on the wrong side.' 'And the book, why the book?' 'It was what he treasured most, what he needed more than me. A book! More than me, so after, after Wimbledon, I took it with me. I always meant to give it back, but after that – I never forgave him, ruining it for me, making me the laughing stock, when it was him, him all along,' and Marjorie clapped her hands, saying, 'I'm glad you never forgave him, otherwise you would not have kept it, would you, and I would not be holding it in my hand,' and it was true. Was not that why he kept Mark's belongings, not because it brought him pleasure, but because it kept the pain acute.

At first light Marjorie had taken him back across the road, to the house she had refused to leave these thirty years, shown him the miniature cricket set that she and Hector had bought him and the sandpit in which he played, even the spot in the fence where he once climbed through, to play among the railway lines, with a boy, she added, herself trying to remember the genealogy of the residence, who had lived in your own house. My house? Richard paled and in response took her further, further than he wanted to, a blind man leading her back into Anglefield Road and that April train journey five years ago and Henry standing where they were standing now, looking all about him, ignorant in his knowledge. Marjorie put her hand to her mouth, falling upon the surface as if to gather the imprint of his footsteps into her arms, Richard bent too under the merciless mystery of the world. Anglefield Road, Anglefield Road, the street turned into a slipway to foaming thought, the lives that had lived here in such presumed order, so of a clockwork piece. Anglefield Road, Anglefield Road, Matty gone four years, back to Greece with his daughter's family, Patsy and Freddie some six months later. They rose together.

'Anglefield Road has been our lifeboat,' he said. 'We have all survived because of it. Without Anglefield Road Freddie would not have started his magazine; without Anglefield Road I would not be working for him, without Anglefield Road your son would not have returned.'

They went back then, up Richard's stairs, to see if there was anything else of Henry's that he had kept. There was nothing as he had assured her, only bits of Ellen, bits of Mark, which he could hear her turning over, discarding them as quietly as she dared, the crackle of a bundle of photographs, the scrape of a school certificate, the rattle of a cassette, Mark singing in a carol service, the voice coming through not one of innocence, but of as yet untested faith. Marjorie had caught the suppressed anguish on his face. 'It must be hard for you, too,' she said, 'living in a house with such memories,' and he took it from her and placed it back in the case. 'Isn't that what houses are for,' he asked, 'to hold down what little we can of our lives?'

They left Anglefield Road in the afternoon, the street deserted, the bare houses staring at their departure, Marjorie with the book in the handbag. They were nervous both, agitated. Going through the tunnel leading to the station a group of youths raced through them, whooping at the echoes. Richard shrank back. It was one thing he still feared, the noise of youth, despite his dog's fierce protection. Marjorie led him to the waiting room, bought him a cup of tea. Sophie too was on edge, sensing her master's fear.

'It's all right, Richard,' Marjorie had told him. 'They meant no harm.'

Richard nodded. How could she tell?

A month after Mark had died, Ellen gone, his severance pay come though, he had driven up to Stevenage one last time. He thought Amy deserved the truth too. How she'd found out about the depth of his deceit, he wasn't sure, Mrs Dixon probably when she went back for the necklace. He'd rung her home but the woman on the other end said she'd upped and left. She'd abandoned her job at the florist's too and if they knew where she was staying they weren't telling him. He wandered round Stevenage all that long day, looking in her old haunts, the leisure centre, the bar where they first met. That pub, the next one, no one seemed to know where she was, or if they did, chose not to tell him, bunches of young men, clusters of young women, answering his questions with scorn.

Later in the evening he'd gone to sit by the park bench where they had sat that night, hoping that she would appear, like in a film. After an hour and a half he decided to return home. It was late, past twelve. Walking back by the side of the lake he had passed a pack of them, half drunk, half stoned, bags of half-eaten chips greasy in their hands. He nodded to them, an older man conscious of his vulnerability and walked on quickly. One of the youths had called out.

'I remember you. You're the bastard who . . .'

And then his collar was grabbed and the lad called the others back. Roach had recognized him then. John, the one who hadn't believed him.

'This is the bloke I told you about,' he exclaimed, 'the one that was all over Amy. Told her he had a son in the Falklands, told her he'd died, just so he could fuck her.'

One of the girls began to walk round him, short, muscular.

'You cunt.' Richard winced. A young girl using a word like that!

John gave him a shove. The others did too, bouncing him around like a deflated beach ball.

'Pretended to be nice to her, interested like an uncle, all the time trying to get her knickers off. And then you know what? She finds out he didn't have a son there at all.'

The girl came up and poked him in the stomach.

'You filthy old fuck.'

Roach could see her now. She had some sort of string vest on and short black skirt, and would you believe it, a pair of Bronco trainers.

'What's the matter,' she had said, 'can't you get anyone your own age?'

Well, that was true.

'No, I . . .'

'Who asked you? What you doing here, then?' Roach stuttered his explanation.

'I came back. Looking for Amy. My son. You see, he *is* dead.'

'See?' John grabbed hold of him again, smacked his forehead against Roach's nose. It didn't seemed to hurt at all. 'Same old story.'

The girl came in close. Her eyes had been very bright, shining with intensity. Recognition crossed her face.

'He was in the pub earlier. Halfway down my dress he was, every time I went up for a drink.'

Richard had squirmed in the truth of her observation.

'No, no,' he protested, 'you've got it all wrong. I was looking at your trainers.'

They had burst into laughter, the remark repeated amongst them in a variety of voices.

'No, honestly. I used to sell them. Bronco's they were called.'

'Oh, yeah? Wear them over my tits, do I? You want a look? I'll give you a good fucking look.'

They dragged him to the water's edge, pinned him to the ground. The girl hitched up her skirt and sat on his chest. Others held his arms and legs.

'Prop his head up,' she complained. One of them knelt behind him and grabbed his ears. The girl leant back and lifted up her vest.

'Is this what you want, you filthy old . . . You got a ringside seat now.'

She held them in her hands. They were ghostly white, full of forlorn youth. He tried not to look.

'This close enough for you?'

He struggled, trying to turn his head away. John was standing next to him. Roach could see his boot, the scuff marks, the lace, broken halfway up, tied back in a clumsy knot. He watched as the foot was lifted back. The sole was coming away from the upper.

'Mind your hand,' he heard John say.

Pressure shot from his side of his face. Then another blow, from the other side. He reared up, trying to remember, lost in a wet rubbery warmth.

'He's got it all over me, the cunt!'

And then he curled up into a ball, curled up tight, his arms hugging his knees, his knees pressed into his chest, so that there was no shape to him that was human, just a sphere without a will or a volition of its own, a shape bereft of antagonism, something that lay on the ground waiting to be scooped up and gathered in a saviour's embrace, and they kicked the ball and rolled it into the water, whooping and laughing as they ran away.

The train lurched to the right to the left, to the left again. Richard looked up. He was intimate with such locomotive signals, the bend of the rail, the hoot of the whistle, the camber of the track. He leant over.

'We'll be at Euston in fifteen minutes,' he said.

Marjorie looked to the window.

Euston, again.

*

That day, all over London, from the circle of Piccadilly outwards, people were on the streets, the city surging, alive with an abandonment that she had never seen before, given over to nothing less than a celebration of the simple fact of being alive, of inhabiting living bodies of blood and flesh, of heat, of singularity, of similarity. There were no lovers there, no sweethearts, no husbands, no wives, no sons, no daughters, just thousands upon thousands of those two-legged things, humans, wanting nothing more than to celebrate their own tumultuous energy.

She had gone up with Jane that afternoon, caught the train up like so many others. Bursting into London out of the huge hall of the station was like walking out from the dark and cool of a cavern to the blinding white of a dazzling sea, squinting at the light and the freedom of tumultuous space. The air was fizzing, like God had taken the capital and shaken it hard, taking his thumb over the dome stopper of St Paul's, and watched London spout and froth forth. There was only one place to go, Jane said, Piccadilly Circus, with all the lights and the crowd and by the time they had walked there it was heaving, a great wheel of people caught in a whirlpool of human current. Seeing the slow moving crush of it, like the great grind of a millstone, Jane wanted to hang back, fearful of getting squashed, but that was what you had to do, plunge in and feel yourself tangled in its relentless current, pulled to its hidden magnetic heart. And it was a heart, pumping the stream of people round, people jostling and shuffling and surging to its pulse, and it was but a moment for Marjorie to take Jane's hand and pull them into its tow, giving up to the momentum, leaning into the thrill of it, shouting a careless 'See you later' as Jane and she were pulled apart, Jane struggling to reach the outer current, Marjorie hurling herself towards the heady danger of it, wheeling round and round, singing above the noise, not hearing herself what she was saying, until she reached the centre and the boarded up statue and the people standing above. That's where she wanted to be. There was a man there, with his hands in his pockets. It looked like he'd been up there for the duration of the war, the way he stood, with his hands in his pockets and his shoes and jug ears poking out over the side, he had that long familiarity of balance and machine about him, like those grinning boys in fairground roundabouts did, who walked round the wrong way with their dark hair and their spotted neckerchiefs flapping who took your money without holding on and who bent down to talk audacious sauce to the curve of your blushing mouth. And he looked down at her and saw the want in her eye, the way her hands were already feeling the smooth of the casing and grinning had put a cocky hand on his hip bent down and called out, 'Care for a pew, sweetheart? Won't cost you nothing, well, not in shillings and pence, any road,' and nodding she had stood on tiptoe and held her hand out. There was a man next to him and he said, 'Hold me fast, Jerry, while I reel this ashore,' and the other man held his one arm as he bent down and grabbed her wrist and hauled up over the boarding. 'Buy Savings Stamps' the sign said, 6d, 2/6 and 5/-, her arms nearly pulled out of their sockets, her body banging against the sides, her pleated skirt blowing up over the back of her legs, dragged up over it all till she stood, unsteady, to their exclamations and exhortations like she was some prize mermaid caught in a trawler's net. Then they turned her round slowly and looking down suddenly she felt slightly giddy and he put his arm around her waist and said, 'Look up, not down. I've just busted a gut getting you up here, love, you're not dropping off now,' and she did, looked across over the great swim of faces with all the flags, the Union Jacks and Stars and Stripes, the Russian one too, hanging from the buildings, secretaries leaning out the windows waving at everyone below. 'Found your sea legs yet?' he asked and she nodded and looked down again to the men and women, washing in and out round the boarded plinth: demob suits, brown and blue uniforms, men in civvies, women in WAACs, dancing and singing and chucking their hats into the air. 'What's your name?' she said to the chap who'd done most of the pulling. 'Jim,' he said. 'Nice up here, isn't it?' and he handed her a bottle of beer, 'What's yours?' he asked and for a moment she felt like giving him a false name, like Kathleen or Elizabeth. She had this sudden intuition that this wasn't going to be like any other day and that she wanted to be an anonymous part of it, herself and yet not herself, 'Marge,' she said, telling the truth, 'though I prefer Marjorie.' 'The thing I like about Marge,' he replied, 'is that it spreads so easy,' and though she'd heard the joke or something similar before, she smiled and took another swig of beer. 'Why don't you give us a kiss, Marge?' 'Why don't I?' she said, and she did, gave one to his friend on the other side and took another drink. In fact it was like Mecca, for they were worshipping in a way, worshipping England and the sea washing against the white cliffs, laying their little bits of history at his pillared feet. They must have had crates of the stuff up on the plinth for by the time she jumped down she felt quite tipsy, a great sway of them linking arms and kicking their legs down to Trafalgar Square, the crowd circling the lions and Lord Nelson. 'Fancy a dip,' he said, 'I do if you do,' she answered back, and without waiting, tucked her skirt into her knickers and jumped in. It was warm, the water, there were about ten or twelve other couples, old Horatio peering down at their tomfoolery. 'What's your name again?' she said, 'Jim,' he said, and they started to prance about in the water, holding on to each other, kicking their legs in the air like they were in a chorus line, then splashing each other, like they were kids on the beach, only they weren't, there was this man who she had never met till a couple of hours ago scooping up water with his hat and throwing it all over her, soaking her to the skin so that he could see her outline, her everything. But she didn't care, didn't mind who saw what. It wasn't that she was drunk or out of control, but rather her spirit was aflame and she jumped into his arms and kissed him full on the mouth, kissed him hard with her legs around him and his hands squeezing into the flesh of her behind, his tongue breaking in, wheeling her round, her head thrown back. And then he swung her over onto the wet steps before chasing her wet through the parting admiring crowd, turning and holding her close. And she kissed him again, only this time it was different, *her* tongue in *his* mouth this time, yes, that was the difference, the signal that she gave him, her tongue wild in the sour tobacco taste of him, his skin hard and scratchy, knowing in that moment as they waltzed through the crowd, his hand held just underneath her cold but unashamed breast, that she could do anything she wanted. They reached a quiet spot and he took another bottle of beer out and levered the cap off with his teeth, spat it across the road. 'What's your name again?' she said, 'Jim,' he said, and she looking at him askance. 'Are you sure?' 'No,' he said, 'are you?' and started pulling her along the street. 'Where are you taking me, Jim?' 'Wherever you want to go, my spring chicken,' and they ducked down a narrow alleyway to a pub on the corner with a lantern hanging out. It was getting darker, and she was young and alive and Jim was older and she liked that, liked the way his breath smelt as he pushed her into the doorway. 'This is where I'm taking you,' he said, 'isn't this where you want to go?' and his hands delved under. It was a tobacconist's, the shop like her uncle Desmond's, she could see a display rack in the bay window, briars and redwood and the type that Dad had that looped up and down like the drain under the sink, she knew all the names of them, and Jim was pressing up against her, moving himself up and down over her and she thought of her dad sitting by the wireless smoking his pipe and Mum darning his socks and the leather armchairs and all they'd gone through, their Arthur lost in the convoy and her Hector coming home in the next day or two and the marriage plans they had made, and she pushed back, knowing this was the first and last time in her life when there was nothing else but her, that there would be nothing like this day, this night, that with the laws of social gravity suspended she was limitless, unassailable; no blackout, no fire wardens, no censorship, no policemen, no MPs, no doodlebugs, no rations, no wife, no mother, no fiancé, no husband, no nothing. It would all be wonderful. 'No time like the present, wouldn't you say?' she whispered, and easing his hand into her elastic slipped them down, shaking her legs free, lifted her off her feet nearly with the sudden work of his hand. Then he looked down the road and stepping back unbuttoned himself and took it out. It was long and thin and seemed to glow, like it was hot. She reached out and touched it and it bounced in the air, as if it was on a spring. 'Now you've done it,' he said, and moved towards her. She felt so powerful, so brazen, God she had never done it standing up before, let alone in the open, in the street. She couldn't quite believe what she was doing. She had done it once on the steps of Hector's house when he came back on leave, but not like this, not in public with everyone walking past, and it was better this way, better than in a room with all the awkwardness and the false intimacy and the admittance that it should be hidden away and paid for. She didn't want that. It had to be here, out in the open. 'Jim, was it?' she said. 'As sure as I'm standing here,' he said and she giggled and said, 'Well then, Jim, pleased to meet you, I'm sure.' 'Not half as pleased as I am to meet you,' he replied and bent his knees as she stood on her toes and worked him in. She thought they were going to fall through the shop door he went at it so hard, his mouth buried in her wet of her hair, but she needn't have worried because he did it right away that first time, couldn't help himself and pushed her off back against the doorway. It was a stupid thing to do, she knew, to do it unprotected, but someone had told her that if you did it standing up you were safe, not that she was worried. Nothing was going to happen tonight. Nothing was going to happen to anyone. It was like they were all caught in a magical time, with everything suspended, like they were all Cinderellas, little pocket mice turned into stallions, scullery maids into princesses, frogs into princes, a night of coaches and foaming beer flowing in the gutter. It was all running out of her anyway and looking down she tried to find her underwear. 'Where are my knickers?' she said, unable to see them. 'You won't be needing them for a bit. Wipe yourself on this if you must,' and he handed her a large white handkerchief. And taking it, folding it in half, she noticed the markings on the corner. 'It's got your initials on,' she said. 'Now I'll know who to blame,' and she held it to the light. 'Here,' she said, 'there's no J on this at all. Have you been lying to me?' and Jim laughed and said, 'That's no handkerchief, that's a table napkin, and strictly speaking it's not mine. It belongs to the hotel where I work.' 'Hotel? I thought you were in the forces,' she said. 'What does it matter who I am? I'm here, aren't I?' It was true, it didn't matter. Hotel porter, soldier, blackout warden, whoever they had been, whatever they had done, they'd all come through it, every one of them, and she wanted to be with every one of them that night, wanted to kiss every one of them, make love to every one of them, and she said, 'Yes, you are. Kiss me up top, Jim, they're all cold,' and dug them out from under the damp rim of her bra before they did it again. 'All the fucking war, I've been dreaming of this,' he said, 'all the fucking war,' and she closed her eyes and felt that word grow in her mouth. She had never used it before and never used it again, but she did then, as they fell down into the well of the door. Whether he put them or himself back in or not she never could remember, nor where they went after that, just the two of them touching and feeling and kissing each other along in the rhythm of the dark. It was every-where, people dancing, kissing, couples clutched in doorways, men some of them, spooning and doing other things she dared not look at. 'Look at that,' Jim had said, 'the whole bloody world's at it at this moment, do you know that, the whole bloody world, at it like there's no tomorrow, and do you know why, cause there is no tomorrow, that's why, not like tonight, don't you see?' and she said yes, she did see and fell in love with idea. There was a couple in this cul-de-sac, a woman on the wall and the man standing, the lamplight shining directly down upon them and they were doing it, and the woman looked over her shoulder and saw them looking and called out, 'Come on in, why don't you, the water's lovely,' and Jim hoisted her on the wall next to them. She couldn't remember much, just the burning sensation on her face, until the man said, 'Fancy a swap, mate?' and she and Jim looked at each other and then she looked at the woman looked at each other and the woman said, 'I will if you will,' and she said, 'Go on, then,' and they did. 'What's your name?' she asked. 'Lucky,' he said, 'don't you think?' and placed a hand on each of her legs. They looked strong his hands, hands that had worked a hard life, thick-knuckled and fat with muscle, hands for lifting cargo and pulling rope, hands for turning into fists, and he had taken off his shirt and running his hands back under had lifted her clean off the wall onto him, walked her round like a circus act. Afterwards the four of them went off to a pub, stood jammed up against everyone, bottles passed back over their heads, someone dancing on the bar. Then there was a conga weaving down the street and they joined it, and there was a Canadian, a happy fellow with big ears and a slow drawl and a bottle of American whiskey, with a name like chocolate biscuits, but somehow she and Jim got separated, it didn't matter, they were all one and the same, and they found this church where there was little graveyard at the side with iron railings and he laid his greatcoat on the ground and wrapped themselves in it, lying there with the recognition that their time had but a few hours to run, and that the dark could no longer hide it, that the dark must not hide it, that now was the moment to affirm it in earnest, the only time she would be allowed this, and she struggled out her damp dress and he out of his uniform, and they began to make love, first buttoned up, wriggling within its scratching envelope and then, despairing of the limitation, throwing the folds open, bearing themselves to the cold damp dawn. She'd never felt so open, so able, so in control of the world, drawing him deep, like she was diving, holding her breath till the bubbles burst out of her lungs. They were the living. The dead couldn't do this; the dead couldn't kiss and make love in the gutter like they could. They could do anything now, anything. It was their world, not the dead's. She wanted to shout. 'The dead are dead and we are alive! The dead are dead and we are alive!'

That how Henry was conceived, she was sure on that day, the day before Hector came back. Though she had never talked about it, she never felt ashamed of what happened, indeed in a way she was proud that her son was a product of VE Night, and wondered often how many other children had come from that night, as if they might be a special race. Whose he was she never knew, could have been any one of them, but what she believed most of all was that Henry was like a mongrel dog, a bit of this, a bit of that. It was what made him such a peculiar mixture, the dark hair, the blue eyes, the big feet, the dainty hands, the slow speech, the quick temper. Hector had wanted to call him James after his own father but she had put her foot down, wouldn't allow it, though she could never explain to him why. He was clever, Henry, clever beyond his ears as Hector would say. Hector was good at saying funny things like that.

In the morning the Canadian walked with her all the way to the station, where she caught an early train. 'I'll never forget this night as long as I live,' he said, 'never,' and he wouldn't, though he began fading from her memory the moment he turned and walked out the entrance. The train was packed with people like her, bleary-eyed, some still drunk, some still singing, most staring out the window, reliving the night before, a clutch of soldiers in one carriage leaning out the window and asking her to join them. She walked past at first, looking down, smiling calmly to herself as any girl would. 'You look as if you've been up all night, sweetheart. You been a naughty girl?' and she had turned and said, 'I hope so,' and they roared with laughter and one of them swung out on the door saying, 'Come on, then, love, we'll look after you,' and made room for her so that she could stretch out for a bit of shut-eye. She had about an hour's sleep before she got home, despite their singing. 'Where in God's name have you been,' her dad said, looking at her clothes all crumpled and damp and she said, 'Oh, you should have seen it, Mum,' she said, 'singing and dancing, doing the conga all round the streets, why I must have danced my way half round London,' thinking of the other word she could have used, and she yawned, like her mouth was a cavern and all of London had roomed there for the night. Mum said, 'You'd better get some sleep. You don't want to be out for the count for Hector, do you,' so she went upstairs and peeled off her clothes, her skin white and soft to touch, like when she sat in Auntie Penny's bath too long. She stood in the tin basin and washed herself down, looking for some trace of what she had done, and there were bruises all right around her thighs and something like a love bite on her shoulder, but although it was a bit tender down there, it looked normal enough, as if nothing had happened. As if nothing had happened! She dried herself carefully and climbed into bed. 'All the fucking war I've been waiting for this,' he said, and she had been the one to give it to him, she and all the other girls, they had all given themselves up to the wonderful simplicity of life, throwing everything they knew out the window, thrown it all to the moment when there was nothing but life running in the gutter.

When she woke it was dark and as soon as she got up and started to dress she could smell that night on her still, smell Jim and his tobacco and the taste of their talk, so she washed herself again and thought that while she was at it she should do the same with her dress. She took it from the edge of the bed and was about to drop it into the water when she noticed the corner of the hotel napkin poking out from the sleeves, all dry and stiff with the initials GM in the corner. It was all there in this quarter of Irish linen, from all the men of that night, all their stuff, all the lost children of VE Day, the abandoned children of peace, soaked into this one napkin, and she thought for a moment that if she held it up to the light she could read what had happened, like you could with blotting paper. She stood in front of the mirror and held the napkin against her skin, thinking of what he did and where he worked and whether she would ever see him again, and then, kneeling by the basin, spread the napkin out over the warm water, like it was a raft, imagining all the little lives soaked into its membrane, imagining their Arthur losing his life in the Arctic, and she put her hand over it and pushed it down and watched the water turn cloudy white, held it fast before taking it out and holding it for a moment to her face, then wringing it out, slipping back into bed and placing it underneath her pillow, before going back to sleep again.

'Welcome back to the land of the living,' Dad said when she finally went downstairs. An hour later Hector came round and they sat in the front room and had tea. He had the bandage taken off by then, but he still held his hand down to the side, like he was ashamed of it, and she'd wished then that Mum hadn't gone to all the trouble of cups and saucers and a half a jar of precious jam because he found implements like that difficult, poor thing, with only one hand to use and that his clumsy left. Later, after she and Mum had washed up and Dad and he had had a long chat, he took her to a dance. She had never considered Hector a natural dancer, but he wouldn't come off the floor for a moment and after a while she understood the reason, for as long as they were dancing the longer he could hide his hand behind her back. His bad hand, that's what he called it. And though she pretended not to notice it, as soon as she realized what he was doing, it burned into her back like a branding iron, the long bony thumb, the great gap, and then, an age away, his deserted little finger, And it seemed to her then that all his quiet, all his shyness, all his apprehension, all that had happened to him was etched on that wrinkled ridge and she wanted to touch it, to look at it closely, tell it everything, confess to it that she had seen life beyond this town too, that they had something else to share outside courtship and plans for the future; outrageous life! But she knew that she couldn't, knew that she wouldn't, not ever and that there were hundreds, thousands of women like her who could never tell what they had done, what they had seen. It wasn't only at the front that unspoken things had happened. Everyone had experienced a secret war, and everyone shared in the hiding of that secret, a secret they all shared and which no one would ever divulge. And so they danced and held each other and despite what had gone before she wasn't tired at all, she was limitless. And then they had the quarrel.

Every time they had circled the floor, she had noticed this girl, standing there. She wasn't bad looking, but there was something in the way she hung her head, the way she scuffed her feet, that suggested a forlorn and unlooked-for presentation and Marjorie, seeing the world still in terms of last night's fraternity, told Hector to go over and dance with her. 'I didn't come here to dance with her, I came here to dance with you,' Hector objected but she pushed him away, saying, 'Go on, she's lonely, it won't kill you,' and he went off, looking back at her funny. And while the two of them were on the floor, this young chap came over and asked her to dance, and whereas any other night out she would have said no, she said yes, straight away. 'What's your name?' he said as they started up, 'Marjorie,' she said, 'what's yours?' 'Jim,' he said. 'Jim!' She started to laugh. 'Something wrong with it?' he bristled, put out by her unreasonable merriment and wishing to atone for this unwarranted slight she said, 'No, it's a lovely name,' and drew him closer than a girl on a date with her fiancée should with a stranger, danced with him twice, strongly, in lovely, leaning rhythm, feeling the pull of his arms and the proximity of his body grow bolder with every turn, ignoring Hector's furious looks, enjoying every captured minute. When it was over and they stood back, faintly out of breath, Hector came across and stood next to her while Jim worked his charm. Hector said not one word and after a minute or two this other Jim, getting fed up, turned round and said, 'Waiting for a bus, mate?' and Hector said, 'No, but I think it's time you hopped off this one,' and she could see how it had all changed. No one would have said that last night. No one had belonged to anyone. That was what revolution must be like. And now, one night later, possession had been restored. Deflated she said, 'Actually, Jim, he's waiting for me,' and Jim looked at her and said, 'Yes, but are you waiting for him?' Hector pulled her to one side. 'Yes, she is,' he said. 'Go and pester someone else.' 'Don't you get funny with me, mush, or you might get your ticket punched,' Jim said and she could see the two of them starting to square off. She jerked her hand out of Hector's grasp and stepped in between them. 'It's my fault,' she said, putting her hand on the young man's shoulder, 'I shouldn't have left him. Now go and find someone unattached you can dance with. A good-looking fellow like you, they'll be lining up,' and she kissed him on the cheek, like she was saying goodbye to a world that she had glimpsed but once. Hector and she didn't speak for about twenty minutes, and she could see it all going wrong, him standing there not saying a word, two, three men coming up and asking her to dance, she shaking her head, not daring even to open her mouth, and she knew that if she didn't do something quick it would be all over, that eventually she'd accept and Hector would walk out and that would be that. Was that what she wanted? It would be so easy to say yes, if that was what she wanted, to be set free and when she saw him coming across again, she was in half a mind to do it, the blue suit, the dark wavy hair, the swagger, why the bloody hell not? And she knew that if he reached her and asked her she would say yes and that would be the end of it. And she wanted to shout, 'It's life I want, Hector, life, with the whole world spilling out before me,' but then she looked at him, and saw the stubborn wound in his eyes, knowing that she couldn't, couldn't jump off like that into the unknown, couldn't grasp the notion of unlicensed sovereignty, a world of Jims and strutting uncertainty, so turned to him and said, 'Dance with me, Hector, don't say a blinking word, just dance,' and she hauled him back onto the floor. He held her out at arm's length like he was dancing with a tailor's dummy. 'Don't be such a ninny,' she told him, and pulled him closer and pushed every bit of herself against him. 'Oh, Marjorie,' Hector said, 'oh, Marjorie,' and held her like that until the last number, sowing her name in the thick folds of her hair. That was all he could say. When he walked her back she thought he might want to make love again, like they had done that one time when he was back from leave and though, walking slowly down to their house, she had felt her heart beat wildly at the thought of repeating what she had done last night, when they got there and he started to kiss her, she realized that it would be wrong, that it couldn't be like Piccadilly, that she and Hector should wait until they could close the door and lie together, in a bed, all romantic and peaceful, like there was no hurry any more. And she pulled away and straightened her dress and stood back, looking at him. 'Not now, Hector, not here.' 'Why not? Last time . . .' 'Last time was different,' she countered quickly. Hector nodded. 'It's my hand, isn't it. I understand. I'd no right to expect,' and hid it behind his back. She loved him then, loved him for his simplicity and his tenderness and the way he thought of her and what he hoped might become of them now, when the decisions were theirs, now there were no more doodlebugs or telegrams, and she felt herself flower for the ordinary promise of it all, the rent and the wage coming in and the babies that would come their way, and wanted to whisper all that in his ear, that she was his and she was glad to be his, glad that he was home. 'No, it isn't, it isn't at all,' she said, 'it's just I want it to be right, you know, right, and it is right, Hector, it is,' and with that she took it and kissed it, kissed the thumb and the little finger and the length of tissue in between, kissed it all and held it to her cheek, kissed it again and took it down to her breast opening the palm over where her heart lay. 'That's where I want it,' she said, 'from the day we marry, that's where I want it, Hector, every night,' and he had closed his eyes and said nothing. There was nothing more to say. They bought the bed the Tuesday following, and eleven days later his hand lay where she had promised.

She'd hardly been to London again after that, and always

avoided Piccadilly and the Grand Metropolitan just around the corner, just in case, but it was Christmastime and she'd promised Henry they'd go to Hamleys and see the lights. She was a bit worried, for there's no knowing what can spring out of the wood-work just when you least expect it, but she needn't have been, for when they got there the place was enveloped in fog, the worst they'd had in twenty years. Jim could have walked by a foot away and he wouldn't have seen her. When they got off the bus they went into a Lyons Corner House, the smog was so filthy, and watching Henry eating his sticky bun she had thought, this is where he started, somewhere round here, this Henry of mine, wondering what would happen if the door opened and Jim came in, wondering if she would even recognize him. 'All the fucking war I've been dreaming of this,' he had said, 'all the fucking war.' No one had ever said that word to her before. The things she did that night. 'Are you all right, Mum?' Henry asked, looking at her, and wishing to cover her confusion she snapped, 'Of course I am,' and hurried them out, pulling him along, in her haste to be rid of the place. They hadn't gone a hundred yards when she remem-bered her purse. In her hurry to leave she'd left it on the table. 'Stay there,' she said, 'Don't move,' and ran back fast, knowing the types that frequented Lyons Corner House, running as hard as she could. It was still there, the waitress had just found it and was in the process of putting it in her apron pocket, for safe keeping she said, but looking at her Marjorie thought different and snatched it back, running back both relieved and anxious to where she'd left him. But he wasn't there. Henry wasn't there! She couldn't have been gone more than three minutes and he wasn't there! An old man came by and breathless she rushed up to him, but before she could get the words out, he had pushed her away, crying, 'Get away from me, you dirty little trollop, I'll have the law on you,' and she backed off, masked her mouth for a moment, looking about, because that would be dreadful, to be mistaken for one of them. Then, as he hurried away, she ran back and forth calling his name until, hearing the muted call of a police whistle, she dashed out into the road where the glisten of a shrouded cape stood, ran out without looking, nearly flattened to the ground by the ghost of a green removal van looming out of the swirl. She fell back against the wet cape, clutching at his stationary slither, pointing to the capital letter on the van's side, caught for an instant by the sweep of the policeman's lamp, the herald of her own baby boy's frantic name. Henry! Her Henry! Her only Henry! And she pulled and jumped at her story, the words in the wrong order, the plot of it garbled, the holes in her tale terrible and ragged, signifying nothing but her boundless neglect. Though he said by rights he shouldn't be leaving his post on account of the troubled traffic, telling her not to fret, madam, that boys are always losing themselves, the little tykes, he folded her arm through his and raising his lamp on high led her back to the Lyons Corner House, not twenty yards away, where he hushed her hysteria, commandeered a pot of tea and a quiet table and, taking out his top-pocket notebook, wrote down Henry's details in quick deft strokes that belied his seemingly slow temperament; one boy, six years old, small for his age, with brown hair, recently barbered, brown eyes, wearing a blue belted mackintosh, a dark red jersey, a green shirt, an Aertex vest, a pair of grey shorts, long grey socks, a brown muffler hand-knitted by his grandma, a white napkin tied around his neck, and oh yes, just the hint of icing sugar round the corners of his mouth, from one of the buns here you see. A napkin? the policeman asked, looking up surprised. Yes, a white napkin, she said, stumbling over the memory of it, Yes, I had it in my handbag. I tied it round his face, you see, to keep out the fog. He has a delicate chest. Very wise, the policeman concurred, very wise, madam, to have him wearing something white. He'll stand out, you see. Any other distinguishing marks? She shook her head. When Henry was born and the midwife handed him to her for the first time, she had picked him up under his arms and held him in the air, turning him this way and that, dreading the discovery of some peculiarity that would mark his debauched conception, a lurid birthmark, an odd configuration of fingers, a deformity of the genitals, or God help him a strangely coloured skin, but he was perfect. She laid him down on her breast, relieved, relieved for Henry, relieved for Hector, relieved for the continuing calm of the accepted history of her self, but now, watching the policeman pick up his notebook and walk with her Henry's shape and her Henry's looks to where the phone lay, how she wished that he had! Yes, he has Jim the waiter's jug ears and the man on the wall's great haunch-holding hands, he has the Canadian's hair running down his back, thick like the pelt of a wolf and a howl to match, and to cap it all he is milk-eyed and staring, as blind as my husband's trust. He has borne all those things through his short life and he is still perfect, do you hear? He is still perfect!

She waited while he rang in, hoping that he had already been found, but the look on his face when he returned told her that he hadn't been. Don't worry, madam, he told her again, we'll find him. She stayed there, drinking tea, walking up and down outside calling his name, stayed there for six hours until the police car came and took her to the station. Then she sent Hector the telegram. They didn't have a phone. It read 'HENRY LOST IN FOG. PLEASE CONTACT VINE STREET POLICE STATION.'

She had lost their son. She had lost their son in the last smog in Britain.

*

They walk from the station down the Euston Road towards King's Cross, Sophie walking alongside her charge, Marjorie trying to hurry the two of them along, passing commuters taking time to look askance as she grabs at his elbow, trying to force a blind man's pace. And there it stands, King's Cross, with its gaping holes and sunken stairs, a myriad of entrances and exits. It is the rush hour now, half-past five, one hundred thousand people flooding through between the evening hours of four o'clock and six thirty, when thought is minimal and herd instinct kicks in, the next step just the next step before the next step, and each one a consciously defiant act, wary of impediment and delay. The eye looks but sees nothing but space and obstacle, the body speeding up towards the gravitational pull of the magnetic, turbine crowd. A merry-go-round that careers up and down, but never moves.

Richard and Marjorie stand at the mouth of the stairs the cold night air tugging at their coats, hesitating before the enormity of their descent, but they cannot stand still for long. The impetus and humour of the crowd propels them down into the broad passageway known as the Khyber Pass, which leads directly into the ticket hall. This is where Richard heard Henry the night

399

before, at approximately the same hour, but he is not there now. There is no busker here at all. Perhaps this evening they have been all cleared out. It happens, regulation stretching its muscle. Some days Roach can travel the underground without hearing a single note played. At other times it's as if there's an importuning minstrel stationed every fifteen yards.

The moment they step in, the drag of the people sucks them towards the ticket hall, but it is an area that holds no interest to them, for that is where officialdom reigns and is the one site all buskers avoid. They turn back, forcing their way across the human stream into the perimeter subway that runs a half-circle round, to see if he might not be stationed in some of the other connecting passageways or by the amenities that describe its circle. They pass the heel bar, a young man in evening dress sitting cross-legged, his red-socked toes wriggling impatiently while a new heel is attached to his patent-leather pump, and after that the tunnel leading to St Pancras Road, lined with telephone kiosks, a good place to busk, loose change not simply in the pocket, but ready in the hand or laid out along the money-box top, but tonight there are genuine callers only, speaking with various degrees of purpose while others stamp their feet outside. Hearing nothing Richard shakes his head and presses on, past the newsagent and the bureau de change, Marjorie noticing the rack of *Lawns and Lawn-Mowing*'s new November edition taking centre stage in the gardening section, a florid celebrity of some sort perched on what looks like a small tractor. Freddie Millen the entrepreneur; who'd have thought it. They continue, past the builder's store and sweep of steps that is the other opening onto the battling ticket hall.

'He's not here.'

Richard can hear the panic in her voice rise above the preoccupied crowd. 'We'd best buy some tickets,' he says, 'see if he's down there.'

But where to go? King's Cross is unique in London in that it is built of five different levels, all connected by a series of passageways and staircases and escalators, though it is possible to move around the tube side of the maze without using the escalators at all, switch-backing through interlinking stairs from one line to another. There are so many escalators and platforms from which to choose, some buried deep in the London clay, others lying just underneath the surface, the life of London bunched at this junction, the earth corkscrewed, flesh for the city's arteries and veins: the Victoria Line, the Piccadilly Line, Metropolitan and Circle, the Northern; London the heart, and its people flowing in and out like the pump of blood.

They buy their tickets, Richard feeling the clunk, clunk of coins dropping through the machine, conscious of the first thread of music that he can hear, somewhere down below. So much noise rushing past them, so much noise wallowing up from the depths, the rumble of trains, the boom of blurred announcements, the tramp of feet, the chattering machines; enough to drown out any solo performance, but it is music they hunt for, music that they listen out for, music that propels them up and down, in and out, round and about for the next hour and twenty minutes, Sophie padding patiently in between them, unsettled in herself, unused to such a purposeless journey, determined it seems by one thing alone, odd notes floating up an escalator, half-played tunes hidden round far away corners, catchy numbers, ballads, folk songs, jazz, snatches of the classical, indifferent or accomplished, any sound will do, banjo, guitar, saxophone, mouth organ, it does not matter, for there is no knowing who might be waiting in the wings to take melody's place, no knowing what the player might know of the one they seek and where he might be; but though they drop the obligatory coin before they ask, they are not vouchsafed much. There is too much agitation in their voices, too much suppressed anxiety in their stance, and besides, they are taking up precious busking time these flustered bloodhounds, and buskers have more practical matters to attend to. But yes, grudgingly some of them acknowledge a truth; that they might have come across someone like that. Keeps himself to himself, one says. Doesn't say much, offers another. Doesn't say anything, her companion adds, taking it almost as a personal affront, but yes, he should be here some time, in need of some warmth, a little money, to keep at bay the damp of the night.

Up and down, up and down they roam, from the fresh night air of a wet London road to the damp and dingy gloom of the Northern Line, trudging through the narrow passages and stairs, patrolling the concourses, standing under the curve of patched ceilings, listening and watching as the platforms fill and empty before moving on. Coming up from the deep gives them hope, as if brighter possibilities must pertain the closer they rise to the surface. Diving back down, their spirit falls, as if they are plunging into a dark sea from which they might never emerge. Marjorie wants to hurry, to take the outside escalator lane and excuse-me on down, but Richard prefers to stand. He plays to his obvious excuse, but in fact it is memory that keeps him stationary, not the invalidity he invokes, remembering the pleasure he took standing on the two long run up Holborn, examining his fellow travellers' shoes, the state of wear and probable comfort, the complexity of design, the simplicity of shape, a rival's triumph, a rival's mistake, the parade of trends and health-defying obstinacy. Now he has other thoughts. Where are they going, these people he cannot see, with their cases and umbrellas and shoulder bags that brush past him so impatiently? To their homes, he assumes, standing half-occupied on a hundred thousand Anglefield Roads, men and women and children waiting for their familial return, some fearful, some joyful, many worn down and indifferent, empty rooms too, like his own, not even a waiting light to greet them, just the cold touch of a switch and the bare revelation of continued inoccupation. What is it of bricks and mortar that we crave? Who is inside, or the fear of what lies beyond? Is that the keeper of one's own self, that lock, that door? And when you leave, what holds you then? The memory of what resides there, or the fear of discovering there is nothing there at all?

Marjorie guides his arm as he steps off. It is not necessary with Sophie in charge, but he thanks her anyway. It is what people feel good about doing, helping the blind off escalators, onto trains, crossing roads. Talking to them is another matter, unless it is in the manner of an adult to a child, in slow capital letters, often shouted. It's helped him in his job, he supposes, on the rare occasions when he comes face to face with a client. It always throws them at first. He doesn't miss the salesman's life, though that is what he's still doing, selling advertising space in Freddie's magazine. The fact that their product is waltzing off the shelves helps. If he had the inclination he would be exultant, sandman to a salesman's dream, but though he takes pride in the product, he feels no passion. Passion has left his life, if indeed it was ever present. He is pleased for Freddie, though, pleased for Patsy, pleased that once a month he is invited to their house for an overnight dinner, pleased that the twins sit on Uncle Richard's knee, pleased that Anglefield Road has only ever been mentioned once. Sell up, Freddie urged. I'll help you find somewhere else, and Richard declined, the reason, he claimed, being that he didn't have to learn anything new as far Anglefield Road was concerned, he could find his way around with his eyes shut (his little joke), but in reality fearing that if he left, turned up the hill never to return, there would be nothing left of Richard Roach either, just a floating hollow of a man, adrift within and without, much like the man they search for, the string of tune, the only anchor he has to this world, the only rope that prevents him from sailing off into oblivion.

At seven thirty they are back down the Northern Line. Marjorie is tired, tired of raised hope and false alarms, tired of the long trekking, chasing a man carrying a flute case, questioning a girl unpacking her guitar, tired of the uncovered trails, the dashes of headlong excitement followed by another retreat back through the echoes of disappointment. She is resentful too of her companion. They should have come earlier as she had suggested. They are moving towards some stairs and an asthmatic accordion when he grabs her arm.

'Listen,' he says. A sea shanty sound, jolly rollicking down from the other direction.

It is Henry all right. Roach recognizes the tune. He can even see the bend of his young arm, the concentration working in his mouth, the lock of hair falling over his face. They turn and move fast, pushing their way back towards the escalators that will take them back up to the Piccadilly Line. Then the playing stops, stops before they are even in sight of it. Richard urges his dog forwards.

Henry packs his violin and takes out a cigarette. Moved on not half a minute into playing, the second time in two days running. He nearly said something. That would have startled him. But that would only be fitting. It is the time for being astonished. Only yesterday he spoke for the first time in five years but his throat still

403

has not got used to the strange feeling. This morning he'd woken with the memory of it, alone in front of the mirror, standing in his underwear, and spoken his name twice, Henry Hawkins, Henry Hawkins, marvelling at the strange contortions his face had to endure, tracing the outline of his lips, pressing them hard as if to hold back the sound seeping though his fingers: sounds of a lost future.

He stands on the escalator and lights his cigarette, dropping the lighted match. Step 48 on escalator 4 on the Piccadilly Line. It is old design, wooden, built in 1939 with metal-backed plywood steps and maple-wood cleats. The risers are made of oak fastened to a metal sheet which forms part of the step, on either side of which is a plywood skirting board, running its full length. The balustrades and decking are made of plywood too, the handrails of fabric-bonded rubber. It rises at an angle of 30 degrees, rising through 17.2 metres. The lighted match falls through the clearance between the steps and the skirting board onto the trench of running track beneath, between the driving chain and the trailer wheels. Its lies there on a bed of glutinous grease and detritus that has accumulated in the years since its installation, forty-eight years' worth of wood impregnation. Nearing the top, he hears a voice shouting from below.

'Henry,' it cries. 'Henry Hawkins?'

The third time he has heard his name today. He looks behind. Richard Roach is standing at the foot of the escalator, a woman trying to force her way past his dog. Henry steps off smartly. The match flickers, the flame reasserting its small strength. A tiny fire begins, a thin pencil line of blue transparency starts on the running track underneath. It is carried up quickly to the vicinity of step 70, heating the balustrades and decking as it progresses, making them susceptible to ignition and the spread of flame.

Henry is in a hurry. He knows this station, knows how to lose this man. He wants to lose Richard, but not his chance at earning a few bob. Last night after that one word he was unable to play a single note. He sat in the corner bar of his favourite pub, nursing his thought, wondering too what would happen if he simply leant across and engaged the man opposite. Would bells ring out; would the pub be stunned into shocked silence; would the man walk away? And what to say after these five years, what could be the first sentence; how could he introduce himself again into the living world? He moves across, take the Victoria escalator down. He does not want to leave King's Cross. His customers are here. He has missed too many of them already this night. He will circle back, pop down to the Victoria Line platforms, move across via the Midland City subway to the Piccadilly Line and resume his station. He'll have lost Richard by that time. Anyway, doesn't he have a home to go to? The fire ignites the dry plywood.

Though he moves quickly voices seem to follow him, not simply Roach's but another, unknown. He jumps onto the escalator, pushing his way down back onto the crowded Victoria concourse. The flow is viscous here, and he worries that in the slowing down he will have been seen, but then finds himself laughing out loud. Richard Roach is blind! He is running away from a blind man! And yet, he was calling him, beckoning almost. How could that be? The spoor of his playing, a question asked to another commuter to identify the violin-carrying villain? Whatever, the danger has gone now. He could stand two foot away from him, reach out with the tip of his finger and still Richard Roach would pass by, oblivious.

Instead of rising vertically to the ceiling and flowing up the apex, the fire runs up the greasy running-track trench. Further up it divides into two streams, the higher rising out of the trench spiralling on the fascia boards and across the ceiling, the lower keeping to the trench, moving stealthily along towards the ticket hall. Henry relaxes, lets the crowd carry him to the flight of stairs that leads to the Midland City connection and the relatively free subway that will take him back to the Piccadilly and his escalator again. He takes the stairs one, two, three at a time, and sets off down the passageway. There is hardly anybody there. He is almost tempted to call his name again, to shout it, hear it bounce up and down the tunnel walls, but it is not in a busker's nature to draw attention to himself before his performance. Maybe he will save it up. Maybe he will play for an hour or two and return to the pub again. Maybe he will talk tonight, say a word or two, throw the rope shore, haul himself in. Would there be any harm in that, just to set a foot on dry land again, see if he could still stand?

When he returns to the Piccadilly escalator the scene has changed. There is smoke coming from the fourth escalator, quite a lot, and the other escalators have been shut down. A station attendant is guiding the crowd out via the Victoria Line. He joins the queue with reluctant grace. There will be no busking here tonight, not for an hour or two at least. It will be crawling with every kind of official, eager to stamp his authority. He shuffles forward impatient to reach the fresh air outside. At least he is no longer being followed. Whatever sixth sense Richard Roach might have had, it has deserted him now. Henry steps onto the escalator, subdued. He'll take himself to Leicester Square, see what he can find there, maybe across over to Waterloo Bridge, for the concert crowd. He likes Waterloo Bridge, the hunched anticipation of the concert goers, their departing discussions, lend him sympathy. Under escalator four the lower stream accelerates, the flame tip poking out, like a rude boy, into the ticket hall. It licks the floor, and the walls, and then begins to lift its long tongue to the smoke above.

The escalator rises, the crowd moving with it. A minute more and he'll be gone. There is the smell of burning in the air, but it is not that which seems to impede the progress of his breath, but the great bank of fog that seems to roll down to greet him. As he reaches the brow it is as if he is on the river with the mist swirling in, or climbing up the final feet of some dark South Atlantic ridge, the dark confusion of shouts and the scramble all around. There are people rushing past him, the fog growing thicker, and he too finds his movements growing quicker. Curiously he feels young again, carrying his box of tricks, and he bends into it, wanting a scarf to muffle his mouth with and a toy gun to shoot through it. He starts to quicken pace, his voice calling (can that be true?), trying to see his feet, unable to remember where he is or where this fog might have come from, the river, the Falklands, one of London's yesteryear treats, trapped all these years in some disused tunnel, let loose by some careless workman's spade, or Richard Roach wrenching open a forbidden door, remembering too when he stood in that road and how it rolled down over the embankment, swirling up around his feet like gaseous sand, and he starts to run, to where he thinks the exit must be, running pell mell as if there is something lying dead ahead of him, something that if he can only reach will scoop him up into the safety of the clear night with his name calling and his life running alongside him, Henry again, Henry with his music, Henry with his voice, Henry with running limbs and love, and he runs his head down smack into someone, both of them cursing and falling, the violin spilling out onto the concourse in jangled chords, a hand clutching at his leg, his own hand grabbing something warm and soft, like a coat, hearing the dog's growl and Richard Roach's voice, choking.

'Henry? Henry? Is that you?'

And then another voice cuts through, a voice he had waited for since he knew not when, a voice that he had never heard but every single day, a voice than he ran in search of and never found, a voice that had told him to stay put and which he had disobeyed, a voice that had lost him, and kept the loss, a voice calling a name he had never heard and yet remembered.

'Henry? Henry Armstrong?'

And he rises to his feet. He can remember it now.

'My name is Henry Armstrong and I live . . .'

And the voice comes back.

'And I live in Anglefield Road.'

Anglefield Road! Anglefield Road! He saw it all, Anglefield Road, the iron gate before the little dip of cul-de-sac and the porch light swinging in the winter wind, the towering embankment he climbed and the flattened pennies on the shining rail, saw the imprint of his knees upon the sand, and the spin of the ball as it curled towards him and a bed and a light and a book on the floor and he turns and there she is, running out of the fog of old London town, her arms open widen her smile boundless, and the years seemed to fall away from her and she was young and lovely and the knowledge of her love swept over him like a wave of joy, a great ship cresting a wave, and then a burst of light blossomed all around her and she was gathering him up as if he was just a boy, her arms indestructible, and the mists cleared and the light spread and there was singing in his ears.

He was with her once again, now and for always and they were happy.